The Houseguest
A Pride and Prejudice Vagary

ELIZABETH ADAMS

ISBN: 1492318744
ISBN-13: 978-1492318743

DEDICATION

To Sasha, who encouraged me to write this story, and to my dear friend Andrea, who made me believe it was interesting enough that someone would actually want to read it!

For all the Pride and Prejudice fans who just can't leave well enough alone, this is for you.

ACKNOWLEDGMENTS

Thank you Ramona, Lyndsay, and Catherine for editing and re-editing.
I am incredibly grateful!

I have to thank Ms. Austen for writing such endearing characters that we can't bear to leave them alone. I hope I've done her proud.

PROLOGUE

27 October, 1811
Darcy House
London

Dearest Brother,

All is well here and I have quite recovered from my bout of cold. Mrs. Annesley insisted I drink a special tea with honey, which, though it tasted horrible, was quite helpful in my recovery. I have kept busy with my studies and am progressing well with French. Do you remember how you and Father used to speak in French in front of me when you did not want me to know what you were saying? Well now I should understand you! If only Father were here to hear me. I think he'd be pleased with my learning French. Do you think he would be proud of me, Fitzwilliam? I do miss him terribly sometimes.

Mrs. Annesley says that I am progressing well with my lessons; I have begun embroidering a new cushion for your study using all your favorite colors. Some of the knots were a bit difficult, but I believe I mended it quite well and that it will be pleasing in the end. I also have been working on a watercolor of Pemberley. Mrs. Annesley suggested I use the painting in your study as a reference. I hope you don't mind, but I had it moved to the music room. It is my favorite room in the house and catches the sun so pleasantly. And it will not do for me to spend the afternoons painting in your study. So far I have made two copies and I will begin the third tomorrow. I believe I improve a little more with each attempt. I shall have so many things to show you when you return!

Are you enjoying your time with Mr. Bingley? Does Miss Bingley play for you every evening? Please tell her I return her greeting and well wishes, and thank her for her praise of my table design. She is too kind. I have started a new song that is rather difficult, but I will master it and play it for Christmas and you shall be so delighted! At least I hope you shall be.

Is Hertfordshire a very pretty place? I would like to see it. It must be quite pleasant if Miss Elizabeth Bennet can traverse it so easily. It is sweet of her to come all that way to nurse her sister. I wish I had had a sister to nurse me while I was ill. Mrs. Annesley is very kind, but she is more a teacher than a sister. I think I would like Miss Elizabeth Bennet rather well. Do you think we shall meet? She sounds so very merry! It would be a nice change to be around someone so cheerful.

Please be careful while you are shooting, Fitzwilliam. I know you are quite proficient, but I would be terribly lost without you.

Your devoted sister,
Georgiana Darcy

1 November, 1811
Netherfield Hall
Hertfordshire
My Dear Georgiana,

I am so pleased to hear of your accomplishments. We shall have to find someone who cannot speak French to converse in front of and confound. Perhaps Colonel Fitzwilliam will do? I do not think he paid much attention to his tutors. And yes, my dear sister, I am sure our Father would be very proud of you.

I am enjoying my stay with Bingley. We have had many hunting parties and yes, I am being very careful. I am afraid I could not bear to leave you, my dear girl. Miss Bingley does play for us most evenings, but her playing is not as pleasant as yours. I did hear Miss Elizabeth Bennet playing at a neighbor's; she played well and sang rather sweetly. I imagine you would enjoy a duet; your styles are not dissimilar.

I think a watercolor of Pemberley is a splendid idea. Paint as many as you like. When we are home in the summer, we can take a ride up to the ridge and you can paint from the original. Perhaps Mrs. Reynolds will pack us a basket and we can have a picnic. Would you like that?

I am so proud of you, dearest, and all your endeavors. I cannot wait to see your progress when I return. You know not how I miss you. Miss Bingley is searching for me, so I must conclude.

Your most devoted brother,
Fitzwilliam Darcy

5 November, 1811
Darcy House
London
Dearest Fitzwilliam,

I have finished the last watercolor. It is much better than the first two. Where would you like to hang it? I should like to put one in the library. I am so glad you have music to listen to, for I know how much you like it. Miss Bingley is quite proficient, but I never know if she is really enjoying the music. I should like to hear Miss Elizabeth Bennet play and sing someday.

I miss you terribly, Brother! I enjoy my time with Mrs. Annesley and she is very agreeable and an able teacher, but I miss our conversations. I know we have letters, but they are not the same. I fear being left with my thoughts too much.

I have a proposition for you. Why do I not come to Hertfordshire? Mrs. Annesley could come with me in the coach, or you could come and fetch me yourself if you like. I would only stay a little while, perhaps a week, and I would not be in anyone's way. I would so like to see you - and of course Mr. Bingley and his new estate. Do you think he will buy it? That is rather exciting for him. Please say I can come and visit you!

Your loving sister,
Georgiana Darcy

9 November, 1812
Netherfield Hall
Hertfordshire
My Dear Georgiana,

I see that you are quite determined to make your way to Netherfield. You know I could never deny you anything that is in my power to give, especially a request as beneficial to me as seeing you sooner than expected. I will arrive in London Monday and return to Hertfordshire with you on Wednesday. I daresay I shall be right behind this letter. Then you shall be able to ask Bingley about his estate yourself.

Your Brother,
Fitzwilliam Darcy

The following Wednesday saw Mr. Darcy and an excited Georgiana headed to Hertfordshire. Georgiana hadn't looked forward to anything in several months; seeing her excitement, Darcy felt that he had made the right decision to bring her here. He had seen the old Georgiana peeking out occasionally in her letters, but not yet with any regularity. She had always been shy and reserved in company, but at home and amongst those with whom she was comfortable, she had been quite charming and even exuberant. She still had so much of the girl about her. How could anyone want to disturb such precious innocence? He could only hope it wasn't lost in her forever.

As they pulled up to Netherfield, Caroline and Charles Bingley were waiting for them.

"Miss Darcy! I am so glad you were able to join us!"

After curtseying to Mr. Darcy, Caroline locked arms with Georgiana and led her inside. As they walked ahead of the men, Georgiana looked over her shoulder to Darcy with a forbearing smile. He winked at her and turned to give directions to the coachman.

Caroline led Georgiana upstairs to her chambers, chattering all the way. "Now should you need anything at all, Miss Darcy, please don't hesitate to ask. I do want you to feel completely at home," she purred.

Georgiana required nothing more than a bath and a rest after her long carriage ride, and after informing Caroline several times that the rooms were quite adequate and she wanted for nothing, Miss Bingley finally took her leave.

~

Elizabeth awoke early, as usual, and looked out at a bright November morning. It hadn't been sunny like this for several days and the morning was beckoning to her to come and greet it properly. With avoiding the newly arrived Mr. Collins as an added inducement, she dressed and crept downstairs. Seeing no one about, she hurried out a side door and quickly walked out of sight of Longbourn. She chose one of her favorite paths and began nibbling on the muffin she had grabbed from the kitchen.

She had walked a little over two miles from home when she saw two riders in the distance. Not recognizing them, she momentarily stopped and looked in their direction. They seemed to be talking to one another; a tall man on an enormous black beast, and a lady riding side saddle and wearing a blue riding habit, sitting atop a grey with black fetlocks. It wasn't Miss Bingley, there was a decided lack of feathers, and Mrs. Hurst had said she didn't like to ride. Curiosity getting the better of her, Elizabeth stepped onto the first tier of the stile and looked over the small dividing fence.

"Brother, look over there." Georgiana pointed to a low fence running along the field they were riding in. Her cheeks were pink from exercise and her eyes were brightened with a curiosity that he hadn't seen in far too long. "Who is that?"

Following her gaze, Darcy saw a woman in a cream-colored dress and green spencer with matching bonnet. She had dark curls escaping around her face and was walking briskly.

"I believe that is Miss Elizabeth Bennet."

"Really? Oh, what a lucky chance! Now I shall meet her!" Looking back, they noticed that Miss Bennet was now also looking at them and had stopped moving. "Come William, you must introduce us!" Georgiana started off in the direction of the fence, Darcy following her a moment later.

As the riders approached, Elizabeth noticed that the man was Mr. Darcy. She had never seen him atop a horse before. It was a pity that such a handsome man had to be so disagreeable. Cursing the curiosity that forced her to stand and wait to greet them, she stepped off the stile and prepared herself for something unpleasant - and hopefully quick.

They were now close enough that Elizabeth could see the face of the lady. She was more of a girl, really. She had honey colored hair spilling down her back, with a few curls around her face, and while she was a little taller than Elizabeth, she still had a very girlish look about her expression. Her figure seemed to be caught somewhere between a woman's and a girl's. Who was she? Why would Mr. Darcy be out with a young girl? Could she be the accomplished Miss Darcy?

"Miss Bennet, good morning." Mr. Darcy nodded down to her.

"Good morning, Mr. Darcy." Elizabeth curtseyed in response.

"Miss Bennet, may I present my sister, Miss Georgiana Darcy? Georgiana, this is Miss Elizabeth Bennet."

"I am very pleased to meet you, Miss Bennet," Georgiana said quietly, looking down as a flush crept up her face. "I have heard a lot about you."

Was this shy creature the paragon of accomplishment whom Miss Bingley praised so thoroughly? Surprised and leaning slightly forward to hear her better, Elizabeth replied, "And I am very pleased to meet you, Miss Darcy. Your brother speaks very highly of you."

At this, Georgiana looked up and smiled genuinely. "My brother is very good to me," she said quietly, glancing at Darcy.

"It is fine weather for a walk Miss Bennet, is it not?" Darcy's loud voice was such a contrast to Miss Darcy's barely audible one that Elizabeth almost startled.

"Yes, sir, a very fine morning it is."

"Have you been out long?"

"Not long, no, barely an hour. I enjoy long walks."

"Yes, I know." At this he looked straight into her eyes, and Elizabeth was momentarily unsettled. Why did she get the feeling he was looking for something in her? *Probably thinking how he should not like for his sister to be walking for hours all alone*, she thought.

Attempting to break the slightly awkward silence that had come upon them, Elizabeth added, "And I daresay it is rather pleasant weather for a ride. Do you ride often, Miss Darcy?"

"When I am not in town, I like to ride nearly every day. Mr. Bingley was kind enough to allow me to ride one of his mares. I have been in London so long that I haven't ridden in quite some time." Her voice trailed off a bit at the end as her eyes began looking for something on the ground. Seeing her shyness was overtaking her, Darcy stepped in to aid his sister.

"Do you ride, Miss Bennet?"

"No, not at all, I'm afraid."

"Truly? Not at all? That is quite surprising!"

"Why should it surprise you, sir? Surely you know many ladies who do not ride," she retorted with a slight bite to her tone. Elizabeth's brow was raised and Darcy felt himself being pulled in once again by her teasing nature.

"Yes, you are correct, many ladies do not enjoy riding. However, I never thought you should be one of them."

"Me? And why do you suppose that, sir?" Her eyes were sparkling now and he felt himself slipping onto dangerous ground.

"You seem to have the perfect temperament for it, Miss Bennet. It can be quite exhilarating. Especially with the right mount," he said in a strange tone as Elizabeth looked down in confusion at the quasi-compliment.

Darcy dismounted quickly and said, "Do horses frighten you?"

Her head snapped up, an angry flash in her eye. "No, Mr. Darcy, they do not frighten me." Trying to cool her temper, she continued in a more subdued tone, "I suppose I never took the time to learn properly. By my third lesson of walking around the stable yard, I confess I was rather impatient to be off and decided I would be quicker on my own legs. I imagine that if I had been able to run and race and jump from the very beginning, I would probably feel quite differently about it now."

While she was speaking, Darcy walked over to Georgiana, who had been listening with rapt attention to the exchange, to assist her in dismounting. Now both standing on the ground, Georgiana on his right arm, the horses' reins in his left hand, Darcy looked Elizabeth squarely in the face and said, "Since you are not afraid of horses, Miss Bennet, shall we continue on together? I am sure you know the area much better than we and we would be most appreciative of the guide and the company."

Knowing she couldn't refuse, especially after her bout of temper, and seeing the hopeful look in Georgiana's eyes, she consented and began to climb over the stile. Darcy quickly handed the reins to his sister and moved to assist her. Taking his hand to climb down the other side, she refused to meet his gaze, not wanting to see his disapproval. As soon as her feet were on the ground, he released her hand abruptly and walked toward his sister. He took the reins from her and allowed the ladies to take the lead, quickly falling behind them.

Feeling some conversation must be necessary, Elizabeth decided to make the best of an awkward situation.

"Miss Darcy, how long have you been at Netherfield?"

"I just arrived yesterday."

"And will you be staying long?"

"I go back to London next Wednesday."

Elizabeth politely asked questions, trying to draw Georgiana out. When they hit on the topic of music, her voice rose above a whisper and Elizabeth could tell this was a favorite subject. They continued on in that vein for the next quarter hour, Mr. Darcy walking a few feet behind them with the horses.

Coming toward a split in the trail, Elizabeth asked Miss Darcy, "What do you think of Hertfordshire so far?"

"It is lovely. I would like to explore the area more, but Fitzwilliam is occupied helping Mr. Bingley with the estate, and Miss Bingley is new to the area herself, so I am afraid my explorations will be limited to the gardens and anything beyond that will have to wait until next time."

"That is too bad. Hertfordshire is a lovely county and there is much beauty to see here. Oakham Mount is particularly nice and not too far. I often walk there myself." Georgiana nodded and they continued walking silently.

After a few moments, Elizabeth had an idea. "Miss Darcy, if you are not otherwise engaged, I could accompany you on your explorations. I have lived here all my life and know every trail in the area; you would be hard pressed to find a better guide. It might be a welcome occupation while your brother and your hosts are seeing to their duties." *And it will give me a wonderful excuse to stay away from the ridiculous Mr. Collins*, she thought.

"Oh, Miss Bennet! That sounds wonderful! I would love for you to show me around the country."

"Miss Bennet." Darcy's deep voice sounded from behind her. *Here it comes*, she thought, *the denial of all things enjoyable.* She had suspected he might not approve, but she could hardly leave this sweet girl alone with Caroline Bingley and Mrs. Hurst all day. The poor thing! Nothing but compliments and doting, gossip and unsolicited fashion advice, morning till night.

Prepared for a reprimand, she looked over her shoulder with a determined and slightly impertinent look on her face. "Yes, Mr. Darcy?"

He looked at her seriously for a moment, and replied, "Thank you for your kind offer. I am sure my sister couldn't be in better hands." His face was a mask, letting no sign of his true feelings show through.

"It is my pleasure, Mr. Darcy."

They walked along a few more minutes before Elizabeth declared that she needed to head home, and took a narrow path in another direction.

"You were right, Brother."

"About what, dear?"

"I do like Miss Bennet."

Darcy smiled softly as they rode toward Netherfield, wondering if he'd made the right decision in allowing Georgiana to visit with Elizabeth. Miss Bennet was delightful, yes, and Georgiana did seem taken with her, just as he thought she would be, but he was beginning to feel that familiar sense of danger. How was he ever to forget all about her when he left this place if she became friends with his sister?

Looking at Georgiana, he saw how happy she was and decided to think on it no more at present. Even if they became friends, they certainly wouldn't see each other often; maybe never again. They would likely write letters and nothing more. Perhaps Elizabeth would be invited to tea or even to dine if they were both in London at the same time, but surely he could handle that. What was seeing her for a few hours once a year?

CHAPTER 1

The Saturday air was crisp and cold as Darcy walked into his London town home; he hated traveling in January, but there was nothing to be done for it. Hearing music drift up from the back of the house, he smiled to himself, happy to hear his sister playing. He handed his hat and gloves to the footman, all the while thinking how relieved he was that Georgiana seemed to be coming out of her despair of the last summer. As he walked toward his study, he was arrested by the sound of Georgiana laughing.

Curious, he walked up the stairs to the music room. Just before he opened the door, he heard something that made him stop in his tracks. He knew that laugh. But surely it couldn't be; she of all people wouldn't be here, in his home, with his sister, playing on his pianoforte? Sure his mind was playing tricks on him, he opened the door and was met by the picturesque sight of his sister sitting next to Elizabeth Bennet on the bench, both playing terribly while laughing so hard they were on the verge of tears. They were so close they were nearly embracing as they giggled and continued to play out of sync.

The sight of Georgiana laughing was so foreign to him that he stood there watching them for a few silent moments before he could force himself to advance into the room. Eventually Georgiana became aware of his presence and looked up, her blue eyes turning to saucers as she gasped and stopped playing. Elizabeth followed her gaze, and her mouth dropped open as her eyes widened in shock at the sight of Darcy before her.

"Brother! I did not know you had returned!"

"Only just. I heard the music and decided to come say hello."

Elizabeth and Georgiana had risen with his entrance, and he made a quick bow as he acknowledged Miss Bennet. The ladies curtsied in return.

"Was your journey pleasant, Brother?"

"Yes, quite uneventful. I'm afraid I have some letters to write. I'll see you at dinner?"

At her nod, Darcy quit the room and headed to his study. He would have to sort out this business of Elizabeth Bennet later. For now he knew he had a stack of correspondence to deal with, and it would be rude to question Georgiana in front of her guest; he would simply wait until Elizabeth went home to wherever it was she was staying and then speak with Georgiana later. Surely there was an explanation for all of this. Didn't Elizabeth have family in town? Maybe she was visiting them and Georgiana had invited her to call; yes that made perfect sense. That must be it.

Darcy walked behind the mahogany desk and settled in the comfortable leather chair; he took a deep breath and stared into the fire. "Focus old man!" He shook off his reverie and decided to delve into his work. There was a large pile of letters in the center of the desk and he set to work organizing them into three neat stacks: the first for business, the second for invitations, and the third for personal correspondence. Seeing that the stack of business letters was the smallest, he decided to start with that one first. After writing several "odious" letters, as Miss Bingley would have called them, he looked at his other two stacks. The stack of invitations was, as always, precariously high and he did not have the energy to deal with it at the moment.

He had vaguely entertained the thought of hiring a secretary, someone to handle his business letters and respond to invitations. But it didn't take up that much of his time, and invitations were only so various when he was in town, which was only half of the year, if that, so it never seemed that necessary, and he pushed it out of his mind.

Darcy liked to be busy. It kept his mind engaged and focused. His father had always told him to stay active, that idleness led to mischief and a soft mind. His aunt, Lady Matlock, liked to remind him that if he would marry, his wife would manage both households and all the invitations, cutting back his workload and freeing up his time considerably. He had responded with, "So would hiring a secretary, and would likely cost a lot less." She had only shot him a withering glare and moved to a new topic.

Darcy turned to his slightly shorter stack of personal correspondence.

As usual, there was one very blotched and ill directed, obviously from Bingley, which he decided to put aside in favor of the letter underneath which was clearly from his sister. Odd, he had received a letter from her the day before he left. He then noticed that it had been directed to his aunt's estate and then redirected to his London town home, as it had arrived on the day of his departure from Somerset.

Breaking the familiar seal, he opened the letter and began to read.

21 January, 1812
Darcy House
London

Dear Brother,

I am sure you will be surprised to receive this letter as you probably just received one yesterday filled with all the latest news on my rather uneventful life and feminine education. Yet something exciting has happened! I will not leave you in suspense, but will get straight to the point.

As you know, I have been corresponding regularly with Miss Elizabeth Bennet since my departure from Hertfordshire last November. Her letters of late have led me to believe she was slightly depressed. Upon questioning, she let me know that her sister Jane was here in London visiting her aunt and uncle and her dearest friend had recently married and moved to Kent. Miss Elizabeth was left quite on her own, with only the company of her younger sisters, and she has admitted she is not as close to them as she is with her sister Miss Jane Bennet.

When I asked her why she did not accompany her sister to London to visit her family, she first told me that she did not think it would be so bad without Miss Bennet, and since she is to visit a friend at the end of March, she did not think it would be necessary. However, having been without her sister these three weeks, she found that she missed her terribly and was rethinking her decision to remain at Longbourn. Her aunt and uncle are also hosting her aunt's family from the North and could not currently extend an invitation to Elizabeth as well. As you have been encouraging me to step out more with my friends and into the role of hostess, as has Mrs. Annesley, I decided to issue an invitation to Miss Elizabeth Bennet to stay with me here at Darcy House, so she might more easily see her sister near Cheapside.

She is to arrive Friday next and will stay for three weeks and then she shall return to Longbourn. I do hope that you approve of my plan, which I am sure you will as you have always spoken so highly of Miss Elizabeth Bennet. I feel she is an excellent friend, and I do enjoy her company. It is so much more pleasant to have friends in the house than to be here all alone with my thoughts. Although I will be an attentive hostess, do not worry, dear Brother, I will not fall behind in my studies. Mrs. Annesley is staying on top of me quite diligently and Miss Elizabeth will be going to visit her sister several times each week which will allow me ample time to complete my work.

I have greatly enjoyed the duties of hostess in choosing a room for her and seeing to its preparation; you were right, Brother; it is not as intimidating as I thought it would be, especially with such a pleasant guest in mind. I hope your trip is going well and that you achieve everything you hoped to. Please give my best to Aunt Preston and Cousin Harold. I will see you in a few weeks. Who knows? Maybe you will get back before Miss Bennet returns home, and the three of us shall a very merry party make.

Your most devoted sister,

Georgiana Darcy

Darcy leaned back in his chair and let out a deep sigh. So she was staying here, in his home, as a personal guest of his sister. He could hardly rescind the invitation once she was already there, even if he had wanted to. Plus, it meant a great deal that Georgiana felt brave enough to invite someone to her home of her own accord. It was the first time she had ever done so and he would be foolish to discourage her at this point.

Hadn't he just spent months pushing her to make friends? Was this not exactly what he wanted her to do? No, there was nothing to be done for it. He would have to stay under the same roof as Elizabeth Bennet for the next three weeks. Now how was he ever going to escape her?

~

"I thought your brother was to be away for some time." Elizabeth looked at Georgiana over the tea service in front of them.

"He was. At least that was the plan. He was visiting our Aunt Preston in Somerset. I didn't expect him back for at least two more weeks, perhaps even three or four."

"Hmmmm," was Elizabeth's only reply.

"Our Aunt has an estate in Somersetshire that my cousin has been learning to manage, and Fitzwilliam has been helping him. He had told me that Cousin Harold's progress would determine the length of his trip, but he had planned to be there at least a month. But it has only been a fortnight! Cousin Harold must be doing very well indeed!" At this thought, Georgiana lit up and her face glowed in delight. Elizabeth decided not to be discomfited by Mr. Darcy's presence, as Miss Darcy could hardly have planned it and she clearly wasn't the type for creating mischief. *I have been too long with impish sisters*, she thought, *I have become suspicious of everyone!*

"Are you close with your cousin?" she asked.

"Not particularly, but I am rather fond of him. I remember him being very nice to me as a child. He has no sisters, is the only child in fact, so he was always very sweet to me and would spoil me terribly! He used to bring me candies wrapped in brown paper that he would hide in his coat pockets. He used to make me hunt them out, all the while pretending there was nothing there." She smiled sweetly at the memory and began to nervously pour the tea.

Noticing this was among the first times Georgiana had served tea to guests, Elizabeth tried to put her at ease. "He sounds very kind. Do you see him often?"

"No, not anymore. Since he went to Cambridge and then on to learn management of the estate, he hasn't had much time to come to Pemberley. It is rather far and I have only recently begun to spend much of my time in town. Fitzwilliam says I should have the benefit of the masters, as does the Colonel."

"The Colonel?"

"Yes, my cousin on my mother's side. He and Fitzwilliam share guardianship of me."

"I hadn't realized your brother shared that privilege."

Georgiana blushed slightly. "I don't know that I'd call it a privilege. I'm sure I cause them undue anxiety." At this a shadow passed over face, and Elizabeth was about to inquire what was wrong when Georgiana changed the subject.

"Would you like to meet the Colonel while you are here, Miss Bennet? I'm sure you would like him very much! He's terribly funny, and always has something pleasant to say. Please say you'll meet him!"

Elizabeth couldn't help but be caught up in her enthusiasm after so quick a mood change. "Of course I should like to meet your cousin. Does he reside here in town?"

"Yes. He is posted at the army college not far outside town, and he often stays at Matlock House, which is just around the corner. Perhaps I'll show it to you on one of our walks! Richard – I mean Colonel Fitzwilliam – will be happy to take us. And you can meet Lady Matlock, too!"

"Lady Matlock? Is she the Colonel's mother?"

"Yes. Lord Matlock is my mother's brother. She calls here quite often, I'm sure you'll meet her soon."

Elizabeth was trying hard to restrain a giggle at Georgiana's desire to escort her about town like a new puppy, showing her to all her relations. How lonely she must have been, to be so excited about finally having a friend. Elizabeth decided she would put every effort into making Georgiana happy while she was here. If she could ease some of her loneliness that would surely go a long way toward helping her make more friends on her own.

Living so far from one another and knowing how her brother only tolerated her for Georgiana's sake, Elizabeth thought having more friends was definitely a good plan, since she had no way of knowing how often she'd be able to see Georgiana. Poor thing, she was all alone without female companionship of any kind, not even a mother. Elizabeth gave a silent prayer of thanks for her sisters and even for her exasperating mama. For while she could try one's nerves, Elizabeth always knew which family she belonged to and believed her mother would do anything for her good, or what she perceived to be her good, even if she was wide off the mark.

~

As Elizabeth was dressing for dinner, a knock sounded on her dressing room door. In only her corset and chemise, she called out, "What is wanted?"

"Miss Bennet," came Georgiana's sweet voice "I thought you might want some help dressing. Hannah will assist you if you desire."

Elizabeth smiled and opened the door. "Thank you, Miss Darcy. That is very thoughtful of you. I must confess I am so used to having someone about for pinning my hair in this style, I have almost forgotten how to do it properly. I was about to resort to something simpler. Jane and I usually do each other's," she rambled cheerily.

At this point she noticed that Miss Darcy was staring at the floor and that there was a light blush over her cheeks. Realizing the cause of this was likely her state of undress, she quickly pulled on her dressing gown.

"Forgive me, Miss Darcy! I am too used to being surrounded by sisters, and I must confess, we are not very private with each other."

"Oh, that is alright, Miss Bennet. I am the opposite, I'm afraid. Do sisters really do this? See each other without all their clothes on, I mean?"

Elizabeth started and her eyes widened slightly. "Uh, well, I can't presume to speak for all sisters, but in the Bennet household they surely do, within our own chambers at least. And I believe my other friends with sisters are the same." Elizabeth looked at her quizzically, then decided that if she was going to help Georgiana come out of her shell, here was an excellent opportunity. "In fact, Jane and I used to sneak into each other's rooms at night and whisper our secrets under the covers. We would often fall asleep together. It's very helpful for staying warm on a cold winter's night!" She laughed.

Georgiana merely looked at her thoughtfully, but not judgmentally, which Elizabeth took to be a good sign.

"Since I don't have my sisters with me, you and Hannah shall have to help me choose something to wear and figure out what to do with this hair." At that, she flipped her long strands over her shoulder dramatically and smiled brightly at Georgiana.

"Oh, I want to choose your dress!" Suddenly Georgiana was running to the closet, intent on finding the perfect gown while Hannah busied herself brushing Elizabeth's hair. It was obviously new to her, but just as obviously welcome; maybe female companionship was just what Georgiana needed.

As they walked downstairs to dinner, Elizabeth caught her reflection in a mirror on the wall. The yellow dress Georgiana had chosen for her was certainly very flattering and the hairstyle Hannah had fashioned suited her features perfectly. Georgiana had insisted on putting pearl tipped pins in her hair. While Elizabeth did feel a trifle overdone, her dress was simple, as was her jewelry, only wearing a simple ribbon with the pendant Jane had given her last Christmas around her neck. *Well, here we go,* she thought. She wasn't looking forward to dinner with Mr. Darcy, but she thought it would be worth it for Georgiana's sake.

It was clear that Miss Darcy was desperate for friendship from a woman her own age. Her companion, Mrs. Annesley, was a very nice woman, but being nearly 30 years her senior, could not possibly relate to Georgiana on the level of a peer. Elizabeth would suffer through dinners with Mr. Darcy, knowing that she was doing Georgiana, one of the sweetest girls she had ever met, a very great favor. And of course he wouldn't always be there; surely social occasions would take him away most of the time, and he did have many matters of business to which he must attend. And since Georgiana was not yet out, they would hardly be expected to accompany him.

She wondered if they would ever be entertaining. Georgiana had told her that she normally had dinner with her brother when it was just the two of them, as neither of them liked to eat alone, but that when he entertained people she would often stay above stairs, mostly because she wasn't comfortable around his friends. Elizabeth wondered if he would be doing much entertaining while she was there; three weeks could be a rather long time to be eating above stairs - she had been out for more than four years and was used to eating with the adults. She suddenly found it rather comical that she might be relegated to having dinner in the nursery. At this thought Elizabeth let a slow smile spread across her face and her eyes sparkled with the image her mind created. It was at that moment that they reached the bottom of the stairs and Mr. Darcy stepped around to greet them.

If Elizabeth had known the picture she was presenting she might have taken a care to control her expression; her eyes were sparkling, her lips parted in a slow and steady smile, her dress clinging becomingly in all the right places, the light yellow color setting off her dark hair perfectly. The pearls in her hair glimmered and her eyes shown in the candlelight.

Mr. Darcy bowed at the appearance of the ladies rather formally and gave Georgiana a light smile. He then extended his arm first to Miss Darcy and then to Elizabeth as he escorted them into the dining room.

Since only three of them were dining, he had asked his housekeeper to make it a simple affair. Darcy sat at the head of the large table with Georgiana on his right and Elizabeth on his left. While this was definitely a more intimate dining experience than Elizabeth had expected, she did not regret it. It would have been rather odd to be spread out over so long a space, practically having to yell to one another to converse throughout the meal.

At first she thought this might offer her more opportunity to tease Mr. Darcy and perhaps wiggle some information about Wickham out of him, but then she remembered she was here for Miss Darcy; to make her comfortable and be her friend, so she decided to leave Mr. Darcy alone - for now.

Conversation was basic and simple; they spoke about the weather and their plans for the week. Mr. Darcy asked whether or not they intended to attend church the next day, and Elizabeth and Miss Darcy both agreed that they had been planning on it. He told them he would escort them and instructed them to meet him in the foyer at 9 o'clock sharp. Elizabeth resisted the urge to salute and say a mocking, "Yes, sir!"

After he asked what they intended to do afterward, Elizabeth mentioned that she had planned to see her aunt and uncle in Cheapside where her sister Jane was currently residing. The hopeful look in Georgiana's eyes gave away the idea that she wished she would be able to accompany Miss Elizabeth, which distracted her from seeing the quick look of guilt cross Darcy's features.

Not knowing Miss Bennet's relations, and armed only with the small bit of information that they were in trade and resided in Cheapside, Mr. Darcy instinctively knew it was not somewhere he wished his baby sister to be going.

"Perfect. I will have Georgiana all to myself. I so rarely spend time with my sister that when an opportunity presents itself, I like to take full advantage."

Elizabeth had a feeling that she knew exactly what Mr. Darcy was taking full advantage of and it had nothing to do with spending time with his sister and everything to do with a certain address near Cheapside. But again, she reminded herself that she was here for Georgiana; not to chide, tease, or infuriate Mr. Darcy. So she let sleeping dogs lie. After all, he was entitled to his opinion just as she was entitled to hers. If he chose to look down and think ill of her relations in Cheapside, people whom he had never met, but judged solely on their business in trade and their address, then she had every right to think him arrogant, conceited, and above his company. *At least he is kind to his sister*, she thought. *Georgiana clearly adores him. There is real affection between them, it is not feigned. How can he be so good to his sister, and so horrid to everybody else?*

It was with these thoughts circling through her mind the Elizabeth undressed, slipped into her nightgown and climbed into the soft feather bed at Darcy house. *Tomorrow I will see Jane and my aunt Gardiner.* She chose not to think about going to church with Darcy, but rather to fall asleep dreaming of the pleasures an afternoon with her family would bring.

Down the hall, Darcy was having a very different experience. What was she doing here? Hadn't she tortured him enough in Hertfordshire? Teasing him, unnerving him, her fine eyes sparkling with some hidden joy he couldn't fathom, no matter how hard he tried. Why could she not leave him in peace? What had he done to deserve this torment?

He was a good landlord, a thoughtful master, a responsible brother, a helpful relation. How many times had he gone to Somerset since his Uncle had died, just to help his father's sister with her estate? There were other relations, but he was the one who went. Would he not perform the same duty for his aunt, Lady Catherine, at Easter? Colonel Fitzwilliam would go, and even Cyril would be willing to go, but no, she wanted Darcy. Only Darcy would do. He listened to their complaints and checked their books and interviewed their tenants. He spoke with their stewards and put their minds at ease. All this he was responsible for. All this he could accomplish without blinking an eye.

Was he not Master of Pemberley? Was Pemberley not one of the greatest estates in the country? Not only in size and beauty, but it was also one of the oldest and certainly brought in one of the largest incomes. And he did this on his own. He had no father looking out for him, not anymore. No thoughtful uncle to call upon, at least not with any regularity. He had no older, wiser cousin to assist him. He was the one called in to take care of things, the one people counted on to make the best decision. The responsible one, the in-control one, the loyal, steadfast, and honest one. *The lonely one.*

This thought struck him as a surprise. He had never thought of himself as lonely. He had Georgiana, and he was very close with Colonel Fitzwilliam. He even got on well with his cousin Cyril, though they had their differences. Bingley was a regular companion, and certainly a very good friend. And yet… and yet, he was lonely.

And now this woman, this siren, had taken up residence in his very home, in his private sanctuary, taunting him with pictures of what could never be. How many times had he thought of her coming down the stairs, her eyes sparkling, a smile on her lips just for him? He would take her arm and lead her through their house. No more sitting at opposite ends of the table, no more Caroline Bingley to put up with. He could sit and enjoy her smiles, and look at her without restraint, because she would be his. And he would be able to look upon what was his as often as he chose. He could look at her while they were eating, or drinking tea, while she was practicing the pianoforte, or reading a book, while she was fixing her hair or getting dressed…

"That's enough!" he said aloud.

He began pacing his room like a caged animal, one hand on his hip, the other raking through his already disheveled hair.

Fitzwilliam Darcy had long prided himself on being a man completely under his own control. He did not have fanciful whims or sudden impulses that, he thought, inevitably led to catastrophic consequences. He weighed his decisions thoughtfully and considered the outcomes thoroughly before engaging in a particular action. He was, therefore, not prone to spontaneity or frivolity, at least not anymore. He could remember a time, before his father died, when he was much freer; when he smiled quicker and laughed easier. But that was before the weight of the world began to press on his shoulders and he realized the far reaching consequences of even his smallest action.

As Master of a great estate, hundreds of lives depended on him directly, and even more were touched in some way by his decisions. When he had first realized this, it had had a sobering effect. Darcy had always been thoughtful and responsible, but this added knowledge turned his reserve into reticence, and his thoughtfulness into brooding, twisting him into the man he was today.

Within two years of his father's passing, he had a working knowledge of every inch of his estate and had increased its income by ten percent. He knew every tenant by name, and was known to be a generous and forthright Master by his servants. His steward handled most everything pertaining directly to Pemberley and its mills and various crops, but he personally handled all other investments and communications with his solicitor, and left the running of the households to his very able housekeepers, only checking the accounts each quarter.

He had thought a few times of taking a wife, someone to ease his burden and comfort and entertain him with smiles and music. But the thought had no more crossed his mind before he had dismissed it. He wasn't against the idea of marrying completely, but he did not want to marry just anyone. So far, he had met nearly every eligible lady between seventeen and twenty-seven in the ton, along with her mother, father, and any other relations in the ballroom at the time.

They had all been pretty, batted their eyelashes coquettishly, and sent simpering smiles his way at an alarming speed. They each seemed fascinated with everything he said, never disagreeing with him, and never having an opinion of their own, unless it was about lace or silk, but even then they were remarkably similar. It had gotten to the point where he could hardly tell them apart.

He had first entered the marriage market six years ago. He had just graduated Cambridge and was willing to be a good sport, letting his aunt, Lady Matlock, cart him around to balls and dinner parties with his two older cousins, imagining it would be a few years before he met someone he was interested in.

The season hadn't been under way a month before his father became ill and he had returned to Pemberley to look after the estate. After watching his beloved father waste away for nearly a year, he became Master of Pemberley and guardian to a very scared ten-year-old girl. He had never felt so adrift. He had briefly entertained the idea that a wife might comfort him and be good for Georgiana, but returning to town 11 months after his father's death to commence the search, he had been sorely disappointed.

Everywhere he went, his reputation preceded him. He felt as if he were being compared against an elaborate checklist; like a horse at the races, he had been reduced to a list of stats. The eldest son and heir, Master of Pemberley, in full possession of his fortune and free will; 10,000 a year, nephew to the Earl of Matlock; tall, good looking, excellent stock for the next generation. It made him ill.

It wasn't long before he started to weigh the ladies on the same scale. Young, pretty, passable, plain; she plays, draws, sings, and can embroider your initials onto any number of personal items; dowry of 20,000 pounds, 30,000 pounds, 50,000 pounds; daughter of an Earl, niece of a Duke; a pleasing dancer and charming hostess; healthy and likely to produce an heir; if you ever need an Italian translator, she may assist you.

Just thinking about it made him dizzy.

That was when he had decided to give up the search. He had the excuse of running the estate, and in the beginning, people mostly left him alone, thinking he was still grieving over his father and would come around in time. Many a young lady put off other eligible suitors waiting for young

Mr. Darcy to come back to town. Each was sure *she* was the one he would want; and each one was disappointed as the seasons came and went and Mr. Darcy hadn't returned.

Finally, two years after his sudden departure, he had re-emerged into society, only to find the same vultures circling the fields. The smart ones got out of the race sooner, choosing to marry less complicated and fastidious men. The not so smart stuck around longer, every season thinking this would be the time he noticed her, until they began to be fearful of never marrying, and would accept the first available gentleman who was remotely qualified. The unlucky, or perhaps the dim, were still lingering about, not considering that if Mr. Darcy hadn't noticed or preferred her yet, he wasn't likely to.

And so it went every year, with the new round of debutantes being introduced to the legend that was Mr. Darcy of Pemberley, master of his fate, the perfect catch who refused to be caught.

And so he thought he would remain. When he was younger and unfamiliar with the ways of the world, he had desired love. His father had loved his mother completely, and she had returned his affection in full. He had asked his father about it as he sat by his bedside, toward the end, trying to think of something to say, and at the same time wanting to know everything his father could ever possibly tell him.

George Darcy had revealed that he and Lady Anne had been childhood playmates. He would pull her hair and steal her toys, and she would tease him and make him give her pony rides. He had been five years her senior, so at first, a romantic thought had never crossed his mind. Mrs. Darcy and Lady Matlock were very great friends and would often spend days at a time at each other's houses. Lady Matlock would bring Anne with her, presumably to play with George's sister Clara, and the three would go gallivanting off in the woods together.

Then one year George went off to school and when he came back for the summer, Anne was with her parents on a tour of the continent. They kept missing each other, one in town while the other was in the country, and five years passed before they were face to face again. George was twenty-one, recently graduated from university, and she had just turned sixteen. Her older sister Catherine had become engaged and they were holding a ball to celebrate. Though not yet out, Anne had been allowed to attend and dance with the family.

George Darcy had described seeing Anne for the first time with moist eyes. He had remembered it like it was yesterday, even though it was more than twenty-five years ago. He had described to his son how she looked like an angel; golden hair framing her cherubic face, blue eyes so wide and deep you could drown in them. He didn't care that she played the pianoforte and the harp, and spoke German, and knew every dance, and came with a dowry of 25,000 pounds. She was lovely, and in that moment, he loved her completely.

He had talked her father into letting him dance with her, since he was as close as family, and the next year when she came out, George Darcy was at the door the day after her ball, officially asking her father for a courtship.

Watching their relationship had shown Darcy what it meant to be mutually respected and cared for, and he would settle for nothing less. If he didn't find it, which was certainly the way it was looking, he would remain a bachelor. When he was much older, he would take a wife and produce an heir, but he wouldn't marry soon if he could help it. And certainly not to just any woman; even one with perfect Italian and 50,000 pounds.

If only Elizabeth came from a good family! But would she have been the same? He would never know, nor would he ever know the comfort of her arms and the sweetness of her voice speaking tenderly to him, lulling him to peace and sweet rest. She was his perfect complement; she possessed all the talents he wished he had, and was forever gracious and enchanting. He had never seen anyone like her.

Never before had he been captivated by a woman's smile. Never before had he awoken from dreams so vivid he thought they were real, only to crash into despair when he realized they were not.

But he knew his duty.

And while Fitzwilliam Darcy was not unaware of the irony of the situation, he knew it could never be. Elizabeth Bennet must remain forever in his dreams, for he could never have her in reality.

CHAPTER 2

Elizabeth made her way to the Gardiner's home in Cheapside in the Darcy carriage. She was accompanied by a maid, Mr. Darcy insisting that she not traverse London on her own, even though there was a burly footman and a driver accompanying the carriage. She had to smile at his solicitude, being more used to neglect, but couldn't help being slightly irritated that she wasn't permitted to go anywhere alone.

He'd insisted that while he was responsible for her safety, she should give him the peace of mind of allowing him to ensure it. She was just a little bit surprised, because in her mind Darcy was not the sort of man who spent his time worrying about the safety of young women who weren't his sister. She was beginning to wonder if there was more to Mr. Darcy than met the eye, but then she remembered that Georgiana was not permitted to accompany her and went back to thinking meanly of him.

Her visit with Jane and Aunt Gardiner was unexceptional. Jane still had a sadness about her eyes that Elizabeth did not know how to breach. Jane told her that she had gone to visit Caroline Bingley and had yet to receive a call in return. Elizabeth was unconvinced that Miss Bingley had even told her brother Jane had come to call and did not really believe in his indifference, but rather thought Miss Bingley was being her pernicious self and causing all kinds of mischief.

For the first time she thought of her position at Darcy House as advantageous. When she had first accepted the invitation, believing Mr. Darcy to be absent, she had thought that seeing Mr. Bingley would be quite unlikely. But now that he was returned, surely the relationship between Mr. Bingley and Mr. Darcy would bring Mr. Bingley over at some point, and she could intercept him and say hello. If he knew she was in town, she could mention that Jane was also in town, and by his reaction she would then know whether or not he had prior knowledge of Jane's presence and if he wanted to see her again. She could give him the address and then the choice to call would be his and not his sister's.

She told her aunt all about Georgiana's family and how she was attached to her aunt, Lady Matlock.

"To hear Miss Darcy tell it, she is quite kind and rather motherly. I think she may be the only mother figure she has ever known. As I understand it, her own mother died when she was but an infant. Miss Darcy wishes me to meet her."

"Of course she should, dear. If she is her mother figure, isn't it quite natural to want to introduce her mother to her friends?"

"Yes, I suppose it is quite natural when you put it that way. I hadn't thought of it like that."

"Yet you seem as if you don't want this meeting to happen," her aunt said.

"No, not at all. It's not that I do not wish it, but rather I wonder if Mr. Darcy will wish it."

"Why on earth would he not wish it? You are, after all, a guest in his home. Why would he not wish for you to meet his aunt?" Mrs. Gardiner was aware of the difference in station between the wife of an earl and the daughter of a country squire, and even more aware of the difference between that same earl's wife and a tradesman's wife. However, she was conscious of the good it could do for Elizabeth, and wanted to know her true feelings about it.

"Miss Darcy was the one who invited me, not Mr. Darcy. And yes, I am a guest in his home, but at his sister's request, not his, and he did not wish for his sister to come with me today to meet my family. I can only imagine he would not wish for me to meet his."

"Did he actually say he didn't wish his sister to meet your family?" asked Mrs. Gardiner.

"No, not exactly. He did not say so, but he did seem relieved when Georgiana told him that I would be spending the afternoon with my family and he said he would be happy to be spending some time alone with her. He did not allow her the opportunity to ask to accompany me, nor me to issue the invitation."

"Yes dear, but is it not possible that Mr. Darcy was actually happy to spend the afternoon with his sister unaccompanied? Did you not say they are rather close for brother and sister? Is he not almost more a father to her than a brother? Have you not spent many hours alone with your father, and are you not happy to have your company uninterrupted?"

"Yes, I suppose that is true. My father does enjoy my sole company, and Mr. Darcy is very fond of his sister, as she is of him. It was just the way it was all worked out so conveniently that made me suspicious."

"Perhaps it would be best to give him the benefit of the doubt. I know you don't think well of him from what you've told me already and, of course, from what we've heard from poor Mr. Wickham. It does not look good." She looked at Elizabeth with eyebrows up and chin tilted down. "However, he is hosting you most generously, and sent you here in his carriage, and is allowing his sister to become your close friend, which is very kind and not exactly in line with what Mr. Wickham told us of him. I wonder if maybe there was some sort of misunderstanding between Mr. Wickham and Mr. Darcy. Perhaps there is more to the story than meets the eye, and after all, you have only got one side of it - you've only heard Mr. Wickham's end of the tale. Mr. Darcy might have something altogether different to say."

"Yes, again I must bow to your wisdom, for as usual you are quite correct. I have only heard Mr. Wickham's part of the story, but I must admit I have not been interested to hear Mr. Darcy's side as my own experience with him, as well as Mr. Wickham's account, cannot put him in a favorable light. I will grant you that he is very kind to Miss Darcy, and she is a very sweet girl and such sweetness might be difficult to attain with such a horrid brother, but I still cannot get past what he did to poor Wickham! If such a man can be so overwrought with jealousy as to destroy another man's hopes, I fear that is not a man I wish to know better." Elizabeth was speaking quickly and motioning with her hands, clearly exasperated with the situation.

"Yes my dear, just make sure you keep your eyes open and your wits about you. It is never wise to go into these things with your mind already made up. You must remember that you hardly know Mr. Darcy, and only saw him on a few occasions when you were in Hertfordshire and the few precious days you spent at Netherfield."

"Yes, but I do believe that my time with Mr. Darcy was telling. He showed his true colors when he was in company he believed to be beneath him, surrounded by people he thought he would never have occasion to see again. Is that not the true test of a person's character? How they behave when they believe there will be no consequences to their actions?"

"Yes, while that may be true dear, you must take into consideration other things. You do not know his nature as yet. Is it possible that Mr. Darcy was behaving unnaturally for some reason? Perhaps he had some pressing business matters or family concerns weighing on his mind to cause him to be so short in company. You know how your uncle is whenever things are not going well in his business; he can become quite short tempered at times, while he is otherwise a very genial man." She sighed at Elizabeth's disbelieving expression. "I am simply saying, my dear, that perhaps you should give Mr. Darcy the benefit of the doubt."

"Yes Aunt, I shall take your advice under consideration, and believe me when I say I will be the picture of cordiality while I am staying in Mr. Darcy's home. I am a guest and I will mind my manners. Besides, as you said, he has many business interests and family matters, which I am sure will keep him away from home the majority of the time. Georgiana and I have many plans, so I shan't be in his company very often and when I am, I will be the picture of politeness." Elizabeth smiled at her aunt.

Mrs. Gardiner smiled at her niece's humor and nodded her head. "I am sure you will, my dear. I never doubted your manners for a moment."

As Elizabeth rode back to Mayfair in the plush Darcy carriage, she smiled to herself. She never would have believed a few months ago in Hertfordshire, when she was verbally sparring with Mr. Darcy, that in just two short months' time she would become close friends with his sister, and be a guest in his home, riding across town in a carriage bearing the Darcy crest.

She smiled wickedly at the thought that they might pass Caroline Bingley, who would see her through the window. Oh, what she wouldn't give to see the look on her face then! Just thinking about Miss Bingley put Elizabeth in a rather teasing mood. How she would turn green with envy if she knew that her dearest friend Georgiana had invited Miss Elizabeth Bennet to stay with her for three weeks while her brother was out of town. And then to find out that that brother arrived only a day after herself to spend the entire three weeks in town, closeted away in their home with only Georgiana, her companion, and Miss Elizabeth.

Elizabeth had noticed that the knocker was not yet put back on the door, which meant Mr. Darcy was not receiving guests, so the chances were that Miss Bingley did not even know he was in residence. It really was too ridiculous not to be laughed at.

At the thought of Miss Bingley and how ill she thought of her, Elizabeth thought of what her aunt had said about Mr. Darcy. Perhaps it was true that he wasn't so very horrible since he also did not seem to like Miss Bingley. For wasn't it true that most horrible people tended to like one another? And, after all, he was a very good friend of Mr. Bingley, who was, as everyone knew, quite amiable and agreeable, and as Jane put it, 'all that a young man ought to be'. She would give Mr. Darcy the benefit of the doubt, if only to prove to her aunt that she was in fact quite open-minded, but she was sure what she would find there; the same arrogant, conceited, and selfish man she had met in Hertfordshire - only now with a London address.

~

"Enter," Mr. Darcy replied after the knock on his study door.

"Brother? You wished to see me?" Georgiana entered the room tentatively.

"Yes, Georgiana. Please come in, have a seat." He ushered her to a chair next to the fire and sat down across from her.

Georgiana looked expectantly at him with her wide blue eyes. Once more, Darcy was struck with how much she looked like their mother. He had always favored their father, whom Darcy was almost a spitting image of; tall, broad shouldered, dark, slightly curly hair, deep blue eyes and a strong jaw. Georgiana, while tall for a woman, was fair with light skin and golden hair. Her eyes were a slightly lighter shade of blue than Darcy's and more open in their expression. *She is still such a child*, he thought.

"Georgiana, how have you been lately? I feel as if I've neglected you, it's been so long since we've talked."

"I am quite well Brother, thank you. And do not worry, you have not neglected me at all. I have had Mrs. Annesley with me and my regular visits to Lady Matlock. Colonel Fitzwilliam, of course, has stopped by a few times. So you see I am not on my own entirely. And of course Miss Bennet is here," Georgiana's eyes lit up at the name, "which is making everything ever so much more fun!"

"Yes," he said hesitantly, "I noticed that you invited her before you had my consent."

"Oh!" Georgiana's eyes became bigger and if possible, rounder as she looked at her brother in surprise and a little bit of fear.

"I did not think you would mind, Brother. You have always spoken highly of her, and you had encouraged me to make new friends and she was so lonely without her sister that it seemed quite the right thing to do. And Mrs. Annesley thought it would be a good idea, and she would be here with me all the time. I thought it would be all right. I did not know how long it would take a letter to reach you and a response sent and received. Two weeks could have gone by, time which I could have spent with Miss Bennet. I thought if I waited much longer, you might come back and then of course you might say no because you would wish to have me all to yourself and not share the house with any guests. We thought the best thing to do was to have her come while you were not here so that I would have companionship and you would not be bothered; was this wrong of me brother? Are you angry with me?" she asked fearfully.

"No, Georgiana. Of course I am not angry with you." His face took on a gentle expression as he looked deeply into her soft blue eyes. "I was simply surprised that you took such a step on your own, and I must say I am rather proud. I don't think you could have chosen a better friend for yourself than Miss Bennet. She is certainly all I would wish for in a good friend for you. Please forgive me for frightening you." He took her hand in his and stroked the back of her knuckles with his thumb.

"Oh, Fitzwilliam! I am so relieved!" Her face visibly relaxed. "It is such a joy to have Miss Bennet here and it would be so disheartening for me to be taking pleasure in something that is upsetting to you. I am having the most delightful time!"

It made Darcy smile to see his sister so happy. He couldn't remember the last time she had looked so innocent, so joyful. It had been before Ramsgate, before Wickham came in and ruined their peace. And she even appeared to be coming out of her shell. Maybe Elizabeth was just what she needed to help her come into her own. She was certainly more vivacious and would probably be a lightening influence on Georgiana.

Lord knows he hadn't seen his sister laugh as much in the last eight months as he had seen her do since Miss Bennet arrived. What was it Elizabeth had said once? 'I dearly love to laugh'? Yes, she certainly did. And apparently she drew everyone around her into laughter as well. Yes, Elizabeth Bennet's presence was definitely welcome, even though it was doing terrible things to his peace of mind. It was with a slight jolt that he came back to the present conversation and realized Georgiana was still there, her hand in his.

"Brother, it is so wonderful to have another girl in the house. It is almost like having a sister!" Georgiana was almost giddy with glee.

"Is it now? I am so pleased you are happy, Georgiana, it makes my heart glad to see you smile." Darcy's eyes crinkled as he smiled at his younger sister.

"Yes! Do you know what we did last night?" When Darcy shook his head no, she continued, "I knocked on her door to offer help from

Hannah, and she opened the door in only a chemise and corset! She seemed to think the whole thing was quite funny and said that when she was home she and her sisters often help each other get dressed and fix one another's hair."

Georgiana was so excited by her tale that Darcy did not want to stop her and tell her that it was completely inappropriate for her to be telling him how she had seen Miss Elizabeth in nothing but a corset and chemise, even though he knew he should; but he was so overcome with the vision it created in his own mind (and embarrassed by the blush that was spreading across his cheeks as he realized what he was thinking), that he could not chastise her without making his own imprudence evident.

"So Hannah and I joined her and while Hannah fixed her hair, I actually chose her dress! I've never picked out another person's clothing before; it was quite exciting! And I also chose the pearl pins in her hair. Did you notice them? I thought the white pearls quite striking against her dark hair. And this is what Miss Bennet does every day! Can you imagine? Actually sleeping in the same bed with another person?" Darcy bit his lip. "It must be so heavenly to have a sister." Georgiana sighed and sank back into her chair, her eyes dreamily looking into the ceiling.

Darcy did not know what to say; it seemed that Georgiana had exhausted herself with raptures of the Bennet sisters and was happy enough dreaming of having a sister of her own. Well, at least she'll have the experience of a sister for a few weeks. And maybe, just maybe… No! He would not let himself think that way. Elizabeth was completely out of the question. Her family, connections, and situation in life were wholly unsuitable. If she had a healthy dowry and a family who adhered to propriety; if even just the family were better, if the connections were better suited! He could overlook the lack of dowry; Lord knew he didn't need any more money; he wasn't using half the money he had! He could well survive not having a well-dowered wife. But in order to fully take his place in society, he must be with someone who knew how society worked. He must have his social equal, and unfortunately, Elizabeth was too far beneath him. There was nothing to be done for it. She had relations in trade and an attorney for an uncle! She had a vulgar mother and three completely inappropriate younger sisters. There was nothing for it; she would not do. And yet…

He got up and paced the room a few times before taking the seat behind his large mahogany desk. He knew it couldn't possibly happen, it wouldn't happen, he wouldn't allow it, but there he sat, at his imposing desk, in his lavish study, daydreaming about a lass from Hertfordshire, and how her eyes shone, wishing it was all for him.

He sighed.

On reflection, her father really wasn't so bad, certainly not worse than Lady Catherine, and Jane was quite perfect actually; beautiful, serene, gracious, and kind. Everything you could want in a sister-in-law. And Elizabeth herself, she was everything he had ever hoped for: a bright mind, a fearless spirit, and that perfect certain something that was just bordering on impertinence, but still maintained enough grace to be sweet. And she was beautiful. Her skin was radiant, her eyes sparkled, her hair shone in the sunlight.

Yes, if she was judged on her own merit alone, Elizabeth would be quite suitable. She had handled Caroline Bingley and her ungracious comments magnificently. Never stooping to her level, but responding with grace and kindness. And the ton was full of Caroline Bingleys; yes, she would handle herself among them rather well. And with people who were amiable, such as Bingley, she got on famously. Derbyshire was rather far from Longbourn; they need not see Mrs. Bennet very frequently at all, and the younger sisters would likely marry someone, though it was doubtful it would be to anyone in the same sphere. Could they not just keep her family in the dark? Was there really any need to introduce anyone beyond Jane and occasionally Mr. Bennet? No! It would not do to think like this, making plans that would never come to be. There was nothing for it; it was not possible. He must forget her and move on.

Both Darcy and Georgiana sat staring into the fire, quietly contemplating what life would be like with Elizabeth Bennet by their sides when the sound of the carriage was heard outside the window.

"She's back!" Georgiana ran to the window and peered outside. "There she is! Come Fitzwilliam, let us greet her!"

Darcy knew he should tell her that such exuberance was uncalled for and that you did not run to the front door to greet someone who was merely returning from an afternoon call. After all, had they not spent the entire morning in company with Miss Bennet? Had they not breakfasted together, attended church together, returned home in the carriage together? Would she not be having dinner with them? Would they not all go to sleep in the same house this evening and wake up to have breakfast together again the next morning? There was no need to become so excited over her return after so short an absence. Yet, he could not quiet the excitement in his breast, and so he rose and followed Georgiana to the door.

CHAPTER 3

That evening, Elizabeth dressed in a pale pink dress and let Hannah fix her hair in what she said was a subdued version of the 'latest' fashion. She had to admit, she did look quite fetching. Georgiana had again chosen her dress and chattered away happily as Elizabeth's hair was done. She decided to let her neck go bare as there was a small lace trimming around the square-necked collar. Hannah allowed a few of her dark curls to hang over her shoulder, contrasting perfectly with the pale dress and her light skin.

"Thank you, Hannah. You truly are gifted."

"Thank you, Miss." Hannah flushed and curtseyed, then ducked out through the servant's entrance.

Georgiana came up behind her with a long piece of green ribbon. She held it out shyly to Elizabeth. "I think this will look lovely around your waist, Miss Bennet." Elizabeth noticed it was the same shade of green as Georgiana's dress, and that she was wearing a pink ribbon almost identical to Elizabeth's dress color.

"I think you are right, Miss Darcy. And just think how well we shall look together coming in to the dining room in all our finery?" Her eyes twinkled and Georgiana's shyness instantly melted away.

As the ladies entered the dining room, they heard the sound of men's voices.

"Richard!" Georgiana left Elizabeth's side and flew toward a tall, broad man with shaggy, sandy-colored hair.

"Georgie!" He opened his arms to her and embraced her fully, leaning back as he did, so that her feet came off the ground a bit. "It is good to see you, my girl!"

They smiled broadly at each other as he set her down and released the embrace. "Ah, but where are my manners!" he said as he looked toward

Elizabeth, an appraising look in his eyes. Elizabeth noted they were the same shade of blue as Georgiana's.

"Richard, may I present Miss Elizabeth Bennet? Miss Bennet, my cousin, Colonel Richard Fitzwilliam," said Darcy.

Colonel Fitzwilliam bowed, "A pleasure to meet you, Miss Bennet."

"I am pleased to make your acquaintance, Colonel Fitzwilliam," Elizabeth curtseyed. "Miss Darcy has told me so much about you."

"Do not worry, Miss Bennet. It can't possibly all be true!" he said with a smile.

Elizabeth smiled brightly in return as she headed toward the chair he pulled out for her. Tonight Elizabeth was seated next to Georgiana, who was still on Darcy's right, with Colonel Fitzwilliam on his left. As the Colonel looked up, he caught the edge of a scowl on Darcy's face. But not having the slightest idea what it was about, he dismissed it as another of his cousin's moods.

As the first course was being served, Georgiana peppered Colonel Fitzwilliam with questions about where he'd been and what he'd been doing in the ten days since she had last seen him. After a short lull, Elizabeth joined in.

"Colonel Fitzwilliam, I understand from Miss Darcy that you are quite the practical joker," Elizabeth addressed Fitzwilliam across the table.

"Oh she told you that, did she? And on whom does my fair cousin accuse me of playing these practical jokes?" he asked with an innocent smile.

"So far I have heard only of ones played on your brother, the Viscount."

"Ah, dear Cyril. If he wasn't such an easy target I wouldn't play so many jokes on him. Although the best one was when Darcy and I here -"

"That's quite enough, Fitzwilliam," Darcy interrupted.

"Oh come, cousin, the ladies want to be entertained," the Colonel said slyly as Georgiana muffled a giggle.

"Surely there are better ways to entertain them than with your sorry stories."

"And what do you suggest cousin? Shall you sing for us instead?" Colonel Fitzwilliam asked.

Darcy glared a hole through Colonel Fitzwilliam and said in a steely voice, "No, I have no such intention. I merely meant that perhaps that particular story was not fit for feminine ears." He gestured slightly with his head toward Georgiana.

"Do you sing, Mr. Darcy?" Elizabeth asked before she could resist teasing him.

Darcy's head turned back towards Elizabeth to make a biting comment, but just before he was about to speak, he saw the gleam in her eye and knew she was teasing him. *Here we are again, Miss Bennet. Who shall be the victor this time?*

"Not in public, Miss Bennet."

"What he means to say is only while bathing!" laughed Fitzwilliam.

Darcy flushed a deep red and his eyes became steely, but not before he caught Elizabeth looking down with a deep blush across her cheeks. She was pursing her lips, trying to stifle a smile. A sideways glance at Georgiana revealed her bottom lip was bitten in a desperate attempt at solemnity. Colonel Fitzwilliam looked rather like a Cheshire cat that had just caught a particularly succulent mouse.

A pain in his hand told him that he was squeezing his cutlery too hard, and with a clang he set it down on the table just as Elizabeth let out a choking sound. As Darcy sat surveying an entire table of people laughing at his expense, all the while desperately trying to hide it, he couldn't help but release a small chuckle. Soon the room was filled with laughter.

Funny, I didn't think Mr. Darcy could laugh at himself. In fact, I don't think I've ever seen him laugh before. But Wickham did say he was agreeable enough in the company of equals. Well Mr. Darcy, am I elevated to the level of equal now? No, I will not think this way! He has been perfectly kind and civil to me and I am a guest in his home. I promised Aunt I would be open-minded, and I shall be. She took a breath to clear her mind.

As all this was passing through her mind, Elizabeth had looked instinctually at Darcy. As the laughter faded away, he met her gaze. For a moment, their eyes locked and a small frisson shot through her. Surprised by the sudden intensity, she quickly looked to her plate.

The remainder of dinner was passed in amiable conversation, mostly between Elizabeth and Colonel Fitzwilliam, with Georgiana partaking occasionally and Darcy barely at all. Colonel Fitzwilliam was all that was pleasant and agreeable, ready to make conversation about a variety of subjects and clearly not put off by the serious expression of his cousin.

Soon they were headed out of the dining room to the music room.

"Georgie, what are you going to play for me tonight?" asked Colonel Fitzwilliam.

Georgiana looked down at her hands for a moment before looking up at the Colonel with brightened eyes. "Miss Bennet and I have been working on a new duet. Would you like to hear it?"

"Of course, dear, I'd be delighted." The gentlemen seated themselves on a small sofa, but not before Darcy noticed a small trace of anxiety cross Elizabeth's face. *Could she be nervous? I've heard her play before, and in front of a much larger crowd than this. And she and Georgiana have been playing together constantly since her arrival.* He noticed Colonel Fitzwilliam in the corner of his eye. *Could it be that she's nervous in front of Richard? But he's so congenial! Surely not! Unless... She couldn't be developing feelings for him already, could she?*

Darcy didn't like where this was going. He knew the feeling rising within him and knew its name: jealousy, plain and simple. How could he be jealous of Colonel Fitzwilliam when he had decided that he would not pursue her? He had decided to give her up and seek someone more suitable, hadn't he? Hadn't that been the purpose of his blasted trip to Somerset? To put her and Hertfordshire and Bingley and all their ridiculous problems out of his mind? That had clearly not gone as planned.

Elizabeth took a deep breath and focused on the difficult music in front of her. Georgiana was far more advanced a player than she was, and she knew she did not compare favorably. *Oh, well! I have no one to impress here,* she thought. *And if Mr. Darcy tries to intimidate me, I will tease him mercilessly. No! Be nice Elizabeth!*

The ladies began to play as he and Richard relaxed on the divan. Richard leaned over to him and whispered in his ear, "Pretty picture they make, isn't it?"

"Yes, they certainly look well together." Neither noticed when Elizabeth struck a wrong chord.

"Quite the scene of domestic bliss, eh? Sweet how they are dressed to match, too."

"Hmmm? Dressed to match?"

"Yes, Georgiana is pink on green, Miss Bennet is green on pink. You didn't notice?"

"No, I didn't. Whose idea was that, do you suppose?" asked Darcy.

"I would imagine it was Georgiana's. She seems rather taken with the idea of having another woman in the house. Well, at least someone closer to her own age. How old is Miss Bennet, do you think?"

"I believe she's somewhere in the neighborhood of twenty."

"Yes, that is a fine age; old enough to be a big sister, but young enough to still remember what it's like to be Georgiana's age."

"Yes, I suppose it is a rather good age."

"They met in Hertfordshire?"

"Yes. She met Miss Elizabeth while there. They got on rather well from the beginning and have been corresponding ever since. Georgiana invited her to stay here while I was in Somerset, but I returned early..." he trailed off.

"Yes, I wondered about that. Not very like you to invite a young single woman to stay in your home, unaccompanied. And a damned pretty one at that."

"Yes, you are correct; it is not very like me. But I could hardly send her home after she'd been invited to come all this way. It wasn't Georgiana's fault I cut my trip short and came home early. Plus I didn't want to discourage her; it was the first invitation she'd made on her own and I have been trying to encourage her to make friends and socialize."

"Yes, she certainly does seem to be recovering rather well. Time seems to be working its magic. Or perhaps time with the help of friendship."

Darcy was about to reply when they were interrupted by the soft melody of Elizabeth singing. He let the waves of music roll over him as he leaned his head back on the divan and closed his eyes. Yes, this would be a pleasant way to end most evenings, his sister happy and smiling, Elizabeth playing and singing for him. Yes, he certainly could get used to this 'domestic bliss', as the Colonel had called it.

~

The next two days were spent in similar fashion, only minus the company of Colonel Fitzwilliam. The two ladies would have breakfast together, and then Elizabeth would take a carriage to visit her aunt in Cheapside, while Georgiana did her studies with Mrs. Annesley. She would come back in time for tea and the two would go upstairs and dress for dinner, Georgiana receiving the same feminine pleasure from the ritual as she had the first time. They would have dinner with Mr. Darcy, and afterward they would take turns playing for him in the music room.

Elizabeth had decided to heed her aunt's words and observe Mr. Darcy with an open mind. She found that he was improving upon acquaintance and that he was not as disagreeable as she had found him before in Hertfordshire, but she still wouldn't describe him as amiable. He seemed too often to be brooding. One moment he was agreeable, the next he stopped talking altogether. She caught him staring at her sometimes the way he had in Hertfordshire. What was he looking for? She tried to ignore him and focus on something else, and on occasion would ask him a question, ending his reverie. Surely he had found all the fault he was going to find by now?

But overall, his manners were improved. She wasn't sure if this had anything to do with him being in his own home, but she was beginning to wonder if he was rather like Georgiana and reserved in company. Only in Georgiana, it came across as a sweet shyness; in Mr. Darcy, it was a reticent haughtiness. Only time would tell his true nature.

Wednesday afternoon, as Elizabeth's carriage pulled up to the Darcy doorstep, she saw another pulling away and wondered who it was that had just left. She stepped into the hall and handed her things to the footman. She went straight to the drawing room, hoping Georgiana was still there.

"Hello, Miss Darcy. Did you have a pleasant morning?"

Georgiana looked up when Elizabeth spoke her name. "I suppose it was pleasant enough. Miss Bingley just left. It's too bad you missed her."

"Yes, it is too bad," Elizabeth said ruefully. "Did you entertain her on your own?"

"Yes. She does not know Fitzwilliam is back yet. He is trying to get his work done without the interruption of callers. He always leaves the knocker off the door the first week after he returns from a trip."

"I suppose that makes sense. Was your visit pleasant?"

"Pleasant enough." Georgiana looked uneasy and twisted her hands in front of her. "Miss Bennet, may I ask you a question? Are you good friends with Miss Bingley?"

"I wouldn't say we were good friends, no, not exactly. We are more acquaintances," she said uncomfortably.

"If I were to confess something to you, would you think me terribly horrible?" Miss Darcy asked nervously.

"Miss Darcy! I doubt there is anything you could confess to me that would make me think you terribly horrible."

Georgiana paused, then said, "Very well, then. Miss Bennet, I find that I am not desirous of meeting with Miss Bingley too often and that I am fearful of being thrown continually into her company." She released all the words in one breath and heaved out a long sigh at the end of her speech, her shoulders slouching.

Elizabeth stifled a laugh but composed herself enough to respond. "Miss Darcy, whatever would make you think you might be thrown continually into her company?"

"Miss Bingley seems desirous of an alliance with my family," Georgiana replied quietly, looking at her feet, twisting her hands again.

"Oh, I see. You are afraid Mr. Darcy will marry Miss Bingley and you will have to live with her?" Georgiana nodded slightly. "Oh, dear! Miss Darcy, how can I comfort you? I understand your concern, and I can only try to assuage your doubts as best I can. From my observations, you are correct; Miss Bingley does desire a greater connection to your family. But without overstepping propriety, may I also say that my observations showed that feeling to be unreciprocated."

At this, Georgiana's head flew up and she smiled brightly. "Really, Miss Bennet? Do you really think so?"

"Yes, I think so. I may be incorrect of course, but it would appear that your 'family' is not desirous of the connection. Does that make you any easier?"

"Yes, it does. Thank you, Miss Bennet!"

With that, Georgiana squeezed her hand and flew from the room.

Elizabeth looked out the window, and noticing that the sun was still shining brightly, she decided to take a short stroll to the park to get a bit of fresh air. After collecting her things from her room, she headed downstairs.

She was almost to the bottom step when she was arrested by male voices coming towards the entry.

"Good to see you again, Darcy."

"You too, Malcolm." They were shaking hands and about to part at the door when they noticed her waiting on the stairs. The man called Malcolm eyed her appreciatively, but as Darcy did not offer an introduction, he merely stepped out the door with a nod of his head in her direction.

"Miss Bennet, are you just arrived?" Darcy asked her.

"No, I am actually on my way out. I thought I'd enjoy the sunshine while it lasted with a turn in the park."

"Does Georgiana accompany you?" he asked.

"No, I go alone."

"Alone?"

"Yes, sir, alone. Good afternoon, Mr. Darcy." She made for the door but was blocked by him standing in her path.

"Miss Bennet, I cannot allow you to walk in the park alone," he said stiffly.

"Allow me, Mr. Darcy?" She raised a brow and looked up at him, her ire beginning to rise. Darcy fought the smile tugging at his lips and pressed his case.

"Miss Bennet, while you are staying at Darcy House, you are under my protection," Elizabeth felt her cheeks growing hot, "and as such I cannot simply watch you go off on your own into a busy city park. This is not Hertfordshire where you are known to every neighbor. Someone should accompany you."

Elizabeth knew that in a way he was right, but for some reason, she did not want to capitulate to this overbearing man.

"And who would you have accompany me, sir? I find my stride is too quick for both Miss Darcy and Mrs. Annesley and neither likes to walk as far as I do. Thus, I walk alone," she stated clearly.

"I will accompany you," he declared.

Elizabeth started and looked up at him quizzically. Why would he want to accompany her? She knew very well he didn't like her. Could he possibly take his role as protector that seriously?

"Mr. Darcy, that is quite unnecessary. As you well know, I am accustomed to walking alone and am not afraid of being on my own. I do not require an escort." She was becoming seriously annoyed now, and Darcy could tell by the look in her eyes that she meant what she said.

"Miss Bennet, I am entirely aware of your walking prowess. However, I would feel much more at ease if I accompanied you. Besides, I have been inside all day and could use a little fresh air and exercise." He gave her a small smile, intending to put her at ease, but only confused her as to his purpose.

"Are you sure you can spare your business that long, Mr. Darcy? I do not intend to take a short walk."

Is she always this stubborn? He looked directly into her eyes, causing her resolve to retreat slightly, and said, "I never thought you would, Miss Bennet. Shall we?"

In a moment he had slipped on his great coat, gloves, and hat and collected a rather ostentatious brass-topped walking stick from a footman. He saw Elizabeth eying it and holding back a smirk, and quickly handed it back to the footman. "I won't be needing this today, Causer."

He turned to Elizabeth and saw the mirth dancing in her eyes. *At least she does not stay angry long,* he thought.

"Something amusing, Miss Bennet?"

"No, Mr. Darcy, not at all. I must say I am rather surprised at your going out without a walking stick, though," she replied with mock solemnity as they headed out the door. Why could she not resist an opportunity to tease him?

"Yes, well, I thought I wouldn't really need it today." Her teasing tone was putting him on edge, but he found that he liked the feeling of anticipation it gave him.

"What if you should lose your footing sir? Would such a fine cane not help you to right yourself?" She looked completely innocent, but he could see a hint of mirth behind her staid gaze.

"Possibly, Miss Bennet. I guess now I shall have to hold on to you." He smiled a little devilishly at her and she started in surprise. *Two can play this game*, Elizabeth.

Was Mr. Darcy teasing her? And so wickedly? She hadn't thought him capable. What had Colonel Fitzwilliam said? That he had played a practical joke on his brother with Darcy as his accomplice? She would have to find out the particulars of that. But how?

As Mr. Darcy held out his arm to her outside the front door, she eyed him carefully and said, "Mr. Darcy, if I am to lend my arm for your support, then I wish to receive something in return." His brow shot up at her statement.

"And what is your request Miss Bennet?" he asked in mock seriousness.

"I wish to be entertained, Mr. Darcy."

"Entertained?"

"Yes, I was thinking you could tell me a story, about a joke you played on a certain cousin of yours?" As his eyes grew wider and his brow shot up, she added, "Or you could sing to me." An impish smirk played on her lips as she awaited his answer.

"Miss Bennet, you drive a hard bargain."

"Yes, sir."

She clearly was not backing down. Darcy looked into her determined eyes and smiled. If he was going to be humiliated, better to take his cousins with him.

"Very well, Miss Bennet. But I warn you, you may not like what you hear. I am afraid it's not fit for the ears of a lady, and I will have to ask you not to tell Georgiana."

"Of course, sir. You have my word." She offered a charming smile in reward for his surrender. *See Aunt, I'm being nice.*

As they entered the park gates, Darcy began his story. "Several years ago, when we were all just boys together, my cousins and I used to indulge in racing."

Elizabeth couldn't hide her triumph in getting the impenetrable Mr. Darcy to divulge information he didn't want to part with; she could hardly keep the smile off her face. Mr. Darcy caught her look, and thinking it was for him, continued with new enthusiasm and uncommon openness.

"I had gotten a new horse for my fifteenth birthday as a gift from my father. As a sort of initiation ritual, Richard, Cyril and I decided to race our stallions through Pemberley's meadows, down a small hill to a river in the valley. The whole distance was about two miles. As we started off, everything was as it usually was. Richard was in the lead, being more daring than his brother, even though Cyril is his senior by two years and mine by three. Cyril and I were right behind Richard, neck and neck. Then out of nowhere, Richard's mount seemed to startle and veer to the right, directly in front of me. We almost collided, but Richard was quick enough to get him back on track and avoid disaster. It was enough of a distraction for Cyril to pull ahead. He ended up beating us by a hair."

Elizabeth was so caught up in the story that she didn't realize she was staring up at Mr. Darcy's profile raptly. When he looked down at her and met her eyes, she smiled eagerly at him and said, "And then what happened?"

Darcy chuckled softly at her enthusiasm and continued, "Knowing Cyril as we did, we suspected he'd somehow made Richard's horse startle. So while he was down at the river, we looked into his saddlebags. Sure enough, there was a blow gun."

"A blow gun?" She peered at him with a confused look on her face. He lifted his hand to smooth her brow, but stopped himself just in time. Luckily she didn't seem to notice his slip.

"Yes. A blow gun is a hollowed out stick or pole in which you place a stone or a dart of some kind. You then put it to your mouth and blow, pointing it in the direction you wish to shoot. In this case, to the hind quarters of Richard's mount. It's not enough to hurt the animal, just startle it off its course. So we decided to get revenge."

Elizabeth's eyes were wide as she looked up at him expectantly.

"It was a hot day in early summer, and we were a little worse for the wear. So we suggested to Cyril that we take a dip in the river. It was not so unusual, we'd done it several times in years past, though not recently. So we all went for a swim and as Cyril was leaning against the banks with his eyes closed, after an hour of bragging about his winning the race I might add, Richard and I gathered up his clothes, quickly mounted our horses and headed back to the stables, leaving a rather bare Cyril with nothing but his stallion for cover."

Miss Bennet's gasp brought him back to the present and he looked down at her shocked face. He was grinning mischievously (and not a little proudly) as she stared up at him with wide eyes. "You mean you were swimming without, without your… I mean you didn't have, you weren't wearing any…" she stammered and trailed off. As Darcy tried to catch her meaning, she blushed and looked down.

"Oh!" he exclaimed as realization hit him. "Yes, I suppose we were. Forgive me, Miss Bennet. This story really isn't at all appropriate for a young lady's ears." He flushed and looked away, embarrassed. He hadn't meant to get so carried away.

"No, Mr. Darcy, you gave me fair warning and I insisted. I was just a little surprised. I am quite collected now. Pray, do continue your story. I'm most interested to hear how it ends." She looked at him playfully and he carried on.

"Well, Richard and I made it back in good time, but we didn't know when Cyril would arrive, or even if he would. We'd left his horse tied to a tree, although Richard did consider sending it off as well, but thought better of it. We thought he might head to a barn or try to sneak in through one of the servants' entrances. We certainly didn't expect him at the stables. So we sat in the courtyard, laughing and congratulating ourselves, when in rode Cyril, bare as the day he was born, red in the face and swearing at the top of his lungs. He lunged straight for us on that enormous stallion and would have trampled us if we hadn't jumped out of the way.

"As it happened, we did make it clear, only to have him dismount and chase us around the stable yard, screaming profanities and hurling rocks at us. Richard and I were laughing so hard at the sight of him, we could hardly dodge the rocks. Eventually, one of the stable hands fetched my father and he came to the yard to put an end to things. He marched us all into his study and gave us a stern talking to, then dragged us back to the stables and whipped us soundly. Cyril was eighteen and didn't care for it, but father was determined. We never raced again; well, at least not with Cyril."

His broad smile was contagious, and Elizabeth couldn't help but laugh softly. "Forgive me sir, but it is a most entertaining story. I can just picture you and the Colonel, running around a stable yard, dodging rocks from a half mad, nude cousin. It really is too much!" She laughed in earnest now, partly from the story, and partly because she just admitted that she was picturing a nude man. A blush spread over her cheeks and she laughed even harder, embarrassed that he must realize her embarrassment. Darcy joined her with his mild chuckle, but mostly he just beamed at her while she blushed and laughed, enjoying the companionship.

They walked a few more feet before Elizabeth spoke. "I believe you are right, sir. That story is not at all appropriate for young ladies. I am glad Colonel Fitzwilliam was unsuccessful in telling it in front of Georgiana. While it is terribly funny, I don't know how quickly she would recover from the shock. And I'm sure the Colonel's version is even less circumspect than yours."

"I fear you are right, Miss Bennet. Richard has a flair for storytelling. The facts are not always accurate, but you will not become bored."

Elizabeth was having such an enjoyable time, she almost forgot she was with Mr. Darcy.

"Mr. Darcy, I'm afraid I am in your debt."

"Oh?"

"Yes. I feel the cost of my escort was not equal to your rather illuminating story. I fear the balance now weighs heavily on your side."

"Does it now? Well, we shall have to even the score then." He smiled at her playfully.

"What do you have in mind, Mr. Darcy?" She smiled back, with a trace of a challenge in her eyes.

"I believe I have some rather tedious meetings scheduled for this week."

"Oh?"

"Yes. I am sure that afterward, I will be in need of fresh air to shake off the business of the day."

"Will you?"

"Yes, quite. And I shall be too tired to read, but will want entertainment."

"Entertainment?"

"Yes."

"And who shall provide this entertainment?"

"Why you, Miss Bennet."

"Me?" He nodded. "And what form of entertainment shall you require? Shall I tell you a story? Or would you rather I sing to you?" she asked archly.

"Ah, Miss Bennet, you forget that you sing to me almost every night already, quite to my delight. I think I would like a story."

"And what kind of story would suit your fancy, sir?"

"One where at least one of the Misses Bennet is behaving rather badly and gets properly punished, preferably you."

"Mr. Darcy!"

His devilish grin was the only reply she was to have.

"Very well, then. I shall do my best," she said with more calm than she felt.

By now they had circled the park and were coming upon the gates.

"Are you ready to return, Miss Bennet?" His voice was serious again.

"Yes, it is rather cold. It's probably best we get back before my fingers lose all feeling!" she joked.

"Are your hands cold?" he asked solicitously.

"A bit. But it is not far now, I shall be fine."

Before she could protest, he took up the hand that rested on his arm and began to rub it vigorously between his own. When he had gone on for a few moments, he gently laid it back on his arm and held out his palm for her other hand. She looked at him questioningly, and then cautiously laid her hand in his larger one. He followed the same procedure, rubbing it between his large, sturdy hands while she self-consciously watched his movement.

When he had finished, he released her hand and asked softly, "Better?"

"Yes, quite, I thank you," she replied quietly.

They walked the remaining block in silence, stepped into the house, and with a shy smile, she went upstairs to prepare for dinner.

CHAPTER 4

Elizabeth sighed and laid her head back on the soft towel rolled up across the back of the enormous tub. Since arriving in London, Elizabeth had enjoyed daily baths, something she had done only thrice weekly at Longbourn. But here, with so fewer people to fetch water for and so many more servants to accommodate, it was a luxury she was quickly becoming accustomed to. She had even entertained the thought of one in the morning and another at night, but dismissed it as being too greedy.

As the steam rose around her, curling her hair and plastering the short tendrils to her forehead, she closed her eyes and relived the events of the day. Her walk with Mr. Darcy had been most enlightening. She wouldn't have thought he had such a devilish sense of humor, and she definitely wouldn't have thought that she would have enjoyed it as much as she had.

Perhaps there was something to what Aunt Gardiner had said; maybe she should give him a chance to tell his side of the story. But hadn't she done that? At the Netherfield Ball, she told him she had heard differing accounts of him. What was his response? 'I can readily believe that reports may vary greatly with respect to me.' Why would he say that? How many reports were there? All she had heard was from Wickham, and their reaction to each other seemed to confirm some animosity between them.

Of course Mr. Bingley certainly seemed to think rather highly of him - now there was an odd relationship. But she didn't have time to think about that now.

Focus, Elizabeth. While they were dancing, what else did he say? 'I could wish, Miss Bennet, that you were not to sketch my character at the present moment, as there is reason to fear that the performance would reflect no credit on either.' No credit on either? If she sketched him according to Wickham, it did reflect badly on Mr. Darcy, but why would it reflect badly on her?

Thinking back, Elizabeth tried to remember everything Mr. Wickham had said about Darcy. That he was proud and disagreeable she remembered, and then the whole story about his father being a generous man and leaving Wickham a living she remembered quite clearly. He had asked if she was acquainted with Miss Darcy, and when she told him they had recently become friends, Wickham said she was a sweet girl and quickly went back to speaking about Mr. Darcy.

A memory was niggling at the back of Elizabeth's mind, but she could not pull it out. She dipped her arms back into the water and drew circles with her fingertips along the surface. Old Mr. Darcy had been an excellent man, yes, she remembered that clearly enough. What else had he said about him? That the father had loved him dearly and remembered him in his will, and Wickham had great respect for him. Yes, yes, there was something else… Yes! Wickham had said that he could not disparage the son out of respect for the father. That was it! Yet he didn't follow that course, did he? After Netherfield was closed and its inhabitants gone back to town, Wickham had freely and loudly told his sorry tale to anyone who would listen. Was that not disparaging the son?

A sinking feeling began to work its way into Elizabeth's stomach. Did Darcy know Wickham was telling tales about him? Is that why he had said it would not be a credit to her to believe what she heard; because what she had heard wasn't true?

But she had disliked him long before she heard Wickham's story. In fact, she had as much as told Wickham this in their first meeting. Suddenly realization dawned. That was why he had told her about Mr. Darcy. He assumed she would believe him because she disliked him as well. When her aunt had asked her why Wickham would divulge such private information to a relative stranger, she had thought nothing of it. But now it was becoming clearer. Mr. Wickham thought he had found an ally.

He had promised to come to the ball at Netherfield, saying he would not be run off by Mr. Darcy, and then he had left, saying he didn't want to cause a scene in Mr. Bingley's home. At the time she had accepted it as a reasonable and even gracious answer, but now she viewed it with suspicion. Could he simply have wanted to avoid Mr. Darcy? It did not seem likely that he would make a scene. Mr. Darcy did not attract attention to himself. *No, his position does it for him*, she thought ruefully.

There had to be more to this story than what appeared on the surface. She must find out what really happened between Wickham and Darcy, for the more she thought about it, the more she was sure it wasn't exactly as Wickham had portrayed it. But how would she ever get Mr. Darcy to tell her?

~

This was getting complicated. What had just happened? Darcy was pacing in his study, back and forth in front of the fire, occasionally stopping to stare out of the large window.

Clearly, his plan to forget Elizabeth wasn't working. He had spent a month in town after quitting Netherfield, celebrating Christmas with his sister, and Elizabeth had been on his mind constantly. He would distract himself with work or family matters, only to have Georgiana bring her up and what she'd said in her latest letter, or worse, he would imagine Elizabeth with him.

He imagined what she would say when he was having dinner with his aunt and uncle, sure that her conversation would brighten the otherwise dull event. When he went shopping for Georgiana's Christmas gifts, he had wondered what she would like, and thought about all the things he would like to give her. In a particularly weak moment, he had even bought her a gift. Believing she would like the small volume of poetry, he had stupidly purchased it and placed it in a drawer of his desk where he would see the bloody thing almost daily, reminding him of his folly. He'd tried to move it once, but ended up putting it back, unable to put her completely away from him.

When he'd opened his gifts from Georgiana Christmas morning, he'd wondered what Elizabeth would have gotten him, had she been his wife. Would she embroider his initials on a new handkerchief? Buy him a new timepiece with a loving inscription? Or would she give him something else altogether, to be enjoyed in the privacy of their chambers? He had to stop himself from envisioning Elizabeth in a large red bow and little else.

After that, he knew he had let it go too far, so he had gone to his aunt's in Somerset. His father's sister's home had always been a haven for him. She was so like his father; generous, kind, wise, and understood him completely. He did not have to pretend to be comfortable where he was not and was not asked to do that which he found repulsive. His cousin Harold, though four years younger than he, had long been a friend and was a good sort of fellow, though a touch on the silly side.

With them, Darcy could relax and be himself; he found conversation easier and laughed more readily, though still not often. He had thought that a month away from everything that had ever reminded him of Elizabeth would help erase her from his mind, but it had not worked.

Every time he read something interesting in a new book, he wished to discuss it with Elizabeth. When his cousin said something ridiculous, he smiled behind his glass, thinking how funny Elizabeth would find it all. No, he could not escape her. She was everywhere, even in his sleep where he dreamt of her; sometimes the dreams were so real he would awaken calling her name.

There was one particular dream that had made Darcy awaken more than once, soaked in perspiration, his bedclothes tangled about him from his thrashing. Elizabeth was in the drawing room at Netherfield Hall, sitting in a small chair, reading a book with a gentle smile on her face. He would enter the room and she would look up at him, her eyes lighting up and her smile brightening. She would hold out her hand to him, beckoning him to come closer, but when he began to step towards her, his arm would be grabbed by Miss Bingley. She would begin chattering and talking about nothing, leading him out of the drawing room.

When he tried to turn back, his Aunt Catherine would appear on his other side, a stern look on her face, and again try to lead him from the room. He looked over his shoulder at Elizabeth who was still holding out her hand to him, but seemed to be getting further and further away. He would struggle and try to get away, but his aunt and Miss Bingley's arms would only tighten their hold, and his uncle Lord Matlock and Cousin Cyril would appear behind him, blocking his view of Elizabeth, a serious expression on their faces. He couldn't hear or understand anything they were saying, but the message was clear: You cannot have her; you must come with us now.

He would catch a glimpse of Elizabeth as she faded away, the hand that was held out to welcome him now waving farewell.

That was when he would call out her name and sit up suddenly in bed. Once, he had thrashed so hard he had actually ended up on the floor. Thankfully, his valet was the soul of discretion, or Darcy would have been seriously embarrassed.

He had left Somerset after a fortnight; his cousin was managing the estate admirably and everything was in hand. He knew he was terrible company and the all-knowing eyes of his aunt had begun to disconcert him. She knew something was wrong, but she respected his privacy too much to ask; she would wait for him to open up to her.

She would be waiting forever. Darcy could not tell. He knew that to say it aloud would make it all the more real, and his overly romantic aunt would not give counsel he could stomach at the moment.

So he had decided to come back to London and spend time with Georgiana. At least she didn't see into him like Aunt Preston. He hoped her sweetness would comfort his soul and her presence would serve as a distraction to release him from his self-imposed imprisonment.

The last thing he had expected was to find Elizabeth at his home. It was as if one of his dreams had come to life and was walking about his house. Living with Elizabeth the last few days had opened Darcy's eyes to what could be. Before he had only dreamt about life with her, with only the few days she spent at Netherfield as a guide. In rational moments he had told himself that no woman could be so wonderful in real life.

Surely, once he lived with her, he would find that she was irritable in the mornings, or that she did not wish to be inconvenienced with playing all the time and would withhold herself and her talents from him. Perhaps she had bouts of ill temper or would be cruel to the servants. Even as he told himself these things, he knew they likely weren't true, but he had to hold on to something or he would never be able to put her behind him.

Now, confronted with the living, breathing Elizabeth, he was more drawn to her than ever. She had done wonders for Georgiana, who was laughing more than he could ever remember, and opening up in a whole new way. The servants clearly adored her. She'd been there less than a week and already knew nearly all their names and always thanked and acknowledged them. She had been nothing but pleasant in the mornings, and had played and sung for him every evening, never complaining of fatigue and willing to try anything, even the songs he knew were too difficult, but Georgiana desperately wanted to play with her.

She was gracious to him, smiling and teasing, and she seemed to enjoy his company, even though she wasn't holding out her hand to him and welcoming him to her bed as in his dreams, which she obviously couldn't do in reality. Not unless he made her his wife. *My wife.*

Darcy looked out the window, his hands behind his back, not seeing the London streets in front of him. Elizabeth as his wife; it was a pretty picture. He wanted her; that was clear. He'd wanted her for months now, ever since he'd seen her muddy petticoats that morning at Netherfield.

Or was it before then? It seemed like he'd wanted her for as long as he could remember. She had worked her way into all his memories, even from his childhood when he had not known her to exist. He imagined her there alongside him; he watched for her reaction and imagined what secret things he would tell her. He could barely remember a time without her in his thoughts, even when he was desperately trying to remove her from them. She had pervaded every inch of his life. He knew this was more than attraction. It had stood the test of time; a passing infatuation would have come and gone long ago.

It was time to make a decision.

He could not continue like this. It was clear he'd never get past her. Wasn't his behavior today proof of that? She had disarmed him completely and made him feel freer than he had in years. Their comfort with each other had only continued into dinner, and when he had requested she play and sing the same song she had at Lucas Lodge last October, she'd acquiesced readily.

If this was how he behaved only five days into her visit, what would happen by the end of three weeks? He certainly couldn't trifle with her; she deserved better than that. He either needed to leave her alone and revert to civilities, or pursue the honorable course and court her properly. He knew in an instant which he preferred. If only there weren't so many obstacles!

What good was ten thousand a year, and position, and clout, if one had no right to personal choices and to live life as one desired? He was the master of Pemberley after all. Hadn't he a right to make his own decisions? Wasn't that why half the women who were after him made chase? He was the head of his small family and the choice was his and his alone. He had resisted out of respect for the opinions of his aunts and uncles, though his Aunt Preston and possibly even Lady Matlock wouldn't be too difficult, but now he had to decide what he really wanted. The answer came immediately.

He wanted Elizabeth.

CHAPTER 5

"Enter," Elizabeth answered the knock on her dressing room door.

Georgiana pushed the door open slightly and smiled at Elizabeth. She was in a night shift and dressing gown, her blonde hair in a long braid down her back, an innocent pink ribbon tied at the end. "May I come in, Miss Bennet?"

"Of course you may, Miss Darcy!" Elizabeth returned her smile. "But I must insist you call me Elizabeth, or even Lizzy if you like. May I call you Georgiana?"

"Oh yes, Miss-, Elizabeth. That would be wonderful!"

Elizabeth couldn't help but smile at her enthusiasm.

"Elizabeth?" she said is a small, sweet voice.

"Yes, Georgiana?"

"You know how you told me that you and your sister Jane used to sneak into each other's rooms and tell secrets under the blankets?"

"Of course I remember."

"Well, I know I'm not your sister, and you may be rather tired and wish to sleep right away, but..." Touched by the sweetness of her almost request, Elizabeth took pity on her and interrupted.

"Georgiana, I am not too tired and I would be only too happy to whisper secrets with you."

"Truly?"

Giggling, they climbed onto Elizabeth's enormous bed and talked of dresses and bonnets, mean French tutors, dancing lessons, and other feminine pursuits.

After a while, Georgiana looked seriously at Elizabeth and asked, "Have you ever been in love?"

"No, I have not. Why do you ask?"

"I just wonder what it feels like, that's all. Have you ever favored anyone?"

"Well, there was this one boy, John. I suppose I would have been about 14 years old. He was the brother of one of my dearest friends. He was 18 and home from university for the summer. I remember that I thought he was so handsome." Elizabeth looked up dreamily. "He used to ride his horse in the pasture adjoining my father's estate. I would climb up into the tree and watch him on his morning ride; dreaming all the while of his attentions. It was really all quite ridiculous." She smiled self-deprecatingly and shook her head.

"Did you ever talk to him?"

"I would see him occasionally while visiting my friend and we'd exchange pleasantries, but nothing significant. And I could hardly call out to him from my perch in the tree!"

"You climbed up in a tree? You know how to climb trees?" Georgiana's eyes were wide and her mouth formed a soft 'O'.

"Of course I know how to climb trees! Doesn't everyone?" Elizabeth could tell by Georgiana's expression that she was one of the few who did not know how to climb trees. "Well, I suppose it isn't a very ladylike pursuit. But as my mother would say, I was always the 'wild one'. And the impertinent one."

"I would never say you are impertinent!" Georgiana exclaimed.

"You are very kind to say so, Georgiana, but I do have it on good authority that I am in fact rather impertinent. Although I hope I am never ungracious."

"So what happened? Did he ever notice you in your tree?"

"No, he never noticed me. I watched him from afar and entertained the occasional daydream. I even went so far as to embroider his initial on one of my handkerchiefs. The next day, Jane was looking through my embroidery basket, and I was afraid she would find it. So I snatched it up, and cut the letter out right away."

"Your sister didn't know about him?"

"No! Of course not! I would have been too embarrassed! We live in a small village and it wouldn't have taken long for everyone to know about my silliness. And knowing my mother, she would have had us paired off in a fortnight. As it was, he went back to university that autumn, and I promptly forgot about him. When I was finally out and saw him at an assembly, I couldn't fathom why I had been so enamored with him in the past. He is now married to a lovely girl, and they have a lovely child and I am sure they are living a lovely life together, without me. And I am happier for it."

"You are?"

"Yes, I am. I never really loved him, and now I know what an infatuation feels like, and I shan't make the mistake of thinking it stronger than it is or something worth marrying over."

"Do you wish to get married? Have you ever been courted?"

"Oh, such questions! Let's see… I think I might like to marry one day, if I were very attached to the gentleman. I think only the deepest love will persuade me to matrimony, so I may likely die an old maid! I have never been properly courted, no, though I did receive one very horrid proposal." Elizabeth made a disgusted face and Georgiana let out a giggle.

"You must tell me all about it! What happened? Did he get on his knee? Did he recite sonnets? Was he terribly in love with you? Is he heartbroken?"

Elizabeth giggled and answered, "Well, he began by asking my mother for a private audience with me. Then he gave me a horrible little flower he'd picked from my own garden. He told me he loved me 'violently' and outlined what he was to inherit, then proceeded to enumerate all the ways that he would make an ideal husband and how he was willing to overlook my lack of fortune."

"Oh no! It sounds so unpleasant! Go on."

Elizabeth smiled at her, trying to suppress a laugh. "He told me all the reasons he wished to marry, chiefly because his patroness wished it! I begged him to stop, but he would not listen, so when he started going on about our life together, I stopped him and told him that I had yet to make him an answer. Then I thanked him and told him I could not marry him."

Georgina gasped. "What did he say?"

"He told me he understood it was the 'usual practice of elegant females' to refuse the first proposal, and accused me of trying to increase his love by suspense." At Georgiana's wide eyes, she gave a short laugh and continued, "I told him I was not the sort to torment a respectable man, and that I did not believe he could make me happy and that I was the last person in the world who could make him happy."

"Oh no! How horrible! Did he believe you? Was he crushed?"

"Unfortunately, I do not think he did believe me. You see, he is a rather ridiculous man and I don't believe for a moment that he actually cared for me. His pride was wounded, I am sure, but he seemed to rally rather quickly. He proposed to my dearest friend less than a week later and they have now wed and settled in Kent."

"Oh my! I've never heard such a story. What a terrible proposal! And then to propose to your friend only a few days later; how odd! It must have been a horrid experience for you."

"Not so horrid, only terribly embarrassing and not something I would choose to repeat. I hope the next proposal will be from the right man, or I should not wish for another one at all."

Georgiana looked at her earnestly, and Elizabeth could tell something was weighing on her mind.

"Georgiana, what is it?"

"I thought I was in love once," she said in a quiet voice.

"You did?" Elizabeth asked gently. She could tell the conversation was taking a serious turn.

"Yes," she said hesitantly. "He was an old friend of the family. I hadn't seen him in several years, but last summer I happened upon him in Ramsgate, where I was spending a holiday with my companion, Mrs. Younge. They seemed to know each other, and he was so happy to see me, and I had such fond memories of him from my childhood that I thought spending time with him would be all right."

Elizabeth simply nodded along, sensing something big was coming.

"He began coming by the cottage we had let nearly every day. He would walk with us by the shore, and take me to the theater or to a concert. My companion encouraged me to spend time with him, saying such an old family friend would always be welcome. I did not know at the time that the two of them were working together. You see, Miss Bennet, I mean Elizabeth, I have a rather large dowry. Fitzwilliam tells me that when I marry I will come into 30,000 pounds. I must confess that at the time, I did not know the exact number, but I did know that I would have a large dowry. George was so kind to me, and paid me such attention. No one had ever paid attention to me like that before. I enjoyed being told how lovely I was and spoken to of music and all my favorite books. He seemed to be so interested in me; I thought he adored me. I was such a fool." She hung her head low.

"Oh, Georgiana." Elizabeth could see where this was going and she knew it wasn't going to end well. She pulled Georgiana's head to her shoulder and put her arms around her, and began stroking her hair.

"It turned out that he had many debts and no profession and no chance of any more money coming in. My father had left him a large inheritance, but he had lost it all already. That's when he came looking for me. I was only ever a fortune to him. It wouldn't have mattered whether I was pretty or plain, whether or not I had any intelligence at all, if I was charming or ungracious; all he saw was my dowry. The worst part of it was that I really did believe him. I can't believe I was so taken in." There was a tinge of anger accompanying the sadness in her voice.

She took a deep breath and continued, "He convinced me to elope with him. He said the whole thing would be romantic, like something out of one of my novels. He said we shouldn't tell Fitzwilliam or the Colonel, but that we should just show up after we were married, and that when my brother and cousin saw how happy I was, they couldn't possibly be angry. Deep down I knew better, but I did so want to please him. And it seemed to make sense when he said it, though on reflection, I can't believe I ever listened to him." She took a deep breath and shook her head.

"The day before we were set to leave Ramsgate to get married, Fitzwilliam decided to surprise me with a visit. He had felt terrible that he couldn't accompany me, but he had so much estate business to attend to that he couldn't get away. Seeing my brother made me realize that I would never possibly want to get married without him there to witness it, so I told him everything.

"I had never seen him so angry. His face became pale and his eyes turned to stone. He didn't say a word for several minutes. He was so quiet that I thought he might have forgotten my presence. Eventually, he asked where George was staying and went to seek him out. Fitzwilliam told him that if he really loved me and was genuinely interested in my well-being, he would wait for me to be out, court me properly, ask permission to marry me, and then have a real wedding, with my family present." She sighed.

"Your brother told you right, dear," Elizabeth said softly.

"George Wickham left Ramsgate that afternoon, and I never saw him again. He didn't even tell me goodbye." Georgiana's head drooped forward with the effort of her story.

"Mr. Wickham? George Wickham?"

"Yes. He was the son of my father's steward. Do you know him?"

"Yes, we are acquainted." That was all Elizabeth trusted herself to say. So this was it. This was the missing piece in the story between Darcy and Wickham. This was why they greeted each other so coldly, and why Darcy didn't want to have anything to do with him. It certainly explained why Wickham wouldn't go anywhere near Darcy. He was lucky he hadn't chased him out of town! But she didn't have time to think about that right now. She had to attend to Georgiana.

"Georgiana, dearest, you mustn't blame yourself. You were very young, and as your brother told you, he is an experienced seducer. He lies with a silver tongue and makes you believe whatever he's saying. He comes across as amiable and pleasing; however were you to know he was not to be trusted? You were but 15 years old. And he was not a total stranger, but rather a trusted figure from your past, from a good family." Elizabeth stroked Georgiana's hair as she reassured her.

"Oh Elizabeth! It is in every way horrible!" The dam of emotions was letting go, and Georgiana trembled with the effort of her story. "After Fitzwilliam found out, he told me Wickham was not to be trusted. But I didn't want to believe him. I knew in my heart I should believe my brother, who has never misled me, but I wanted so badly to believe that Wickham loved me. Seeing I doubted him, William told me the most horrible things about him. He had been so horrible to William, racking up debts and leaving my brother to pay them. And my father left him a living in Kymptom, but he refused to take orders.

"That was the hardest part. I pictured living at the parsonage, so close to Pemberley, able to see my brother and my home any time I chose. But it was not to be. Wickham demanded money in place of the living and was given it; William later showed me the papers Wickham had signed. 3,000 pounds! He was given 3,000 pounds, plus the 1,000 my father had left him in his will, and he gambled it all away in a few short years.

"After Fitzwilliam explained it to me, I understood why I had appealed to Wickham. He was desperate for money, to pay his creditors and further his habits, and wanted to punish Fitzwilliam for not giving in to his demands. And I was foolish enough to believe him sincere. And to this snake I would have been bound for all my life!" Georgiana was vehement, outraged, and grieved, hot tears burning her cheeks. Elizabeth was struck by how much older she suddenly seemed, and just stroked her hair to comfort her, knowing she wasn't finished.

"You don't know how it relieves me to tell someone. Only my brother and Colonel Fitzwilliam know. And I don't want to talk to them about it. It's too awkward and humiliating. I know they must be terribly angry with me. I am angry with me. I caused them so much trouble, and all because of my own blindness and silly romantic notions."

"You mustn't think like this Georgiana. I am sure that neither your brother nor Colonel Fitzwilliam is angry with you. Their anger is directed where it should be, at Mr. Wickham. Yes, you were deceived. But in the end you did the right thing when your brother came. You did not lie to him or try to conceal your plans. Instead you saw your error and you chose to take the right path and confess all to him. That was very brave, Georgiana. You must believe that. You could have snuck off in the night with Mr. Wickham and never looked back. But you did not."

"It would have broken Fitzwilliam's heart."

"Yes, it would have," she said feelingly. "So you see, dear girl, in the end you chose to do the right thing, and that is what you must remember. Now that you know there are men in the world like Mr. Wickham, you will know how to recognize them and avoid them in future. Look at it as an invaluable lesson. Then think about it no more."

"That is good advice. Thank you, Elizabeth." Georgiana sighed tiredly.

"When we were little and Jane wasn't feeling well, she liked for me to sing to her until she fell asleep. In truth, we still do it upon occasion. Would you like me to do that for you?"

"Yes, that would be nice." Georgiana closed her eyes and snuggled into Elizabeth's side.

Darcy was walking down the hall toward his bedchamber when he saw a light under Georgiana's door. He knocked quietly, but when he didn't get a response, he thought she'd fallen asleep reading before blowing out her candle again. He opened the door quietly and tiptoed into her room. A few feet away from the bed he could tell no one was in it, and looking around he saw no trace of her. He heard a quiet humming coming from the dressing room door, and stepped towards it. He heard the sweet sound of Elizabeth's voice singing a lullaby. Realizing that Georgiana must be in bed with her and that she was likely singing to his sister, he involuntarily reached out and touched the door between them.

"'Domestic Bliss.'" He smiled slightly and headed to his own room.

CHAPTER 6

Elizabeth looked up at the canopy with unseeing eyes. After Georgiana fell asleep, she lay awake and thought about what she had told her. How had she been so taken in? She, who prided herself on her judgment and strength of character. *Oh, what a fool I have been!* she thought.

She had listened to Wickham, sympathized with him, and sided against Darcy, and for what? Wickham had lied to her and abused her trust. He had taken advantage of an innocent girl. He was a cad and a rake and a liar of the first order.

Stupid, stupid girl! Wretched, wretched mistake! Even though she was alone, she felt everyone could see her folly. She had not made her preference for Wickham a secret. Even when he had ceased his attentions to her in order to pursue Miss King, she had excused him, thinking him realistic; when in fact he was simply mercenary, and nothing else. She felt the heat of shame burning through her.

She had been so willing to believe him! She had readily bought everything said about Mr. Darcy, even though she had known Wickham but a moment and Darcy for a month. Bingley trusted him, and what she herself knew of Darcy spoke to truth and honesty. He may not have been the most cordial or amiable man, but she had not believed he could be so despicable when she first heard Wickham's tale. How quickly she had capitulated!

Wickham had flattered her and favored her, and she had rewarded him with her trust. Darcy had insulted her vanity, and she had returned in kind with contempt and hostility, often teasing him mercilessly. And if she were being honest with herself, she often did it with the intent of making him uncomfortable or angry. She'd thought he deserved it.

How long must the man be punished for one rude statement, spoken in an assembly months before? Elizabeth felt wretched. Here she lay in a soft bed in his more than comfortable house, enjoying his hospitality, befriending his sister, and all the while thinking contemptibly of him. How could she have made such a grievous mistake? She must rectify her behavior. She would be nice to Mr. Darcy.

With this new resolution in mind, Elizabeth closed her eyes and found a fitful sleep.

~

The next morning Elizabeth sat up quickly and slid off the bed. She tiptoed to the dressing room and shut the door gently behind her. She washed up in the basin, which thankfully had been filled with warm water, *God bless Hannah!*, donned a lilac morning dress and sprinkled lavender water in her hair. Twisting her hair up into a simple braided knot, she headed downstairs to the breakfast room.

Checking the clock at the bottom of the stairs, she realized it was still rather early, and began planning what she would do until Georgiana awakened. As she walked down the wide hall, she noticed a half-open door on her right. Looking swiftly inside, she saw a massive library filled with books from floor to ceiling. She let out a light gasp, then afraid she would be caught snooping, quickly made her way to the breakfast room. *Well, now I know how I will spend my time when Georgiana is unavailable.*

Stepping into the breakfast room, Elizabeth was surprised to see Mr. Darcy sitting at the table with a newspaper. She quietly made her way over to the sideboard and began to fill her plate. The soft clinking of dishes made Mr. Darcy aware that someone else was in the room, and he peeked around the side of his paper.

"Good morning, Miss Bennet," he said with a smile as he rose and bowed.

Slightly startled, Elizabeth turned around and curtsied. "Good morning, Mr. Darcy," she said with a bright smile. *See how nice I'm being?* Darcy looked somewhat surprised, but recovered quickly.

Elizabeth was walking to the table with her plate when she noticed Mrs. Hawkins entering the room. She set her plate down in front of her chair and walked to her side. She quietly addressed the housekeeper.

"Mrs. Hawkins, would you please let Hannah know that Miss Darcy can be found in my chambers this morning?"

"Yes, Miss Bennet. Thank you."

"Thank you, Mrs. Hawkins," Elizabeth nodded and headed back to the table. Darcy had been standing the entire time, waiting for Elizabeth to be seated.

His curiosity piqued, he couldn't resist asking her, "Miss Bennet, what business could you possibly have with my housekeeper?"

Elizabeth looked at him oddly. But deciding he looked more curious than put out, she decided to tell him. After all, she was being nice now. "I simply asked her to let Hannah know that Miss Darcy was to be found in my chambers this morning and not in her own."

"Oh, did she stay with you all night?"

Elizabeth found this line of questioning a little odd, especially coming from someone as formal as Mr. Darcy.

"Yes, we were speaking together until rather late and she fell asleep. I did not want to wake her," she answered hesitantly, her look clearly telling him she would give away no more.

Slightly embarrassed for his awkward question, Darcy went back to his newspaper. After a few minutes spent quietly sipping her tea and reading the lines on the back of Darcy's paper, she interrupted him.

"Mr. Darcy?"

"Yes, Miss Bennet?"

"I wonder if I could possibly use your library this morning, unless you had other plans for it?" She looked at him expectantly, a small sparkle in her eyes.

"Of course you may. I am surprised you have not already availed yourself of the library. Did Georgiana not give you a tour when you first arrived?"

"She showed me the drawing room, dining room and breakfast parlor, the music room, and of course my own chambers, but I'm afraid we quite missed the library," she said with an impish grin.

"Ah, I see," he said with a grin. "Well, I shall show it to you after breakfast. You're welcome to use it any time of course. My study is in a separate room, so you will be disturbing no one."

"I thank you, sir."

Elizabeth finished her breakfast in silence, wondering why Mr. Darcy was being so friendly. He had already smiled at her several times and even offered to escort her to the library. This was not the Mr. Darcy of Netherfield Hall.

Armed with new information from her conversation with Georgiana, Elizabeth was beginning to look at Mr. Darcy in a new light. Everything Mr. Wickham had said was false, she knew now, but she had disliked Mr. Darcy before Wickham. Why was that again?

Oh, yes! How could she forget? He had refused to dance with her and said she was merely tolerable. Elizabeth knew she wasn't as beautiful as

Jane, but no one was. Jane's beauty was only enhanced by her sweetness, something Elizabeth knew she would never have. But she was pretty in her own right, and had a bright complexion. Several people had told her so, and she had eyes and a mirror.

Yet he had been disdainful to her then and was solicitous of her now. Why the change?

Oh, Mr. Darcy was an enigma. Just when she thought she was getting a feel for his true nature, he surprised her. *Well, he certainly makes for an interesting character study. And now I have something else to do during my stay in London*, she thought with a grin.

"Miss Bennet," his voice broke through her reverie. "Is something amusing?"

"I'm sorry? Amusing? No, why do you ask?" she asked, slightly chagrined to be caught thinking about him in his presence.

"You were smiling."

"Might a person smile without anything being particularly amusing?" She knew it sounded weak, but she was irritated at being caught and annoyed with herself for not saving her thoughts for when she was alone. "One can think of something pleasurable without it being amusing."

"Indeed," he said, not fooled in the slightest. "And what pleasures were you pondering, Miss Bennet?"

"The library, sir. And all the treasures I might find therein." She smiled innocently.

He set his napkin down on the table and rose. "Then let us be on our way, Miss Bennet. Far be it from me to suspend any pleasure of yours." His expression was smooth, but neither missed the significance of his words, nor had they forgotten the first time he had spoken them. She swallowed hard and rose to follow him.

The library was on the main floor and not too far from the breakfast parlor. Thinking they would head to the room she had passed earlier off the main hallway, she was surprised when Mr. Darcy turned a corner into a short corridor and opened the door at the end. No wonder she hadn't seen it on her own; it was rather out of the way.

When she entered, Elizabeth gave a small gasp. Her eyes widened as she stepped into the room, her gaze falling upon shelf after shelf of books. The cases went from floor to ceiling, which was rather high, and there was a rolling ladder in the corner to reach the highest volumes.

The far wall had three large windows, beginning knee height off the floor and extending nearly to the ceiling, twice the width of a normal window, and bathing the room in light. Each had a seat built into it, covered by a thick cushion. Between each window was another bookshelf, filled with leather spines and gold leaf print.

Elizabeth turned around slowly, taking it all in. Her eyes only became wider as each new view showed more bookcases overflowing with perfectly kept books. There was a fireplace on one end of the narrow room, flanked by a pair of wingback chairs. In the center of the room, there was a round table with four chairs and a sofa and smaller tables on the other end.

Every wall was covered in bookcases, each shelf filled to capacity. The only sound was Elizabeth's breathing and the crackling of the fire.

She had forgotten Darcy was there, fascinated as she was with this incomparable room. As she turned back in his direction, she noticed his expression. It was different somehow; softer, less guarded. His eyes met hers and they regarded each other silently for a moment. In his eyes she saw something she had never seen there before; generosity, warmth, a sense of comfort she wasn't used to seeing in him.

"Forgive me, Mr. Darcy. I fear I am a bit overcome," she said quietly.

"There is nothing to forgive, Miss Bennet. Please, enjoy the library as much as you'd like on your stay here. If you'll excuse me," said Darcy, and with a slight bow, he turned and left, retreating into his mask of civility once again.

Elizabeth shook off her shock and began to explore the library. She found the cases to be organized according to subject, and within that, according to date.

"An organized and fastidious library, for an organized and fastidious master," she murmured to herself. She found a shelf with poetry, and choosing a volume, she quickly made herself comfortable in the soft chair in front of the fire.

On the other side of the wall, Darcy was in his study trying to concentrate. It was becoming increasingly difficult with the knowledge that Elizabeth was, at this very moment, on the other side of the wall, relaxing in his library.

Alone.

He was manfully fighting an intense urge to take her by the hand and show her his favorite books in the library, then lead her to settle in front of the fire where he would hold her in his arms and read to her - among other things. "Get a hold of yourself, man! You can withstand this. You shall withstand this!"

The look on her face as she'd taken in the library, the expression in her eyes, was unforgettable. She was completely enraptured, perfectly happy, and totally genuine. She was so unguarded, so utterly artless, he could not fail to be drawn into her joy. His pleasure at her enjoying his home so much – his library, his favorite room in the house – was immeasurable. He couldn't fathom how he could feel so happy over something as small as Elizabeth liking his library. It made him want to make her happy again, and before he knew what he was about, he was envisioning all the places he would like to show her and see that look of wonder in her eyes again.

~

Friday afternoon brought Lady Matlock to Darcy House. As it happened, Darcy was fencing with Sir Malcolm, and as usual, Georgiana and Elizabeth were working on their latest duet in the music room when the butler announced her Ladyship.

"Lady Helen!" Georgiana sprang up from the bench and walked quickly to her aunt, clearly holding back a skip.

"I hope you don't mind dear, I just had Hawkins bring me straight back. I hope I'm not disturbing you? Do you have guests?"

"Of course you're not disturbing anything, Aunt! May I introduce my friend, Miss Elizabeth Bennet of Longbourn in Hertfordshire."

Elizabeth curtseyed.

"It is a pleasure to meet you, dear. Georgiana has gone on and on about you." Georgiana blushed and looked at the carpet.

Elizabeth smiled widely and said, "She has told me much about you as well, your Ladyship."

The three ladies spent the next hour discussing all manner of topics and doing a great bit of laughing, when Lady Matlock suddenly interjected, "Oh, Georgiana! I have been having such a pleasant time, I almost forgot what I came here to tell you. I am hosting a ball in a fortnight and I want Fitzwilliam to bring you. And you must attend as well, Miss Bennet, of course."

Georgiana went pale. "You want me to go to a ball? But I am not yet out."

"Yes dear, I know, but you did just turn sixteen, and it is not unusual for girls your age to attend family functions such as this. Of course you will only be permitted to dance with family members, but between the Earl, Fitzwilliam, and your cousins, I imagine you'll have a lovely time. And it will give you practice so that you'll be better prepared for next season."

Seeing her distress, Elizabeth reached over and grabbed Georgiana's hand. It did not go unnoticed by Lady Matlock.

"It will be a small affair, dearest. Only the family, and our oldest and closest friends. That is why I thought it would be the perfect time for you try out your dancing and get familiar with the workings of a ballroom. No one shall ask you to dance that isn't family, which will allow you to acclimate to the surroundings. Next year, however, you are likely to have a full card, and you'll want to know what you're about," she said with authority.

"Yes, Aunt, I know you are right. It is wise for me have some practice. What should I wear? I suppose I have nothing appropriate."

"We shall have to go shopping, of course. I've made an appointment for Tuesday. You will join us, of course, Miss Bennet." It was not a request.

"I should like to accompany you, Lady Matlock."

"It's all settled then. I shall pick you up Tuesday morning at eleven o'clock." She smiled at them, kissed Georgiana, told Elizabeth how pleasant it had been to meet her, and departed.

Lady Matlock left Darcy House in high spirits. She had heard about Miss Bennet from Georgiana, and knowing her nature, she knew how difficult it was for her to make friends. And knowing how attractive her brother, or rather her brother's wealth, was to so many ladies of the ton, she knew Georgiana was inundated with requests for friendship by women wanting nothing of the sort, but who only wanted to ingratiate themselves with Darcy's beloved sister. It was widely known how devoted he was to her, and more than one lady had tried to take advantage of that fact.

A certain Miss Bingley came to mind. Lady Matlock had been able to scare off all the others, but because Mr. Bingley was Darcy's good friend, she could hardly make Darcy House forbidden to his sister. At least she wasn't on the guest list for the ball; there was one simpering smile she could forego for the evening.

As the mother of two rather eligible bachelors and the aunt of another, she knew her fair share of blushing ladies and their scheming mamas. She was ever diligent to protect her family from those whose sole purpose was mercenary.

That was one reason she had 'surprised' Georgiana with this visit today; she wanted to see this Elizabeth Bennet for herself. She was quite relieved to find that she was a genuine friend, and she hadn't mentioned Mr. Darcy once, which was a singular occurrence. When talking to Caroline Bingley, Lady Matlock had given up counting how many times Mr. Darcy or Pemberley was mentioned in one conversation when she got to fifteen. She found Elizabeth unaffected and charming, and that is exactly what she told her husband when she returned home.

CHAPTER 7

Elizabeth had taken to sitting in the library the mornings she didn't visit Gracechurch Street. While Georgiana worked on her French, she would search through the tomes for something she hadn't yet read, and cozy up by the fire in one of the large wingback chairs. The housekeeper had taken to bringing her a cup of tea and a plate of lemon biscuits while she read. Elizabeth would always thank her for her thoughtfulness and smile brightly, genuinely complimenting the blend of the tea or the flavor of the biscuits. She even went so far as to request that Cook send the recipe home with her to give to the Longbourn cook, as she was sure she had never tasted better. Cook was so flattered, she sent the recipe straightaway, and made sure Elizabeth was never without lemon biscuits, and planned to send a tin of them home with her when she left.

Elizabeth had just finished a small volume of Wordsworth, and was now ready for something different. Leaving her comfortable place by the fire, she headed to the opposite side of the room and began perusing the shelves there. When she turned, something caught her eye. Near the corner, there was a small patch of wall not covered in shelves. There was a painting of a house hanging there, simply framed. She stepped closer to look at it and saw that it was a large stone house, with a lake in front and a small forested hill behind it. There was a sense of serenity about it, and a natural beauty that was elegant, but unforced.

She was standing quite close to the painting now, and did not notice when the wall behind it began to move until it nearly crashed into her, sending her jumping backward, but not before it caught her foot with a stabbing pain. She closed her eyes tightly and bit down on both lips, sucking in a painful breath, her hands curling into fists at her side. She took a steadying breath and opened her eyes to reveal a very stunned and horrified Mr. Darcy.

"Miss Elizabeth! I am so sorry! I didn't know you were there. Are you injured?" He felt terrible and was quickly at her side, not knowing what to do with his hands, but clearly wanting to help.

"I shall be fine, Mr. Darcy. Wherever did you come from?" Elizabeth tried to keep the irritation and pain out of her voice, but was not entirely successful.

"My study is just on the other side of that door. I came to get a book. I am so sorry Miss Bennet, I-" she cut him off.

"Door?"

"Oh, of course. The door only opens from the other side, that's why you won't have seen the handle. My grandfather had it installed so he could leave his study without being noticed."

"He did not wish to enter it without being noticed, as well?"

"No, I suppose not." He half-smiled.

Elizabeth began to hobble toward the fire, but he was by her side in a moment. "Allow me to assist you, Miss Bennet." He put a hand under her elbow and steered her toward the chair.

"I thank you, Mr. Darcy."

"Not at all."

He helped lower her into the seat, then grabbed a small stool and placed it at her feet.

"May I?" He gestured to her foot.

Not sure what he was going to do, she nodded. He then gingerly lifted her foot and placed it on the stool. Then he began to remove her slipper, keeping one hand on her ankle, the other around her heel. As he slid it deftly off and placed it on the floor, her eyes never left him. His face was turned down, but she was watching him carefully. His hands were large and warm, but somehow still gentle. She enjoyed the feel of his touch on her foot, and she began to breathe more shallowly, not fully aware of her own physical sensations but knowing that she liked his nearness and inexplicably wished for more. As she stared at his unruly hair, he suddenly looked up at her, their eyes meeting.

His deep blue eyes were soft and fathomless and filled her with a warmth she didn't understand. *Why is he looking at me like that?* She didn't know what she was about, but she couldn't look away. As she stared into his blue depths, her expression went from fascination, to confusion, to a welcoming understanding. The longer she looked at him, the more she felt she understood him. Only not in words as much as she felt the very essence of him. He was so very open; there wasn't a trace of the arrogance or haughtiness she had come to expect.

He released her foot and sat in the chair opposite her. "You should be fine, Miss Bennet. It shouldn't swell too much if you keep it elevated."

"I thank you, Mr. Darcy," she said in a small voice. They were both clearly unnerved, but neither knew what to say next.

"I was looking at the painting in the corner. It is very beautiful. Where was it painted?"

"In the music room."

"Excuse me?"

"Uh, Georgiana painted it in the music room from an original I have in my study. It is Pemberley."

"Oh." Again searching for words, she said, "Is it very like?"

"Yes, quite, though without doing a disfavor to my sister's talents, I think the actual subject much more beautiful." He had recovered himself, and was now returned to his usual demeanor.

Elizabeth noticed the change and wondered what had happened or if it had all been in her imagination.

"I shall have to compliment her on her work."

"Miss Bennet, please allow me to apologize again for coming upon you in such a way. It was unforgivable. I should have thought and been more careful." His voice was steady, but his eyes were troubled.

"Do not worry yourself overmuch, Mr. Darcy. You are used to being on your own with an unoccupied library, and even if you had known I was here, you couldn't have possibly known that I would be standing directly behind the door."

He looked at her sheepishly, feeling guilty for hurting her, and not wanting to admit to knowing that she had been in the library and that he had come with the hope of a quick glimpse of her. He always knew exactly where she was in his house and was painfully aware of her presence at all times.

"Miss Bennet, can I get you anything, some wine perhaps?"

"It is a bit early for wine, Mr. Darcy," she gave a small laugh, "but I shall have a cup of tea. Would you like one as well? This blend is particularly good."

She quickly leaned forward and began pouring her own cup of tea, then looked at him questioningly. He nodded for her to continue and she poured him a cup as well. She added a drop of milk to each, then a touch of lemon, and handed him his cup on a saucer.

It usually annoyed him when people prepared his tea without asking him how he liked it, but he couldn't feel irritated.

"I hope you don't mind Mr. Darcy, but this is really the best way. I should know as I've tried several combinations and have discovered this one to be my favorite, especially if you're going to have a biscuit. They are remarkably good," she said as she cheerfully nudged the plate of lemon biscuits in his direction.

"Thank you for allowing me the advantage of your previous study, Miss Bennet," he said as he took a sip of the tea. His eyebrows went up slightly and he looked at his cup appreciatively.

"Good, isn't it? This blend is quickly becoming my favorite."

How was it that he was beginning to feel like her guest instead of the other way around?

"You are quite right, Miss Bennet, this blend is delightful, as is the way you have prepared it." She nodded in response and ate her biscuit as they sat in companionable silence for a few minutes.

"I gather you didn't have any tedious meetings this morning?"

"Excuse me?"

"You did say that when you have tedious meetings, you are too tired to read, and you were coming to fetch a book, were you not?"

"Yes, I was," he said, understanding dawning on him, "but I'm afraid I did have a rather tedious meeting earlier. I would prefer another source of entertainment, since the weather is not suitable for exercise," he said with a sly grin.

"And what sort of entertainment are you looking for, sir?"

"I was hoping to hear a story."

"Shall I read to you then? I have found several lovely volumes of poetry. Wordsworth is particularly fine on such a day."

"I'm afraid I am not in the mood for poetry."

"No? Shall I fetch 'Fordyce's Sermons'?"

"Miss Bennet." He looked at her reproachfully, but with a hint of humor in his eyes.

"What did you have in mind then, Mr. Darcy?"

"I believe you owe me a story, Miss Bennet."

"So I do. Would you like to hear anything in particular?" God, he loved it when she looked at him like that. *Be careful, Elizabeth.*

"I should like to hear anything you should like to tell me."

"Hmmm, let me see. Would you like to hear about naughty little Lizzy, or troublesome Elizabeth?"

"I think I'd like naughty little Lizzy best."

"Very well, then." She made a face as if thinking about something very important, and then began.

"At Longbourn, there is a tree near the edge of the estate where it borders Lucas lodge. It is perfect for climbing. There is a branch that hangs down particularly low to make it easier to climb up." She gestured with her hands and Darcy leaned back in his chair, his eyes in rapt attention, his hands steepled in front of his mouth.

"One summer, my father's sister came to stay with us and brought my cousins, Thomas and Michael. They were horrid boys, always stealing our dolls and hiding them in tops of trees, strapping them to branches with our favorite ribbons. Kitty and Jane would cry inconsolably, and they would just laugh at us before their mama would make them give our toys back.

"One afternoon, our parents and aunt went to a party and weren't due back home till late that night. Jane and I were playing merrily when Thomas ran in and stole Jane's new doll. It had been a birthday present from our parents, and she'd only gotten it the week before. It had a lovely porcelain face, with blue eyes just like Jane's and a lace gown. She loved that doll and carried it with her everywhere, even sleeping with it at night. Which is why, of course, horrid Thomas stole it in the first place." She made a disgusted face and Darcy hid his smile behind his hands.

"So Thomas ran off with the doll, shrieking that he would hide it where we'd never find it. He passed it off to Michael and the two of them ran into the pastures, towards the tree on the property line. We all ran behind them, Jane and Kitty crying, Mary holding little Lydia by the hand. Of course they outran us and were well into the tree by the time we arrived at the bottom. They had fashioned a noose out of ribbons and put it around the doll's neck, and there she was, hanging from the tree." Darcy clamped down hard on his jaw to suppress a laugh and nodded for her to continue.

"Well, you can imagine how it was. Jane was in a terrible state over seeing her prized possession being executed, and there was Kitty, wailing in the background, Mary trying to console her; it was quite a sight. They jumped down from the tree and began taunting us, saying that we'd never get it down and their mother wouldn't be home until later, so we couldn't go to her. The doll would have to stay up there all night. Then they began talking about what would happen if it rained and how the doll would be completely ruined.

"Eventually, I had had enough. I told them that I would climb up into the tree and retrieve the doll. They didn't believe me and said that girls can't climb trees and even if they could, our skirts would get in the way. That was when I got an idea. They were to be staying another month and we couldn't continue doing this every day, so I challenged them."

"You challenged them?"

"Yes. I told them we would race to the top. If I got to the doll first, they could not take any more of our toys and must behave like gentlemen the rest of their trip. If they got to the top first, we couldn't tell their mother about any of this. We shook on the deal and they decided horrid Thomas would be the one to race me, since he was taller and had longer limbs.

"I tied my skirts up around my waist and Jane counted us down. When she said go, we both began to climb furiously, but I knew the way better." She couldn't hide the air of pride she felt in her accomplishment. "I had climbed that tree hundreds of times and knew exactly where to step. I had made it to the top and was reaching for the doll long before Thomas. He was so angry with me, he reached out to grab the doll from my arms, but I hit him with my elbow."

She released a sigh.

"Unfortunately, he lost his balance and fell all the way to the ground. His arm was twisted terribly behind his back and he was screaming in pain, and cursing me with words I had never heard. Michael ran for Mr. Hill and the doctor came and declared he had a broken arm.

"They couldn't set it until our parents returned several hours later, so he was given laudanum and laid in the kitchen crying and writhing in pain. Eventually all was set right, but he ended up having to stay with us another six weeks until the doctor declared he was ready to travel."

She slumped back into the chair and exhaled loudly. "It was horrible! My mother went on and on about how unladylike my behavior was and said that if I wasn't so wild, none of this would have happened. As my punishment, whether for climbing or pushing, I don't know, she made me act as Thomas's nurse while he stayed with us. I had to bring him tea and give him his medicine. Mother said it would teach me how to take care of a man, which was what I should be doing, instead of keeping my nose in books all day and climbing trees." She rolled her eyes.

"And did you?"

"Did I what?"

"Learn to take care of a man?" he asked with a smirk and a glint in his eye.

"I hardly think a twelve-year-old boy can be called a man, Mr. Darcy," she replied with an impish smile.

He let out a deep, rumbling laugh. "No, he cannot, Miss Bennet. He certainly cannot."

CHAPTER 8

Tuesday morning rolled around, and Elizabeth searched for something appropriate to wear to go shopping with Lady Matlock. She wasn't obsessed with ribbons and bonnets like Kitty and Lydia, but she was sensible of the fact that she would be going to considerably nicer shops than she was used to, and that Lady Matlock was a recognizable figure. She did not wish to look like a charity case next to her.

She finally selected a newer gown she'd had made only a few months ago. It was pale green velvet with a simple scoop neck and straight sleeves that reached just below the elbows, a narrow lace ruffle at the collar and sleeves, and three tiny pearl buttons down the center of the bodice. It was cut a little lower than she was used to, thanks to her mother, but it was very flattering and made her merely adequate assets appear ample. Hannah put her hair up in a simple but elegant coiffure, and Elizabeth declared herself ready.

Lady Matlock picked them up at exactly eleven o'clock, and they were off. After pouring over patterns and fabrics for hours, they had finally made their choices. Georgiana's dress was to be white, of course, and had a square neckline that was high enough to be modest but not so high as to be prudish. It had a sheer overlay and capped, puffed sleeves out of the same sheer fabric. She had decided to wear a blue ribbon around her waist and more wound through her hair.

Elizabeth's dress was also white, but her neckline was much lower, befitting her age, and the bodice was crossed, creating a 'V' where the two sections met. The sleeves were short and capped and trimmed in a very thin white lace. Mindful of how much she was spending, Elizabeth wanted to keep it simple. Her aunt Gardiner had told her to have the bill sent to them, but she didn't want to take advantage of their kindness and she knew this modiste would charge much more than the one she typically used. Besides, she liked simple styles and didn't feel that overly done dresses and satin turbans suited her.

"Is your dress going to be white as well?" Georgiana asked her as she looked at the different bolts of fabric.

"It is the proper thing, isn't it? I must admit, I have always wanted to wear a red gown. But mama says I am too young for such a strong color and that I can wear red when I am forty." She gave a short laugh and looked wistfully at the fabric.

"I think you would look lovely in red, Elizabeth! Maybe you can wear red flowers in your hair?"

"Perhaps." She carefully fingered a white silk fabric in front of her, then the red one next to it.

They made a few more stops; at the glovers, they each bought a pair of white satin, elbow-length gloves, and at the boot-makers, they looked at new dancing slippers. Elizabeth declared her old ones were fine and in no need of replacement, but Georgiana picked up a pair of delicate satin ones that were embellished with pearl beads.

After handing their purchases to the footman, the three ladies headed off in the direction of the bookstore. Elizabeth wanted to pick up a gift for her father, and Georgiana was looking for something for Darcy's birthday, which was coming up in March.

When they stepped inside, Elizabeth saw a tall man with jet black hair, a handsome face, and arresting blue eyes. His skin was pale in contrast to his hair and his nose was long and straight, giving him a somewhat angular look that was not unattractive. He looked at her and smiled, as if he knew her. She recognized him from somewhere, but couldn't quite place him.

"Lady Matlock! Miss Darcy!" the man exclaimed.

"Sir Malcolm, how nice to see you again." Lady Matlock smiled and he bowed over her hand.

"Sir Malcolm, allow me to introduce Miss Elizabeth Bennet. Miss Bennet, this is Sir Malcolm Rutherford. He and Mr. Darcy were at Cambridge together and our families are old friends."

"It is a pleasure to meet you, Miss Bennet." He bowed over her hand.

"I am pleased to make your acquaintance, Sir Malcolm." Elizabeth curtseyed slowly, feeling a blush creep over her cheeks from the way he was looking at her.

He bowed over Georgiana's hand as she whispered a greeting and turned back to Lady Matlock.

"Are you ladies shopping for anything in particular?"

"Miss Bennet is looking for a gift for her father, and Miss Darcy looks for something for her brother. His birthday is in a few weeks."

"May I assist you in your search?" He gestured to Elizabeth.

"Of course." He and Elizabeth walked toward the back of the store to the area designated for histories while Georgiana and Lady Matlock went to see the first editions.

"Will you be attending the Matlocks' ball, Miss Bennet?"

"Yes, I will be. And you, Sir?"

"Yes, I am planning on it. Our families are very old friends. My father and Lord Matlock were at Cambridge together, as were Darcy and I."

"I see," she said noncommittally. Sir Malcolm seemed nice enough, and was just the sort of engaging, amiable man Elizabeth usually liked to converse with. However, her recent experience with Mr. Wickham made her leery of strange, charming men.

"Are you staying with the Darcys?"

"Yes, Miss Darcy is a friend. How did you know?"

"I saw you there last week. You had just come down the stairs as I was saying goodbye to Darcy. I must not have made a very good impression if you do not remember me," he said with a warm smile as he leaned his shoulder against the bookshelf, his arms crossed in front of him. He had a natural easiness about him that showed confidence, but was not conceited.

"Yes, I do remember you, so do not feel too wounded." She returned his smile. "I was trying to place you earlier when I first saw you."

Somehow, knowing he was a current friend of Mr. Darcy's made her more easy with him. *How strange*, she thought.

"How long will you be staying in London?"

"I am afraid I leave right after the ball."

"That is too bad, Miss Bennet. I had hoped for the opportunity to get to know you better." He looked at her sincerely and she wondered what she could say without being flirtatious, but she didn't want to send him off completely.

"There will be the ball, Sir Malcolm, so you mustn't despair completely." She smiled sweetly to soften her teasing.

"Then may I take this opportunity to secure a set with you, Miss Bennet?" He straightened formally, and she noticed his eyes had a slight gleam in them when he grinned.

"You may, Sir Malcolm. Would you prefer a particular set?"

"The supper set, if you please. And perhaps I shall secure another when the night arrives, if you are not too inundated with requests."

"You may be tired of me by then, sir," she answered.

"Somehow I doubt that, madam."

Elizabeth just shook her head and began perusing the books in front of her. After Malcolm helped her choose between a history of Russia and one about the Spanish armada, she headed for the front of the store to find Lady Matlock. She and Georgiana were looking through the shelves of first editions, each holding a volume.

"Ah, Miss Bennet. Perhaps you can help us; we are trying to decide. Do you think my nephew would prefer Milton or Wordsworth?" She held up two volumes, one older than the other, but both in good condition.

"I do not claim to know Mr. Darcy's reading preferences, but I believe he would likely enjoy either. He seems to like most books."

"That is exactly the problem, my dear. It is impossible to buy a gift for a man who has exacting tastes, and purchases everything he desires himself," Lady Matlock said, slightly exasperated.

"Perhaps there is a way to make it more personal. Georgiana, maybe you could make a bookmarker or two for Mr. Darcy and place it in the book next to your favorite selection. I believe he would like that."

"What a good idea, Elizabeth! Now we only need to choose the book." She looked at the shelves in consternation as they all began picking up books and perusing titles. Finally settling on a volume of Milton, they paid for their purchases and headed outside.

"It has been a pleasure, ladies." Sir Malcolm bowed.

"It had been nice meeting you, Sir Malcolm." Elizabeth curtseyed.

"The pleasure has been all mine. Lady Matlock, I look forward to your ball with great anticipation." He smiled broadly and stole a glance at Elizabeth. "Miss Darcy, until we meet again."

"Good day, Sir Malcolm." Lady Matlock curtseyed and headed to the carriage. "Well, Miss Bennet, I believe the Baronet was quite taken with you."

"Do you? He only just met me." Despite her effort to remain calm, Elizabeth blushed slightly.

"I have known Sir Malcolm since he was in his cradle. He was a very sweet boy, and rather intelligent. He and Richard used to play together and his mother was a friend of mine. I am still friendly with his aunt. I am sure she will be asking me about you at the ball."

"About me? Why? Surely you don't think him interested enough to warrant his family asking questions!"

Georgiana let out a giggle. "This is exciting, Elizabeth! Now you'll have a suitor that isn't horrid!"

Lady Matlock raised a brow, but chose not to pursue the comment. "What is your situation, Miss Bennet? I hate to be so blunt, but as you will be my guest at the ball, and young men will be dancing with you, it only follows that their mothers will ask me questions and I wish to be as prepared as possible. I hope you do not mind, dear." Her expression was kind but determined, and Elizabeth knew it was more of a command, simply framed as a request to be polite.

"I believe I understand you, Lady Matlock. I am not engaged, neither am I currently being courted. My affections are unattached at present." Lady Matlock nodded in approval.

"I come from a small estate in Hertfordshire called Longbourn where my father's family has resided for more than a hundred years. I have no brothers and the estate is entailed away from the female line, so my four sisters and I are the last generation of Bennets to be born there, as the recipient of the estate is a man named Collins, a cousin of my father's. I have no dowry to speak of, but stand to inherit fifty pounds per annum upon marriage. I play the pianoforte and sing, but I do not draw and only speak French, and not very well. I can read some Latin, but not with ease. Does that answer your question, Lady Matlock?" Elizabeth recited her pedigree without emotion, not wishing to over- or under-state her circumstances.

Elizabeth was fully cognizant of her situation in life, but she had mixed feelings regarding the match-making gleam she recognized all too easily in Lady Matlock's eye. Fundamentally, she disliked the idea of having a suitor chosen for her; she wished to make her own decision regarding something as important as her companion in life. However, she also knew that she could not simply wander through Hyde Park approaching gentlemen and requesting their marital status while trying to discern whether or not they were amiable.

She did not wish to develop an interest in someone only to have it dashed once he knew her circumstances. She also didn't want to be at the mercy of Mr. Collins after her father's death, and she knew Jane wouldn't be home forever to soften the blow. With her beauty, she would likely be snatched up soon and Elizabeth was not looking forward to living at Longbourn without her.

And she did wish for love and companionship; she was human, after all. And Sir Malcolm did seem interesting… *Oh, why must everything be so complicated!*

Lady Matlock looked at her kindly, with soft eyes. For the first time, Elizabeth noticed they were green. "Yes, that answers my question perfectly, my dear. There are some things you should know before the ball. I always invite more gentlemen than ladies. Partially because they are more likely than ladies to change their response and decide the day before that they'd rather be in the country"- she rolled her eyes slightly-"but mostly because I remember being at balls when I was your age and I hated it when the ladies outnumbered the gentlemen." At this she smiled a little impishly and Elizabeth let out a small chuckle.

"I see why you presume my dance card will be full."

"Yes, I am sure it will be. You should also know that I will choose in advance some young men that I believe will suit you. I'll inform you beforehand so you'll be sure to know who they are. They will be of good family, well bred, no one with bad habits." At this she raised her eyebrows and looked pointedly at Elizabeth.

"I understand you perfectly, Lady Matlock."

"I believe Sir Malcolm will ask you to dance as well. He is certainly very eligible and a good sort of man. " Elizabeth looked out the window, feigning interest in something in the street.

"Ah, he already asked you, didn't he?" Elizabeth's blush and guilty expression was all the answer she needed. "Good. That's very good." Lady Matlock smiled knowingly, and they rode the rest of the way in silence.

Elizabeth was slightly irritated at the idea of Lady Matlock arranging her life for her, but she found it too amusing to be truly angry. Besides, it would be entertaining if nothing else. There would be plenty of dancing, which she always enjoyed, and from the sound of it, plenty of partners, so it was likely she wouldn't sit out more than a dance or two. If she tried to push any really horrid partners on her, Elizabeth knew what to do. And she would be leaving shortly after the ball anyway, so why not let the lady have her fun?

~

Nearly six hours after they left, an exhausted Georgiana and Elizabeth walked back into Darcy House. They had a few small packages from their immediate purchases, and their new gowns would be delivered next week. As Elizabeth thanked the footman who took their things, Darcy came around the corner.

"Good afternoon. I trust your shopping trip was fruitful?" He smiled at their exhausted expressions.

"Yes, I bought a new ball gown! It's so pretty, I cannot wait to wear it!" Georgiana's eyes looked dreamy as she hummed and swayed up the stairs, Darcy and Elizabeth following.

"And you, Miss Bennet? Did you find a pretty new ball gown?" he asked with a smirk.

She laughed lightly. "Yes, I believe I was quite successful. We did run into someone while we were out."

"Oh? Who did you meet?"

"Miss Bingley, but only for a moment. We were leaving as she was arriving."

He started slightly, but quickly composed himself. When he looked at her, his face was a mask of civility. "Was Miss Bingley well?"

"Yes, quite well. She hadn't known I was in town and was surprised to see me with Georgiana and Lady Matlock. I asked after her brother, Mr. Bingley." Darcy looked straight ahead. "She said he is well and here in town." Elizabeth looked at Mr. Darcy, trying to discern if he knew about Caroline's deceit, but as usual, his countenance gave nothing away.

"Yes, Bingley is here in town. I saw him at my club a few days ago."

"I think I'd like to see Mr. Bingley while I'm here. Do you think I might have the opportunity?" she asked with one raised brow.

"I cannot say for certain, Miss Bennet. He occasionally stops by; perhaps you will see him then."

Elizabeth nodded and let the conversation drop. It was clear he would say no more, and pushing him on so delicate a matter would not help her cause. Distracted with thoughts of how to alert Mr. Bingley to Jane's presence in town, telling him of meeting Sir Malcolm completely slipped her mind.

"Did you have a good time with Lady Matlock, Georgiana?"

"Yes, it was rather fun. I have to tell you something, Fitzwilliam." She looked at Darcy gravely. "Aunt Helen is sending the dancing master over tomorrow. He will come several times before the ball next week."

"Well then, we shall have to let Mrs. Hawkins know to open up the ballroom." Seeing her worried expression, he added, "I'm sure you will do very well, Georgie."

"Alright, I will try not to worry! If you'll excuse me, I'm going to rest before dinner. Shopping is exhausting." She sighed and headed down the hall to her room, leaving Elizabeth alone with Darcy.

"Are you exhausted, too, Miss Bennet?"

Not knowing if he was teasing or in earnest, she replied, "Tired, yes. I don't know if I'd go so far as to say exhausted."

"Then I shall leave you to rest. Until dinner, then." He left her in the hall and continued down another corridor, she supposed towards the master's chambers.

How odd. He seemed so happy to see us, then he became so quiet. Why can I not understand that man?

~

That night, and for the third time that week, Darcy had a familiar dream. He was in the drawing room at Netherfield. It was a sunny day, the afternoon light filling the room with a cheerful glow. Elizabeth sat in a chair near the fire, embroidering a handkerchief. When he saw her, he was filled with a familiar warmth and began to walk towards her. She looked up at him and smiled, reaching out her hand to him, a welcome expression on her face. He moved near her and took her hand. Raising it to his lips, he kissed it tenderly.

"Elizabeth," he whispered.

"Fitzwilliam," she called his name so sweetly, it was almost painful.

Slowly, he pulled her closer and with his free hand, reached out and touched her cheek. She tilted her face up to him, her eyes looking into his with complete and total trust. As he leaned down to kiss her, he saw the handkerchief she'd been embroidering where she had left it on the chair. The initials 'ED' were nearly completed in the corner. *Elizabeth Darcy.*

His heart swelled with adoration and he kissed her, her response everything he had hoped it would be. He held her in his arms, her head resting lightly on his chest, her hair tickling his chin where it rested on the top of her head.

"Elizabeth," he spoke aloud. "My own Elizabeth."

Darcy drifted into a deep and peaceful sleep, and had to be woken by his valet, a singular occurrence.

CHAPTER 9

The next morning, Elizabeth donned a sky blue morning dress and hurried down to breakfast. She found she was too hungry to wait for Georgiana and hoped to catch Mr. Darcy in the breakfast room. Always attracted to riddles, Elizabeth was determined to crack the enigma that was Mr. Darcy. She felt that with enough time, she would figure him out. *Knowing him, he'll change just as I get my bearings.* Oddly, the thought made her more amused than annoyed.

She was in luck; Mr. Darcy was seated in his usual place at the head of the table, newspaper in hand, coffee steaming in its cup.

"Good morning, Mr. Darcy," she greeted him cheerfully.

He lowered his paper and smiled at her warmly. "Good morning Miss Bennet. I trust you slept well?"

"Very well, thank you. It's rather like sleeping on a cloud. I don't know how I shall go back to my regular bed."

She smiled brightly, clearly in a good mood. *I knew she would be cheerful in the morning*, he thought. He felt a small sense of triumph at this piece of evidence that he had made the right decision in choosing her.

"I am glad to hear you are comfortable." He smiled, visions of Elizabeth in a sheer nightdress, curled up sweetly next to him in his enormous bed, filling his mind. *Sleeping on a cloud, indeed.*

"Did you sleep well?" she asked innocently.

"Better than ever."

Elizabeth was slightly surprised at his answer, but quickly covered her expression with a smile and tucked into her food.

She had gotten about halfway through her meal when she was arrested by something on the back of Darcy's paper. Tilting her head to read it better, she began to raise and lower her head with the motion of his paper so as not to lose her place, causing her to duck and straighten in an odd and rather noticeable fashion, completely unbeknownst to her.

"Miss Bennet?" His voice was soft and inquisitive.

"Yes?" She took her eyes from the paper and saw him peeking around the side of it, looking at her with what looked like amusement in his eyes.

"Would you like the paper?"

"I do not wish to deprive you of your morning ritual, Mr. Darcy. My attention was caught by an article, that is all. Please, continue."

Wordlessly, he shook out the paper, removed the inner page that he was reading, folded the outer page in half, and handed it to Elizabeth.

"Now we may both read in comfort." His expression was kind and open.

"Thank you, Mr. Darcy," she responded sincerely. *An enigma, indeed.*

Ten minutes later, her article complete and her breakfast nearly finished, Elizabeth looked up to find Mr. Darcy watching her.

"Miss Bennet, I wonder if I might ask you a favor."

"Of course, Mr. Darcy."

"The dancing master is coming today, and Georgiana is quite nervous about it. I wondered if you might consent to staying with her throughout the lesson? She will have Mrs. Annesley, of course, but she has grown rather attached to you and I believe your presence might make her more comfortable."

She smiled sympathetically. "I will be happy to stay with her. I must confess that I was half planning on it myself. She did seem rather nervous when Lady Matlock mentioned it yesterday. I will try to lighten her spirits."

"Thank you, Miss Bennet. I appreciate it." He looked into her eyes until Elizabeth began to feel self-conscious.

"Not at all, Mr. Darcy," she replied, her voice barely audible, even to her.

~

The dancing master arrived promptly at one o'clock. Elizabeth had spent the morning in the library, only giving half her attention to her book, the other half contemplating Mr. Darcy's ever-changing behavior. When Georgiana fetched her for the lesson, she was only too glad to leave her thoughts in the library, where she was sure they would be safe until she could entertain them further.

The dancing master was a small, thin man, with gray hair slicked back firmly on his head and a beak-like nose protruding over his thin lips and weak chin. He looked to be about fifty, and Elizabeth thought how funny it was that a maid was required to remain in the ballroom as chaperone, as if this man would present a temptation for either of them.

He walked Georgiana through the steps, doing a remarkably good job at the lady's part, and then attempted to lead her through it. Georgiana had been at finishing school the year before, so she knew the basics, but the girls had always danced with each other and this was the first time she had danced with an actual man, old or young.

It was obvious that she was nervous and she mis-stepped a few times, once on the instructor's foot, causing him to give a small yelp. Georgiana blushed red with mortification while Elizabeth tried to stifle a laugh. The instructor suggested a brief break, which Georgiana agreed to readily.

"Oh, Elizabeth! This is horrible! What am I going to do? If I cannot dance with the master, how am I supposed to be able to dance in a crowded ballroom?"

"Now, do not fret! It is not that bad, truly. No one is perfect when they are first learning. You must be patient with yourself. How did you do when you danced with the girls at school?"

"I did fine with the girls. But it is so much easier to be close to another female. I'm afraid being so near a man makes me a little uncomfortable."

"I see. Well, I have an idea. How about you practice with me? Then you can get a feeling for the steps and refresh your memory before dancing with a gentleman. And remember, at the ball you will only be dancing with family, so they will not be unfamiliar to you."

"That is a wonderful idea! Are you sure you don't mind?"

"Not at all. My sisters and I often practice together. Now let's get started."

They walked into the middle of the room and Elizabeth began counting out the numbers of the steps for a quadrille.

"You were right, Elizabeth! It is much easier with you!"

They continued through the steps, laughing intermittently, until the dancing master returned and cleared his throat. Georgiana was able to get through the rest of the lesson without stepping on his foot again, though not without the occasional look of terror sent in Elizabeth's direction.

With a few hours remaining before they needed to prepare for dinner and both too animated to rest, they decided to bundle up and head into the garden. It had snowed the night before, and there was a thick blanket of white across the courtyard and beyond it on the lawn. As they stepped out, more snow began to fall. They quickly went to work rolling large balls of snow to make a snowman.

"Do you think I will still be able to make snowmen when I am out?" Georgiana asked as she placed a carrot where the snowman's nose would be.

"Of course, should you wish it. I have been out since I was sixteen, and I am building a snowman right now."

"Oh, I didn't mean to imply that you were doing anything improper, Elizabeth. Forgive me. I didn't think before I spoke."

Elizabeth laughed and said, "Do not worry Georgiana. I know you meant no offense. I think some women stop doing things such as playing in the snow because they are too busy with their duties as wives and mistresses of estates. It does not mean they do not wish to be more free in their play. And of course, some are altogether too decorous to play in the snow at all." A picture of Miss Bingley building a snowman briefly flashed through Elizabeth's mind, eliciting a mischievous smile. "Let us enjoy our freedom while we have it!" Elizabeth laughed and twirled in a circle, her arms out to her sides. Georgiana quickly joined her, laughing and spinning until they fell into a heap on the ground, dizzy and smiling.

"Miss Bennet certainly is a spirited one."

"Fitzwilliam! What are you doing here?" Darcy looked over at the Colonel, who was now standing next to him at the window, watching the girls play in the snow. "I didn't expect you until dinner."

"I thought I'd come over early and help you work through that brandy of yours." He looked longingly out the window. "Almost makes you want to join them, doesn't it?"

"Yes, the snow is very inviting."

"The snow is not the only inviting thing. Look at them!" He nodded as he looked out the window appreciatively. "Come, Darcy! Let's get our coats and head to the garden. The ladies have been on their own for far too long."

Colonel Fitzwilliam headed out of the room, leaving Darcy no choice but to follow him. They quickly got their hats, scarves, coats and gloves on and headed out through the courtyard. When they came upon the ladies, they were still lying on the ground, opening and closing their arms and legs to make snow angels.

They didn't hear the gentleman approaching until they were only a few feet away from them and Elizabeth saw a flash of black boots in the corner of her eye. Quickly reaching out to grab Georgiana's hand, the two girls scrambled up, beating the snow off their cloaks.

"Richard!" Georgiana ran to her cousin and embraced him. "I didn't know you were coming today. Did you see our snowman?"

"Yes, Georgie, I did. And a fine figure of a man he is. I see you ladies have been amusing yourself with the recently fallen snow."

"Yes, we have. I don't remember when I've had so much fun." Georgiana was smiling from ear to ear, her cheeks red from the cold, her eyes bright with merriment.

Elizabeth was looking away, slightly embarrassed to have been caught lying down in the snow flopping her limbs in such an unladylike fashion.

She was also worried that Mr. Darcy would think it improper for his sister to behave in such a way, and would look on Elizabeth as a bad influence. *What do I care for his bad opinion? He certainly never thought well of me before.*

Feeling her courage rise, Elizabeth looked up, straight into the eyes of Mr. Darcy.

"Are you enjoying the snow, Miss Bennet?"

"Yes, Mr. Darcy. It doesn't snow very often in Hertfordshire, so I like to enjoy it when I can." She had a slightly defiant look about her eyes, daring him to disapprove of her behavior.

Unfortunately, it had quite the opposite effect on Mr. Darcy. Seeing her with cheeks flushed, eyes sparkling, and hair disheveled from her recent tumble in the snow, his opinion of her was far from disapproving.

"And so you should. I fear I do not feel the same about snow, as it happens quite regularly in Derbyshire and I have grown used to it. It can be rather deep and close in Pemberley for weeks at a time."

"It sounds lovely." If Mr. Darcy was not going to disapprove of her or provoke an argument, she was happy to go back to her jolly mood. "How much fun you must have had playing in the snow every winter."

"Yes, we did. I'm sure the Colonel here can tell you some interesting stories," he said with a knowing look.

"Perhaps you will tell me a story, Mr. Darcy. I'm sure you remember it all quite clearly," she said with an impish smile.

Before he could answer Colonel Fitzwilliam interrupted them. "What do you say, Darce? Shall we show the ladies how we used to play in the snow?" He had a wide grin on his face and a mischievous glint in his eye.

"I'm sure our snow games are not fit for the ladies, Fitzwilliam."

"What sort of games do boys play in the snow, Colonel?" Elizabeth looked directly at the colonel, ignoring Darcy's protest, curious to see what he would suggest.

"We did nothing so ladylike as make snow angels, Miss Bennet!"

"I am glad to hear it, Colonel. Growing up in a house full of sisters, I am afraid I have never had the benefit of a brother to teach me what was common to boys. I must confess I am rather curious now."

"Well, Miss Bennet, it would-be ungentlemanly of me not to grant your request. Darcy, shall we show the ladies how the boys play in the snow?" He looked to his cousin with a twinkle in his eye.

Before Darcy could answer, Georgiana interrupted, "Oh yes, Richard!

Please show us!"

Seeing how Darcy was not going to intercede, Colonel Fitzwilliam began to show the girls how to make a small wall out of snow. "Now the idea here is to have a barrier between you and the opposition."

"The opposition?" Georgiana's eyebrows shot up.

He went on to explain how they were to roll up snow into small balls and create a pile of them, rather like miniature cannons which they would throw at the other team. Darcy assisted them silently, still not saying a word.

"Miss Bennet, you seem to be rather adept at making snowballs."

"I confess, Colonel, that I have made many snowballs in the past and thrown them at my sisters. I have never done it behind a barricade, however, nor with such military precision," she said teasingly.

"One of the many things they teach us in the army, Miss Bennet," he said with mock gravity.

After building two small walls on opposite sides of the garden and filling each with a mound of cannonballs, they decided it was time to open fire.

"Who will be on each team?" Georgiana asked.

"I don't know about you Georgiana, but I would certainly like to get a hit on your brother there," said Colonel Fitzwilliam as Darcy scowled at him.

Realizing that she would have to hit her cousin, her brother, or her friend and guest, Georgiana decided that Miss Bennet would probably be most comfortable on a team with Mr. Darcy, since she knew him significantly better than Colonel Fitzwilliam, whom she had only met once before, and she knew they wouldn't stand a chance if the men were on a team together.

Proud of her quick, hostess-minded thinking, Georgiana announced, "I think that sounds like a fine idea, Richard. You and I shall be a team. Now how do we play?" Georgiana's excitement was palpable, which quieted Elizabeth's nerves about hiding behind a snow barricade with Mr. Darcy. She didn't know why, but she suddenly had a nervous feeling in her stomach.

Colonel Fitzwilliam explained the rules; they would each retreat behind their barricade, and on his count, they would begin firing. "How do we know who wins?" she asked.

"When we were children, it was according to who cried first, but I suppose that would be an inappropriate gauge now." He grinned. "How about whoever has the most direct hits, wins."

They retreated behind their barricades, Elizabeth wondering if Mr. Darcy was ever going to say anything at all, or merely brood behind the snow-wall. Looking up at him, she saw the ghost of a grin.

"Miss Bennet, shall we decide on our plan of attack?" Elizabeth looked at him questioningly, wondering who this man was who had suddenly decided to become engaged in the game. *Could he be more mercurial?*

"I suppose we should, Mr. Darcy, though I have never devised a plan of attack outside a game of chess. Perhaps I should leave it to you."

He looked at her quizzically for a moment, then appearing to briefly come to a decision, he laid out what he thought would be a good way to breach their defenses. Elizabeth couldn't help but smile at how seriously he was taking a simple snowball fight.

"Am I amusing you, Miss Bennet?"

"A little, yes sir. I am unused to the games of boys and find it all extremely diverting." *And I have never seen you like this.*

"Horrid Thomas and Michael never played in the snow with you?"

Smiling, she answered, "They usually only visited in summer, so it was never an option, although I am sure they would have immensely enjoyed pelting us with snowballs!"

They laid out the rest of their plan just before Richard stood up to announce it was time to begin. They started out simply, Darcy popping over the top to lobby a snowball toward Richard, while Elizabeth rolled more to restock their pile. After a few shots, Elizabeth announced that she wished to throw one. Peering around the corner of the barricade to watch the opposition, Darcy signaled her when Colonel Fitzwilliam had just thrown a large snowball over their heads.

"Now, Miss Bennet!"

Elizabeth leapt up and threw the ball as hard as she could, landing a few feet in front of the barricade. Quickly ducking back down, she asked, "I didn't get close enough, did I?"

"Not quite. Perhaps we built them too far apart."

"You are too gracious, Mr. Darcy. I will try again. I'm sure I can do better."

He looked at her approvingly as she readied herself. Once again, he told her when it was clear and she jumped up to throw her ball, hitting the top ledge of their snow-wall.

"Was I closer that time?" she asked breathlessly.

"Yes, you hit the wall." He smiled at her and quickly looked away.

He shot a few more, one hitting Richard's hat and gaining them a point, when Elizabeth said she was ready to try again. "I think I can see the Colonel's hat," she said.

"If you aim just to the left of center, you'll be right above him."

Waiting for just the right moment, she once again jumped up and threw the snowball with all her might. As she fell back to the ground, she heard a loud squeal.

"Hit!" came Georgiana's voice.

"Oops! I was aiming for the Colonel." Elizabeth unsuccessfully tried to hide her smile.

"Well done, Miss Bennet. That's two points for us, and they have yet to make a single hit." He looked at her proudly, liking the way it sounded when he said 'us'.

Before they could wipe the smiles off their faces, three enormous snowballs came flying over them, one landing firmly on the side of Mr. Darcy's head.

Closing his eyes, whether in pain or mortified pride, Elizabeth didn't know, he called loudly, "Hit!"

Georgiana and Colonel Fitzwilliam could be heard laughing and congratulating themselves on the other side of the garden. As Mr. Darcy brushed the snow off his hat and hair, Elizabeth put her hand over her mouth to cover her smile. It wouldn't do to laugh at her own teammate, but he did look funny with snow dripping down the side of his face.

When he looked up and saw her eyes dancing, he said, "As ever, I am glad to be a source of amusement, Miss Bennet." He smiled ruefully.

Suddenly a large snowball landed on Elizabeth's bonnet and slid down to her neck. She squealed from the cold and called loudly, "Hit!" She looked at Darcy who was trying manfully not to laugh at her. "You may laugh, Mr. Darcy. I did the same to you." She shook her head and shoulders to dislodge the snow, Mr. Darcy chuckling quietly, his shoulders shaking. "I see it is my turn to be a source of amusement, Mr. Darcy."

A moment later, he quickly sobered and refocused on the game.

"Now it's time to take action."

They decided on an offensive plan where Elizabeth would run behind a nearby tree while Darcy continued to lobby snowballs from their current location, thus confusing the enemy as to their whereabouts. She would pile up more snowballs until he signaled her. Elizabeth smiled at his serious attention, but found herself being drawn into the game nonetheless.

When the coast was clear, she made a mad dash for the large elm to her right. She quickly ducked behind the tree and began rolling up snow and making a small pile of cannons. Despite knowing it was all a game, she couldn't stop her heart from racing. She peered back to her left and saw Mr. Darcy rhythmically throwing balls over the barricade.

Once she had about fifteen made, she looked to him for the signal to run to the next tree where she would repeat the process, while he ran to her previous location. At his nod, she dashed off again, this time to a tree about fifteen feet from her, about midway between the two barricades. She looked back and saw Darcy give her a nod that she hadn't been seen and she began to make more cannons.

She heard Georgiana call out "Hit!" once more before looking back to Darcy to see if it was time to move to the next tree, which would put her only a dozen feet from the opposition's barricade, setting up their final attack.

At his signal, she ran for the next tree, but a few steps out, she saw Georgiana's back popping up over the snow-wall and turned around before she could be seen and hit. Just as she was scooting behind the tree, she ran headlong into Mr. Darcy.

The force of the impact sent them flying into the air; Mr. Darcy, being the taller of the two, was positioned to land on top of her, but quickly grabbed her and somehow twisted partially underneath her, so that he landed on his shoulder with a loud "Oof!" and she landed halfway on top of him.

"Mr. Darcy! Are you alright!" Elizabeth asked between giggles. "I am terribly sorry! I always laugh when someone falls down, especially myself. It is a terrible habit; do forgive me." She laughed more but tried desperately to control herself. "Are you alright? Have I injured you?"

Darcy lay on the ground, his hat a few feet away and snow scattered through his hair, his eyes closed. He still held tightly to Elizabeth, who was so surprised from the impact, she hadn't yet noticed the extremely indecorous position they were in.

Instinctively, she reached up and brushed the hair and snow away from his eyes, and suddenly worried, asked, "Are you alright, Mr. Darcy?"

Darcy had been enjoying the sensation of lying in the snow with Elizabeth partially on top of him, his hands locked tightly about her waist. He was reveling in the sound and feel of her laughter in such an intimate position, when her voice changed and she touched his face.

Coming to, he opened his eyes and said, "I am quite alright, Miss Elizabeth. You have not injured me in the slightest."

Just then she realized their position and colored brightly. She began to pull away from him, but his hands held her fast. "Mr. Darcy," she said, her voice less steady than she wished it to be, "I must ask you to release me."

He looked at her blankly for a moment as if he didn't understand, and then he loosened his grip. "Forgive me, Miss Bennet. Are you alright? Are you injured at all?" he asked as he reluctantly let her go.

She sat up, brushing the snow off her cloak, and answered, "No, I am quite well. Thank you for breaking my fall." She smiled somewhat awkwardly.

He was still lying on the ground in front of her, propped up on one of his elbows, wiggling his shoulder carefully. "Have I hurt your shoulder?" she asked guiltily.

"Do not worry, Miss Bennet. I shall be fine." Elizabeth reached her hand out slightly in front of her, as if she would touch him, but pulled it back before she could make contact.

She was just about to insist he have it looked at when Colonel Fitzwilliam and Georgiana came around the tree, their arms filled with snowballs, mercilessly pelting them at Darcy and Elizabeth. Darcy groaned and turned his back to them while Elizabeth ducked her face in her knees and covered her head with her arms.

"We surrender! We surrender!" she called.

They finally relented and Elizabeth was able to poke her head back up to see a triumphant Georgiana and Colonel Fitzwilliam beaming down at them.

The Colonel reached his hand out to help Elizabeth up. "I thank you, sir," she said upon rising. The Colonel did the same for Darcy, and Elizabeth noticed how he winced when Fitzwilliam pulled his arm.

"I think I am ready to warm up and have a cup of cocoa," she said to no one in particular.

As they were walking in, Elizabeth looked at Darcy questioningly, but getting no response, she stepped next to him as they were entering the courtyard and spoke quietly.

"Mr. Darcy, I am so sorry for running into you. It was completely my fault. I know you must have fallen rather hard and I feel terrible that you were hurt because of me." Seeing he was about to protest, she held up her hand and continued. "Please take care of your shoulder, I can see you are in pain. It will only compound my guilt to know you are hurting and not receiving any relief. Please take care." She lightly touched his arm and looked up at him imploringly.

Touched by her solicitousness, he nodded silently and strode into the house.

Chapter 9, Part II

After requesting a mug of cocoa and relinquishing her wet cloak to a maid, Elizabeth gratefully sunk into a hot bath. She let the warm water relax her sore muscles and soothe her nerves. *I'm starting to sound like my mother*, she thought. She closed her eyes and tried to empty her mind, but it was proving to be a difficult task.

She felt guilty about running into Mr. Darcy and wondered how badly he was hurt. She was sure it was a bad bruise at the least, and felt silly that she had run into him so clumsily. As she recalled lying on the ground, half her weight across him and his arms about her waist, she felt a blush spread across her cheeks. She had never been that close to a man unrelated to her. It had been oddly comforting and warm despite the snow she was lying in. Had she actually touched his face? How inappropriate! What had made her do that? Elizabeth was tiring of all the mixed emotions inside her and wished, again, that this could just be simple.

Once again, she wondered why she cared whether Mr. Darcy thought she had breached propriety. Had he not always been rude to her and quarreled with her every chance he got? That was how he had behaved at Netherfield. *But*, she reminded herself, *he is not behaving like that here*. He had been quite polite, ever the gracious host, and even kind to her. She had actually begun to enjoy his company. A sobering realization began to dawn on her.

Could it be? Could she be friends with Mr. Darcy?

~

"How on earth did that happen?" Colonel Fitzwilliam gestured to the bruise beginning to turn purple on Darcy's right shoulder.

"I took a spill," he said wryly.

"Uh-huh." The Colonel was not convinced.

"Fisher, you may go. I'll ring when I need you," Darcy dismissed his valet. Colonel Fitzwilliam moved to sit on the chair in the corner.

"So are you going to tell me the real story or do I have to drag it out of you?"

Darcy shifted in the tub and released a sigh. "I ran into Miss Bennet. Or rather she ran into me. She is a surprisingly powerful runner," he said as he shifted his shoulder painfully. The movement made him wince and Fitzwilliam looked at him incredulously.

"How the devil could you have run into each other?"

Darcy heaved an exaggerated sigh. "She was running to the next tree when Georgiana stood up, and not wanting to be seen, she turned back and ran into me running for the tree she had just vacated." He looked around uncomfortably. "We collided."

Fitzwilliam let out a great guffawing laugh. "So that's why you were on the ground! I wondered about that but didn't want to ask in front of the ladies." He leaned forward, and putting his elbows on his knees, looked at Darcy conspiratorially. "So how was it?" he asked suggestively, his eyebrows raised.

"Fitzwilliam!" Darcy waved him off, intending to splash water on him, but only succeeding in sprinkling him faintly and making his injured shoulder smart.

"I see. That good." Colonel Fitzwilliam nodded his head in silent appreciation.

It took Darcy a moment to respond as his mind was occupied reliving the moment after the collision when Elizabeth had brushed the snow off his face. She had been so caring and concerned for him, at least after she had stopped laughing at him. She was the only woman he knew who could laugh at him and make him feel cared for at the same time. And she had fit so perfectly against him.

His reverie was lost as he realized Richard was talking again. "I'm sorry, Richard. What did you say?"

Fitzwilliam only laughed and said, "Nothing of import cousin. I shall leave you to dress in peace."

Now on his own, Darcy had the chance to plan his next move. He wanted to propose to Miss Bennet, but how to go about such a thing? He'd never done it before, and it wasn't exactly the sort of thing men talked about in the club. He had to struggle to keep his thoughts on task and not dwell on the feeling of Elizabeth in his arms, or the way she felt when her body shook with laughter against his, or the touch of her hand on his face, or the look in her eyes when she asked him to take care of himself; she had been so sincere and tender. Yes, she would make him a very good wife.

Pondering how he would propose, Darcy came to a few conclusions. He knew he would have to go to Longbourn shortly after the proposal to ask Mr. Bennet for his consent. He wasn't looking forward to it, but it had to be done.

He didn't want to leave while Elizabeth was still in London and give up what little time he had with her. Once they were engaged, it wouldn't be proper for them to stay under the same roof together, either. He decided he should ask her right after the ball, just before she was due to depart. Eight more days.

Then he could offer her his carriage home, which he had planned on arranging anyway, and escort her, buying him a few more hours with her, without the presence of her family. Georgiana would have to accompany them, but surely she wouldn't mind. And Georgiana always fell asleep in the carriage, so they would have plenty of time to themselves to talk and make plans for their life together. He leaned his head back with a sigh, content with the plans he had made.

That night dinner was a jovial event. Georgiana and Colonel Fitzwilliam were still high from their victory, Darcy was feeling particularly pleased with his recently made plans, and Elizabeth felt a newfound freedom in acknowledging her friendship with Mr. Darcy. They talked and laughed and joked and had altogether the most pleasant evening of her visit so far, and one of the loudest the staff could remember in quite some time.

After dinner, as they sat in the music room, Georgiana was excitedly telling Elizabeth how much snow they had in Derbyshire and was already planning the massive snowball battle they would have at Pemberley next winter.

Everyone was grinning at her enthusiasm when she looked at Elizabeth and said bluntly, "You must come to Pemberley, Elizabeth! It's the most wonderful place on earth!"

"Next winter is so long away! You can't possibly be making plans so far in advance," Elizabeth said in an attempt to dispel the awkwardness caused by Georgiana's unapproved invitation.

"Of course. You must come sooner than that, Miss Bennet." Darcy's deep voice startled her and made her look up at him quickly.

"Oh, yes! You should come for the summer! Pemberley is beautiful in the summer! And we already planned to be there. Didn't we, Brother?" Georgiana was looking at Elizabeth expectantly, obviously waiting for her acquiescence.

Elizabeth looked from Georgiana to Darcy and back again, not sure what to say. Mr. Darcy, seeing her conflict, stepped in. "We would be honored to have you at Pemberley this summer, Miss Bennet. If you can arrange it, of course."

"I don't know whether my father can spare me, I am already doing much traveling this year, but I shall consider it."

"Good. We can talk about it more later, then."

"Where will you be traveling, Miss Bennet?" asked Colonel Fitzwilliam.

"In March, I will go to Kent to see my friend Mrs. Collins, who has recently wed a cousin of mine. I will be staying through Easter."

"What a coincidence! I shall be in Kent for Easter as well, visiting my aunt Lady Catherine, as I do every year at that time. Where does your cousin live?"

"I believe it is more of a coincidence than you originally imagined, Colonel. My cousin lives at Hunsford Parsonage. He is Lady Catherine de Burgh's rector."

"Well that is lucky for me! And Darcy as well. We always make the Easter pilgrimage together. I dare say Kent just became a little more appealing." He smiled openly at her and she grinned back.

"When will you arrive, Miss Bennet?" asked Darcy.

"I shall first travel to London to spend a day with my aunt, then we expect to be in Kent by the middle of March; I believe it is the eleventh. I am traveling with Sir William Lucas and Miss Maria Lucas, Mrs. Collins's family. I intend to stay six weeks with Mrs. Collins, then another week with my family in London on my way back to Hertfordshire."

"We will be arriving the week before Easter, I believe. At least that's what we usually do. And staying a fortnight, or something like that. We'll have to call on you at the parsonage, Miss Bennet."

"I hope you will, Colonel."

Darcy was silently planning, and looked up in time to catch a smile between Elizabeth and Richard. He hoped Richard wasn't falling for Elizabeth; that could prove to be awkward.

Darcy didn't like the sound of all of Elizabeth's travels; it might make it difficult for him to see her regularly after they were engaged. Of course he could always stay at Rosings to see her while she was at the parsonage, but Lady Catherine would not look kindly on this engagement, and he didn't want to expose Elizabeth to her wrath, so that idea wasn't really plausible.

In fact, she may need to rethink the trip altogether once their engagement was announced. He probably wouldn't want her anywhere near Lady Catherine, especially without him to protect her. Perhaps she could stay in London with her aunt and uncle? Then he could still see her every day and wouldn't have to deal with her mother. But then he would have to deal with her Cheapside relations. They couldn't possibly be as bad as Mrs. Bennet! Could they? Maybe he should meet them before he decided on a plan. He wouldn't want to commit to a course of action only to find he had made the poorer choice.

"I believe my cousin is woolgathering, Miss Bennet."

"What was that, Fitzwilliam?" Darcy snapped out of his reverie.

"Where were you just now, Darcy? You clearly weren't here. And judging by the expression on your face, it wasn't pleasant."

"Forgive me; I was thinking about some business I need to attend to."

Fitzwilliam knew he was lying, but decided to get the truth out of him later – in private. Standing to leave, Fitzwilliam wished the ladies a good night and told them he would see them at the ball.

At the door, he turned and said, "Oh, Georgiana, Mother tells me that you will be permitted to dance with the family. May I take this opportunity to secure a dance?"

Georgiana's face brightened and she answered, "Of course Richard! Which would you prefer?"

"The first, if you are not otherwise engaged."

"Actually, she'll be dancing the first with me, Fitzwilliam." Darcy was standing next to Richard and the two gave each other a look, knowing they were reverting to an old game they used to play with Georgiana when she was little where they would fight over her affections. They each puffed up their chests and put on their most courtly faces, trying to win her favor.

"Then I shall dance the first with Miss Bennet, and the second with Georgiana, if that suits you ladies."

"I would be happy to accept you for the first set, Colonel Fitzwilliam," smiled Elizabeth, seeing the game they were playing. Darcy found he did not particularly like her choice of words.

"And I shall accept you for the second, Richard." Georgiana was trying very hard to act like a lady and not giggle.

"Miss Bennet, may I be so bold as to secure your second set?" asked Mr. Darcy formally.

"I would be honored, Mr. Darcy." Elizabeth curtseyed, and both gentlemen bowed, Colonel Fitzwilliam a little deeper and more dramatically than Mr. Darcy.

"I believe I shall retire before every dance is taken and there are none left for the other gentlemen." Elizabeth smiled coyly, and taking Georgiana by the arm, walked toward the door. They nodded and gave a tiny curtsey to the gentlemen as they passed by and continued down the hall.

The gentlemen watched them walk away for a little longer than was necessary, then headed downstairs. "Shall we see you before the ball, Richard?" Darcy asked him as they descended the stairs.

"I don't know. I hadn't planned on it, but seeing how there is more to see here now, I may adjust my schedule." He gave a roguish smile and Darcy glared at him.

"Watch yourself, Richard. Miss Bennet is a lady and not to be trifled with. She has no dowry; you could never afford to marry her."

"Who said anything about marriage? Must you always be jumping to conclusions? You're as bad as Mother." He shook his head in mock disapproval. "But now that you mention it, I just might be persuaded to give up my bachelor ways for the right woman. She is something else, isn't she?" he looked up the stairs longingly.

Seeing Darcy's dark look, he clapped his back and said, "Don't worry, Darce. You're right; I cannot afford to marry her, or any woman for that matter, unless she comes with a large fortune. And most of those are taken by men with equally large fortunes, so it seems I may be a bachelor forever."

Suddenly Darcy felt bad for needling his cousin and gave him a sympathetic look, but Richard cut him off before he could speak.

"Don't feel sorry for me, William. I am not to be pitied. There are certainly those worse off than I am. I could be Cyril." He smiled broadly and shrugged his shoulders.

He and Darcy had always agreed that if you had to be like Cyril to inherit the title and the estate, he'd rather be poor, title-less, and like himself. And they both always knew that should Cyril cut Richard off, Darcy would support him. They had never spoken it aloud, but they knew it just the same.

Darcy laughed unconvincingly and ordered the carriage.

"Apparently I am not the only one who would rather be happy than rich," added Richard thoughtfully.

"What do you mean?"

"Miss Bennet. Hasn't a penny to her name, or not enough to count on anyway, and turned down a perfectly good marriage proposal."

"She did? How do you know this? Who did she refuse?" Darcy asked attentively.

"Georgiana told me, said Miss Bennet and she stayed up late talking and she told her about it. She didn't tell me his name, but said he was set to inherit an estate and was an advantageous match, but Miss Bennet didn't love him, so she refused. I think Georgiana may have found a new hero." He laughed. "Her mother was set to tan her hide, from what Georgiana says, but she said she wouldn't have him, and they couldn't make her! Ha! Can you believe that?"

"Interesting. Very interesting." Darcy spoke quietly and looked down, deep in thought. "Do you know when this happened? Perhaps she was young and headstrong. She might not do the same today."

Richard looked at him thoughtfully and answered, "Georgiana made it sound like it was rather recent; I'd guess in the last few months." He looked at his cousin carefully and made sure he had his attention. "She said Miss Bennet would only marry for the deepest love, and that she suspected she might end up an old maid because of it. Would be a pity. Women like that don't come along every day." He shook his head and headed for the door. "There's my carriage. I'll see you soon, Darcy." He clapped his back and headed out the door.

Darcy finally looked up as Richard was climbing into the carriage. He mumbled a goodbye and signaled to Causer to close the door.

Colonel Fitzwilliam leaned his head against the plush seat and let out a chuckle. "Who would have thought? The incomparable Mr. Darcy of Pemberley, in love! And with a penniless girl from Hertfordshire! May wonders never cease."

He smiled all the way to back to the barracks.

CHAPTER 10

Thursday morning Elizabeth awoke feeling equally rested and famished. She quickly washed up, dressed in her yellow sprigged morning dress, twisted her hair up simply and went downstairs to breakfast.

Mr. Darcy sat at the head of the small table, pretending to read the newspaper as he waited for Elizabeth to arrive. He had come to look forward to having her to himself at breakfast.

"Good morning, Mr. Darcy!" Elizabeth entered the breakfast room cheerfully.

She headed to the sideboard to fill her plate as he lowered his paper. "Good morning, Miss Bennet. Did you sleep well in your cloud?"

"As a matter of fact I did," she answered with a smile. "And you sir? Are you still sleeping better than usual?"

He made a face and she interjected, "I hope your shoulder didn't bother you too much. Does it hurt very badly?" she asked tentatively, making a slight wincing gesture.

"Only minimally, Miss Bennet; do not trouble yourself. My valet applied a salve and I am feeling much better."

"I am glad to hear it. I would hate to be the cause of your discomfort." She gave him a relieved smile.

They ate in companionable silence for a few minutes before Darcy's resonant voice filled the air. "Miss Bennet?"

"Yes, Mr. Darcy?" Did she know what she did to him when she looked up at him like that?

"Have you given any thought to coming to Pemberley this summer?"

"A little. Derbyshire is very far from Longbourn. How long is the trip?"

"Two days in good weather and no trouble with the carriage, plus several horse changes. Three if it's muddy or raining. Four if it is particularly bad." He looked at her thoughtful expression. "I assure you, the destination is worth the trouble."

She gave him an arch smile. "Is that because Pemberley is the most wonderful place in the world?"

"Come to Derbyshire, Miss Bennet, and see for yourself." Something in his eyes made Elizabeth blush and look down.

Suddenly, he stood and held out his hand to her. "Come. I wish to show you something."

She looked at his hand as if it might bite her, then slowly took it. He helped her from her chair, and without letting go of her hand, led her down the hall to a door she'd never gone through before. He released her and opened the door, gesturing for her to walk in before him.

As she stepped through the tall doorway, she realized that this was the room she had originally mistaken as the library. The far wall was covered in bookshelves from floor to ceiling with a large double window set in the center. On the left was a large fireplace flanked by two leather chairs and a small leather divan facing the fire. To the right was a massive mahogany desk, a large dark leather chair behind it and two smaller chairs in front. There was another window behind the desk and plush oriental carpets on the floor. The room was at once intimate and intimidating.

"This way." He motioned for her to follow him and walked over to a painting to the left of the door. "This is Pemberley."

Elizabeth stepped closer to view the painting. It was a more intricate oil version of the watercolor Georgiana had done, filled with rich colors and warm light.

"When you first emerge from Pemberley Woods, you will be on a ridge. There will be trees blocking the view until you get to a bend in the drive and you come upon this spot. There is a clearing in the trees and you can see straight down to the house over the lake." He was standing slightly behind her, reaching over her shoulder to point to the painting.

Elizabeth couldn't stop looking at the grand house. If Pemberley were this beautiful in a painting, how much greater would it be in person?

"So what do you think, Miss Bennet? Will you come to Pemberley?" He spoke quietly over her left shoulder; she hadn't realized he was so close. Feeling a mischievous impulse, likely from her nervousness at his proximity, she said the first thing that came to her mind.

"It is tolerable, I suppose, but not handsome enough to tempt me."

Mr. Darcy's face went from shocked and angry, to hurt and confused, and finally to understanding as her words sunk in. The words were no sooner out of her mouth than Elizabeth regretted them. She watched the changing expressions on Mr. Darcy's face, her hand clapped over her mouth in embarrassment.

"I am so sorry," they both said at once. He meant to continue, but Elizabeth beat him to it.

"I am so sorry, Mr. Darcy! I don't know why I said that!"

"I would imagine, Miss Bennet, that you are angry with me. Please allow me to apologize for what I said at the assembly. I never meant for you to hear it, and indeed, I was unsure you had until now." He was beginning to look guilty and his voice faltered a little as he spoke. "Even so, I never should have said it as it was most untrue and more a reflection of my bad mood and annoyance with Bingley than your appearance. I do apologize, Miss Bennet."

Elizabeth blushed red in mortification.

"It is I who should be apologizing, Mr. Darcy. I am a guest in your home and I never should have spoken so out of turn. Please accept my deepest apologies." She was looking quickly from him to the floor and back to the painting. "It really is a lovely painting. I can imagine it is even more beautiful in person."

He looked at her silently for a moment, his expression unreadable, then answered evenly, "It is. And I would still wish for you to see it, if you'd like to."

"I would, thank you," she whispered to the floor. She finally looked up, first making it to his cravat, then his chin, on to his nose, and eventually to his eyes.

They looked at each other for a long moment, Elizabeth's cheeks flaming red, and finally Mr. Darcy spoke, "Shall we say all is forgiven and move on to more pleasant topics?"

"Yes, let's be friends again," Elizabeth agreed willingly, relief written all over her face.

"Shall we set a date for your visit?"

He led her to a chair in front of his desk and moved to sit behind it. Elizabeth regarded him from her small seat and noticed how very formidable he appeared in his large chair behind his enormous desk in his oh-so-masculine study. She felt almost like a child about to be disciplined.

"If we weren't friends, Mr. Darcy, I believe I should be a little frightened," she teased.

"Whatever do you mean, Miss Bennet?"

"Surely you see how sitting across from such a gentleman, behind his large, important desk, might be intimidating. But I shall not be afraid."

"I know you well enough to know, Miss Bennet, that I could not frighten you, even should I wish it. Which incidentally, I do not." He smiled at her easily. "Now, I suggest you come in mid-June and stay through summer's end. We will be just leaving town, so you will be able to journey with Georgiana and Mrs. Annesley, which I hope will be more convenient for you. We can easily stop in Hertfordshire to collect you. The grounds are particularly nice that time of year, which I believe you will enjoy. My Aunt Preston and cousin will be coming up from Somerset in the beginning of July. Colonel Fitzwilliam usually comes for a few weeks every summer and Lord and Lady Matlock will likely come for a short stay, as Matlock is only twenty-five miles away."

"It sounds like it will be mostly family. Will I not be in the way?"

"Not at all, Miss Bennet. They will likely not all be there at the same time, anyway. Everyone is considerably older than Georgiana. I'm afraid she often feels out of place and I'm sure she would appreciate having a friend with her."

"I see. Well, it sounds like you have thought of everything, Mr. Darcy. Are you always this prepared?"

"I do what I can, Miss Bennet," he said with a modest smile.

"I shall speak to my father when I return and let Miss Darcy know as soon as I am sure, but I believe it's safe to say I will be seeing you at Pemberley this summer." She smiled and rose to leave. He stood behind his desk, resting his hands on the warm wood. As she reached the door, he called out to her.

"Miss Bennet."

"Yes, Mr. Darcy?" she said looking over her shoulder. She was framed perfectly in the doorway and looking at her, his breath caught slightly.

"You are much more than tolerable," he said seriously. She smiled and looked down, a light blush on her cheek, and turned to walk away.

Darcy sank into his chair and let his head roll back, his hand over his eyes. He couldn't believe he had been caught in so uncomfortable a position. She had overheard him at the assembly! He had wondered at the time if she had, but she had been friendly and polite to him and didn't behave as if she were angry. And here in town they had actually become friends. She seemed to be of a forgiving nature, at least after he apologized, and she was sorry for her spiteful comment. All would be well, he decided; and so he resolved to think on it no longer.

~

"Oh Jane! It was horrible! I don't know what made me say that to him. I half expected him to demand I leave his home directly!"

"Dearest Lizzy, it cannot be as bad as you say. He still asked you to come to Pemberley, did he not? That must be a sign of his forgiveness."

Alone in the back sitting room of the Gardiner's town house, Jane and Lizzy were sitting side by side, hands clasped together earnestly.

"I do not know. He didn't seem very angry; well, he was at first, but it passed quickly. He then apologized for insulting me in Meryton and said he'd never meant it." She looked away and said quietly, "Before I could leave he said I was much more than tolerable."

Jane regarded her sister for a moment, noticing the light pink on her cheeks, and said carefully, "I believe Mr. Darcy meant his apology and is truly sorry for what he said. He does not seem to hold your comment against you. It sounds as if you have become friendly."

"Yes, we have. It is strange; when I first met him I disliked him, and the more time I spent with him and the more I heard of him, I only disliked him more. Now, seeing him with his sister and in his own home, I find him quite different."

"I always saw value in him and never understood why you disliked him so heartily, besides his comment at the assembly. Then, of course, there is the story of Mr. Wickham."

"Oh, Jane! There is something I must tell you!" Elizabeth retold the story of Wickham's seducement of Georgiana, only leaving out her name and saying it was a woman the Darcys were close with.

"No wonder they did not wish to see each other! But perhaps Mr. Wickham is sorry for what he did and is anxious to re-establish his character."

"Jane, you are too forgiving. Now the question remains on what I should tell our family and whether his reputation should be made known. He is frequently at our Aunt Phillip's and with our younger sisters. We must warn them somehow to his true character."

"Yes, I believe we should, but not publicly; we do not wish to make him desperate if his intention is to begin anew." Elizabeth smiled at her sister's forgiving nature. "Perhaps we could send a letter to Father so that he might more carefully watch our younger sisters?"

"Perhaps. Though you know as well as I that such a step may not produce the desired result." The sisters shared a look of understanding of their father's indolent nature and continued to ponder the problem at hand.

"Perhaps Mary can be alerted and keep an eye on Kitty and Lydia?" Jane suggested.

"I thought about that as well, but they are not likely to listen to Mary, nor is she likely to be discreet. Mother and Aunt Phillips are definitely out of the question. Perhaps Uncle Phillips? We could ask him not to mention it to Aunt. As an attorney, he is certainly accustomed to being discreet. And he may know something of Wickham's habits in the village, which would allow us to know if he has truly mended his ways." *Which I doubt.*

"You may be right, Lizzy. Though, I cannot believe something so terrible of Mr. Wickham. He has such a look of goodness about him. Gaming and seducing young girls!" Jane blushed and put a hand to her cheek.

"Sweet Jane! I wish it were not true, but I assure you, it is."

They went on to talk of more pleasant things, agreeing that Elizabeth would send a letter to her Uncle Phillips straight away.

While having tea with her Aunt Gardiner and Jane, Elizabeth mentioned her invitation to Pemberley. "Do you think I should accept? I suppose I have in a way, but I am not committed yet if I want to change my plans."

"I see no reason not to accept, as long as Mrs. Annesley is there to chaperone." Elizabeth rolled her eyes. She had always thought the rules of chaperones to be a bit ridiculous and overly restrictive, especially to one of her independent nature. "It is necessary for propriety, my dear. Do not look so glum. As a matter of fact, your uncle and I have been planning a pleasure tour this summer. We are not sure how far it should take us, but perhaps to the Lakes, and we were set to invite you. Now we may at least offer you a way home at the end of our journey."

"The Lakes! I have always wanted to see them! Oh Aunt, when do you travel? Perhaps I might do both? You will be passing through Derbyshire, will you not?"

Mrs. Gardiner smiled at her niece's excitement. "Yes, we will be spending a few days in a village where I spent many years of my youth; it is called Lambton and is but five miles from Pemberley. Perhaps we could collect you and continue on our journey, or carry you home so you do not have to travel so far by post."

"I will speak to Miss Darcy and see what she has to say. Oh, I do hope it can be arranged! I have always wanted to see the Lakes!"

"I'm sure you would like to see Pemberley as well. The grounds alone are worth the visit. They are said to be some of the finest in the country. Yes, Lizzy, you should accept the invitation and go to Pemberley. You will have a wonderful time, and I see no reason why your father should not allow it; we can grant you permission in his stead. You should go ahead and tell the Darcys so they may make proper arrangements."

In the carriage on the way back to Darcy House, Elizabeth reflected on all she had discussed with Jane. They had carefully avoided the topic of Bingley, though it was clear to her that he was on her sister's mind. She had hoped to broach the topic with Darcy this afternoon, but given her outburst this morning, she thought it best to wait. *Maybe Bingley will be at the ball*, she wondered. Lady Matlock had said it was to be a small gathering, but Elizabeth did not know what exactly constituted small for the lady, nor did she know whether she was even acquainted with Bingley. She would have to ask Georgiana.

~

"Darcy! I didn't expect to see you here today! Care for a go?"

"Sir Malcolm. That is what I am here for." They acknowledged each other and donned their fencing vests. Darcy had always preferred to fence without a helmet, as did Malcolm, and their strengths were such that they were each other's most challenging opponent. It was a good thing, because he was feeling especially tense today after his conversation with Elizabeth.

Stepping into the center, they bowed, raised their foils, and waited for the signal to begin. "EnGarde!"

They circled one another, each waiting for the other to make the first move. Malcolm was the first to advance, Darcy easily dodging his attack. They went back and forth, parry, feint, glide, a small crowd gathering to watch them, as was usual. They were both skilled and equal in size and strength, though it may be said that while Malcolm was slightly more liked, Darcy was infinitely more feared.

By the third round, they each had a win behind them and were growing bored. Toweling off before they began, Malcolm looked slyly at Darcy.

"I ran in to your aunt the other day, Darcy."

"Did you?"

"Yes. Your sister was with her, as was a certain guest of yours." He looked at Darcy from the corner of his eye. "Quite enchanting, Miss Bennet."

Darcy's jaw clenched slightly. "She is a good friend of Georgiana's."

"I thought as much. She has excellent taste in books."

"Books?"

"That's where I ran in to them, at the bookstore. I helped her select a gift for her father. I was surprised by her knowledge of literature. Fancy having an intelligent conversation in a bookstore, with a lady no less! Singular." Malcolm was smiling abstractedly. He came back to the present. "You've been keeping her quite to yourself, Darcy. That's not very gentlemanly of you, you know."

"I am not in the habit of introducing my sister's friends to all my acquaintance," he said evenly.

"Well, no matter. I shall have a chance to get to know her better at the ball next Thursday. Are you attending?"

"Of course. It is at my uncle's home."

"I don't seem to remember that ever being a good enough reason for you to attend in the past, Darcy."

"Yes, well, Georgiana will be going, so I will be there."

"As will Miss Bennet. Tell me, is she here in town alone or are her family also staying with you?"

Darcy didn't like where this was going. "She is here on her own, as Georgiana's personal guest."

"So if I wanted to call, I'd have to go through you then?" Malcolm gave him a taunting look, but there was seriousness behind it.

"Malcolm, what are you getting at?"

"Nothing at all, Darcy. Just asking an innocent question. I suppose Miss Bennet can tell me at the ball." He was clearly enjoying this.

"Lady Matlock is fond of making her balls a bit heavy on the male side, so you may not get a dance." His face was smooth, without a trace of emotion, but his eyes were stormy.

"I've already secured the supper set, but thanks for the warning. Shall we?"

His jaw clenching, Darcy stepped again to the center and lifted his foil into position. "EnGarde!"

This time there was no circling. Darcy immediately attacked Malcolm, quickly backing him into the corner. Surprised by his aggression, Malcolm took a moment to respond, but managed to hold his own. Darcy was relentless; attack, counterattack, cut. Malcolm parried and feinted and defended admirably, but it was no use. Darcy was unstoppable; within minutes, he had a direct hit and the match was his.

The men stepped back, bowed to each other, and headed to the dressing rooms. Darcy had no intention of talking to anyone. He nodded thanks to the various words of congratulations, quickly changed, and headed out before Malcolm could talk to him again; he didn't trust himself to speak.

How dare he insinuate that Darcy was keeping Elizabeth to himself! Of course, that was exactly what he was doing, but not for the reasons Malcolm implied. His intentions were honorable; he was going to marry her, for God's sake! He didn't need Malcolm butting in and mucking things up. How dare he ask him to call? He was not Elizabeth's father; far from it!

And to think he'd had the audacity to secure the supper set! Darcy knew what he was doing; he'd be able to escort her to the dining room and likely sit with her, prolonging their time together.

With a sigh, Darcy admitted to himself why he was really angry; he had intended to ask Miss Bennet for the same set, so that he might be the one to sit with her through dinner. Now he would have to watch her smile and laugh with Malcolm. Ladies always smiled and laughed with Malcolm.

Well, he wouldn't let this get the better of him. He had determined to have two dances with her, and two he would have. And damn what anybody said about it!

That night after dinner, as they were walking to the music room, Darcy stepped next to Elizabeth.

"Miss Bennet, it occurs to me that I have only secured one dance with you at next week's ball."

"That is correct, Mr. Darcy."

"May I also request the last set?"

"The last set?" Her eyebrows shot up. "You may."

"Good. I look forward to it." He smiled and entered the music room, leaving a bewildered Elizabeth in his wake.

□

CHAPTER 11

Lady Matlock handed her things to the footman and asked to see Miss Bennet. Hawkins showed her into a small sitting room at the back of the house and went to find Elizabeth. Ten minutes later, Elizabeth found herself sitting across from Lady Matlock sipping tea, and wondering what on earth this was about.

"Miss Bennet, I am glad I've got you on your own for a moment. I wanted to discuss the upcoming ball with you."

"I'm listening, your ladyship."

"I have located a few eligible gentlemen that I wish you to dance with and consider on Thursday."

"Excuse me?" Elizabeth stopped her cup in mid-air and stared blankly at Lady Matlock.

"My dear, I'm sure you know how this works. You meet in a ballroom, you dance, he calls, if he likes you, he asks to court you. If you find this favorable, you accept. Most courtships end in proposals, and most proposals end with weddings."

"Yes, Lady Matlock, I understand that perfectly. What I don't understand is why you are taking it upon yourself to find me a suitor – or is it more than one?"

"Miss Bennet, I do not wish to upset you, but I feel I must speak frankly. May I?"

"I would prefer it if you did." Elizabeth was trying very hard to keep her voice steady.

"I like you. I believe you are honest and good, and are an excellent friend to my niece. My son Richard raves about you. Even Fitzwilliam, who seldom enjoys the company of women outside his family, has taken a liking to you." Elizabeth's face betrayed her surprise at this statement.

"I assure you, Miss Bennet, I speak the truth. I know you have not known them long, but the Darcys are a loyal bunch. Georgiana will be your friend for life. And if I can believe my son, so will he and Fitzwilliam. I don't know that you realize how powerful a position Georgiana is about to be in. The Darcy family is almost as old as England. They have lived at Pemberley for more than twenty generations, and each has prospered more than the last. The Fitzwilliam family is barely less ancient and holds more than one title.

"Lady Anne Darcy, formerly Lady Anne Fitzwilliam, was a dear friend of mine. We were in school together along with Georgiana's aunt, Clara Preston, then Clara Darcy. It was through Anne that I met my husband Henry. He wasn't Lord Matlock yet, and I was visiting Anne for the summer. Little did I know that I would be married to her brother in a year and that a few months later, Anne would marry Clara's brother. So you can see why I care about this family. We have been bound together through blood and friendship nearly our entire lives." She looked at Elizabeth earnestly and clasped her hands in her lap before continuing.

"Georgiana will be much sought after when she comes out, and I am afraid that she has no true friends like I had in Clara and Anne. She has just the sort of disposition that makes her easy prey to those who would take advantage of her position. And the fact that she has a large dowry would be temptation to anyone. This is part of why I want to help you. You are an honest person, I can tell that about you, and you are just who Georgiana needs by her side to navigate these treacherous waters."

"But surely I do not need to be married to do that! I will be her friend as long as she wishes it. I fail to see how a suitor plays into this." Elizabeth was feeling very perplexed and it showed on her face. She did not like not understanding what was happening.

"Yes, my dear, you are quite right. However, you do not live with Georgiana, and with her being under her brother's guardianship, you will hardly be able to make prolonged visits with any regularity. Besides, being so close to her, you will also be sought out, and I am afraid you will not always receive the best treatment. The first circles can be very cruel and are often closed to those who are not their own."

"I see. So do you wish to protect me or to buy me entrance?"

"Both. I do not want to be crass, but I must tell you that everything will be easier for you under the protection of a husband. Especially the right husband."

"Lady Matlock, I appreciate your interest in me and I understand that it is an honor to be singled out by you, but I must tell you that I do not wish to be auctioned off to the highest bidder. And I cannot believe that finding me a husband of the first circles will be as easy as you make it appear. I wish to marry for affection. I am afraid that I cannot enter into a union without it, regardless of the material gains. I am sorry and do not wish to upset you, but I must be firm on this."

"My dear Miss Bennet, surely you know there are ways to access the first circles, without being in the first circles. But we shall get to that; you have just confirmed that I have indeed judged you correctly." Lady Matlock smiled broadly at her. "Please, allow me to tell you a story." Elizabeth reluctantly nodded her agreement.

"When I met Lord Matlock, the viscount then, I thought he was self-important and dull." Elizabeth choked slightly on her biscuit. "I was spending the summer with my friend Anne Fitzwilliam and wasn't interested in men as of yet. I was nearly seventeen and I knew I was coming out the following spring, as were Anne and Clara Darcy, and I wanted to enjoy the last summer of my youth.

"Little did I know that Henry Fitzwilliam had other plans. He took one look at me and decided I was the one for him. I didn't know if it was my youthful bloom or my 25,000 pounds that attracted him, so I decided to have nothing to do with him. I thought that if he was after the dowry, he could get in line the following spring along with everyone else. If he truly loved me, he would be willing to wait, or at least find a better way of showing it." She laughed lightly at the memory.

"I gave him the hardest time. Every time he came around, I found an excuse to leave the room. I refused to sit by him at dinner and would never play what he asked me to at the pianoforte. If my mother had known I was behaving so rudely to a potential and extremely eligible suitor, and a titled one at that, she would have had my head.

"But I knew it would be alright in the end and I would marry eventually. I was rich and pretty and all that is considered accomplished, and that will always bring suitors around. I wanted to enjoy my last summer of freedom, and he was ruining it."

She shook her head and smiled at the memory. "Lady Anne was a little bit wild, which is probably why we were friends, but she was everything ladylike in public. Only those closest to her, and possibly not even all of them, knew her true nature. Fitzwilliam is like her in that way. She would be the image of perfect obedience and manners, and then sneak off to climb trees when no one was about. She never did anything really bad, she was just a bit naughty and perhaps not what everyone thought a perfect lady should be, which is probably what George saw in her.

"Anyway, one afternoon it was terribly hot and Clara and Anne and I decided to sneak off to a little cove and go for a swim. Proper ladies weren't supposed to bathe, at least not without a screen and a chaperone, if then, but we were all raised in the country with our brothers and saw no reason to adhere to those ridiculous rules.

"We made sure no one was about and went swimming in our shifts. We were all fairly good swimmers and knew how to be careful. Unfortunately, I wasn't careful enough. I jumped off a nearby rock and somehow got my foot tangled in the branches and vines under the water. I was struggling to swim to the top, but I couldn't break free. Just as I was sure I was going to drown and began to say my prayers, I felt something grab my ankle. All I could see through the murky water was a figure moving around my bound leg, and then I was free."

Elizabeth released the breath she was holding. "Who saved you?"

"The last person I expected. When we reached the surface, I saw it was Henry Fitzwilliam. He pulled me to the shore and wrapped me in his riding coat to keep me from shivering. My hands and feet were blue and he was rubbing them briskly, trying to restore the color. He kept talking to me, asking me if I could hear him and saying my name. I was vaguely aware of Clara and Anne crying in the background. I could hear his voice, but I couldn't respond. I suppose it was the shock." She took a sip of her tea, then continued in a faraway voice. "I couldn't stop staring at him. I watched everything he did; his hands, his face, his eyes, and finally, I saw it."

"What?"

"It was in his eyes. He was terrified - for me. He loved me and he was afraid I was dying in front of him. And that's when I knew. I knew I could trust him and that he would love me the way I had always wanted to be loved. It wasn't about the money, it never had been. And then I knew that I loved him, too. I called out his name and he looked at me with such tenderness. I felt that I could see his very soul in that moment." She let out a small sigh and came back to the present. "We were practically inseparable the rest of the summer. Even after I went home, we would send each other letters through Anne. We married a year later to the day and have spent thirty-four wonderful years together."

"That is a beautiful story," Elizabeth sighed.

"I told you this so that you would understand that I do know what it feels like to not want to give up your independence to a man. And I know what it means to love, and feel love in return. I've seen good and bad marriages amongst my various friends, and I wouldn't trade mine for any of theirs.

"But hear this, Miss Bennet: there is often more to a man than meets the eye, and if you are too quick to look away, you may miss it, as I almost did with Henry." She reached across and put her hand over Elizabeth's, a sincere look on her face. "It is just as easy to love a rich man as a poor one. I would not want to see you in a bad marriage, nor in dire straits. So please, let me help you."

"Alright, Lady Matlock, you may help me. But I make no promises to leave your ball engaged," Elizabeth acquiesced. Lady Matlock smiled and gave her hand a squeeze.

"We shall see, Miss Bennet, we shall see."

Just then, Georgiana came bounding in. "Lady Helen! I didn't know you were coming today!" She kissed her aunt affectionately.

"Miss Bennet and I have just been having a little chat while you finished your lessons. Are you all through now?"

"Yes, quite."

"Good. Now you can help Miss Bennet and me sort through the men coming to the ball."

Georgiana's eyes grew wide and she sat down slowly. "What do you mean, 'sort through them'?"

"You will be out next year, so this is as good a time as any to teach you how these things work. Now, here is who we have to work with." She drew a small piece of paper out of her reticule and unfolded it.

"Lady Matlock! You have an actual list?" Elizabeth asked disbelievingly.

"With something as serious as this, Miss Bennet, it is best to be prepared." She gave her a somber look. "Now let's get started. First we have Sir Malcolm Rutherford."

"Sir Malcolm! Lady Helen, what exactly are we doing?" Georgiana asked with trepidation.

"We are sorting through possible suitors for Miss Bennet."

"Oh!" Georgiana's eyes became even wider, and she decided to just listen for now.

"As I said, there is Sir Malcolm. You have already met, and he does seem to be attracted to you. You will dance together?"

"Yes, the supper set."

"Oh, that is good." Elizabeth had to stop herself from rolling her eyes. At least this was a much more private way of matchmaking than her mother's method. She told herself to be a good sport and let Lady Matlock lead the way.

"Sir Malcolm has an estate in Staffordshire. He comes from a respectable family and has already inherited, so his decisions are his own. That moves him to the top of the list. And his aunt is a friend of mine. He also has a house here in town, of a good size, and has an income of about 8,000 a year. And he is very handsome," she added with a sly smile.

"But would a baronet take a wife without a dowry?" Elizabeth asked.

"Most would not, I grant you, but Sir Malcolm is healthy financially and a bit sentimental, though he wouldn't want you to know it, so I believe it is a possibility. And his close relationship with the Darcy and Fitzwilliam families can only be beneficial."

Seeing Georgiana's growing alarm, Elizabeth told her, "Lady Matlock would like to introduce me to some gentlemen at the ball this week and wishes me to know of them beforehand. I shall be introduced to them and if we get along, we can see what comes of it. Don't worry, my dear, I shall not be sold like a slave on the market," Elizabeth teased and squeezed her hand.

Georgiana smiled and nodded, then began to get involved with the conversation, adding bits and pieces that she knew about each, mostly those who were friends of Darcy's or the Colonel's.

"Another thing to consider is second sons. Now, a younger son from a noble family brings very good connections to the table, so he is likely to marry a lady with a large dowry and similar connections."

"Like Richard!" piped in Georgiana.

"Yes, quite. But not all second sons are from noble families. Now, many of these men will have made their way in the world through alternate means, as clergymen, in the army, or sometimes the law. Occasionally their parents will give them a house in town as a wedding gift, and as long as they remain in good graces with the elder brother, they will usually be welcome at the family's country estate and have a decent allowance.

"A few others will marry a lady with an estate, which is rare, and more still will inherit a smaller estate from a relative or will be gifted one from their father. Those men will be looking for wives who know how be mistress of such a home and who will be comfortable in those circumstances, but who are ladies nonetheless. Some of the more well-dowered, and more attractive," she added quietly "ladies are not willing to entertain this, and will pass these gentlemen over."

"I see. So my coming from a small estate and not expecting a grand home is to be in my favor."

"Precisely, Miss Bennet. One such man is Mr. Thomas Bradenton, of Bedfordshire. His aunt, Mrs. Braebury, is an old friend of mine and speaks quite highly of him. He is the younger son of her youngest brother. He is not as handsome as Sir Malcolm, but they can't all be, now can they?"

Elizabeth wondered when Sir Malcolm had become the scale against which every man was measured, but Lady Matlock just continued down her list.

"Mr. Alfred Kirkland. He is the third son of Mr. George Kirkland. His mother and I served on a charity board together. He is a barrister, and lives here in town. His mother has hinted that should he marry, they would purchase him a house. He is quite his mother's favorite."

And so she went down the list, until Elizabeth was so confused, she couldn't remember who was a barrister or a navy captain, let alone who was the son of whom.

"I see why you have this written down, Lady Matlock. It is quite overwhelming!"

Lady Matlock just smiled and patted her hand, and, after tea, she took her leave.

Despite her earlier protestations, Elizabeth had enjoyed herself. It was rather like an elaborate game. Meet Mr. Worthing of Oxfordshire, 3,000 a year and a house in town. Mr. Swanson of Bristol, a little older, but very kind. She laughed a little at herself and shook her head. As much as she hated to admit it, she was rooting for Sir Malcolm.

CHAPTER 12

Sunday morning dawned dark and raining, thunder booming loudly outside the windows; all knew making their way to church was out of the question in such weather.

Georgiana snuck into Elizabeth's room early and requested they order a tray and eat together in their dressing gowns, something one of the girls she knew from school had told her she did with her sisters on rainy days. Elizabeth was happy to oblige, but had to admit to a slight twinge at the idea of missing breakfast with Mr. Darcy, something that had become a regular and welcome occurrence in her day.

They drank tea and ate toast with jam in the comfort of Elizabeth's chambers and their warm winter dressing gowns, giggling about nothing and everything at once. They talked of the ball and what they would wear and how they would fix their hair, and what they thought all the other ladies would wear, and how their hair would be fixed. They eventually moved on to who would be there and Elizabeth thought this was a perfect time to ask about Mr. Bingley.

"Georgiana, do you know if Mr. Bingley will be at the ball?"

"I am not certain, but I do not think so. Lady Matlock has rarely met him here and she did not know his parents. Most of the people at her balls have known our family for more than one generation. That's part of what makes them so exclusive," she said with her nose in the air and a mocking voice, causing Elizabeth to laugh lightly. "Why do you ask?"

"I have not seen him at all while I've been here and I wish to renew the acquaintance, that is all."

"Shall I send a greeting through Miss Bingley next time she calls? She will probably come the day after the ball to ask me all about it."

"No, not Miss Bingley, but if you see Mr. Bingley directly, please give him the heartfelt greetings of the entire Bennet family, and let him know that my sister and I hope to see him while we are in town."

Eventually they dressed and went downstairs, Georgiana to the music room and Elizabeth to the library. When she entered the warm space, her eyes flew to the door she knew connected to Darcy's study. Surprisingly, it was open. She walked slowly toward it and gingerly stepped into the doorway, careful not to go too far. Seeing no one at the large desk, she looked to the fire and saw no one there either.

She was about to head back into the library when she heard a murmur. Oddly, it almost sounded like her name, but she couldn't be sure. She looked toward the sound and for the first time noticed something hanging off the end of the small sofa facing the fire; it was a rather large foot.

Curiosity getting the better of her, she walked into the room and approached the fireplace. When she was a few feet away from the sofa, she craned her neck forward, and found Mr. Darcy sound asleep.

She had never seen a man asleep before, except for her father, and that was years ago when she was a little girl. She found herself once again wishing she had a brother so these things wouldn't seem so mysterious and stepped a little closer. The light from the fire was flickering across his face, which was more relaxed than she had ever seen it. He looked so peaceful, not formidable or proud or any of the other words she usually used to describe him.

A lock of hair had fallen casually across his forehead and his coat was unbuttoned, made more noticeable by the regular rise and fall of his chest. How disheveled and harmless he appeared! And almost endearing… Elizabeth stood watching him a few moments more, knowing she was intruding on his privacy, but not quite able to make herself leave.

Suddenly he shifted and made a murmuring sound, and she hastily made her way to the library.

Darcy had waited in the breakfast parlor for Elizabeth to come down, and when she hadn't made an appearance, he had begun to worry if she was ill. He had finally asked Hawkins if Miss Darcy was still sleeping and was informed that she and Miss Bennet were sharing a tray in her chambers. Relieved she was not ill, and slightly annoyed she had elected to eat without him, he had gone to his study in an attempt to be productive.

He had slept fretfully the night before, awakening in the middle of the night after a particularly stimulating dream, and had been unable to fall back asleep for several hours. After reading the same letter three times without comprehending a word of it, he decided to lie down and attempt to relax his overactive mind. Hoping Elizabeth would head to the library, as she usually did when she wasn't calling on her aunt, he had left the adjoining door open so that he might hear her when she came in.

He had unwittingly fallen asleep and was now in the midst of his favorite dream, only instead of finding Elizabeth in the drawing room at Netherfield, she was in the library in his townhouse. When he kissed and held her, she whispered his name sweetly and he closed his eyes in contentment.

A few minutes later he awakened and was surprised to find himself in his study. Remembering his purpose, he looked toward the open door and listened carefully. Hearing nothing, he glanced at the clock and thought it was past time when she should have come down.

Darcy tensely rose and went to stand in the open doorway, looking around the library in agitation. As soon as he saw her, he felt the tension leave his body and warmth fill its place. She was standing across the room, her back to him, reaching up to a shelf just out of her reach, trying to grab a book. He smiled at the sight of her on her toes, stretching her little fingers as far as they would go. In a few strides he was at her side.

He stood behind her and grabbed the book she was grasping for, his hand brushing hers as he did so. Elizabeth froze when she felt his touch.

"Miss Bennet." He handed the book to her as she turned around.

"Thank you, Mr. Darcy." She was almost in his arms, pinned as she was between him and the bookshelf. She blushed at his proximity.

"Any time, Miss Bennet." He stepped back and walked to the fire, gesturing for her to take a seat across from him.

"Did you enjoy your breakfast with Georgiana?" He tried to keep his voice free of accusation, knowing his feelings of neglect were more like a petulant child's than a grown man's.

"Yes, we had a lovely time together. I think she is immensely enjoying another female presence in the house," she said, smiling.

He sat quietly for a moment, basking in the warmth of her smiles. They spoke about the books they were each reading and what they thought of them, noting how their opinions were the same on certain points and completely opposite on others, each a little surprised at the other. Eventually the conversation turned to the poetry of Wordsworth and his many poems about the Lakes, when Elizabeth remembered her proposed trip with her family.

"Oh! I wanted to tell you something. When I told my aunt about visiting Pemberley this summer, an invitation she gave me leave to accept, she told me they are planning a northern tour and were going to invite me to join them. Now that she knows I will be at Pemberley, she thought perhaps I could journey back to Hertfordshire with them, and even go with them for a portion of the trip. They will be spending a few days at Lambton where my aunt spent her youth. She said it is quite close to Pemberley."

"Yes, Lambton is only five miles away. Do you know when they will be going?"

Mrs. Hawkins interrupted them to bring in the tea and Elizabeth's favorite lemon biscuits, giving Darcy a moment to think. His original intent in inviting her to Pemberley was to secure her plans for the summer so she couldn't go anywhere else. She seemed to be issued many invitations, and once they were engaged, he did not want any obstacles to an immediate wedding. He did not think he could handle more than a three month engagement at the most, and would prefer less. It would seem he had been right to plan ahead.

"I am not sure exactly as their dates are not yet fixed, but they are planning on departing mid-June and traveling roughly six weeks. I can inform you in more detail as we approach the summer."

Darcy briefly thought how much simpler this conversation might be if they were already engaged. As it was, she did not know if or when he would ask, though he believed she was expecting it at some point.

"I am sure something can be arranged to suit all parties," he said diplomatically. *Such as me taking you to the Lakes on a wedding tour.* ***Alone.*** She smiled at him again and handed him his tea, prepared in his new favorite way.

"Miss Bennet, I wanted to speak with you about your journey back to Longbourn. Are you still set to leave Saturday?"

"Yes. My uncle will take me as far as Islington and then I will take the post to Meryton."

"And you will return to town three weeks later?"

"Yes. I am to spend two days with my aunt and uncle before going on to Kent."

"Can we not persuade you to remain? You will only be at Longbourn three weeks; that is barely worth the journey."

She smiled indulgently. "That is very kind of you, Mr. Darcy, but I am afraid my father would not like to have me away for three months altogether, especially if I am to spend the summer away as well."

"You are close with your father?" He sipped his tea.

"Yes, very. I suppose because I am the most like him of all my sisters."

"He will miss you greatly when you are gone."

Elizabeth looked at him quizzically for a moment, then answered, "Yes, but the visits are not overly long and as one's friends marry and move away, it is inevitable."

He looked at her, wondering at her meaning, and asked, "So you will not consider staying until you remove to Kent?"

"I am sorry, but I cannot." He thought she looked regretful, but wasn't sure.

"Then please allow me to return you to Longbourn in my carriage." Elizabeth opened her mouth to protest and he gently held up his hand. "It is the least I can do. I haven't seen Georgiana this happy in months."

She looked at him through narrowed eyes, wondering if he had known she would refuse the offer of the carriage, and believed she would not decline two offers in one conversation out of politeness. *Well played, Mr. Darcy.*

"I should not accept. How would it look, for me to travel all that way in your carriage without Georgiana?"

"It would look like you are a very dear friend of the Darcy family and a lady who is well protected. Miss Bennet, I would be much more at ease if you traveled in the carriage instead of by post." Elizabeth had been enjoying teasing him, but now she saw something in his eyes that arrested her response. He was sincere and seemed genuinely concerned for her.

"Very well, Mr. Darcy. If it will make your mind easier, I shall take the carriage."

"Thank you, Miss Bennet. You have greatly relieved me." He smiled and they continued to discuss whatever topic entered their minds for the next hour.

~

Monday, as Elizabeth returned from her visit to the Gardiners, she heard music coming from the back of the house. She gave her things to the footman and followed the sound to the ballroom.

Peeking around the door quietly, she saw Georgiana and Mr. Darcy dancing together, slowly going through the motions of a quadrille while the housekeeper played the pianoforte in the corner. Georgiana stumbled through a few of the turns, but after several minutes, her confidence grew greatly and her eyes danced in merriment as the tempo increased. They danced through a faster jig, twirling and hopping, and Georgiana could not contain her giggles. Darcy's deep laugh joined hers, his head thrown back and his eyes crinkling at the corners.

Elizabeth couldn't help but smile at their antics and wondered, again, what it would be like to have a brother. Someone to practice dances with and look after her, someone who always had her best interests at heart.

If she had her choice of brothers, she supposed she would choose one like Colonel Fitzwilliam. She had a sort of familial affection for him, and they got along famously, having similar temperaments and senses of humor. She gathered that he thought of her in a similar manner, judging by the way he spoke to her and the jokes he was always telling her.

Yes, Colonel Fitzwilliam was the ideal older brother. Georgiana was like another sister and Mr. Darcy was, well, she didn't know what Mr. Darcy was. She knew she did not have a familial sort of affection for him. He was a friend, even though it still seemed odd to call him such.

With her thoughts thus organized, she left the siblings to their dance and went upstairs to change for dinner.

Chapter 12, Part II

The next few days passed much as the days before, with Darcy only dining out once, and Elizabeth going to Cheapside twice more, each time in the Darcy carriage. Final fittings were done and their new gowns delivered, until, at last, the day of the ball arrived.

Elizabeth and Georgiana ate a light repast in Georgiana's sitting room, then separated to prepare. Georgiana was beside herself with excitement and nervousness, wanting to have a good time but afraid she wouldn't, and terrified of all the people and all that was expected of her.

Elizabeth relaxed in the tub, all too aware that this would be one of the last times she would enjoy it. Friday morning would be spent sleeping, then she expected Caroline Bingley to call in the afternoon and she had decided to remain with Georgiana during the visit. Dinner would likely be a subdued and languid affair, but she hoped the Colonel might come to say goodbye, and then Saturday morning, she was off to Hertfordshire. Elizabeth would miss this place. *I will especially miss this tub*, she thought.

She slid down, allowing the water to come to the nape of her neck, and let her mind flood with memories of her visit. She had become infinitely closer with Georgiana and had enjoyed meeting and getting to know Lady Matlock and Colonel Fitzwilliam. She had even become friends of a sort with Mr. Darcy, something she never would have imagined when she first came to London. Not wanting to ponder on things she didn't understand when she did not have the time to do them justice, she turned her mind to the ball.

She could not believe she was participating in Lady Matlock's scheme to marry her off. At least the first two dances were with men she knew. Colonel Fitzwilliam was very amiable and she knew he would become a favorite acquaintance. He would probably be an excellent source of information throughout the evening and was likely to know everyone in attendance, so Elizabeth could apply to him with her questions. She wondered if he would ask her to dance a second. *Probably not, I doubt his mother will allow it!*

She was set to dance twice with Mr. Darcy. She had been surprised when he asked her for a second dance; she was under the impression he disliked the activity. *Maybe it is only country balls he dislikes.* She had made headway in her sketching of his character, and she felt she had a better understanding of him than she had had in Hertfordshire, but he was still an enigma in many ways. *I will have to consider this when I have more time, perhaps in the carriage*, she thought.

There was one more person to think about; Sir Malcolm. She was to dance the supper set with him, which probably meant she would be eating with him as well. It would give her an excellent opportunity to get to know him, and she already knew him to be intelligent and agreeable, and he was handsome. Tonight will certainly be interesting, if nothing else, she mused.

Darcy sat in his dressing room, his chin in the air while his valet shaved him. He wanted to look perfect tonight. It was a special day, though no one knew that but him. He was dancing twice with Elizabeth, and he would be able to watch her easily in the crowded ballroom, though he did not relish seeing her smile and dance with other men. He couldn't wait to see her in all her finery and believed all her efforts were for him.

He remembered how she had looked at the Netherfield ball and knew that tonight would be even better. Tonight they would not argue or talk about Wickham. They would dance and be together until dawn, and when they came home, he would ask her to speak with him in the library. He would tell her that he loved her and ask for her hand. He hoped she would allow him to kiss her, and he entertained warm thoughts of holding her hand, or perhaps just holding her, by the fire, discussing plans for the wedding and their future together.

An hour later, Darcy stood in the entry waiting for the ladies to come down. He was just becoming impatient when he saw a flash of white and looked up.

Elizabeth stood at the top of the stairs, her white dress flowing elegantly, her hair upswept with two perfect curls hanging over her shoulder. As she descended the stairs, her eyes met his and held them the rest of the way down, until she was standing on the bottom step, eye level with Mr. Darcy.

He noticed her cheeks had a becoming flush and her eyes were sparkling in anticipation. Without meaning to, he had walked towards her and was now face to face with her, blocking her path. He stood staring at her, unable to move a muscle.

Elizabeth smiled brightly at him, not sure what he was doing but finding it amusing, and was surprised to see him smile back brilliantly.

"Mr. Darcy."

"Miss Elizabeth."

After a few moments, she smiled nervously and waited for him to move, but he did not. Beginning to be uncomfortable with the unusual closeness, she nodded toward the entry.

"Shall we?"

Wordlessly, he held out his arm and led her toward the door, releasing her to collect her cloak. Georgiana came down a moment later to compliments from Elizabeth and Darcy and the three of them boarded the carriage to travel the short distance to Matlock House.

~

They were the first to arrive, having come slightly early at Lady Matlock's request.

"Lady Helen, Lord Matlock." Darcy bowed formally. They nodded and he turned to Elizabeth. "Allow me to present Miss Elizabeth Bennet of Longbourn in Hertfordshire."

Elizabeth curtseyed and Lord Matlock bowed slightly. "It is a pleasure to meet you, Miss Bennet. I hear interesting things of you from my wife."

"I am pleased to make your acquaintance as well, Lord Matlock. Her ladyship has been equally interesting in her stories about you." She smiled at him.

"Oh has she now? And just what has my wife been telling you?" he asked good-humoredly.

"Henry, why don't you and Darcy have a glass of port while I speak with the ladies?"

"Yes, dear." He smiled at his wife, knowing she was getting rid of him before he heard something she didn't want him to know. "Come, Darcy. Let the ladies convene on their own." He clapped Darcy's back, and after giving Georgiana a kiss on her cheek and telling her how grown-up she looked, led Darcy to his study.

"How are you holding up, Darcy?"

"What do you mean, Uncle?" Darcy looked at him warily.

"Georgiana at her first ball, meeting gentlemen for the first time. They'll be watching for her next year when she comes out. Now would be a good time to see who's out there and start asking questions."

"Already? I thought I wouldn't need to start interviewing suitors until half way through her first season."

"It wouldn't be interviewing exactly, just getting to know who the potential players are. It is a big decision and not one you want to make quickly. Georgiana is a sweet girl; we don't want her taken in by a reprobate."

"Of course, you are right, Uncle. I will keep my eyes open tonight."

"Good. Now, tell me about Miss Bennet." Lord Matlock sat back in his chair as if waiting for a treat.

"Sir?" Darcy had a twinge of fear that his uncle knew his plans.

"Helen seems to have taken quite a liking to her. She has determined to find Miss Bennet a husband."

"She what?" Darcy blurted, nearly choking on his port.

"She says she wants Miss Bennet close by, at least socially, for Georgiana's sake. She doesn't want her to lose a friend. But between us," he grinned at Darcy, his eyes twinkling with humor, "I think she just wants to play matchmaker and happens to like Miss Bennet."

Darcy returned the smile uneasily and asked, "Who does she have in mind?"

"Who does she not? Anyone who is appropriate and shows the least amount of interest will be considered, I imagine. And judging by the looks of her, there will undoubtedly be some interest." He looked meaningfully at Darcy.

"Has Miss Bennet expressed an interest in the prospect?" He tried to keep his voice even as he thought of hordes of suitors dancing with his Elizabeth.

"From what Helen told me, she had to talk her into the idea. Said she wanted to marry for affection and wouldn't consider anything less, no matter the material gain. From what I've heard, and what I've seen myself this evening, she is a spirited one." He laughed softly. "Reminds me of Helen," he said to himself.

"Yes, I have heard something of the same," Darcy said thoughtfully. A hint of doubt was creeping over him, but he tried to ignore it.

"Shall we get back to the ladies?" Lord Matlock led the way while Darcy contemplated what he had heard.

How had he not known about this? It was happening under his own roof! And what was Lady Matlock thinking, playing matchmaker for Elizabeth? She didn't need a match, she had him!

He brooded over why Elizabeth would choose to participate in such a scheme when he had clearly made his preference known. *But how could she say no to Lady Matlock?* he justified. He knew from experience that the countess could be very persuasive when she wanted something, and Elizabeth was a guest; she probably felt obligated to go along with the plan.

After all, you have not proposed. Yet, he told himself.

Could she doubt him? Surely not! Surely she knew him better than to think he would court her and disappear? She must be playing along out of politeness. It was the only explanation.

They returned to the ladies to see Georgiana receiving instructions for the evening from Lady Matlock, Elizabeth watching with a polite smile on her face. Darcy looked at her until she felt his gaze and turned toward him. Her smile immediately brightened and he moved to her side. *See how she smiles at me. She does not doubt me,* he thought with satisfaction.

Before he could speak to her, Colonel Fitzwilliam joined them.

"Miss Bennet, Darcy." He bowed. "You, madam, are looking very lovely this evening." He smiled at Elizabeth.

"Thank you, Colonel Fitzwilliam. You look rather dashing yourself," she said brightly.

"I hope you are well rested for this evening, Miss Bennet. I fear you will not sit out a single dance."

"You are too kind, Colonel. But do not fret, my feet can take it and I dearly love to dance." Darcy sent a dark look to Fitzwilliam, which his cousin chose to ignore.

"Miss Bennet, I fear I must warn you of imminent danger," he said seriously in a low voice, but she saw the twinkle in his eye.

"And what danger might that be, Colonel?" she asked just as quietly.

He leaned towards her and whispered loudly, "My brother, the viscount. I fear that your toes are in grave danger if you accept a dance with him."

"But surely you know, sir," she replied, leaning toward him and matching his tone, "I cannot refuse him should he ask."

"Well, it is no loss to me as I have your first dance. But if he stomps on your foot and you are forced to sit out the rest of the evening, do not say I didn't warn you." He smiled brightly and she gave a small laugh.

"Richard, what on earth are you going on about now?" came a loud voice.

"Ah, just the man I wanted to see. Cyril, may I present Miss Bennet of Longbourn in Hertfordshire? Miss Bennet, my elder brother, Cyril Fitzwilliam, the Viscount Selton." Colonel Fitzwilliam was obviously having fun baiting his brother, and Elizabeth had to cover her smile with a formal curtsey.

"Miss Bennet, it is a pleasure to meet you." He bowed deeply, getting a good look at her décolletage as he did so. He arose with a small smile on his face.

"I am pleased to make your acquaintance, Lord Selton."

"Miss Bennet, may I request a dance? Are you free for the second?"

"I am already engaged for the second, milord, but the third is available."

"The third it shall be then. Thank you, Miss Bennet."

Elizabeth smiled and nodded, and he turned back to his parents.

"Well, Miss Bennet, surely now you see my point. I can see you barely survived the introduction!"

"Colonel Fitzwilliam, I found your brother to be perfectly agreeable and civil. I am quite looking forward to my dance with him," she teased him casually as she plucked nonexistent lint from her skirt.

Fitzwilliam shook his head and offered his arm. "May I escort you to the ballroom?"

"You may, but do you not have to greet your guests with your family?"

"A benefit of being a second son and living in a barracks - I can avoid reception lines."

She took his arm and they started off, smiling and laughing. Darcy extended his arm to Georgiana, and they followed them into the ballroom, Darcy scowling all the way.

CHAPTER 13

Elizabeth stayed to the side with Georgiana, helping her calm her fears and review her dance steps and how to accept a dance properly. The ballroom quickly filled with guests and the gentlemen came to claim the ladies for the first dance.

Elizabeth laughed and smiled throughout the first set, Richard either telling her something amusing, or doing something to make her laugh. When it was over, he escorted her to Darcy for the next dance. She had drawn attention with her smiles and light movements and several men were looking her way. It did not go unnoticed by Darcy, or by Colonel Fitzwilliam, who winked at Darcy as he handed her off and took

Georgiana's arm, leading her away.

"Miss Bennet, would you like some refreshment before the next dance?" Darcy asked her.

"Not at present, Mr. Darcy, I thank you." She looked at him carefully, noting he was more serious than a ball required and wondered if something was troubling him or if that was his usual demeanor at a ball. Having too much fun to be brought down, she decided to ask him.

"Forgive me, Mr. Darcy, but is something troubling you?"

"Not at all, Miss Bennet." He attempted to smile unsuccessfully. "Why do you ask?"

"You seem rather serious for a ball, sir," she said with an arch smile while lifting one brow.

"Forgive me, Miss Bennet. I find I am never completely at ease in large crowds of strangers. My cousin and I differ greatly in that respect."

Beginning to comprehend his shyness, and not completely understanding why he referenced his cousin, she smiled brightly at him.

"Then I shall have to distract you, Mr. Darcy." Her smile and words had the desired effect and he smiled in return. He wasn't as uncomfortable in the ballroom as he'd intimated, though he certainly didn't enjoy it, but he could hardly tell her that seeing her laughing with his cousin made him want to grab her and kiss her in front of all these people, publicly claiming her, so they would all know she was his. And possibly throw Colonel Fitzwilliam out the window in the process.

"And how do you propose to do that, Miss Bennet?"

"I'm sure I shall think of something."

The music began and they took their place in the line, Darcy never taking his eyes off Elizabeth. She smiled at him and began moving through the steps. When she got to Colonel Fitzwilliam, he winked at her and she couldn't help a startled laugh, and was chuckling when she returned to Darcy.

"What is so amusing, Miss Bennet?"

Remembering his comment about his cousin and not wanting to imply Fitzwilliam was more amusing than he, she thought quickly about what to reply.

"I find that I am having a difficult time keeping a straight face around your cousin," she saw his face become a mask again as they separated and circled back to each other, "the Viscount. I'm afraid your story keeps playing in my mind, now that I have a face to put to the actions." She looked up to see Darcy looking slightly startled, his expression quickly breaking out into a wide grin.

"I understand your predicament completely, Miss Bennet. I often find taking the viscount seriously to be a difficult task as well." They completed the dance in light conversation, smiling and laughing frequently, creating questions amongst the guests as to who the woman was who could make the stern Mr. Darcy smile.

He escorted her off the floor and brought her some punch, returning just before the Viscount arrived to claim his dance. Elizabeth gave Darcy a meaningful look and tried to hide her smile as he led her onto the floor. Darcy was relishing the idea of having a private joke with her, and chose to stand on the side and watch her instead of finding his own partner.

After nearly 3 hours of dancing, Elizabeth's mind was whirling. She had met several men, all nephews or cousins of Lady Matlock's friends, plus the occasional younger son of a wealthy landowner. She didn't really think any of them would be seriously interested in her, thankfully, but she was having a good time and they were all polite and kind, some even intelligent or funny.

In between sets, Lady Matlock approached her.

"How is it going, dear?" She had been introducing Elizabeth all evening as a dear friend of the family, leaving no doubt of the countess's loyalty or intentions.

"As well as can be imagined, I believe."

"What do you think of Mr. Hargrove?"

"Is he the parson from Northampton?"

Lady Matlock gave a light laugh. "Buckinghamshire. Though I am not surprised you can't remember. There have been a great many this evening, and there are more to come." She looked at Elizabeth meaningfully. "He seems to like you."

"He does?"

"Yes. His aunt is a friend of mine and was asking me about you. He may call. Would that be welcome?"

"I hardly know. I only spoke with him a few minutes after the dance and what little conversation could be had during. He seems like a nice enough man." Elizabeth was slightly shocked at herself for discussing such a thing in a ballroom, and with Lady Matlock, but if she was going to play along, she may as well play heartily.

"You have yet to dance with Sir Malcolm. The supper set is coming up; I daresay it will be telling." She gave Elizabeth a pointed look, patted her hand, and walked toward her husband.

Elizabeth considered Mr. Hargrove. He had sandy hair, light grey eyes, and a warm smile. She could not doubt he was a genuine man, but maybe a trifle good for her tastes. She thought about the duties of a parson's wife and whether she could envision herself in the role. She didn't have long to think on it; her next partner, a Mr. Fielding, arrived for the next set.

Mr. Fielding was a barrister in London and seemed to be hardworking and intelligent. She would guess his age to be near thirty-two; he was just shy of being considered tall and had warm hazel eyes. He wasn't very handsome, but they couldn't all be. She enjoyed the intellectual stimulation and thought he seemed to be a decent man, though her feelings did not go beyond that. Elizabeth imagined that he would not be in a position to marry for at least a few years, which gave her leave to relax a little, letting her humor and vivacity flow freely; until he dropped into the conversation that he had inherited a house in town from a childless uncle. She instantly knew she wasn't interested and it was with relief that she heard the music come to an end.

If only mama could be here! How she would be crowing about all the eligible men and how I don't have a single set free! Elizabeth couldn't help but smile at the thought of her mother in this fashionable ballroom and she let out an amused sigh.

"I hope that is not a sigh of exhaustion and that you would not try to avoid our dance, Miss Bennet?" She looked aside to see Sir Malcolm smirking at her.

"I wouldn't dream of it, Sir Malcolm."

"I am glad to hear it. Shall we?" He led her to the floor and they took their place in the line.

"How do you know the Darcys, Miss Bennet?" he asked her as they danced.

"I met them in Hertfordshire. Mr. Darcy was staying with his friend Mr. Bingley, and I met Miss Darcy when she came up for a short visit."

"I am surprised Bingley isn't here. He and Darcy are thick as thieves."

Elizabeth looked at him quizzically. "Yes, they seem to be very close friends. But it is not Mr. Darcy's ball."

"You are right, Miss Bennet, it is not." They danced in silence for a while until Elizabeth felt conversation was needed.

"And how are you acquainted with the family, Sir? You were at Cambridge with Mr. Darcy?"

"Yes, I was. I knew him a little before that. My father was a friend of Lord Matlock's and Colonel Fitzwilliam and I saw each other often as children. Sometimes Darcy was present."

"I see. Do you have any other family?"

"Both my parents are gone, and I have a sister, Arabella, who was recently married to Lord Ashland. She is in the country now at her new husband's estate."

They separated in the dance and when they came together again, he had a teasing look in his eye.

"And what of you, Miss Bennet?"

"What about me, Sir Malcolm?"

"Do you have any family?"

"Yes. My family lives in Hertfordshire on my father's estate."

"And your brothers and sisters?"

"I do not have a brother, and am the second of five sisters." She expected a reaction, but he didn't miss a beat.

"And are all your sisters as lovely as you?"

Elizabeth blushed despite herself.

"I could not say, Sir."

They separated again and when she came back to him, he was smiling again.

"Sir Malcolm, is something amusing you?"

"Nothing at all, Miss Bennet. I am merely enjoying the uncommonly good company." Elizabeth looked down and when she raised her eyes, the music was at an end. He offered his arm and began to escort her to the dining room.

Darcy had been watching Elizabeth all night. His aunt had tried repeatedly to get him to dance and had gone so far as to introduce him to a lady, knowing he couldn't refuse if she were standing right in front of him, but after the dance, he could not even recall her name.

After leaving the forgettable girl with her mother, Darcy was accosted by Mr. Graves, an older man with a daughter in her third season.

"Mr. Darcy! How are you this evening? What a fine party it is! You remember my daughter, Letitia." He gestured to the round-faced girl next to him.

Miss Graves – how could he forget: 20,000 pounds, plays the pianoforte and the harp, sings, draws, speaks French. He nodded out of politeness and continued around the ballroom, only to be stopped twice more, once by Mr. Harvey and his daughter, 25,000 pounds, the harp, sings, Italian, cannot draw though – a pity – and Mrs. Trantham and her daughter, 30,000 pounds, pianoforte, draws, German. He paid no attention to any of the daughters and barely acknowledged the parents.

His attention was entirely focused on Elizabeth Bennet. He watched her every step, wondered at the cause behind each laugh, and worked to control his anger each time she blushed from another man's compliments.

He knew his aunt was watching her and scheming, and judging by the way she had rushed to the dining room, he could only imagine she was placing Elizabeth next to Sir Malcolm at the table. He waited until she went back to the ballroom, then walked over to where she had been standing and saw he was right.

Elizabeth was placed to the right of Sir Malcolm, a man Darcy didn't know was on Malcolm's other side, and Georgiana was placed next to Elizabeth. He located his own name on the other side of the table and a few places down and switched it with someone named Worthing on Georgiana's right. He then moved himself to Elizabeth's right and Georgiana next to him. *That's much better*, he thought.

As people began filing into the dining room, Darcy was quick to prepare his and Georgiana's plates, and was just returning to his place at the table when Sir Malcolm arrived with Elizabeth.

"Malcolm, Miss Bennet." Darcy nodded and waited for Elizabeth to be seated. Colonel Fitzwilliam arrived with Georgiana and Darcy held out her chair as the Colonel left to find his seat. Malcolm offered to get a plate for Miss Bennet and he headed toward the buffet table as Darcy seated himself between his sister and Elizabeth.

"How is your evening going, Georgiana?" he asked her.

"I hardly know what to think! Everything is so grand and there is so much to see!"

"And you, Miss Bennet, are you enjoying the ball so far?"

Elizabeth laughed gently. "I daresay I am. I don't know when I last danced so much in one evening!"

Georgiana leaned across her brother. "Elizabeth! You have not sat out a single dance. Are you not tired? I should think you could hardly feel your feet!"

"I am a little weary, but sitting for a spell and eating should put me to rights again." She leaned slightly closer to Georgiana, putting her in close proximity to Darcy, which of course had been his design all along. "How are you enjoying your first ball? Have you enjoyed dancing with real partners?"

"Oh yes! I am so glad I came! I can't imagine doing this for the first time next year with gentlemen I had never met before."

Darcy was sitting back in his chair to give the two women in his life room to speak to each other across him. It wasn't the best manners, but it was late and everyone was half in their cups in the noisy dining room, so he didn't think it very important to be perfectly decorous at the present moment. And he was enjoying it too much to say anything.

"I think your aunt was right to insist on a practice ball for you. Though it remains to be seen whether she was right about other things," Elizabeth said in a low voice, with eyebrows raised, but of course Darcy heard her.

She was speaking more freely than she usually would and he wondered if she'd had too much punch and was a little tipsy. An inebriated Elizabeth was something he would very much enjoy seeing. He could imagine how delightful she would be when completely unencumbered. Though preferably not at a ball. He could think of other locations better suited to that particular display.

Georgiana's only answer was a giggle and a pointed look toward Sir Malcolm where he was approaching with two plates filled with food.

"Here you are, Miss Bennet." He sat down next to her and for a time everyone's attention was given to the food in front of them.

After a few minutes, Sir Malcolm began to speak with Elizabeth about her home in Hertfordshire. Darcy was trying to be polite and give his attention to Georgiana, but she was being rather quiet, understandable since she had rarely been up this late before and she was looking sleepier by the minute, but he couldn't help being drawn in by Elizabeth's laughter.

"Yes, I often walk about the countryside. Is that so terribly shocking?" she said laughingly to Sir Malcolm.

"A little shocking, but not terrible, Miss Bennet. Do you walk alone or do your sisters accompany you?"

"I prefer to walk alone. None of my sisters enjoy it much and I am afraid they dislike long rambles, which are my favorite sort."

"And do you ride alone as well?"

"I do not ride."

"Not at all?"

"Not at all."

"That is interesting. I would have thought you to enjoy riding immensely."

Elizabeth laughed. "You are not the first person to tell me so, Sir. Mr. Darcy shares the same opinion." She looked to her right slightly and noticed Mr. Darcy was looking straight ahead, but appeared to be listening to their conversation and had shifted slightly when she said his name. Knowing he was listening gave her a strange feeling, but she could not name it.

"Does he? That should not surprise me. Darcy and I often agree on a number of subjects." He gave her a sly smile. "May I ask why you do not ride?"

"My father tried to teach my sister and me when I was very young, but I quickly became impatient and gave it up when I had mastered only circling the stable yard and sitting properly. My sister is much more patient than I and can ride fairly well. I much prefer to walk."

"Perhaps, with the right animal, you would feel differently." Elizabeth remembered Mr. Darcy saying the same thing and knowing he was listening, considered her answer carefully.

"Perhaps you are right, Sir Malcolm. Maybe I will try again when the weather is warmer and the right horse presents itself." He smiled at her answer and they moved on to other topics until the footmen brought out the dessert.

In the adjoining room, some of the ladies were beginning to entertain with music, and the four of them stood to leave the dining room. They listened and applauded for the next three quarters of an hour, then headed back to the ballroom, where Georgiana was led to the floor by Lord Matlock, and Elizabeth was swept up by her next partner, giving Georgiana a quick smile over her shoulder as she headed to the floor.

Several sets later, Elizabeth was waiting for her latest partner to bring her some refreshment when she saw Mr. Darcy and Sir Malcolm in conversation only a few feet away. She didn't intend to eavesdrop, but their words caught her attention.

"I wonder that Bingley isn't here tonight. I saw him at the club last week, poor man looked terrible. What on earth has happened to him?" Elizabeth perked up her ears to hear Darcy's answer.

"I do not believe the Bingleys were invited. My aunt is not overly fond of Miss Bingley," Darcy answered quietly.

"Surely the brother can come without the sister! Though I do know what you mean." Sir Malcolm gave Darcy a knowing look. "I think I shall call on Bingley tomorrow and see what's eating him. He had the devil in his eye last I saw him, very un-Bingley like."

"It would be helpful if you could cheer him. I have had no success."

"So you know what's going on then? Poor fool looked as if he'd had his heart broken! I would have thought someone had died if it weren't for the absence of black."

"You are not far off the mark. I'm afraid he became entangled with a young woman recently. The match was most imprudent; it is better this way." Darcy looked away, clearly not enjoying the conversation.

"What was so imprudent about it? Was she terribly mercenary or just not pretty enough?"

Darcy ignored his sarcasm and continued, "She was quite beautiful, actually, but her family was unsuitable. I do not know that she herself was mercenary, but her mother certainly was, and the daughter wasn't likely to go against her."

"Ah, the mother! Are not they all, Darcy? There is hardly a sincere one in all of London. If the lady isn't objectionable, cannot the mother be avoided?"

"I wish it were that simple. She is not merely mercenary, but wholly without propriety. The younger sisters are no better. It would be an unfortunate connection at best," Darcy said quietly and with some distaste. Elizabeth held her breath, unable to believe what she was hearing.

"Well, at least you got him away from her in time. Was the poor girl heart-broken?"

"I doubt it. Why must you call her poor girl? I cannot see that her heart was touched. She will likely move on to the next gentleman and forget all about Bingley, though he seems to be having a hard time forgetting about her. I had hoped he would have fallen in love with someone else by now – you know how he is," replied Darcy in a resigned tone.

Malcolm nodded in agreement. "Yes, I know Bingley. I hope he did not raise her hopes too much. Even if she was not in love with him, surely she must have realized that he would make a good husband."

"Yes, he would." Darcy's voice trailed off and he looked about him uncomfortably.

Elizabeth, not wanting to be seen, quickly turned and fled the ballroom. She headed toward the front door, hardly knowing where she was going. She only knew she had to get out of there.

She could not believe it. Mr. Darcy! He had taken Bingley away! She had suspected Caroline Bingley all along, and had initially wondered if Darcy was involved in convincing Bingley not to return, but since she had gotten to know him better, she had not been able to believe it of him. Her eyes were stinging from the tears she was holding back.

She quickly asked the footman to fetch her cloak and as she was waiting for it, Colonel Fitzwilliam appeared, having seen her flee the ballroom.

"Miss Bennet, are you alright?" He looked at her worriedly.

"I am well, Colonel Fitzwilliam, I assure you. I simply wish to leave. Will you please convey my thanks and excuses to your mother and wish her a good evening for me?"

The footman arrived with her cloak and she quickly put it on.

"Allow me to wait with you for the carriage," he said as he watched her cautiously.

"I have not called for the carriage. I will walk. It is not far."

"Miss Bennet! Surely you cannot be serious! It is the middle of the night and this is London. Madam, I beg you, please reconsider and allow me to call Darcy's carriage."

Hearing that name reminded her all too keenly of why she needed to leave and she looked squarely at Fitzwilliam.

"I do not have time to wait for the carriage, Colonel. If you will excuse me." She curtseyed and headed for the door. The footman was about to swing it open when the Colonel jumped into her path and blocked the doorway.

"Miss Bennet, if you insist on walking, allow me to escort you." He signaled the footman to fetch his things. "I can see you are in some distress and I cannot let you leave alone."

The footman arrived with his coat and hat and he quickly pulled them on.

Not having the energy to argue further and not wishing to cause a scene, she agreed and let him lead her out the door. They walked in silence for a few minutes before the Colonel spoke.

"Miss Bennet, if you would like to tell me what is troubling you, I am a very good listener," he said gently.

She was momentarily disarmed by his kindness, but could not bring herself to confide in him. "I appreciate your kindness, but I must decline your offer." She noticed his sympathetic expression and added, "I merely heard something I was not meant to hear and it was not pleasant, and now I find myself rather disillusioned – that is all."

Concerned and slightly bewildered, he stifled his curiosity and said, "I am sorry you are distressed and I hope everything will work itself out."

A few more quiet minutes passed and they were in front of the Darcy townhouse. Colonel Fitzwilliam rang the bell, and a surprised Hawkins answered, no doubt wondering where the carriage was, not to mention the Darcy's, and why these two were walking alone together in the middle of the night.

"Hawkins, Miss Bennet has a bit of a headache. Could you please send a maid to her room and send up some tea?"

"Yes, sir." The butler hurried off to do his bidding, and Colonel Fitzwilliam looked down at Elizabeth with a mixture of sympathy and affection. He really had come to like her very much and rather liked the idea of her joining the family. He did not like seeing her distressed. "Miss Bennet, I must return. Will you be alright on your own? Should I send Georgiana home to be with you?"

"Thank you for your kindness, Colonel Fitzwilliam, it is most welcome. But I assure you I shall be fine on my own."

He bowed to her and headed back to the ball, wondering what on earth she could have heard to send her running away in such a state. And how was he going to explain it to his mother?

Elizabeth went upstairs to her chambers and met Hannah in the dressing room. Hannah asked if she would like a bath. She considered it for a moment, but then decided she wouldn't be able to enjoy it. Hannah helped her out of her dress and began letting her hair down. Glancing at the clock, Elizabeth realized it was nearly four o'clock in the morning. The ball would be over by five. And then Georgiana and Darcy would be back. She could not face him, not after what she had heard.

She quickly asked Hannah to fetch her trunk and began gathering her things. Hannah looked at her askance, but did as she asked. Elizabeth sat down to pen a note to Georgiana. She didn't want to lie, but she could not leave her house in the middle of the night without some explanation, and she couldn't bear to say the truth. She briefly considered waiting until she returned and saying goodbye in person, but she was likely to run into Darcy and she did not think she could maintain her composure if she saw him now.

She decided the reasons behind that were better left unexamined at present, and wrote that something urgent had come up and she must return to her family. She would write soon and not to worry, everyone was well. She apologized for leaving abruptly and wrote of her affection for her friend in the hope of softening the blow. She did not mention Mr. Darcy.

As Elizabeth was sealing the letter, a sleepy footman arrived with the trunk, Hannah following behind him. Elizabeth asked Hannah to place the letter in Miss Darcy's room where she would be sure to see it and quickly began grabbing dresses and shoving them into the trunk. Hannah took the letter and disappeared into the adjoining room, returning moments later. She wordlessly began helping Elizabeth pack, neatly folding her clothes and putting them into the sturdy trunk.

Between the two of them, it only took a few minutes to complete. Hannah closed the lid and rang for the footman.

"Hannah, would you please ask Mr. Hawkins to find me a hackney cab? I wish to leave immediately."

Hannah's eyes widened slightly, but she did as she was asked.

Elizabeth took one last look around the room, knowing she would likely never see it again. She noticed a book on the table next to the bed, and reaching for it, she recognized it as the book of sonnets Mr. Darcy had reached for her only a few days before. She picked it up and headed downstairs, silently saying goodbye to the rooms as she went.

She gingerly stepped into the library, which was lit only by the moonlight, and made her way over to the bookshelf next to the window. She could not reach high enough to set the book upright, so she laid it on its side on the intended shelf, pushing it into place with her outstretched fingers. She blushed at the memory of Mr. Darcy finding her reaching for it and how close he had been when she turned around.

She knew it was silly, but for a second, she had thought he might kiss her. She chastised herself for her foolishness and shook her head to rid herself of the memory. With a look over her shoulder to her favorite room, she walked toward the entry and saw Hawkins holding her cloak.

"Your trunk is loaded and the carriage is waiting, Miss Bennet."

"Thank you, Hawkins." Elizabeth smiled as best she could, but it was halfhearted and it showed.

"Not at all, Miss Bennet." He opened the door and she gasped slightly to see the Darcy carriage. She could not see Darcy, not now. She waited for someone to emerge, but the door remained closed. Realizing it was vacant, she looked at Hawkins.

"I requested a hackney, Hawkins. I do not wish to impose and use Mr. Darcy's carriage without permission."

"If I may, Miss Bennet, Mr. Darcy would be most displeased if I allowed you to go in a hackney. I am sure this is what he would order if he were here, and I would not wish to incur his disapprobation."

Elizabeth did not want him to get into trouble because of her, and she had a strong feeling he was right, so she swallowed her urge to stubbornly resist and nodded her agreement.

"Very well. Thank you, Hawkins. I have enjoyed my stay here. Please pass on my thanks and farewell to Mrs. Hawkins and Cook."

"I will, Miss Bennet. It has been a pleasure. Safe journey."

The footman handed her into the carriage and she gave him the address in Cheapside. It would be just after five when she arrived at her uncle's and the servants would soon be up, beginning preparations for the day. She looked out the window as the carriage pulled away and unconsciously put her hand upon the glass, saying a silent farewell; whether to the house or its inhabitants, she could not say.

CHAPTER 14

"What do you mean, she's gone?" Darcy's voice boomed through the house, causing more than one housemaid to look up in astonishment.

Hawkins stood before him in the study, a calm expression on his face.

"She is no longer here, sir."

Darcy looked at Hawkins with barely concealed rage. He wanted an explanation, and he was not keen on having to drag out each individual answer.

"When did she leave? Where did she go?"

"She left almost immediately after she returned, and I believe she went to her relations in Cheapside."

"You believe?"

"I can check with the driver, sir. I ordered the carriage for her. I did not think you would want Miss Bennet to take a hackney."

"Certainly not! Did she suggest such a thing?" Darcy was dangerously close to completely losing his composure.

"Yes, sir. I told her you would prefer her to take the carriage."

Darcy could not make sense of any of it and knew he was not going to get anywhere with his mind so disturbed. He asked Hawkins to bring him some food and slumped in the chair behind his desk and rubbed his temples.

What had happened? He had thought the night had gone well; even he was having a good time. He had talked with some old friends from Cambridge, and when it was time for the last dance, he had gone in search of Elizabeth. After searching nearly the entire house, he had asked his aunt if she knew where she was.

Her answer could not have shocked him more. She informed him that Miss Bennet had left nearly an hour ago, claiming a sudden and harsh headache, and had been escorted home by none other than Colonel Fitzwilliam. What? Why had she not asked him to take her home? Why had the Colonel not informed him of it himself? He had bid his family goodnight, collected a barely awake Georgiana, and called for the carriage.

By the time they arrived at Darcy House it was after five, and he hurried inside to inquire after Miss Bennet. Hannah was seeing to Georgiana, who had gone straight to bed, so he asked Hawkins to send her to his study when she came down from attending Miss Darcy. He wanted the most direct information possible.

He sat at his desk for a few minutes, trying to find something to occupy his time while he waited for Hannah. He was exhausted, and his eyes were drooping. He saw the sun rising outside and decided that Miss Bennet was likely sleeping and that he should do so as well. He headed upstairs to his room, telling Hawkins not to worry about sending Hannah, and took himself to bed.

His proposal would have to wait. It would not do to ask her while she had a headache, especially if it was bad enough to cause her to leave the ball early. It didn't sound like Elizabeth to be ill, but he thought perhaps she had drunk too much punch, which would explain the headache and the sudden departure if she had been afraid of losing her composure. He could not really see Elizabeth over-indulging in such a way, but as it was the only explanation his tired, agitated mind could think of at the moment, he accepted it and gratefully crawled into bed. When he woke up, he would find her and ask her to join him in the library.

All would be well; he just needed to be patient.

Now, several hours later, he was pacing his study like a caged lion and kicking himself for not asking more questions earlier. What had prompted her to leave? That was not like Elizabeth to be so rude, to not even say goodbye or leave word. Maybe she had left a note for Georgiana. He quickly rang for a servant and asked him to summon Miss Darcy.

Hawkins appeared at the door and informed him that Miss Darcy would await him in her chambers.

~

Elizabeth sat back in the carriage, her heart heavy and her head pounding. She barely registered the sun rising over the buildings or the clatter on the streets as the city awakened. She felt utterly foolish. Now, alone with her thoughts, she could finally look at things clearly.

She was beginning to care for Mr. Darcy, as more than a friend, and not as a brother as she had tried to tell herself so many times. The way his deep eyes bore into hers, the sensation he created in her when he stood nearby – these could not be mistaken. Foolish, foolish girl!

She felt completely humiliated by her feelings and her recent actions. Had her behavior led him to believe she cared deeply for him? Elizabeth knew she wasn't in love with him, not yet, but she was in a fair way to getting there. Did he think she was?

She ran over their past conversations in her mind, desperately searching for a clue, something that would prove her indifferent – that would prove this all to be in her mind. Unfortunately, she realized much of her behavior with him had been playful, but could easily be considered flirtatious.

She had been alone with him several times in the library. The door was always left open, of course, and servants were coming in and out as needed, but still, she had never done that with any other man besides her father or uncle. She could only pray she hadn't made too big a fool of herself, and that he did not think she was in love with him.

That was a humiliation she could not bear. He would obviously never associate himself with her "low connections" and "vulgar, mercenary mother".

Her feelings of embarrassment were soon overcome by her anger at Mr. Darcy. How dare he interfere with Jane and Mr. Bingley! It was not as if it was he who would be marrying into the "unsuitable" family! If his dislike was so strong, he could simply refrain from visiting or attending events when they were present. The arrogance of it! Who did he think he was? He might be Master of Pemberley, but that did not give him the right to play with the hearts of young women, or to manipulate the lives of decent men for his own gain or comfort.

What did it do for him to separate them? What was his gain? Why would he do such a thing? Bingley was still in love with Jane and apparently heart-broken over her. At least, that was what Sir Malcolm had said. And Darcy, Bingley's closest friend, had not denied it.

Elizabeth felt her heart hardening toward Mr. Darcy and a blackness filling in what had become soft and vulnerable. How could she have begun to care for such a selfish, unfeeling, prideful man? She was ashamed of herself and of her feelings, and of her gullibility in believing he was better than she had first assessed him to be.

It would seem that her first impression had been correct: he was proud, conceited, and overly impressed with his own importance.

Elizabeth felt her cheeks grow hot with indignation when she remembered walking with him, or talking in the library with him, or how she had looked forward to their breakfasts together like an idiotic school girl. At that point, she did not know who she was more disappointed in: herself for making such a mistake, or Mr. Darcy for turning out not to be the man she had believed him to be.

She looked up to see her uncle's home. She stepped down from the carriage to ring the bell and was greeted by a surprised house maid.

"Hello, Sarah. Is Mr. Gardiner awake yet?"

"He is just rising, miss. He should be down soon."

"Thank you, Sarah."

Elizabeth directed the footman to leave her trunk in the hall, thanked him, and headed to the breakfast room to await her uncle. When he finally entered, and after expressing his surprise at seeing her there, Elizabeth asked if he could possibly arrange for her to travel home that day. When he asked her about the hasty departure and if Mr. Darcy had rescinded his offer to see her home in his carriage, she told him she merely had a sudden desire to be home and that she did not want to take advantage of the Darcys' kindness.

He knew something was terribly wrong, but did not press her, knowing well enough she would only talk when she was ready.

Elizabeth watched her uncle eat, barely touching her own food, and followed him silently to the carriage. No one else was up yet, it was only nearing seven, so she was able to escape without the prying questions of her aunt and Jane.

An hour later, she was sitting in a mail coach, waving to her uncle out the window, a smile she did not feel plastered to her face.

~

Darcy knocked lightly on Georgiana's door and let himself in at the sound of her soft voice. He took a seat by the fireplace and looked at Georgiana.

"Georgiana, did you have a good time last night?"

"Yes, I did. I do not know how I will become accustomed to staying up all night, but I did enjoy the ball."

"Did you, perchance, speak to Miss Bennet before she left?" His eyes searched her tired face.

"No, I did not. I saw her standing next to you and Sir Malcolm between sets, and then I did not see her again."

Darcy did not remember talking to her with Sir Malcolm, but continued his questioning.

"Did you have a note from her when you returned?" He tried to keep his voice even.

"Yes, I did." She stood to retrieve the missive and handed it to him. He quickly grabbed it and read.

Dear Georgiana,

I have so enjoyed my time here with you and thank you again for the gracious hospitality. I hate to leave without speaking to you, but something has occurred which requires my immediate presence at Longbourn. Do not worry, everyone is well, but I must return home as soon as possible.

I will write to you when I arrive so you will know I am safe and I look forward to hearing all about your impressions of your first ball. I had a wonderful time with you and have greatly enjoyed furthering our friendship these past weeks. Please know I would not leave you without saying goodbye if there was any other way.

Farewell, dear friend, and I hope to hear from you soon.

Yours etc.,

Elizabeth Bennet

Darcy read the letter twice more, hoping to glean something from the script besides what was written there. She did not mention him. She did not ask Georgiana to send her regards. That was very unusual given how close they had become. Perhaps she had left him his own letter? But no, she could not write to him unless they were engaged, which, unfortunately, they were not. He decided to check his study and the library, just in case.

He had a short conversation with Georgiana, ensured that she was not overly distressed by Miss Bennet's precipitous departure, and headed downstairs to speak with Hawkins.

"Hawkins, can you please tell me everything about Miss Bennet's departure?"

"Everything, sir?"

"Yes. When did she arrive, what did she do, did she say anything, how did she seem?"

"She arrived shortly before four on foot with Colonel Fitzwilliam. He said she had a headache and asked for tea to be sent upstairs to her room. He then asked her if she would be alright on her own to which she replied that she would."

"And how did she seem, did she appear ill, distressed?"

"I cannot say for certain, sir, though she did appear somewhat distraught and was rather flushed. Though that may have been from the walk in the cold air, sir."

"Hmm, yes. Continue, Hawkins."

"She went directly upstairs and soon requested her trunk. She sent Hannah to ask for a hackney to be summoned, and I took it upon myself to order the carriage. I did not think you would like her to travel across London so early in the morning in a hackney, sir. I hope I have not overstepped."

"Not at all Hawkins, you were quite right to order the carriage." Darcy looked out the window thoughtfully, then turned back to the butler. "Did Miss Bennet receive a letter today? Was there anything waiting for her when she returned?"

"No sir, nothing at all."

"Well, finish it for me man. What next?"

"The trunk was quickly packed and loaded, Miss Bennet expressed surprise when she saw the carriage, I convinced her to take it, and she asked me to bid farewell to Cook and Mrs. Hawkins. Then she left." Hawkins looked at Mr. Darcy sympathetically. "She did seem rather distressed, sir."

"Thank you, Hawkins. That will be all."

Darcy sat in his chair and pondered this new information. Fitzwilliam told Lady Matlock and Hawkins that Elizabeth had a headache. Alright, that might be enough reason to leave the ball early, but with Colonel Fitzwilliam and without speaking to Lady Matlock or himself, or even Georgiana? Then she packed up almost as soon as she returned and headed to Cheapside, in a hackney! Or at least she would have if Hawkins hadn't stepped in.

She left Georgiana a note saying something required her immediate attention at home, but she was due to head back to Hertfordshire tomorrow as it was. Why go only a day early? She wrote no one was unwell and she had received no letter from Longbourn that day.

It would appear she had fled. Fled the ball and fled Darcy House. Why on earth would she do that? And not even say goodbye to him? She could have mentioned him in her note to Georgiana, or even asked Hawkins to give him a message. She had asked him to say goodbye to the housekeeper and the cook, why not to him?

Elizabeth knew how he felt about carriages, they had recently discussed it. If she wanted to go home, surely she knew that he would send her in his carriage directly. *For some reason she did not want my assistance in leaving the ball or getting back to Hertfordshire. She wouldn't even use my carriage! What has happened?*

~

Elizabeth climbed down from the coach onto the streets of Meryton. She asked the innkeeper if she could please leave her trunk with him until her father sent for it. She then said goodbye to her uncle's servant and began the mile long walk to Longbourn.

By most standards, Elizabeth was an excellent walker. She was fast, never tripped, and possessed great stamina. But now, after a full day of activity, a night of dancing, and another half day on the road, with nothing more than the half hour of sleep she had managed in her uncle's carriage, she felt herself flagging. Once she was out of sight of the town, she ducked into a little copse of trees and sat on a fallen log. She rested her elbows on her knees and held her head in her hands.

She had not yet let herself cry. She had had a few moments of privacy on her way to her uncle's, but she was too filled with thoughts to release her emotions completely. She was about to do so now, when she remembered that her eyes would be red and in conjunction with her unexpected arrival, would send her mother into a fit of questions she did not want to answer. She got up, shook off her anxiety, and continued home.

She slipped into a side door at Longbourn, hoping she could go up the back stairs and make it to her room without being seen. She could hear Mary practicing on the pianoforte in the music room, but otherwise the house seemed quiet. She imagined her father was in his bookroom as usual, and not hearing them, she assumed Kitty, Lydia and her mother were out. She gratefully entered her own room and untied her bonnet, throwing it onto a nearby chair. Mrs. Hill heard her and came in to welcome her home and offer tea. Elizabeth accepted readily and asked her to send a man to the inn to fetch her trunk.

Elizabeth was now so overcome with exhaustion that she unceremoniously stripped off her dress, turned down the bed, and went to fetch her nightgown. That was when she realized that all three of her winter nightgowns and her dressing gown were in her trunk, at the inn at Meryton.

Giving an exasperated sigh, she swiftly ran into the hall to Kitty and Lydia's room, hoping none of the male servants would choose that moment to come upstairs and see her in her shift. She quickly took one of Kitty's gowns and dashed back to her own room. She let her hair down and brushed it out, put on the nightgown, and crawled into bed. Mrs. Hill entered with a tray of tea and biscuits, a little ham and bread on a plate next to it.

"You seemed to be a peckish, Miss."

"Thank you, Mrs. Hill." Elizabeth found herself near tears at her kindness and sent her away, asking her not to let anyone know she was back until she had gotten a few hours of sleep. She picked numbly at the food and sipped her tea, staring unseeingly into the fire. The curtains were drawn and though it was the middle of the afternoon, her room was dim, the glow from the fire the only light.

She lay back on her pillows, her eyes heavy, and tried to sleep. She finally released her pent-up emotions as silent sobs wracked her body and hot tears spilled down her cheeks, soaking her pillow and exhausting her further. She eventually drifted to sleep, images of brooding countenances and stormy eyes filling her dreams.

~

"Miss Bingley is here, sir. Are you at home?" Hawkins asked Mr. Darcy.

"Miss Bingley? Isn't she here for Miss Darcy?" He looked up from his desk warily.

"Miss Darcy will not be down for a quarter hour, sir. Should I send her away or ask her to wait?"

"Send her to the drawing room. I shall be there shortly." The last thing he wanted to do was talk to Caroline Bingley, but she was here and the sister of his good friend. Where was Georgiana? He quickly climbed the stairs, careful to avoid Miss Bingley, and knocked on her door.

"Georgiana? It is William. May I come in?"

She opened the door slowly, and he saw she was wearing a dressing gown and her hair was let down over her shoulders.

"Georgie, are you well?"

"Yes, Brother, I am well. I am simply tired."

He could tell by her eyes that something else was amiss, and he was afraid it was the same thing that was ailing him. "Are you missing Miss Bennet, dearest?"

"Oh, William!" She ran into his arms and buried her face into his chest, her shoulders shaking with gentle sobs.

"Dearest, do not cry. All will be well." He rubbed her back and kissed the top of her head, just as he had done when she was little and hurt. "You will see her again soon." He dearly wished it was true, for at that moment, he was so confused and angry he almost wanted to join Georgiana in her crying and rid himself of the questions torturing his mind. He led her to a sofa by the fire and they sat down, Darcy softly stroking her hair.

"I know I am being silly. I so wanted to tell her all about the ball and sit together once more before she left. I hate that I didn't get to say goodbye. I know she wrote me and that she would not have gone if it weren't very important, but…"

"You love her and worry for her and wish she was here with you now," he finished for her.

"Yes," she said in a small voice. "Does that make me terribly selfish?"

"No dearest, it is not selfish to love your friend or to wish she were not in distress or even to want to spend time with her. You became very close while she was here and your feelings are perfectly natural."

"Thank you, William." She snuggled into his chest and he comforted her for a few more minutes before speaking.

"Dearest, Miss Bingley is downstairs." Georgiana burrowed deeper. "Will you come down or shall I send her away?"

"Oh!" she sighed heavily. "Do not send her away; I shall see her. Will you join me?"

"Of course, sweetling. Now run along and get dressed. I'll go down and entertain Miss Bingley until you are ready."

Georgiana kissed his cheek. "Thank you, William. I will be quick." She rose and headed into her dressing room.

Downstairs, Darcy went straight to the drawing room. It was one of his least favorite rooms in the house, only used for formal gatherings and brief acquaintances. Close friends and family were received in either the music room or the sitting room upstairs, or in Darcy's study. He stepped into the opulent room, done in emerald green and deep gold, and steeled himself for the interview that was to come.

"Miss Bingley, I am sorry to keep you waiting. Georgiana will be detained a few minutes longer." He took the seat across from her, putting as much distance as was polite between them.

Caroline seemed quite pleased by his presence and their tête-à-tête. "It is no trouble at all, Mr. Darcy."

How was it that with only one sentence, she was already annoying him? There was something in her tone; the words seemed to drip from her mouth, and the way she said 'Mr. Darcy' made him shift uncomfortably in his chair.

"Are you well, Miss Bingley? And Mr. and Mrs. Hurst?"

"I am quite well, sir, as are all my family."

"I am glad to hear it."

"Did you attend the ball last night, Mr. Darcy?" she was looking at him as if they shared a secret, and it reminded Darcy of how he and Elizabeth had shared a private joke last night, only that had been much more pleasant.

"Yes, I did, Miss Bingley. It was quite enjoyable," he added, hoping to stem off her next question.

"Really? I thought you did not enjoy balls as a rule."

Darcy only smiled. "It was Georgiana's first ball and she was able to dance with the family. It was pleasant to see her enjoying herself."

"I do wish I could have been there to help her. It is so important to have another woman with you at your first ball," she simpered.

"I am sure you are right, Miss Bingley, but she did have Lady Matlock," Miss Bingley nodded, "and of course Miss Bennet."

Caroline's mouth dropped open most unbecomingly. "Miss Bennet?" she asked a little too loudly. She saw Darcy looking at her critically and quickly recovered herself. "I suppose she and Miss Darcy have become friends while she was staying in London."

"Yes, they have become closer, though they were friends before this visit."

Caroline would not be beat out by that country chit again. "I suppose she enjoyed calling here, as it must have been a pleasant change from her uncle's home in Cheapside," she nearly spat the last word. "And of course you would never permit Miss Darcy to travel there."

Darcy did not like her tone and knew what she was doing, just as he had known what she was doing in Hertfordshire when she had so emphatically criticized Elizabeth at every possible opportunity. He conveniently ignored the fact that it was true that he had not allowed Georgiana to travel to Cheapside.

"There was no need to call, Miss Bingley. Miss Bennet has been staying here, as Miss Darcy's personal guest."

Caroline's mouth dropped open and her eyes widened, giving the impression of a fish gasping for air. As ungentlemanly as he knew it to be, Darcy had to fight the urge to laugh.

"They have gotten along splendidly. I do believe they are closer than ever now," he added. "I am surprised you did not know she was staying here, Miss Bingley. Miss Bennet mentioned that she saw you while out shopping with Lady Matlock."

Caroline gave her head a little shake and spoke unsteadily, "Yes, I did see them at the modiste. I suppose I thought it was just a shopping trip together, though I did think it a little odd for Lady Matlock to be in company with Miss Eliza Bennet." She could not keep the derisive edge out of her voice.

"Oh, yes, Miss Bennet has become quite the favorite of my aunt. She was her personal guest at the ball last night. I should not be surprised if Lady Matlock issues her an invitation to her future balls."

Caroline was perilously close to losing her temper completely. "Miss Bennet was her personal guest at the ball?" She had never been invited to one of Lady Matlock's exclusive balls. They were talked of and looked forward to with great anticipation, and the following days' society pages were always filled with news of who was there and what they were wearing. How dare that country chit come in and take her invitation? She should be Lady Matlock's particular guest and personal favorite!

"Yes, and quite sought after, I might add." Darcy was never this voluble with guests, especially with women, and certainly not with Caroline Bingley, but since he had decided in favor of Elizabeth, he could not bear to hear anything said against her, and thought it was high time he put Caroline Bingley in her place. And he had to admit, he enjoyed doing it. Perhaps Elizabeth's teasing nature had worn off on him more than he'd realized. "I don't believe she had a single set free."

"Oh?" Caroline did not like his gaze or this conversation, and she was not blind to the fact that he had never spoken to her like this before. "And did you dance every dance as well, Mr. Darcy?" Caroline knew it was imprudent, but she wanted to know for certain if he'd danced with Elizabeth and couldn't stop herself from asking when so convenient an opening was before her.

"Only twice each with Miss Bennet and Georgiana, and one or two others." He had only danced once with Elizabeth, but he had asked for and been accepted for a second, so he felt this little untruth was permissible.

Miss Bingley lifted her nose and chin in the air and was about to respond when Georgiana entered the room.

"Miss Bingley, I am so sorry to have kept you waiting!"

"My dear Miss Darcy, it was no trouble at all," she smiled ingratiatingly.

Darcy wanted to leave, but had promised Georgiana he would stay, so he sat back and watched their interactions, only interjecting when necessary.

"Miss Darcy, your brother tells me you danced at the ball last night. Did you enjoy yourself?"

"Yes, Miss Bingley, it was a lovely occasion. All my family were kind enough to dance with me." She sent Darcy a thankful smile.

"It was our pleasure, Georgiana," he replied, and smiled back at her.

"Tell me everything! I want to know all the details!" Miss Bingley leaned forward and put her hand on Georgiana's.

Georgiana reflexively leaned back. She couldn't explain it, but she did not want to have this conversation with Miss Bingley. She had wanted to discuss this with Elizabeth, and somehow sharing it with Caroline first just seemed wrong.

"I must beg you to excuse me, Miss Bingley. I am afraid I am rather tired and I could not currently do the ball justice. Let's speak of it next time we meet." She tried to smile sweetly.

Caroline did not like it, but she could not force her, so she replied, "Of course, dear Miss Darcy, you must be exhausted! You are not used to dancing so much or being up so late, I agree you must feel quite tired."

"Thank you, Miss Bingley."

They spoke of uninteresting topics, such as the weather, for another quarter hour, until Miss Bingley took her leave.

Georgiana sighed heavily and went to the music room to play, and Darcy headed to the library. He sat in front of the fire, trying to glean what was left of Elizabeth's presence from the room, and brooded until dinner.

Tomorrow morning he would go to Gracechurch Street and seek Elizabeth. He could only hope that the coach would be sold out and she wouldn't have already left. He wished Caroline Bingley hadn't come; he might have been able to go to Gracechurch Street today, but now it was too late to pay a call. He would simply have to wait till morning.

Then he would get some answers.

CHAPTER 15

Saturday morning began foggy and cold. Darcy had spent half the night in the library, alternately pacing and sitting in Elizabeth's chair, trying to understand her actions and know her thoughts. He finally retired but slept restlessly.

He had had another dream about her: She was in the library, reading, and when she saw him she smiled, as was usual, but when he advanced towards her, a great distance seemed to come between them and the harder he tried to reach her, the farther away she became until she faded away completely. He had awoken calling her name and reaching into the air, his hair soaked in sweat.

As soon as propriety allowed, he was on his way to Gracechurch Street to call on the Gardiners. He had thought about bringing Georgiana along, but he didn't want to take her into a completely unknown situation with total strangers. Plus, he didn't want her to be upset if Elizabeth was already gone.

The carriage pulled up in front of the Gardiner's townhouse and he noticed it was neat and well kept, with a small but pleasant garden. The remainder of the street seemed to be much the same, and he thought Cheapside wasn't as bad as he had feared. That bode well for his future plans.

The maid entered the drawing room and handed a card to Mrs. Gardiner. "To see Miss Bennet. Shall I show him in, ma'am?"

"Yes, show him in. Thank you, Sarah."

"Who is it?" Jane asked.

"It is Mr. Darcy." She couldn't say more before the man himself appeared in the doorway.

"Mr. Darcy, what a pleasant surprise." Jane curtseyed and he bowed, quickly searching the room for Elizabeth.

"Miss Bennet. It is a pleasure to see you again."

"May I present my aunt, Mrs. Gardiner?"

"A pleasure to meet you, madam." He bowed, noticing her clothing was modern and looked expensive, and that she was quite attractive and not much older than him. He would have guessed she wasn't more than thirty-five.

"I am pleased to make your acquaintance, Mr. Darcy."

He was invited to sit and Mrs. Gardiner ordered tea. Jane, being the only one known to both parties, put her serenity and pleasant manners to good use and struck up a conversation. At first they asked after their respective families' health and commented on how cold it was. The pleasantries behind them, Jane mentioned that Mrs. Gardiner had spent her youth in Derbyshire.

"I do miss the Peaks sometimes. London is very diverting and has much to entertain, but beautiful countryside cannot be replaced."

"I could not agree with you more, Mrs. Gardiner. I would spend all my time at Pemberley if I could."

"Are you often there, Mr. Darcy?"

"Usually every summer, and the rest of the year is divided between Derbyshire and town."

They spoke of places they both knew, Mrs. Gardiner's skills at hosting and directing a conversation being shown to full advantage.

"My aunt and uncle will be taking a tour to the lakes this summer and will pass through the Peaks," Jane said. "I know she is looking forward to seeing her home county again."

Darcy thought this was an excellent time to bring up Elizabeth. "Miss Elizabeth mentioned it. She was to visit Pemberley this summer and hoped to somehow combine the two."

Mrs. Gardiner had been watching Mr. Darcy closely, wondering when he was going to bring up Elizabeth. She did not want to push him, but from everything Lizzy had told her, she suspected he had some tender feelings toward her, though how strong she did not know.

"Yes, I believe with a little finesse we will be able to arrange it." She did not miss that he had said 'was' instead of 'is'.

He looked slightly relieved. "That is good to hear. My sister Georgiana has become quite attached to Miss Elizabeth."

"Elizabeth has become equally attached to your sister. She speaks very highly of her."

Darcy nodded, not knowing how to ask if Elizabeth was there. It would appear that she was not, but what if she was only in another part of the house and he left without seeing her?

"Did Miss Elizabeth make it safely to you yesterday?" he asked, carefully controlling his voice.

"Yes, she arrived quite early. I did not see her before she left, but my husband informed me that she made it onto the coach safely and as the weather was fine, I imagine she was at Longbourn by three o'clock."

Darcy tried to control his emotions, but he could feel his temples throbbing. He knew he should say something, but he did not trust his voice. Mrs. Gardiner noticed his distress and tried to assuage him.

"We usually hear from her within a few days of her arrival. Elizabeth is very good about letting us know when she has arrived safely. I imagine we will have a letter by Tuesday, and Miss Darcy will likely have one as well. I'm sure Elizabeth will give her all the details of her trip." She looked at him pointedly at the last statement.

"I am sure you are right, Mrs. Gardiner." He knew she had told him what she had to alleviate his concern and he silently thanked her for it. Perhaps it would be alright to have the Gardiners as family. Mrs. Gardiner, at least, seemed very genteel and pleasant.

"I wish you could have met my husband, Mr. Darcy. We have heard so much about you from Elizabeth, I am sure he would like to put a face with the name."

Darcy smiled a little at hearing Elizabeth had spoken of him, and felt a slight ache in his chest from the lack of her presence. "I am sure Miss Elizabeth's uncle could be nothing but agreeable."

"Indeed Mr. Darcy, we would be honored to have you for dinner, if you could join us Tuesday?"

Normally he would never have dinner with a man in trade, but he was desperate for news of Elizabeth; it did not escape him that Tuesday was the day she had said she was expecting a letter. He was sure she would find some way of informing him of its contents, as she had informed him of her niece's travel arrangements earlier. "I would be happy to accept, Mrs. Gardiner."

"We shall look forward to it, then." She gave him a warm, open smile.

"Yes, it will be good to see you again, Mr. Darcy. It has been a long time." He looked into Jane's face as she spoke; she was serene and graceful as ever, but he thought he could see something in her eyes. It reminded him of what he saw in Bingley's eyes ever since they had left Hertfordshire. But she had not mentioned him the entire visit. He knew from Caroline Bingley that she had finally returned Jane's call and made it clear that she was not anxious to continue the acquaintance; he had felt the duplicity of it and did not like deceiving Bingley, but he had told himself it was for the best, and that the ends justified the means.

"It has been too long, Miss Bennet." He stood and bowed and headed towards the door. "Until Tuesday, Mrs. Gardiner, Miss Bennet."

"Good day, Mr. Darcy."

~

Elizabeth had been able to dodge her sisters' questions easily enough, saying she was just homesick and could not wait to return, and that Saturday's coach was fuller, and she thought she'd be more comfortable on Friday's. Luckily, she had never told them about Mr. Darcy's offer of his carriage. Her mother believed it readily, as well as allowing Elizabeth to remain in bed for the evening, taking her dinner on a tray to hide her eyes from her father. She would have to face him eventually, but she thought a little sleep beforehand wouldn't hurt.

Saturday morning she took a long, solitary walk, and then joined the family for breakfast. Her father looked at her skeptically over his paper, but she smiled slightly and took her usual place. I will not think about Mr. Darcy, she told herself. She joined in conversations and tried not to talk too much, lest her ill-humor give her away.

After breakfast, she went to the sitting room to write to Georgiana. There was no use putting it off; it would have to be done. And she would have to find some way to get out of the trip to Pemberley.

She had not yet asked her father to allow her to go. She rarely asked him permission for anything, as he rarely required it, but traveling across the country was something he would want to be consulted on. She supposed she could say he had refused, but would they believe that? Her aunt and uncle had already given her permission to say yes, and they were proxy guardians while she was in town, and she had told Mr. Darcy that.

They had made arrangements and planned everything but the exact date. She decided she would find a way to cancel later. There was no reason to upset Georgiana further right now. Elizabeth knew her feelings would be hurt badly by her premature departure, especially since she had not said goodbye properly. She hated hurting her friend, but she knew she could not have remained in Mr. Darcy's home and maintained her equanimity. Elizabeth couldn't bear to hurt her again so soon. They could talk about the summer later.

Her letter, as well as a brief note to her aunt to let her know she had arrived, completed and sealed, she asked her sisters if they would like to walk into Meryton with her to post it and call on their Aunt Phillips. She walked behind Kitty and Lydia with Mary, preferring her quiet and contemplative attitude to the exuberance of her youngest sisters. The walk helped to clear her mind, and she decided it was time to talk to her Uncle Phillips about Mr. Wickham. *I might as well get it over with*, she thought. *It's been an unpleasant two days, why not get all the unpleasantness out in one go?*

After posting her letters, Elizabeth left Kitty and Lydia at the milliners and she and Mary went to see their aunt. While drinking a cup of tea, Elizabeth inquired after her uncle. Her aunt informed her he was in his office, which was located below her apartments on the main level. Elizabeth asked if she might take him a cup of tea, to which her aunt replied in the affirmative, stating effusively what a thoughtful girl Elizabeth was.

Elizabeth's soft knock was answered by a gruff voice calling, "Enter!"

She stepped into the small, square room and smiled at her uncle.

"Lizzy! What a pleasant surprise! I thought you were in London still."

"I've only just returned, Uncle." She handed him the tea and took a seat in front of his desk.

"Thank you, Lizzy. Now tell me, girl, what can I do for you? It's not often you visit me in my office. Especially after sending me such a letter as I recently received from you. I assume that is what you are here to talk about." He gazed at her over the rim of his spectacles.

"You assume correctly, Uncle. I wanted to make sure you received my letter and to ask if you have heard anything about Mr. Wickham."

Mr. Phillips was a medium-sized man, not too tall, but a bit round in the chest. He wore gold-rimmed spectacles and had soft gray whiskers on either side of his face, covering his slackening jaw. He was a jovial man, a bit boisterous like his wife, but not overly vulgar and intelligent enough. He was not ambitious, but he was good at reading people and had a small but successful business.

"I asked around, discreetly of course, and it is as you suspected. He owes money to every shopkeeper in town, in addition to several debts of honor. He is due to be paid soon, and everyone has been told they will receive payment when he does. Unless the militia is paying very well indeed, I doubt that will come to pass."

"Oh no!" Elizabeth slumped a little in the chair. "What can be done?"

"Nothing, really. The tradesmen will go after him for what they can get, as will the officers he owes money to. If he does not pay, he may be challenged, though I think that highly unlikely." He shrugged.

"What about Miss King?"

"There is talk of an engagement, but nothing has been announced yet. I fear his intentions there may not be entirely honorable."

"What do you mean?"

"Surely you've heard of a man marrying a woman and running off with the dowry, never to be heard from again?"

Elizabeth gasped. "Do you really believe he would do such a thing?" She was not friends with Miss King, but she did not wish her ill.

"You tell me. You certainly know as much as I do, perhaps more." He looked at her shrewdly.

"You are quite right, Uncle. I believe he would, I simply do not wish to think of it. What can we do? We cannot simply warn Miss King. She would probably never believe us, anyway."

"I will discreetly let the tradesmen know that he has a history of not paying in full and not to issue him any more lines of credit. I will speak to your father about keeping your sisters away from him, and I will let Mrs. Phillips know not to include him in any more invitations. She won't like it, but something must be done. Hopefully, he will find it too difficult to run his schemes here and look elsewhere. If he does anything truly illegal, we can contact the magistrate."

This was so much more complicated than Elizabeth had originally imagined. She was now thoroughly grateful to have handed this over to her uncle, who was undoubtedly more experienced in such affairs.

"Don't worry, Lizzy. I'll take care of it."

"Thank you, Uncle. That is a great relief to my mind." She smiled and stood to go, giving him a quick kiss on the cheek and heading back upstairs to her aunt, all the way saying a silent prayer of thankfulness that she had never really been in love with Wickham. Oh, what a narrow escape she had had!

CHAPTER 16

"Did you save any for me?"

Darcy looked up from his glass of brandy to see Colonel Fitzwilliam eying him questioningly.

Darcy tilted his head in the direction of the decanter. The Colonel poured himself a glass and settled in the chair across from Darcy, Elizabeth's chair, or so he had come to think of it.

"Rough day?" asked the Colonel quietly.

"Did you escort Miss Bennet home from the ball?"

Surprised by the sudden question and the lack of formality, he answered slowly, "Yes, I could not let her walk here alone."

"She did not wish to call for the carriage?"

"No, she declared she had no intention of waiting for the carriage."

Darcy shook his head in irritation at his own bewilderment. "Why would she do such a thing?" he said quietly, almost to himself.

"Why did you not ask Miss Bennet, Darcy? She seems to be a rather forthright woman."

"Believe me, Cousin, I would have, but she was not here to ask," he said acidly.

"Not here? Where was she?"

"She was at her Uncle's home in Cheapside, then on a mail coach to Hertfordshire."

"A coach? I thought you were sending her in the carriage?"

"I was. At least I thought I was. I only know that when we arrived home after the ball, she was gone." He swallowed the last of his brandy and refilled his glass.

"Darcy, I think you had better tell me what happened," Fitzwilliam said over his glass.

"I was going to say the same thing to you."

Seeing the Colonel's raised brow, he added, "Very well. At the ball, I went in search of Miss Bennet for the last set, which we were to dance together. I could not find her and applied to your mother, who informed me that she had left with you nearly an hour before. Imagine my surprise when I found out Miss Bennet had a headache and requested you escort her home – on foot." His voice became steely and his eyes flashed as he continued. "After questioning Hawkins, he informed me that Miss Bennet immediately ordered her trunk, had it packed and loaded and headed to Cheapside before the clock struck five."

Colonel Fitzwilliam sat up straight in his seat. "She what?"

"Yes, my feeling exactly." He took another swallow of brandy.

"Did she give any reason? A note? A message?"

"She left a short letter for Georgiana." He pulled it out of his coat pocket and passed it to his cousin.

Fitzwilliam quickly read it, then passed it back to Darcy. "What was so immediate she needed to return to Hertfordshire?"

"I had hoped you could tell me."

"You mean there was no urgent letter waiting for her here?" Darcy shook his head.

"Hmm."

The two men looked into the fire and quietly thought through the last day and a half's events.

Suddenly, Darcy drained his glass and thrust it down on the table with a loud thud.

"Richard, I would appreciate it if you would tell me everything that occurred between you and Miss Bennet two nights ago, or I should say yesterday morning."

Seeing his cousin more disturbed than he had in years, Fitzwilliam quickly agreed.

"I saw Miss Bennet leaving the ballroom. She looked quite agitated and headed directly for the door. I followed her and asked where she was going and if all was well. She said she simply wanted to leave and as soon as she had her cloak, she made for the door. I offered to wait with her for the carriage when she told me she intended to walk, and that's when I insisted I accompany her. It is London, after all." He made a face at Darcy, who nodded for him to continue.

"We walked along and I asked her what was troubling her, as it was obvious that she was quite distraught. She said she was not ill, but that she had overheard something unpleasant. We arrived here and I asked her if she would be alright on her own, and I asked Hawkins to send a maid and tea to her room. That is all."

"So the headache was a farce?"

"Oh, yes, that was me, I'm afraid. She never said any such thing. She asked me to make her excuses to my mother, and I decided a sudden headache was the most plausible excuse. I said the same to Hawkins."

Darcy stood and began to pace in front of the fire. "It doesn't make sense," he mumbled to himself. He raked his hand through his hair and his free hand alternated between hanging limply and propping on his hip.

"She overheard something? What did she overhear?"

"She did not say exactly. Let me think…" He looked up as he searched his mind. "I believe she said, 'I merely heard something I was not meant to hear and it was not pleasant, and now I find myself rather disillusioned.' Yes, that was it."

"'I merely heard something I was not meant to hear'," Darcy mumbled to himself. "What could she possibly have heard?"

"There were a lot of rich young ladies there who would not take lightly to a country girl coming in and stealing attention from them. You saw how the men took to her. Maybe she overheard someone speaking about her?"

"Possibly, but Miss Bennet would have laughed them off. She does not intimidate easily. What was the last thing she said? She was disillusioned?" he furrowed his brow in thought and resumed his seat.

"Let us think about this logically," replied the Colonel. "If she said she was disillusioned, she must have overheard someone she had already formed an opinion of, or something about them, in order to hear something contrary."

"Yes. So that leaves Lady Matlock, the two of us, Georgiana, and could possibly include any man she danced with, though I doubt she would let such a short acquaintance bother her, even if such a man had insulted her." He remembered how he had slighted her at the assembly, and she had not run off, but merely laughed and continued dancing. Of course, she had not yet formed a favorable opinion of him, and he did not know if that could be said of all of her dance partners.

"And there is Sir Malcolm," Fitzwilliam added quietly.

"Yes, but I hardly think he..." Darcy stopped mid-sentence and snapped his head up. With wide eyes he said, "Surely not, surely she didn't hear... oh no." He suddenly remembered Georgiana saying she had seen Elizabeth standing next to him and Sir Malcolm, but he had not remembered seeing her in the crowd.

"What, Darcy? You look as if you've seen a ghost!"

Darcy rose again and began to pace, his left hand clenching and unclenching at his side, his right holding his temple. "I spoke with Malcolm a bit at the ball. He asked about Bingley and mentioned how horrid he'd been looking and hinted that he was heartbroken. I confirmed his suspicions and told him that Bingley had fallen in love but was persuaded to leave the country before he could do anything rash. She must have heard us!"

"Surely Miss Bennet was not the woman Bingley fell for?"

"Worse. It was her sister." Colonel Fitzwilliam's eyebrows shot up. "Her favorite sister. The sister she walked three miles through the mud to nurse when she was ill. She is her closest confidante and I daresay her favorite person in the world."

"So you were the one she overheard and was disillusioned with. Well, you or Sir Malcolm."

For a moment Darcy considered that Elizabeth might have harbored tender feelings for Malcolm and that she would be disappointed in his agreement with the separation of Jane and Bingley. But it was not his carriage she had refused, nor his house she had fled in the dark of night.

She had said more than once that they had become friends, and he believed that she had forgiven him for his rude comment at the assembly. If she still had an unfavorable opinion of him, she would not have been disillusioned, but would have thought it in keeping with what she already knew of him. *She was disillusioned because she had come to believe better of me than that.*

There was some small consolation in that, but it did not last long.

"No, Fitzwilliam, it was me. It is all me. It's my fault she's gone." He sank into the chair and put his head in his hands, the realization of what had happened beginning to take effect as well as the brandy.

Fitzwilliam looked at his cousin, not knowing what to say. "She may come round, Darcy. Perhaps all is not lost."

Darcy merely looked at him through unseeing eyes and hung his head.

Dinner at Darcy House was a somber affair. Elizabeth's absence was felt acutely, even by Colonel Fitzwilliam, who attempted to cheer his despondent cousins with stories of young cadets at the army college. He was not overly successful. Georgiana retired immediately, claiming fatigue, and Darcy and Fitzwilliam went to his study for a glass of port.

"I went to Gracechurch Street this morning," Darcy said in a faraway voice, leaning against his desk.

"And?"

"I met Elizabeth's aunt. She seemed very genteel. She hails from Derbyshire."

"Does she?"

"Miss Jane Bennet was there. Bingley's Jane."

Colonel Fitzwilliam observed his cousin, knowing his presence wasn't really necessary for this conversation.

"She seemed much the same as ever, but perhaps her eyes were a little sad." He swirled the dark liquid in his glass. "I watched her, at the Netherfield ball. She was not as attached to Bingley as he was to her. She seemed to like him well enough, but not more than any other. I did not want Bingley to marry so far beneath him to a woman who didn't even love him."

"What if she had loved him?"

Darcy raked his hand through his hair and looked at the carpet. "I do not know. Never before have I deceived a friend, Richard – knowingly deceived. Bingley trusts me implicitly; he is the easiest person to convince, but perhaps that makes my deception that much more reproachable.

"If I tried to convince you of a certain course of action, you would listen, but would also ask your own questions and follow your own judgment. Bingley's trust in me is such that he would never question any advice from me. He would assume I had considered all the options and chosen the best course, and that he naturally would come to the same conclusion on his own, so he saves time and effort by simply agreeing with me immediately. It is convenient in most situations and a minor nuisance in others, but this…"

Darcy took a slow sip of his port and looked around him thoughtfully. "When Miss Bingley came to me and requested my assistance in getting her brother away from Miss Jane Bennet, I confess I was relieved she had taken the initiative. I had already decided to talk to Bingley about the imprudence of it, and if need be, share my observations with him. Miss Bingley informed me that she and her sister would leave Netherfield directly after Bingley went to London, and that they would have the house closed and convince him not to return." He looked at the floor and studied the pattern in the carpet.

"She told me she would send a letter to Miss Bennet, informing her of their leaving the country, and would make it clear that they were not to return." He looked up at Colonel Fitzwilliam, who was watching him closely, a slight look of displeasure on his face – though he was covering it admirably.

Fitzwilliam had never liked Miss Bingley, and he liked this story even less. He gestured with his hand for Darcy to continue.

"Of course I never saw the letter, but knowing Caroline Bingley as I do, I can imagine she did not let Miss Bennet down easily. When Jane Bennet came to London to stay with her family in Cheapside, she called on Miss Bingley. Miss Bingley waited over a fortnight to return the call. I saw her at a dinner, and she informed me that Miss Bennet would not be bothering her anymore. I found the whole thing distasteful."

He made a face and took a gulp of port. "I did not like having a secret with her. I especially disliked coming home to see Miss Elizabeth happily playing duets with my sister, while I was out plotting against hers," he spat out the last sentence.

"I can see how that might disgust you," said the Colonel, his voice unusually level.

A few minutes went by in silence.

"I've been thinking, Richard."

"I would imagine so, Cousin."

"Miss Elizabeth is not mercenary."

Colonel Fitzwilliam's eyebrows shot up. "No, I daresay she is not."

"I do not believe her sister Jane is either, though I do not know her as well."

Fitzwilliam could tell he was coming to his point, so he sat silently and waited for Darcy to grapple with his own thoughts.

"Why would Elizabeth be disillusioned with me?" The Colonel did not miss the familiarity in his speech. "If Jane Bennet did not love Bingley, or hold him in special regard, she would have accepted him only for security and to save her family from the entail. I am sure she would have accepted him, her mother would have assured it, and Miss Bennet does not have Miss Elizabeth's fortitude. The only disappointment would be in losing a valuable suitor."

He began to pace slowly, standing behind a chair and grasping its back for support. "Miss Elizabeth is an intelligent woman. She understands the ways of the world. If she knew I had separated her sister from Bingley, and if her sister did not love him, would that cause disillusionment? Perhaps anger for preventing an advantageous match for her beloved sister, but then Jane would be free to find someone else whom she did love and, as we both know, Miss Elizabeth places a high priority on love. And we can presume she would also wish for Bingley to be married to someone who loved him."

Fitzwilliam nodded, seeing where his cousin was going and not liking it. "She was obviously so distressed by the knowledge of their being forcibly separated that one can easily assume there was a deep bond between Bingley and Miss Bennet, or at least that Miss Elizabeth believed there to be. Otherwise…" His voice trailed off, clearly exhausted.

"So you separated a couple who loved each other, and broke Miss Elizabeth's favorite sister's heart."

Darcy stood in front of the fire, his arm on the mantle, and let out a heavy sigh. "It would appear that I did."

"What exactly did you say to Malcolm?"

"Besides what I've already told you, I told him I had been unsuccessful in cheering Bingley, and that Miss Bennet was very beautiful. I mentioned that her family was unsuitable, that the mother and younger sisters were intolerable and uncouth, and that the connection was unfortunate at best."

Fitzwilliam let out a bark of a laugh. "And you cannot imagine why she would feel distress?" He looked at Darcy as if he were the stupidest man alive.

"I said nothing that was not true." Darcy stood straighter and squared his shoulders defensively. "Miss Elizabeth herself has been embarrassed on numerous occasions by her family. It's no secret that they are coarse and ill-mannered."

"Darcy," the Colonel took a deep breath and looked his cousin in the eye. "I know you like to keep your own counsel, and that is your right. But let me ask you a few questions." Darcy nodded, looking skeptically at Fitzwilliam.

"Are Miss Jane and Miss Elizabeth Bennet sisters?"

"Yes, of course they are." Darcy looked surprised at the simple question.

"And they have the same mother and younger sisters?"

"Yes."

"They have the same undesirable connections?"

"Yes."

"And Miss Bennet is well-mannered and graceful, and all that is beautiful and kind?"

"Yes."

"And you felt that Miss Bennet, who is all that is desirable in her person, was not suitable for Mr. Bingley, because of her status and family?"

"Yeeeees," he said hesitantly, his eyes squinted in confusion, clearly not seeing where the colonel was going.

Fitzwilliam released an exasperated sigh. "Would you say that Bingley has the same social status as yourself?"

Darcy almost laughed. "No, of course not." Where was the Colonel going with these ridiculous questions?

"And he does not have an ancient estate or an important family to impress, does he?"

"No, he does not."

"And yet, according to you, the beautiful Miss Bennet was not good enough for *him*."

"I ..." Darcy was about to speak, but he was caught by the emphasis in Fitzwilliam's speech as well as the sharp expression he was giving him.

"As I said Darcy, you have every right to keep your own counsel, but I like Miss Elizabeth – I would hate to see her hurt. I don't want to see you hurt either."

Darcy looked warily at his cousin.

"I also think she'd make an excellent addition to the family." Darcy's eyes widened in shock. "I'll see myself out."

Colonel Fitzwilliam set down his glass and walked out the door, leaving a stupefied Darcy staring after him.

~

An hour later, Darcy was still in his study. That Colonel Fitzwilliam knew about his feelings was not the most surprising thing. They had known each other their entire lives and Fitzwilliam was observant and understood him well. What was surprising was that Darcy had behaved like a prize idiot. Even after he knew Elizabeth had overheard him, it took Richard pointing out that what he'd said was insulting for him to realize he had probably wounded her with his words. She was likely mortified that someone she regarded as a friend would say such things about her family. Even if it was true, he should not have said it, at least not in public, and certainly not to someone wholly unacquainted with them who had absolutely no business knowing her private affairs.

And Richard had made a point of Darcy's rank, and more importantly, his opinion of his own status. If Bingley was too high for the Bennet sisters, would Darcy not be completely out of reach? Did Elizabeth think his speech meant he would never consider offering for her? Did she think she had been trifled with? Was she heartbroken? Was that why she had fled? Or was she merely angry at him for ruining her sister's happiness?

There was another thing troubling his mind. She had said they were friends. Twice. He wondered if she had made that point on purpose, or was she just saying it because it was the only proper description of their relationship?

Her recent actions in combination with what Richard had just told him were causing Darcy to feel doubt; something he had not entertained until this moment.

He did not like it.

He was Fitzwilliam Darcy of Pemberley. There wasn't a woman in the ton who wouldn't accept him; he had everything to offer and was a good man in addition to all of that. He would not gamble away his inheritance, or get drunk and beat his wife, or humiliate her in public. He was a catch, and he knew it.

He began to feel indignant at her sudden removal; she should have allowed him a chance to explain, or at least had the courage to tell him goodbye properly. He had been about to propose to her! She should be grateful he was willing to offer to someone so beneath him. To connect himself permanently with people as crass as her mother and younger sisters was a degradation at worst, and a folly at best.

He paced until his anger began to cool, and he finally stretched out on the couch in front of the fire, his aching head on the cushion Georgiana had embroidered for him. He read the dedication on the back before settling: *For My Brother, The Best of Men.*

A new wave of guilt washed over him, and he lay silently contemplating his thoughts and actions, waging a war with himself until his mind drifted to his time with Elizabeth.

The Colonel had said she would only marry for the deepest love. For the first time, he wondered whether Elizabeth loved him. He believed she cared, but beyond that he couldn't be sure. She had refused a man before, a man set to inherit.

But surely he wasn't just any man! He had more to offer than any other single man he knew; she must accept him.

But did she love him?

All of a sudden, Darcy realized that he wanted her to love him. With a twinge of embarrassment, he understood he'd never thought about her feelings before. He had planned his proposal, and gone straight ahead to planning their life together. The thought that she might not want him had never occurred to him. Was he really that arrogant?

And did he want her to accept him out of gratefulness or duty? Yes, they were friends and that was an excellent basis for marriage, but was it enough for him? Suddenly, and with great force, he knew it was not.

He didn't want to marry his friend and take her home and make love to her. He wanted a wife. He wanted all her passion and fire and tenacity turned to him. He wanted to be the reason for the brightness in her smile, to hold her and know she needed him as much as he needed her. He wanted to see desire for him burning in her eyes and know that he was the only man she would ever look at that way. He wanted her to want him. Not Pemberley, not the house in town or his ten thousand a year, but him.

Now how the devil was he supposed to accomplish that?

CHAPTER 17

Elizabeth spent the next week hiding from her family. If her mother only knew that her own behavior had cost Jane Mr. Bingley!

Elizabeth remembered the ball at Netherfield with shame. She had sat next to her mother at dinner, across from Mr. Darcy, while her mother went on and on to Lady Lucas about the advantageous match Jane was making. Elizabeth had asked her repeatedly to lower her voice or change the topic, but to no avail. She had even told her Mr. Darcy was listening and that as a close friend of Mr. Bingley's, it could not help her to anger him. Her mother had loudly replied that she did not care what Mr. Darcy thought and that she would say what she liked. Elizabeth felt herself blush from the memory.

Her feelings toward Mr. Darcy alternated between indignation for what he had said to Sir Malcolm, anger that he had interfered with her sister and his friend, which was really none of his business, and sadness that their brief friendship was at an end.

Any time a feeling of melancholy tried to creep over her, she would push it away and remind herself that he was not the man she had thought him, that he was arrogant and self-serving and cared for nothing beyond his own interests. How can you miss a person that does not exist? Despite her careful regulation, her emotions did not always comply with her wishes. Her sense of fairness would insist on being heard.

Wasn't what he had said about her family true? He should not have said it, and to Sir Malcolm of all people, and certainly not in a ballroom, but she could not fault him completely for thinking it. Bingley was his very dear friend, and he wanted him to have a happy marriage; was that so wrong?

He had said that Jane's heart was not touched. He was completely wrong of course, but he did not know that. Jane was modest and did not show her feelings to the world – his presumption was understandable – even Charlotte had said Bingley might not see her regard because he did not know her character as they did. Elizabeth did not like these thoughts, but her good sense demanded she be reasonable.

She pulled out the letter she had received from Jane, praying for good news to distract her from her own relentless thoughts. She hoped her sister was in better spirits.

Elizabeth couldn't help but be angry at Mr. Bingley for leaving Jane like he did, no matter how convincing the argument. He had made his preference known to the whole neighborhood, only to leave Jane in the lurch, humiliated for her trust in him. How could anyone be so easily persuaded? Had he no backbone at all? *If I really loved someone, I would not care what my friends or my sisters said*, Elizabeth thought.

She broke the seal and began to read.

20 February, 1812
Gardiner Residence
Gracechurch Street, London

Dear Elizabeth,

The most extraordinary thing has happened! But I must tell you from the beginning. Saturday, Mr. Darcy called. He stayed half an hour and asked about you and if you were safe. Aunt told him you had already gone to Longbourn. They spoke of Derbyshire and he mentioned your planned trip to Pemberley and Aunt invited him to dinner for the following Tuesday.

He came, and made pleasant conversation with everyone. He was quite different from his behavior in Hertfordshire! He was so pleasant and amiable - though I never thought so ill of him before. He and Uncle spoke of fishing at great length and seemed to enjoy one another's company. Then Mr. Darcy brought up Mr. Bingley. Oh, Lizzy! I faltered only for a moment, and managed to maintain my composure. He would bring him up several more times throughout the evening, sometimes to me directly - it was rather odd.

The strangest thing was yet to come. Who should call the next day but Mr. Darcy again, this time with Mr. Bingley! He said he had had no idea I was in town until Mr. Darcy had shown up at his home that morning to inform him. And he insisted on calling on me right away!

Can you believe it Lizzy? You were right about Caroline all along. I am grieved to think how deceived I was in her character.

The gentlemen stayed for nearly an hour, then Mr. Bingley came again this morning! We walked out and he asked if he may court me - I have never been so happy! Oh Lizzy, I hardly know what I have written!

Your Sister,
Jane Bennet

Elizabeth stared at the page and reread the letter. What had happened? Mr. Darcy delivered Mr. Bingley to Jane? But why? Had he changed his mind about her unsuitability? Questions began rushing through her mind at an alarming speed. She did not trust her feelings and decided she would apply to her aunt; that was the best place to get clear answers.

Before Elizabeth had a chance to write to her Aunt Gardiner, she received a letter from the lady herself. It said much the same as Jane's, only less excited and added that Mr. Darcy had seemed quite agitated and disconcerted when he visited on Saturday, and that he was relieved to receive the dinner invitation. Elizabeth's head spun. That did not sound like Mr. Darcy!

Her aunt went on to say that she had shared with him that she had arrived safely and all was well in Hertfordshire. He had asked many questions about Elizabeth and the rest of their family, and seemed genuine in all his discourse.

What was going on? Why had he called on her aunt? Her heart whispered that it was for her, but she could not fully believe it. He had considered an alliance with her family a degradation.

Yet, he had restored Bingley to Jane. What could it mean? Did he somehow puzzle out the true reason for her sudden departure? He must have been greatly concerned for her to go to Cheapside. Three times in one week! What could cause such a change as this?

~

My Dearest Elizabeth,

I dreamt of you again last night. You wore a yellow dress and smiled at me, then held out your hands. I took them, so small in my own, and held you in my arms. I can hardly wait to see you again, my love. You fill my every thought and are ever present in my heart. I have never before looked forward to my annual trip to Rosings, but knowing you will be there makes me count the days to my departure.

Are you well, dearest? Do you miss me at all? I miss you beyond what I ever thought I could experience – I feel an ache that cannot be subdued except by your presence. I long for the day I will see your sparkling eyes and hear your laughter once more.

Your Aunt and Uncle came to dinner last night with your sister and Bingley. Georgiana was quite pleased with them. It looks like she and Miss Bennet will become good friends. I imagine the three of you will spend many happy hours together.

I have called at Gracechurch Street several times in the last fortnight – I've gotten to know your uncle and find him to be intelligent and well-informed. We have become friends. Your aunt is very pleasant and she has done much to make Georgiana comfortable in their home. I can see why you enjoy spending time with them.

I am greatly looking forward to your visit to Pemberley this summer. I invited your Aunt and Uncle to stay with us while they are visiting the area. Does that please you, my dear? In a fortnight I will see you at Rosings. I can hardly wait.

Until then, I remain,

Yours,

William

Darcy held the letter in his hand and read its contents with a cynical expression. Shrugging his shoulders and shaking his head, he crumpled it into a ball and threw it into the fire. He watched until it burned to ash, then sat at his desk. A few moments later, Hawkins announced that Mr. Bingley had arrived.

"Bingley! What brings you here this morning?"

"Darcy! I am the happiest of men! I have asked my sweet Jane to marry me and she has accepted! Can you believe it?" Bingley was practically bouncing in excitement.

"Congratulations, Bingley! I couldn't be happier for you!" Darcy clapped him on the back as they shook hands.

"I can hardly believe my luck! My angel will be by my side all my days! I am truly the most fortunate of men!"

"Do you plan to go to Longbourn to ask for Mr. Bennet's consent?"

"Mr. Gardiner has been given leave to consent in his stead, which he has granted. I have sent a letter to Longbourn and hope to hear from Mr. Bennet within the week."

"Will Miss Bennet remain in London?"

"She was meant to stay on until after Easter and return with Miss Elizabeth, but her plans may change now."

"Do you have a wedding date set yet?"

"Not yet, no. We are waiting to hear from Mr. Bennet. I do not want to wait overlong, though."

More congratulations followed, toasts were made, and Bingley asked Darcy to stand up with him, which of course his friend quickly agreed to do.

~

Elizabeth watched her sisters in dismay. Kitty and Lydia were running through Lucas Lodge, one carrying a saber and the other a lieutenant's hat. They were shrieking and shouting out dares for the officers to catch them.

Elizabeth had tried twice already to calm them, only to be told by Lydia that she didn't know how to have any fun and that just because she was a bore, she should not force them to be bores alongside her. At that point, Elizabeth had given up and wished that Jane or Charlotte could be there with her.

Another week and I shall be away from all of this.

Ever since her return, she had not looked at her family the same way. What had been merely annoying antics and slight embarrassments now became deeply troubling and intense mortifications. What was to become of girls such as these?

"You seem troubled, Miss Elizabeth." She turned around to see Mr. Wickham watching her intently. Obviously, he had only been taken off the guest lists for her family's gatherings.

"Not at all, Mr. Wickham. I was merely woolgathering."

"I heard you have recently spent some time in London."

"Yes, I returned a little over a fortnight ago."

"Did you enjoy your stay?"

"Yes. London is quite diverting."

"Your sister tells me you stayed with Miss Darcy."

"That is correct."

"And how did you find Darcy House?" he asked intimately.

"It was all that was inviting, Mr. Wickham."

"Yes, it is quite comfortable. It is too bad the Darcys are not as inviting as their home."

"On the contrary, I found them to be very amiable and welcoming."

"Both of them? Really?" He looked at her with mock incredulity, as if they were enjoying a private joke. "Miss Darcy is not so bad, I suppose, but rather averse to entertainment – like her brother. But I can hardly believe you find Mr. Darcy amiable."

"I do not find Miss Darcy averse to entertainment at all. In fact, she is rather pleasant company and a charming girl. She has become a very dear friend."

"Well, perhaps she has improved in the years since I have seen her."

"Has it been that long, Mr. Wickham? I was under the impression that it was not above eight months," she replied with practiced innocence.

He lost his carefully constructed expression for a moment, but quickly reverted to his pleasing demeanor. "I believe I did run into her last summer, but it was not an overly long visit."

"I can imagine that your relationship with Mr. Darcy would make overly long visits rather uncomfortable, and of course it would be difficult to establish a relationship with Miss Darcy without her brother's presence."

"Yes, you are quite right, Miss Bennet," he answered carefully, wondering what she was getting at.

"I also met Colonel Fitzwilliam while I was in London," she said with a false air of distraction.

Wickham's face became a little paler. "You did?"

"Yes, we were frequently in company. I found him to be very agreeable. Did you know he was decorated in the army? He has received two special commendations for courage in battle. Is that not extraordinary?" Elizabeth leaned in as if she were telling especially juicy gossip. "And he did not buy in as a Colonel. He started as a major and earned his rank. Such a man cannot help but be respected. I understand he is quite revered by his men."

Wickham swallowed visibly. Elizabeth pretended not to notice and continued.

"You know, I met a fellow officer at a ball, and he told me that Colonel Fitzwilliam has survived more battles than any other officer of his rank. He could not give me particulars, but I got the impression that his affable manners are not always so affable when one gets on his bad side. I am happy to be called a friend; I imagine he would be a frightening enemy indeed! Would you not agree, Mr. Wickham?" She pertly tilted her head to the side and looked at him with clear eyes, a small smile on her lips.

"You are quite right, Miss Bennet. I have seen the Colonel angry on occasion. It was a memorable sight," he said, as he self-consciously straightened his collar.

"I daresay it would be. I hope I never have cause to see it myself." She looked at Wickham meaningfully.

"I understand you perfectly, Miss Elizabeth."

"I am glad, Mr. Wickham. Good evening." She curtseyed and walked toward her mother.

~

The next week went by rather quickly, and before she knew it, she was in the Lucas's carriage and on her way to London. She was anxious to see Jane and find out what was happening with Mr. Bingley. All of Jane's letters had been filled with him and she was expecting to hear of their betrothal any day.

They pulled up in front of the Gardiner's, and Elizabeth was the first one out of the carriage. She practically ran into Jane's arms, and the two stood in the passage hugging and talking over each other for several minutes before their uncle interrupted them.

"I hope the men you marry live close together, or they will face very large travel bills."

"Uncle!" Elizabeth improperly hugged her uncle, who had always been a favorite of hers, and she of his, and went in search of her aunt.

"Aunt! It is so good to see you!" Elizabeth found she was close to tears. It had been a difficult three weeks, and she'd had no one to speak to except in letters. No matter how often she wrote, it was not the same as having a confidante close by.

"Come dear! Let's get you upstairs. You probably want to freshen up."

Elizabeth was lead up the stairs by her aunt and Jane, who followed her into the room they would share while the Lucas's were there.

"Jane, you look wonderful. You're positively glowing!"

"Oh, Lizzy! The most wonderful thing has happened! I am engaged to Mr. Bingley!"

"Oh, Jane, I am so happy for you!" She kissed both her cheeks and held her hands in front of them. "You must tell me everything about it!"

As Elizabeth washed and changed out of her traveling dress, Jane told her the story.

"Mr. Bingley had come for a morning visit. We were all sitting in the parlor when Nanny Kate came down and said she needed Aunt for something. Afterwards, Charles told me he had asked her to take Aunt out of the room so he could be alone with me." She smiled giddily. "After they left, Charles sat next to me and took my hand and told me how sorry he was that he had left Netherfield without leaving word, and that if I would let him, he would spend the rest of his life making it up to me. He said he never wished to be parted from me ever again and that the idea of living without me was agony to him, and would I please end his misery and agree to be his wife."

"I had no idea Mr. Bingley was so poetic!" Elizabeth smiled at her sister.

"I believe he had been practicing it for some time." Jane smiled and looked at the floor. "It was very sweet and endearing."

"Then what happened?" She could always tell when Jane was holding back.

"Lizzy, you must promise not to tell Aunt, or she will never let me be alone with Charles again!"

"Jane, whatever could you have done that is so horrible?"

"I let him kiss me." Her face flushed bright red and she cast her eyes down, unable to hold back a small grin.

"That's wonderful! You had just got engaged! What other occasion could warrant a kiss more?" She gave her sister a teasing look as she brushed her hair. "So, what was it like?'

"Oh Lizzy, it was wonderful! At first it was awkward and I was surprised, but once I relaxed, it was everything I had hoped it would be and more."

"Dearest Jane! I am so happy for you!"

Jane began laughing and could hardly speak for smiling. "Can you die of happiness? Lizzy, if there were such a man for you! If you could be so happy!"

"I am content to see you happy, dearest. When is the wedding?"

"I wanted to speak with you about that. We just received a letter from father yesterday giving his consent, so we have not really had time to discuss it. Charles does not want to wait long, and I am inclined to agree with him. There will be much to plan, though. What do you think of May?"

"I think it sounds perfect. The flowers will be blooming and the churchyard will be beautiful," she gave Jane a meaningful look, "and it gives us plenty of time to shop for your trousseau."

"Oh, do not tease me, Lizzy! Wait until it's your turn!"

They laughed together for the next quarter hour, until their aunt rejoined them.

"Lizzy, we will be leaving for the theatre in an hour. Are you hungry? Cook has made a light meal if you want something sent up. We won't be having supper for several hours, so it's probably best to eat now."

"Yes, a tray would be lovely, thank you, Aunt."

"Amy will be here shortly to press your dress and help with your hair. I suspect the carriage will be early; you know how Mr. Darcy is."

"Mr. Darcy?"

"Yes. He is coming with us to the theatre tonight. Or I should say we are going with him, it is his box. Mr. Bingley will also be joining us, of course. Don't worry, we shall be comfortable between the two carriages."

Elizabeth turned pale and stared ahead of her. "Lizzy, are you alright?" Jane asked.

"I'm fine, only surprised, that is all."

Her aunt looked at her suspiciously. "Take care, Lizzy. I imagine you are tired from traveling, and it will be a late night. We are having supper at the Darcys' afterwards."

"We are? All of us?"

"Sir William and Maria will come back here, as they are tired from the journey and Sir William does not think Maria is old enough to be attending such functions. The rest of us will go to the Darcys' to celebrate Mr. Darcy's birthday. Miss Darcy has planned something special. But he does not know anything about it, so you mustn't say a word, Lizzy. I'm surprised she hasn't written of it to you."

Elizabeth's head was spinning. How had no one informed her of this? She knew Mr. Darcy had called a few times with Bingley, and he had come to dinner at the Gardiners' and she knew they had gone to Darcy House once for dinner, but she had yet to figure out why. Was Mr. Darcy friends with her aunt and uncle? The same aunt and uncle he refused to let his sister visit? And whose idea was this birthday dinner?

Suddenly Elizabeth wished she had brought a nicer dress. She didn't have a proper theatre dress, only a few ball gowns and evening dresses. She brought the gown she'd worn to the Netherfield Ball, as it was her nicest next to the one she'd purchased with Lady Matlock, and suitable for an evening with her family and the Lucases. Oh well, there was nothing to be done for it now.

Amy curled her hair and piled it atop her head, leaving a few curls hanging temptingly over her shoulder. Elizabeth knew she would not look her best after a half day of travel and several stressful weeks, but when she looked in the mirror she saw her color was high and it made her look healthier than she felt, as long as one didn't look too deeply into her troubled eyes.

She walked down the stairs behind Jane, who looked lovelier than ever, of course, intending to wait in the drawing room for a short while until the carriages arrived. But her aunt was correct – Mr. Darcy was early. She saw Mr. Bingley standing at the bottom of the stairs, staring raptly at Jane, a silly grin on his face. She could partially see Mr. Darcy behind him. She couldn't help but remember the last time she had walked down the stairs toward him; it had been a decidedly different experience.

She focused her eyes on the back of Jane's head and walked steadily down. She refused to look at Mr. Darcy. She greeted Mr. Bingley and said hello to Darcy, staring at his waistcoat buttons the entire time. They walked outside to the carriage and she saw that the Gardiners and Sir William and Maria Lucas were getting into the Gardiners' carriage, and that she was to ride in Mr. Darcy's carriage with Bingley and Jane. Oh, dear!

If Darcy had had any doubts about Elizabeth's anger toward him, he didn't anymore. Never, in the entire time he had known her, had she been unwilling to look at him. She had always looked him in the eye, even when they were arguing. She had never before shown fear or backed away from a confrontation. *It's going to be a long night.*

Georgiana was waiting in the carriage, and Elizabeth's genuine joy in seeing her friend helped her to overcome her discomfort. She decided there was nothing to be done about Mr. Darcy's presence, and she had been looking forward to this event for over a month. And now she was to see the show from the comfort of a private box. She decided to be happy about her improved comfort and enjoy the company of her friends, and not think about the dark man brooding across the carriage.

When they arrived at the theatre, Bingley offered his arm to Jane, of course, Sir William to Maria, Mr. Gardiner to Mrs. Gardiner, leaving two women to one Mr. Darcy. He looked between Elizabeth and Georgiana, trying to decide who to offer to first, and slightly afraid Elizabeth would refuse him, when Sir William stepped in to rescue him.

"Miss Elizabeth! Come, let us see what raptures await us inside!" He offered her his free arm and she accepted it gratefully, walking briskly behind her aunt and uncle.

Darcy's mouth set in a thin line as he and Georgiana followed their party inside. They were greeted by many acquaintances and they bowed and curtseyed and nodded where needed, until a gong sounded that it was time to be seated.

The Darcy box was as she expected it to be: One of the best in the theatre and very comfortable. Georgiana waved to Elizabeth to sit next to her and she settled into her chair between her friend and her aunt. Mr. Darcy was on the other side of Georgiana, desperately trying not to look at Elizabeth.

Afterward, he could not remember anything about the play except that Elizabeth had laughed in the middle of the first act. And Elizabeth could only recall that the central actress had worn a purple dress and died just before the end.

Back in the carriage on the way to Darcy House, she was silent, happy to listen to Georgiana telling her everything that had happened in her absence.

As she looked out the door at the familiar façade, she couldn't help but feel a sense of homecoming. It was almost as if she were seeing an old friend again after a long absence. She didn't know it, but her face betrayed her thoughts, easily seen by Mr. Darcy who was watching her closely. The men got out and handed down the ladies, Elizabeth exiting last, her eyes still absorbing the house in front of her. Mr. Bingley was already heading up the front stairs with Jane on his arm and Georgiana behind them. As Elizabeth reached her hand out, she was surprised to find it grasped by Mr. Darcy and not the footman. She was even more surprised that she recognized the feel of his hand without seeing him. She looked up into his face and saw he was watching her intently. There was a glimmer of something behind his eyes; was it pleasure? She gave a polite smile and headed inside.

CHAPTER 18

Darcy was sufficiently surprised when he entered the drawing room and saw everyone. Georgiana was beaming with the triumph of having planned an entire dinner party, with Lady Matlock's assistance, of course.

She ordered all of Darcy's favorite foods and planned the seating arrangement – something she had enjoyed a little too much. Lady Matlock had checked the menu and helped send out invitations, adding Sir Malcolm to the guest list.

At dinner, Elizabeth found she was seated between Colonel Fitzwilliam and Sir Malcolm, Mrs. Gardiner on his other side. Caroline Bingley sat across from them. After the first course, Georgiana peeked around Fitzwilliam to whisper to Elizabeth.

"What do you think?"

"I think it's lovely! Did you do it all yourself?"

"Mostly, though Lady Matlock helped with the menu and invitations."

"I am very impressed. Did Mr. Darcy suspect anything?"

"He seems to be completely surprised! I can't believe he didn't figure it out sooner. Though he has been distracted of late," she added thoughtfully.

"It truly is impressive, Georgiana! Well done!" Colonel Fitzwilliam joined the conversation.

"I'm surprised I didn't hear of it before tonight. You were very good at holding your secret!"

"I'm afraid that was my fault, Miss Bennet. I told Georgiana it would be fun to surprise you when you came to town." Fitzwilliam smiled guiltily at her.

"You accomplished your mission, Colonel Fitzwilliam, I am certainly surprised." She wondered what the Colonel was up to, but decided there was nothing to be done for it now and settled in to enjoy her dinner and company.

Conversation continued on happily between Fitzwilliam and Georgiana, and Elizabeth turned her attention to Sir Malcolm on her right.

"Miss Elizabeth, are you pleased to be back in London?"

"Yes, Sir, very pleased. I have missed my sister immensely," she said with an affectionate look towards Jane at the other end of the table.

"I understand congratulations are in order. When is the wedding?"

"Thank you. A date has not been set yet, but I believe they are hoping for some time in May."

"That is not that far off. Will they be joining the party at Pemberley this summer then?"

"I cannot say." Elizabeth searched for a way to change the topic, but he beat her to it.

"I must say I am glad your sister is here this evening."

"Why is that, Sir?"

"Now I may call you Miss Elizabeth. I have always liked that name."

Elizabeth flushed slightly. "Have you? It is only fair; after all, I have always called you by your given name."

"Have you given any thought to riding?"

"Pardon me?"

"At the Matlocks' ball, you said when the weather improved, you would consider learning to ride again."

"You have an impressive memory, Sir! I did say that. Well, I suppose I should be true to my word."

"Now we need only find you the proper mount and teacher."

"That may be hard to come by, Sir Malcolm. I'm afraid I can be a rather difficult student."

"I cannot imagine that." He looked at her teasingly.

"It requires a very patient master to offset my lack of the quality. And I doubt I will have much natural talent for riding."

"I doubt that very much, Miss Elizabeth. I'm sure the right teacher could have you riding in no time. And I am sure you are very talented."

"You are too kind, Sir. First, I must find a teacher willing to take me on."

"I am such a teacher. And I am very willing." He gazed at her pointedly.

Elizabeth blushed and smiled nervously. Something in his look spoke of more than innocent dinner flirtation and she found it unnerving.

"We shall see, Sir Malcolm."

Seeing her discomfort, he swiftly changed to a neutral topic and they continued speaking pleasantly for the next half hour.

Caroline Bingley was not pleased with her seat. She was at the very end of the table, between Mr. Hurst, who never had anything of interest to say, and the empty hostess chair at the foot of the table. She was as far from Darcy as was possible and several seats away from Georgiana or anyone else in Darcy's family. She was left to converse with Mrs. Gardiner, who sat across from her.

She couldn't help but notice how Sir Malcolm, on Mrs. Gardiner's left, was completely wrapped up in Eliza Bennet. Why was he bothering to pay attention to that country chit anyway? Didn't he know she had absolutely no dowry? Her thoughts tended thus for quite some time, during which she inserted jagged barbs into her conversation with Mrs. Gardiner about living in Cheapside and having a husband in trade, conveniently forgetting that her own fortune was similarly tainted.

She was about to interrupt Elizabeth and Malcolm and insist on her due of attention from the gentleman, when she looked up to the head of the table at Mr. Darcy. It wasn't difficult to see that his eyes kept wandering back to Elizabeth and her dinner companion. His expression was unreadable, but he was watching her nonetheless, and it did not go unnoticed by Caroline.

She remembered how he had watched her in Hertfordshire and had called her eyes 'fine'. He had been drawn into more than one conversation with the vixen, quite to the exclusion of everyone else in the room. She did not like the attention he paid her, even if it wasn't openly romantic.

She had known Darcy for years and had never seen him look at any woman for any length of time, regardless of the expression on his face. She also had never seen him willingly enter into conversation with a lady, especially one he appeared to enjoy. She did not think he would ever do anything as ridiculous as court or offer for her, his sense of honor and duty would forbid it, but she was certainly a distraction and Caroline had waited long enough.

Miss Bingley was coming into her fifth season and she had had her sights set on Mr. Darcy since her second. She thought her brother's close friendship would cement her chances and in many ways it had; after all, she was here at an intimate party in his home. But even though she was included in more invitations than she previously had been or was entitled to by rank, personally, she had not gained any ground.

She knew next to nothing about Mr. Darcy's person. She could not name his favorite books and had no idea what he did when he was not in her presence. That was why she had become so bitter toward Eliza Bennet: Mr. Darcy had begun to reveal himself to her. He had told her of his thoughts on more than one subject and even described his temperament. What did she have that Caroline didn't? Why could he not confide in her?

Everything was going so well until Charles found out about Jane's presence in London. She had thought she was rid of the Bennets forever; now she was to be inundated with their presence for the rest of her life. The sooner she married and got out of her brother's house, the better.

Seeing Darcy looking at Elizabeth only strengthened her resolve and she was struck with an idea. Darcy may never actually do anything, but he was certainly wasting time being distracted with her. And who knew? Perhaps he would go so far as to ask her to be his mistress. As a country girl with no prospects, Elizabeth would be a fool to say no.

If she were truly honest with herself, Caroline wasn't sure that she herself would say no if the opportunity presented itself. But Caroline had never been known for her honesty; to herself or anyone else.

She knew a man with a mistress, especially one he cared for, might wait years to take a wife – what would be the need? She could not afford any more delays. Elizabeth Bennet needed to be taken out of the way, and Sir Malcolm seemed like just the man to do it.

"Sir Malcolm," Caroline purred, "have you heard Miss Elizabeth play and sing?"

"I have not had that pleasure, no." He smiled at Elizabeth.

"You have missed a great pleasure indeed, Sir! Miss Eliza, you must play for us after dinner – I insist!"

"I would like that very much, Miss Elizabeth," added Sir Malcolm.

Elizabeth looked at Caroline dubiously and shot a sideways look to her aunt before answering. "Of course, I will be happy to oblige you Sir Malcolm, Miss Bingley, if our hosts do not have something else planned."

"Sir Malcolm, I assure you, Miss Elizabeth is indeed a very accomplished musician. Never will you have heard such a – pure voice." She stumbled a bit on the compliment but covered it well with a sickening smile and heavily batting her lashes.

"Thank you, Miss Bingley. Such praise coming from you is a compliment indeed," Elizabeth said graciously. Caroline merely nodded as Elizabeth wondered what on earth had happened to Miss Bingley.

Malcolm turned his attention back to Elizabeth. "How long will you be in London?"

"We are to leave for Kent tomorrow and will be gone six weeks. Then I will be back in town for a week before returning to Hertfordshire. However, depending on the date they set, my sister's wedding may change that."

"I imagine you would never miss such an important event."

"No, I would not. I am to attend her, so I'm sure she would be upset with me if I was not present," she replied.

"It is too bad you are leaving so soon after your arrival. I would have liked to see you again."

Elizabeth smiled openly. "Perhaps you will. Lady Matlock wished me to visit with her for the season, but I have told her I must stay with my sister until the wedding. She was not pleased, but I told her there was nothing I could do. She just may work a miracle; I would not put it past her."

He laughed – a deep, friendly sound. "I would not either, Miss Elizabeth. Perhaps I will see you at Matlock House later in the season then." He smiled into her eyes, and she noticed how clear a blue they were, not stormy or brooding, just clear and open and endless.

Due to the lateness of the hour, the gentlemen did not depart after dinner but went with the ladies directly to the music room. Caroline was asked to play, and to everyone's surprise, she deferred to Elizabeth. Confused, Elizabeth took the seat behind the pianoforte, and Sir Malcolm offered to turn the pages for her.

She chose a simple song with a pleasant melody, and each time the page needed to be turned, Sir Malcolm would rise and reach across her, his sleeve and then his side lightly brushing against Elizabeth's right arm. She got a whiff of his cologne when he moved so close to her. It was a mixture of a fresh, grassy smell that she could not place, and a touch of a warm kitchen flavor. Vanilla maybe? It was not unpleasant, and she felt it suited his character – interesting, but uncomplicated. *A girl wouldn't spend hours trying to understand him.*

Darcy had never been more frustrated in his life. Elizabeth was finally here, back at his house, and he had barely been able to say two words to her. In the drawing room before dinner, he had been so surrounded by well-wishers that he hadn't been able to speak to her beyond a thank you when she wished him a happy birthday.

He was sure his aunt was responsible for Sir Malcolm being invited and seated next to Elizabeth, who was irritatingly placed at the other end of the table. He tried to be attentive and polite to his guests. After all, Georgiana had gone to a lot of trouble for him, and he was proud of her and touched that she would do something for his birthday beyond a gift. His aunt was on his right and talking about something meaningless – he couldn't even remember the topic. She finally turned her attention to Mr. Gardiner on her other side, leaving Darcy free to watch the others.

At first Darcy was surprised she was sitting next to a tradesman, but it didn't take long to realize what she was doing. He could hear many of the questions she asked Mr. Gardiner, and was pleased when he answered intelligently and correctly, as he knew he would.

She was interviewing him – and it wasn't difficult to guess why. As Elizabeth's self-appointed patroness in society, she was assessing the supposed weakest link in her family. Darcy laughed silently to himself as he imagined his aunt's impressions of Mrs. Bennet and Elizabeth's younger sisters. He chided himself for being uncharitable, but could not help the irony of the situation.

'Surely Sir Malcolm would not find fault with Mr. Gardiner! He is so genteel and intelligent!' Darcy could see the thoughts as they ran through his aunt's mind, having been on the receiving end of her matchmaking machinations several times before. He had to hand it to her, she seemed to be doing an excellent job; Malcolm did appear quite taken with Miss Elizabeth. Which of course only made Darcy more agitated.

When they removed to the music room, he had decided he would sit near her and possibly turn the pages for her when she played, if Georgiana didn't. That would allow him a chance to speak with her and assess her feelings. She had seemed distant and unhappy when he first saw her that evening at the Gardiner's, but as the night wore on, she mellowed into being merely cold to him and subdued to everyone else.

When they arrived at Darcy House, she had actually seemed happy, like she was coming home after a long time away. It pleased him to no end that she felt that way about his home, and he had wanted to prolong the moment of intimacy between them, but it was not to be with a house full of guests and a dinner party to host.

Now, Sir Malcolm was ruining all his plans. Of course, Darcy had had no idea he was to be there, not knowing anyone but the theatre party was coming for dinner. And now here he was, sitting next to his Elizabeth at the pianoforte, turning the pages for her, brushing against her arm as he did so. Darcy fought a feeling of revulsion as he saw Elizabeth blush the first time Malcolm leaned across her. *She can't be falling in love with him, can she?*

And was it his imagination, or did Malcolm smirk at him as he sat back down? *I am losing my mind!*

Malcolm was one of his oldest friends; they had only ever been competitive in the sporting field, never with women. Of course, they had never before been interested in the same woman. Darcy decided to keep an eye on his old friend, even though he was mostly sure it was all in his own head.

It was well into the early morning hours before the party broke up. Lady Matlock had pressed Elizabeth again to come and stay with her for at least part of the season, and Elizabeth had promised she would speak with her sister and parents and let her know her plans.

Darcy had managed to speak two sentences to Elizabeth: one about her journey to town, and one about her trip to Kent the following day. He was exceedingly frustrated with the night, especially when Sir Malcolm, not he, handed Elizabeth into the carriage. No matter, he told himself, she is to Kent tomorrow, and he would follow in a week's time.

There would be no Sir Malcolm at Rosings.

CHAPTER 19

"Charlotte!"

"Lizzy!"

The two women embraced and laughed together outside Hunsford Parsonage, where Charlotte and Mr. Collins had stepped out to greet them. The two women slipped inside while the latter was busy welcoming Sir William and Maria Lucas.

Mr. Collins was as effusive as ever. He repeated every offer Charlotte made of refreshment and insisted on immediately giving them a tour of the parsonage. He pointed out all the wallpaper specifically chosen by Lady Catherine, and commented on the superior quality and elegance of design, as if the lady had painted it herself. He waxed poetic on the shelves she had had installed in the closets, which left nowhere for the guests to hang their garments, and he spent fifteen minutes on the benefits of a well-appointed stairwell and the proper length of a corridor.

Elizabeth couldn't help but feel that Mr. Collins hoped to make her see what she had given up when she refused him. Charlotte seemed to have developed a system of ignoring her husband when he said something embarrassing, and redirecting the conversation before it became too mortifying, though her cheeks were often flushed during his more ebullient speeches. At first Elizabeth felt sorry for Charlotte, but when the two had a moment alone together she changed her mind.

"I am quite happy, Lizzy. I so enjoy having my own home." She looked around the room proudly and Elizabeth had to admit it was a nice house. There were no younger sisters or brothers or overbearing mothers to contend with - though there was Mr. Collins.

"I am glad to hear it, Charlotte. How are you getting on with Lady Catherine?"

"She is very considerate, and often condescends to drop by unannounced and make helpful suggestions for where I should place the furniture and what cut of meat we should order. She is a very involved patroness." She gave Elizabeth a pointed look.

"Oh, Charlotte, I can imagine! Lady Catherine will have guests soon, so perhaps she will find herself too busy to assist you." She smiled slyly.

"So you know her nephews are coming?"

"Yes, they informed me of it in February while I was in London."

"Her ladyship will not like not being able to make the introduction – it is one of her favorite things to do. Any relationship that comes of it she then feels was of her design." The smile on Charlotte's face took the bite out of her words, but Elizabeth understood her sentiment. "Miss Darcy is to accompany them now, though originally it was just the gentlemen, and they were not to arrive until just before Easter."

"Yes, I saw Miss Darcy just last night, and she informed me that she and her brother and cousin will be arriving in a week's time."

"Then we shall likely not be invited to Rosings overmuch if Lady Catherine has other guests to entertain her." Charlotte looked slightly relieved, though she was trying to keep her expression neutral.

They continued to talk of their families and familiar friends in Hertfordshire, carefully avoiding the topic of Charlotte's marriage to the man Elizabeth had refused.

The week passed quickly, with Mr. Collins gladly spending most of his time working in his garden at Charlotte's encouragement, leaving Elizabeth and Charlotte to spend many happy hours together talking and taking walks to explore Rosings Park.

Despite everything she had heard, and was disinclined to believe, it was a beautiful park. There were many walks and trails and a particularly lovely grove that easily became her favorite place to wander. The gardens closer to the great house were overly manicured and stripped of all natural beauty, and Elizabeth found herself avoiding them in favor of the more natural wood paths and surrounding fields.

The most interesting event of the week was an invitation to Rosings the day after their arrival. The time had come to meet Lady Catherine. Maria was beside herself with nerves and could hardly brush her hair, she was so nervous. Sir William appeared brave and gave the impression that this was an everyday occurrence for one of his rank, but by the time they were approaching the house, he was stunned into silence – a singular occurrence, indeed.

Elizabeth did not feel frightened of meeting the great lady or being in her enormous house. Her courage did not fail her; once inside, she found it to be dark and overdone, with furnishings covered in the most expensive, though not the most tasteful, fabrics, and walls burdened by imported papers in decadent designs. The entire house seemed to be designed to impress one with the wealth and consequence of its owner, with no real concern for comfort or livability.

Lady Catherine herself was a tall, large woman, with strong features that may have once been considered handsome, but now gave her a rather unfortunate expression, not distant from a horse's, but less gentle. Her daughter Anne was a mousy creature that might have been pretty had she had some color and thoughts of her own. Elizabeth wondered how such a young woman had come from such a mother. Miss DeBurgh's companion, a Mrs. Jenkinson, was not much larger than her charge, but significantly older and bore a slightly haunted expression. It didn't take long to find out why.

Lady Catherine sat in a large, throne-like chair in the center of the room, the other chairs placed strategically around hers so that when seated, all would face her. Mr. Collins wasted no time introducing his father- and sister-in-law, saving his destitute cousin for last. Elizabeth curtseyed politely and took a seat, preparing to be extremely diverted. *If only Father were here to see this!*

After listening to Mr. Collins and Sir William clamoring over each other to flatter Lady Catherine, practically prostrating themselves in the process, the grand lady turned her attention to Elizabeth.

"Miss Bennet, are both your parents living?" she asked in a loud, imperious voice.

Elizabeth was startled by the abruptness of the question, but responded civilly, "Yes Lady Catherine, they are."

"And do you have any siblings?"

"Yes, ma'am, I have four sisters."

"Four sisters! That is most irresponsible! And how many brothers?"

"I have no brothers, your ladyship."

"No brothers? No wonder the estate is entailed! That was very silly of your mother. No brothers, indeed!" She huffed indignantly, as if it was her estate entailed away. "I daresay it is good for Mr. Collins, but I see no reason for estates being entailed away from the female line. If my estate had been entailed, you can be assured I would have produced a son."

The entire room was quiet, not daring to hold even a whispered conversation while Lady Catherine was talking, even if it was not to them. So Elizabeth continued the dialogue, feeling almost like a player on the stage before a small but attentive audience.

"Indeed, Lady Catherine."

"How many elder sisters have you?"

"One elder, three younger."

"Is your eldest sister married?"

"No, ma'am, she is not."

"Is she engaged?"

"Yes, ma'am."

"Well, at least that is something!" She looked around as if she was expecting to see a pig flying by at the mere idea of an elder sister not being married already.

"And you, Miss Bennet? Are you engaged?"

Elizabeth fully felt the impertinence of the question, but remained civil. "No, I am not."

"Are you being courted?"

"No, your ladyship, I am not."

"That is quite careless! Two girls out and neither married, nor you even being courted! Why does your mother not take you to town to meet suitable gentlemen?" Lady Catherine seemed seriously offended. "She must move quickly so your younger sisters may come out." Mr. Collins made a small whimpering sound. "Are any of your younger sisters out?"

"Yes, ma'am, all."

"All! What, all five out at once? Very odd! And you only the second.

The younger ones out before the older ones are married! Your younger sisters must be very young?"

"My youngest is not sixteen." Mr. Collins studied the floor carefully as Lady Catherine's eyes grew wide, and her nostrils flared, and her head bobbed curiously back and forth, as if she didn't know where to look.

"I think it would be very hard on younger sisters, not to have their share of society and amusement just because the elder do not have the means or inclination to marry early. And to be kept back for such a reason! It would scarcely encourage sisterly affection," Elizabeth added.

"Upon my word, you give your opinion very decidedly for so young a person! Pray, what is your age?"

"With three younger sisters grown up," she smiled, "your ladyship can hardly expect me to own it."

Lady Catherine looked quite shocked and Charlotte employed her newly learned skill of changing the subject when things became unbearable. The conversation moved on, Elizabeth saying as little as possible and not being addressed again by the great lady, until finally the visit was at an end.

~

"Did you see her, Louisa? Shamelessly flirting with Sir Malcolm! Who does she think she is?" Caroline was alternately pacing and sitting with her sister in her private sitting room at the Bingley townhouse.

"Caroline, weren't you just saying you were relieved Sir Malcolm seems to be distracting her from Mr. Darcy?" Louisa asked.

"Yes, I am. I really wish she wasn't here at all! What do they see in her? I don't understand it!"

"Men are not meant to be understood, Caroline, do not trouble yourself. Use Sir Malcolm to keep her away from Mr. Darcy. When all this is through, you can easily exclude her. Sir Malcolm will probably never offer for her anyway; he is likely just flirting."

"Do you really think so? He seemed to genuinely like her." Uncertainty filled her voice. The only thing worse than Elizabeth stealing Darcy's attention away from her was Elizabeth marrying before her. That would be unconscionable. And to a man with a title, too! "Ridiculous as the notion is."

"Perhaps he did like her. What he liked her for is debatable." She sneered and smiled unkindly.

"Louisa, you are wicked!" Caroline said with wide eyes, followed by a malicious laugh.

"I wish Mr. Hurst would get on with finding a mistress. I am utterly exhausted!" She leaned back against the sofa cushions.

"You must produce your heir, Louisa! You know your duty." Caroline gave her sister a teasing look and dodged the pillow Louisa threw at her.

"One day it will be your turn to fulfill your duty, Miss Caroline, and we shall see who is laughing then!"

"Somehow I think performing my duty for Mr. Darcy might be a trifle less unpleasant than doing the same for Mr. Hurst." She pursed her lips and smirked bawdily at her sister.

Louisa sighed, suddenly serious, and leaned back on the settee, a bitter look on her face. "Caroline, you speak of what you know not of. Mr. Darcy is a fine specimen, I grant you. But you never know how a man will behave behind closed doors. You should hear the stories amongst the married women."

"You have told me many stories. I heard nothing unexpected or too terrible."

"I kept the more horrible things from you. I did not wish you to be too frightened to marry!"

Caroline had a doubtful look in her eye, wondering what her sister had kept from her and if it was possible she was making this up.

"How bad could Mr. Darcy be, Louisa? He is such a gentleman!" she cried disbelievingly.

"He is a man accustomed to having his own way and being in control of everyone and everything around him. He is also powerful, in every way. You could not fight him." She raised her brows at Caroline. Throughout the illuminating conversation, Louisa's demeanor was superior and knowledgeable, and more than a little bitter and angry.

"Surely you do not mean… Mr. Darcy is a gentleman! He would never… he would never, never demand of a lady what she did not wish to give!" she said haughtily, her pert nose up in the air. She was slightly shaken but trying to hide her naiveté from her elder sister.

Louisa leaned forward and looked tauntingly at her. "As I said Caroline, you never know. We hardly know Mr. Darcy. How well can you know a man from a few games of whist and dinner conversation?" her voice betrayed her own disillusionment. "He is close with Charles, which I must admit is in his favor, for we know Charles would never hurt a fly. But, I must remind you that he is a man accustomed to having his way and might not take lightly to someone opposing him, especially when it comes to his marital and legal rights." She pointed her finger for effect.

Caroline was beginning to look frightened and Louisa, struck with a comforting instinct, took her sister's hand. "I do not wish to frighten you; I simply want you to realize that there is more to marriage than choosing the husband. Once you have been courted and proposed to and said your vows, you are at his mercy. He becomes your master and you cannot choose another. You should think very carefully about your choice, Caroline. If Mr. Darcy does not look your way, perhaps it is for the best. You may wish to begin looking elsewhere."

Caroline nodded her head and was silent a moment, thinking about what her sister had told her. She knew Louisa was not happy in her marriage to Mr. Hurst. How could she be? The man did nothing but drink and sleep and, according to Louisa, demand his marital rights. When he was courting her, he had seemed quite dashing. He had walked out with her and complimented her and played the attentive suitor well. How things had changed!

Caroline could not believe Mr. Darcy would be a cruel husband. Everyone knew him to be an honorable man, at least that was what Charles said, but among the women he was known less by his character and more by his possessions, all of which Caroline was acutely aware.

She had to admit that Charles was easily led, and that she did not know Mr. Darcy very well personally, so it was possible she was mistaken in her opinion of him. They had hardly had more than two dozen true conversations in private. Usually she would speak, and he would add a comment here or there.

She had thought being together at Netherfield would do the trick, since they would be in company for long periods of time and as hostess, she could orchestrate more events that put them together, and he wouldn't be as busy with business as he had been when she had visited Pemberley in the past. When they had agreed on the insufferable neighbors and the unsuitability of the Bennet family, she had thought she was finally getting somewhere.

And then came Eliza Bennet and her dirty petticoats.

Thinking of Elizabeth filled Caroline with anger and she leapt up and began pacing quickly behind the sofa, Louisa looking over the back at her suddenly energetic sister.

"The nerve of that girl! Everything was going so well! Mr. Darcy was finally turning to me – to me! She had to come in with her fine eyes and mind broadened by reading," she said in a mocking tone, her hands gesticulating wildly.

Louisa did not understand the sudden change in her sister, but she was accustomed to it. Caroline had always been moody and easily angered, and the situation with the Bennets had only served to push her character into further extremes.

"What does she have that I do not? She is impertinent and argumentative! Her gowns are old and reworked, and she cannot play half as well as me. She doesn't even have a lady's maid! She shares one with her sisters. And no dowry! What on earth do they see in her?"

"Is this about Mr. Darcy, or about Miss Elizabeth getting more attention than you?" Louisa asked. She usually agreed with Caroline about the Bennets, but Caroline's ranting was getting old. Louisa had her own problems.

"What?" Caroline rounded on her sister. "I might remind you, Louisa, that you have always agreed with me about the Bennets and were just as ready to get Charles away from them as I was! And I saw how you conveniently sat quietly by while he was berating me for not telling him Jane Bennet was in town."

Louisa sighed exasperatedly. "I know, Caroline. I do not like the Bennets any more than you do. But Jane is now engaged to Charles, and I don't see how there is any way to change that. I am simply trying to make the best of a difficult situation, something I seem to be doing a lot of lately." She muttered the last bit quietly. "I honestly do not know what the men see in Eliza Bennet. I myself do not like her and would be happy to never set eyes on her again, but that is not likely since she is Jane's sister and Jane is to marry our brother. You are correct that she has no style and her beauty is wanting. However, I believe our attention would be better spent trying to find you a husband. If you are set on Mr. Darcy, then we should pursue your idea of encouraging Sir Malcolm in her direction so she cannot further distract him. If not, we need to widen the search."

Caroline released her anger in a deep, aggravated breath and sat next to her sister. "I still want Mr. Darcy," she mumbled grumpily.

Louisa gave her a resigned nod.

They discussed ways to push Elizabeth toward Sir Malcolm and agreed to say nothing but good things about her when the baronet was near. Caroline was walking a fine line – disparaging Elizabeth to Darcy and building her up to Sir Malcolm. This would require finesse, and Caroline was determined to do it well.

CHAPTER 20

"Are we almost there?"

"Georgie, relax! We'll get there when we get there. Why don't you try to get some sleep?" Colonel Fitzwilliam looked at Georgiana across the carriage and tried to hide his smile.

"We're about two hours out," Darcy spoke in a low voice. He had been staring out the window and had hardly spoken since they left London.

Georgiana released a deep sigh. "Alright. I shall try to rest." She curled into the corner and wrapped her cloak about her. Within a few minutes, she was breathing regularly in a steady sleep.

"That was quick!" Colonel Fitzwilliam laughed.

"She hardly slept last night, she was so excited about the trip," Darcy answered.

"Imagine actually being excited to see Lady Catherine! What is the world coming to?" he joked and looked to his cousin, who was clearly not in a laughing mood. "Although I doubt it is our aunt who has inspired such feelings."

Darcy looked at him out of the corner of his eye. The colonel continued, "Who do you suppose she is so anxious to see? Could it be a dear friend perhaps? A slip of a thing with dark hair and sparkling eyes?"

"She's not a complete slip," Darcy muttered, remembering how she had been softer than he would have thought when he had held her in the snow.

"Ah! You are aware then! Well, dear cousin, as a military professional trained in the art of strategy, I must ask you what your plan is."

"I do not have a plan, Richard. Mind your own business," Darcy answered grumpily, his arms across his chest.

"I hardly believe that Fitzwilliam Darcy does not have a plan. Come! Out with it! You know I shall weasel it out of you eventually, so you may as well go ahead and tell me – save us both some time."

Darcy took a deep breath and let it out slowly. "Alright. I do not have an exact plan, but I will tell you what I intend to do."

The colonel smiled in satisfaction. "I'm listening."

"She obviously was not happy with me, as I'm sure you saw at dinner last week." Fitzwilliam let out a low whistle. Darcy gave him a withering look.

"Sorry, Cousin. Continue."

"She did seem to mellow somewhat as the evening progressed, but I did not have a chance to speak with her and ascertain her state of mind. So my first intention is to call on the parsonage in the morning and make a point of speaking to Miss Bennet. Without knowing her current feelings on the matter, I cannot proceed properly."

"Very wise, Cousin. How do you plan to know her feelings?"

"I haven't the foggiest idea." He looked dejectedly out the window.

The Colonel laughed softly, trying not to wake Georgiana. "May I make a suggestion, William?" He only called him William in very playful or very serious situations. Darcy wasn't sure which this was.

"You may."

"I suggest a spy. Someone to do a little reconnaissance behind enemy lines." He waggled his eyebrows.

"And just who do you have in mind?"

Richard gestured towards Georgiana sleeping in the corner. "Richard! Surely you cannot be serious! She knows nothing about this. I cannot tell her and raise her hopes, only to have them dashed."

Colonel Fitzwilliam looked at Darcy closely, quickly becoming serious. "Do you really think her hopes would be dashed?"

Darcy ran his hands through his hair. "I don't know, Richard. She looked at me so coldly. And that was when she was willing to look at me at all! Mostly she simply pretended I wasn't there. It was my worst nightmare come true – Elizabeth's complete indifference. I would almost rather have her angry with me. At least then there would be something to grasp onto."

"I was under the impression she was angry at you, some of the time anyway."

"What do you mean?"

"Cousin, I was sitting next to Miss Bennet at dinner, watching her talk and laugh with Sir Malcolm," Darcy cringed "but it was dinner chatter. She did not laugh with him the way I have seen her laugh with you. Nor did she look at him as I have seen her look at you."

Darcy felt a moment of hope, then sank down again. "That was before. Before she knew what I had done."

"Perhaps. But I also noticed her watching you after dinner last week. I was under the impression she was avoiding you because she was angry – and sad. And I would wager she is a good bit confused about who you really are."

"So what are you suggesting, Cousin?"

"Show her who you really are. Of course, apologizing for attempting to ruin her sister's life couldn't hurt either," he said lightly. Darcy glared at him, then sank his face into his hands as his cousin continued. "I suspect Georgiana will be able to tell us much if we simply ask her about her time with Miss Bennet. Perhaps a planted question here or there wouldn't hurt."

Darcy groaned and leaned back, looking out the window with a forlorn expression. "I made this mess, Richard. I will clean it up."

Fitzwilliam squeezed his shoulder affectionately. "Do not worry, Darcy, all will be well. I have a good feeling about this one."

"That's what you said about the battle in _________."

"And I made it out alive, didn't I?" The Colonel nodded his head as Darcy chuckled slightly and closed his eyes. Sleep was long in coming.

Their first evening at Rosings was uneventful enough. Lady Catherine instructed Georgiana on how many hours and in what way she should be practicing her music, informing them that no one in England had better natural taste than she. She chided Colonel Fitzwilliam for not being married yet, and told him he had better get on with it as he was looking rougher every year. He had merely thanked her graciously and rolled his eyes to Darcy.

When she spoke of marriage, Lady Catherine looked pointedly at Darcy and back to Anne. She insisted Anne was looking very well that day and would not stop speaking of her improved health until they each agreed that Anne was looking well and seemed much stronger than on their last visit, though she said not a word and had barely moved since their arrival.

Georgiana made Darcy and Fitzwilliam promise to take her to the parsonage in the morning to see Elizabeth. It was the only reason she had come, and she was already beginning to question the wisdom of exchanging entire evenings with Lady Catherine for a little time each morning with Elizabeth Bennet.

No one slept well that night, and not just because no one ever sleeps well at Rosings. Georgiana stayed awake for several hours, trying to think of responses to her aunt's many questions and criticisms, and clever ways to avoid conversation with her in general. Unfortunately, all she could think of was foisting her on her brother – he did seem to be Lady Catherine's favorite.

Darcy spent the first few hours tossing and turning, and could only sleep after his third glass of brandy had taken effect. Besides the fact that he couldn't stand this uncomfortable relic of a bed, he hated being at his aunt's, he hated her constant insinuations that he would marry Anne, and he was beyond nervous about his meeting with Elizabeth tomorrow.

He knew he should tell his aunt once and for all that he was never going to marry Anne and that if she wanted to see the future Mrs. Darcy, she should take a walk down the lane to the parsonage, for that was where the lady in question could currently be found. But he had tried to dissuade his aunt before, to no avail. She would believe what she would believe, and Darcy had given up trying to convince her otherwise years ago. It was simply easier to be quiet and let her ramble on.

Colonel Fitzwilliam beat the pillow under his head, trying to fluff it properly, but with little success. He shifted on the mattress, trying to find a place without lumps, knowing Darcy was in the newly renovated room and he had been sent to the same old guest room he'd always had. Darcy had always been Lady Catherine's favorite, and the Colonel had his own opinions about why that was, but nevertheless, the great lady was about to be in for a rude awakening. Fitzwilliam just hoped he had enough time to pack before she threw them all out. With a grunt, he gathered his flat pillow and coverlet and laid down on the floor.

"Ah, much better!"

~

Before anyone could leave Rosings the following morning, Mr. Collins came to call. He fawned and flattered, and poor Georgiana had not the slightest idea what to do with him. Luckily, the visit was not overlong and when he rose to leave, the gentlemen informed him that they had planned to call on the parsonage themselves and that they would accompany him thither and bring Miss Darcy, too.

They followed him down the path, noticing how he walked as if he were on a leash, never getting too far ahead, and calling over his shoulder to warn them anytime there was a stone or twig in the path, lest they lose their footing. This, of course, caused him to stumble more than once.

Colonel Fitzwilliam's face was red with holding in laughter, and he was forced to study the foliage diligently just to keep a straight face. Georgiana refused to look at her cousin. She knew she would completely lose her composure if she did.

"My dear, look who has condescended to call!" Mr. Collins produced the guests as if they were prizes won at a fair. Charlotte rose and greeted them politely, curtseying with each introduction.

"Elizabeth has stepped out for some air, but she will return shortly." Charlotte rang for tea and did not miss the looks of depression and disappointment on all three guests' faces. A few minutes later, Elizabeth walked briskly in, her cheeks flushed with exercise and her eyes sparkling, a ready smile on her lips.

"Georgiana!" Miss Darcy was out of her seat in moments, enveloping Elizabeth in a tight hug. Elizabeth felt tears pricking the back of her eyes but held herself together admirably. Colonel Fitzwilliam and Darcy rose, waiting for the girls to stop smiling and holding each other. Eventually they broke the embrace, and Elizabeth moved to greet the others.

Colonel Fitzwilliam, in a fit of gallantry, knelt over her extended hand and kissed it, winking at her as he rose. Elizabeth smiled crookedly at him and thought how much she had missed his easygoing manners. *If I had a brother, I would want him to be just like Colonel Fitzwilliam.*

She moved to Darcy, who repeated the motion. Elizabeth's hand tingled slightly when his warm lips met her bare skin, and she felt heat rising in her cheeks. His eyes met hers as he rose and they looked at each other silently for a moment.

Elizabeth looked away first, seating herself next to Georgiana. Darcy sat opposite her, though he was not far away in the parsonage's small parlor. Conversation was genial and stuck to common topics, and was frequently seized by Mr. Collins, who agreed with everything Mr. Darcy or Colonel Fitzwilliam said, even when they disagreed with each other. Georgiana, uncomfortable with strangers, said a few quiet words to Elizabeth, but otherwise remained silent.

When it came time to depart, Elizabeth walked them to the door. She and Georgiana agreed to meet for a walk in the morning, and with a quick glance into Darcy's deep blue eyes, she turned back inside.

CHAPTER 21

"Father, how did you know you loved Mother? Truly loved her, and that it wasn't just an infatuation?"

Mr. Darcy looked at the worried face of his son and asked, "Is there someone you are interested in, Son?"

"No, no one as yet. I just wondered in case, that is... when there is... someone, in the event that you, if you..."

"In case I am long gone when you find someone?"

Darcy hung his head. "Forgive me, Father."

"There is nothing to forgive, my boy. I am happy you are thinking of these things, instead of rushing headlong into it like so many do. And I am proud that you would come to me for advice. It means a great deal to me. Now tell me, what do you want to know?" Mr. Darcy sat a little higher in his bed and leaned closer to the chair his son was sitting in.

"How did you know you loved Mother?"

"I knew it here." Mr. Darcy clenched his fist and held it to his stomach. "She was beautiful and wonderful and sweet, but you know, I think that even if she were not, I would have loved her still. She was my destiny."

"So you basically had a feeling? That is how you chose your wife?" young Darcy asked in disbelief.

"More than a feeling. We had long been friends and I was well acquainted with her character, which led me to know that she would make a good wife and mother." Mr. Darcy looked at his son seriously. "But if you want to know how I knew I loved her with all my heart, yes, it was a feeling. She was air to me. I could not breathe without her."

Darcy looked at his father strangely, seeing the older man's eyes looking at some far-off place.

"Air," the son repeated quietly.

A loud knock disturbed Darcy's reverie, and he looked toward the door to see Colonel Fitzwilliam walking in.

"My God, Darcy! You look like the devil! Did you not sleep at all last night?" Fitzwilliam walked over to his cousin.

"I was just thinking about my father, and something he told me," he answered quietly. Fitzwilliam was silent for a moment, then walked over to the window and looked out.

"It is a fine day."

"Hmm."

"I imagine Miss Bennet is already out walking. She expects to meet Georgiana in a quarter hour. I've talked Aunt into inviting the parsonage for dinner. I was going to accompany Georgiana now and issue the invitation personally. Care to join us?" He was still speaking to the window.

Darcy inhaled sharply. "I'll be with you in a moment, Richard."

The colonel smiled and headed to the door. "I'll wait for you in the entry."

~

Georgiana spotted Elizabeth first and ran ahead to meet her. The two ladies chatted happily until the colonel's loud voice interrupted them.

"Good morning, Miss Bennet!" Elizabeth looked up.

"Good morning, Colonel Fitzwilliam!" She looked past him and saw Darcy a few steps away, advancing toward her. "Good morning, Mr. Darcy," she said politely, though not coldly.

"Good morning, Miss Bennet." *Air.*

She noticed his voice was somber and he looked as if he hadn't slept well. There was something missing in his eyes and something present that wasn't usually there – almost a haunted look.

The four of them walked together for a half hour, Georgiana and Elizabeth in front, Darcy and Fitzwilliam a few yards behind them. Eventually, the men approached the ladies.

"Miss Bennet, my aunt has issued an invitation for your party to join us at dinner this evening," the colonel stated.

"That is very kind, Colonel Fitzwilliam."

"Georgiana, would you accompany me to the parsonage to inform Mrs. Collins of the summons?" He smiled jovially, but he had a firm look in his eye that Georgiana knew would not brook opposition.

"Very well, Richard. I shall see you soon, Elizabeth." She squeezed Elizabeth's hand as she walked away with her cousin.

Elizabeth followed them with her eyes until they disappeared around a curve in the path, carefully avoiding looking at Mr. Darcy, who stood silently to her right a few feet away.

She began slowly walking in the opposite direction, looking over her shoulder slightly at Mr. Darcy, encouraging him to follow her.

Elizabeth had been through so many emotions over the past month she could not begin to name them all.

Her first impression of Darcy last autumn led her to believe he was haughty, arrogant, and unfeeling, all of which had been confirmed by Mr. Wickham. After finding out those stories were completely false and learning Darcy was actually blameless in his dealings with the man, she had gotten to know him better personally, as well as his family. She had become friends with him and had begun to feel a small regard for him, one that, if she was honest with herself, she knew had the potential to blossom into something much deeper.

And then everything had come crashing down around her when she heard what he really thought of her situation and family, and she learned he had been instrumental in separating Bingley from Jane. And then, in a mad plan to confound her, he brought Bingley back to Jane and was to stand up in their wedding! What was she to think?

Now, he clearly wished to speak with her, and she agreed it was probably a good idea to clear the air. She needed to tell him that she would not be visiting Pemberley that summer, or any summer. She could not bear it.

"Miss Bennet, we must speak." Darcy's voice was low and quiet, its intensity sending chills down her arms.

"Yes, Mr. Darcy, we should." She stopped on the path and turned to look up at him.

"Miss Elizabeth, I believe you overheard a conversation the night of my aunt's ball that you were never meant to hear; actually, a conversation that should never have been spoken."

She searched his eyes and saw nothing but honesty and sorrow there, so she decided to listen with an open mind and not to lose her temper, no matter how tempted she might be.

"Yes, I did," she said slowly.

"Miss Bennet, I must tell you how incredibly sorry I am to have caused you discomfort and pain. I should not have said such things to someone so wholly unconnected to you. I should not have been speaking of such things at all, especially in a ballroom. It was thoughtless and I can only beg your forgiveness." He looked at her earnestly, his deep eyes pleading with her. She nodded for him to continue.

"As for the matter of your sister and Bingley, please allow me to say I hold nothing against Miss Jane Bennet personally, and I believe she is very amiable and all that is good and kind."

Then why did you do what you did!? Elizabeth screamed internally, but outwardly she held her composure.

Darcy continued, "Bingley is a very dear friend. He is almost like a brother to me. I knew he felt strongly for Miss Bennet, but I thought he would get over her quickly as he had done in the past. Bingley is one who often fancies himself in love. What he felt for Miss Bennet was deeper than anything that came before, but I believed that he would recover as he always had.

"I watched your sister, knowing the neighborhood believed an engagement forthcoming, to ascertain her feelings for Bingley. She seemed to enjoy his company and accepted his attentions gladly, but she did not appear overly partial to him and seemed to be happy with everyone."

Elizabeth was breathing deeply to control her indignation and could feel her cheeks darkening. Darcy saw the fire in her eyes, but went on, "I must confess I did not know your sister well at the time and while I did not, and do not now, think her mercenary, I believed she would accept Bingley because of his position, whether she had a deep regard for him or not. I did not want my friend to be in a marriage where he was not loved. Bingley has a lively and giving disposition. He would give and give and give until he had nothing left, and years from now would be a shadow of his current self." He ran his hand over his face.

"I did not wish such a fate on my friend. I followed him to London at his sisters' bequest, and did not inform him of Miss Bennet's presence there, until last month, that is. I am disgusted with myself for the part I have played in this deception, for disguise of any sort is my abhorrence. That is why I must tell you one more thing." He took a deep breath and looked at Elizabeth's waiting face. Her eyes seemed to have softened, but her mouth was set in a grim line.

"When Bingley lamented not seeing Miss Bennet again, I convinced him that she did not care for him. He had believed she loved him." Elizabeth's eyes grew wide, but she listened silently. "Bingley trusts my judgment completely; it was not overly difficult. I was proud of my achievement, believing I had saved my friend from a terrible fate."

He began to pace in front of her.

"When I came home from the ball and found you were gone, it was one of the worst moments of my life." Elizabeth was surprised at the turn in his narration and watched as he continued to pace quickly. Four steps, turn. Four steps, turn. *Even in distress he is methodical.* Suddenly, she found herself stifling a small smile, but quickly returned to the seriousness the conversation demanded.

"After speaking with Georgiana and Richard, I realized you had overheard my conversation with Sir Malcolm, and I was filled with agony at the idea of you being hurt by me. I went to Gracechurch Street to find you – you weren't there." He stopped pacing and stood a few feet in front of her, looking into her face intently.

"I realized I must have been wrong about Miss Bennet, as you are too reasonable to be upset about my interference if she hadn't really loved him. That's when I went to Bingley and told him everything. He was not happy, but upon hearing that Miss Bennet still cared for him and was at that moment in London a mere thirty minute carriage ride away, he insisted we call on her immediately. Bingley forgave me and our friendship has survived." He looked deeply into her eyes and took both her hands in his larger ones.

"Miss Bennet, will our friendship survive this? Can you forgive me my arrogance?"

Elizabeth's mouth dropped open in surprise. She had not expected the proud Mr. Darcy to apologize in such a way. In fact, she hadn't been sure if he would apologize at all. She felt like he was *her* Mr. Darcy again; Mr. Darcy of the library, of the walk in the park, of the breakfast room. Not Mr.

Darcy of Netherfield, or of the ball, or of the assembly in Meryton.

Taking a deep breath, Elizabeth decided honesty was the best course.

"Mr. Darcy, I do not know what to say. You have wounded me, and my sister, deeply." His eyes darkened at her words. "Jane did not deserve your interference, and she would never tell a man she loved him if she did not mean it. She would not even imply it. She is all that is good and kind and gracious and forgiving. How could you do it?" She looked at him with dark, pain-filled eyes, pleading – begging him to explain his cruelty.

She released a breath. "I thought… I thought you… I thought you were…" She stammered, barely retaining her composure as weeks of emotional turmoil came to the surface.

Darcy had been prepared for her wrath, he had even steeled himself for her indifference, but he could not handle her disappointment in him. He lifted her hands to his chest and held them tightly to him.

"Miss Elizabeth, I am. I am who you thought me to be. At least I want to be, I believe I can be. I have made a grievous error and I will continue to seek your forgiveness. I was full of my own importance and was not thinking justly. I am seeking to correct that, and I fervently hope one day to win back your approval. Please, tell me we are friends again."

He looked pleadingly into her eyes and lifted her hands to his mouth, first one, and then the other, to bestow a gentle kiss on the back of each. Elizabeth was surprised by the desperation and depth of feeling in his voice. She lowered her eyes to the ground, not knowing how to respond in this intimate moment.

She was never one to stubbornly remain angry, and his sincerity was so clear that she felt her choler for him leaving her body. She began to relax her rigid stance.

"I forgive you, Mr. Darcy. We may be friends again."

His expression quickly changed into one of obvious relief, a wide smile making his eyes crinkle, and he kissed her hands again and released his held breath. "Miss Elizabeth! Thank you!"

Elizabeth released a nervous laugh and pulled her hands away, turning to continue their walk up the path. He moved to her side, but did not offer his arm, and they walked quietly for some time, occasionally speaking of lighter topics until they reached the parsonage.

Colonel Fitzwilliam and Georgiana were just on their way out.

"I wish we were staying together, Elizabeth!" Georgiana told her as she pulled her aside to say goodbye. "It is so much more fun getting ready for dinner with you instead of on my own."

"Georgiana! I believe you have become quite spoiled!" she teased her. "What color are you wearing tonight?"

Georgiana's eyes brightened. "I had thought I would wear my pink gown, with the yellow trim and a yellow ribbon in my hair." She looked hopefully at Elizabeth.

"Hmm. I was going to wear my yellow gown this evening. I believe I may be able to procure some pink ribbon from Charlotte." She smiled widely at her young friend.

Georgiana's glee was clear as she practically skipped away with her guardians.

CHAPTER 22

Elizabeth went inside to find a letter from her sister and another from her mother. She went to her room for privacy and settled onto the window seat to read.

18 March, 1812
Gardiner Residence
Gracechurch Street, London

Dear Lizzy,

I have so much to tell you! We have set a wedding date. It is to be the 4 of May. I know it is only a little over a month away, but Charles just received word that his cousin in Scarborough is to marry in the middle of June and wishes for Charles to stand up with him. Apparently they have been quite close since they were children. Charles had wanted to take me on a wedding tour to Scotland for a month, then on to Scarborough to meet his family there. If we waited until mid- or late May to wed, we would have to skip the tour, which neither of us wishes to do.

Oh, Lizzy! Everything is happening so fast! I have never been so excited in my life. I hope the change of plans does not cause too much trouble for you. I received a letter from mama informing me that she requires our presence at Longbourn a week before the wedding to make sure everything is in place. I know we are due to arrive in Hertfordshire at that time anyway, but I wondered if you might come to London earlier?

I have always envisioned shopping for my trousseau with my dearest Lizzy, and I cannot imagine doing it without you. I hate to ask you to cut your holiday short, but Charles made me promise to ask instead of silently fretting about it, as he calls it. He is so dear! Never has a man been so attentive to me. I feel every need I have is met before I know I have it. It is a most wonderful feeling to be so looked after! Please say you will come, dear Lizzy! I am lost without you!

Charles sends his greetings and says that if you cannot reach London on your own, he will gladly send a carriage to Kent for you. He also wishes me to tell you that should you wish to return later in the year to complete your holiday with Charlotte, you may do so at his expense. What a dear man he is!

I hope you can come in time, as I must begin shopping soon in order for everything to be ready before the wedding. Please come, Lizzy! I need my sister with me!

Yours affectionately,
Jane Bennet

P.S. Soon I will be signing Jane Bingley! Can you believe it? I must practice a new signature.

Elizabeth smiled at Jane's enthusiasm and reached for her mother's letter. They were rare and always short, or at least short on actual information. She was sure it would be filled with wedding plans and warehouse recommendations for their shopping expedition.

Dear Lizzy,

I am sure you have heard from Jane by now. She is to be married the 4 of May. A daughter married! And to such a rich and handsome man, too! And so agreeable! I always said he would come back for her. How could he not?

Now if only you would have accepted Mr. Collins, you would be married now and I would have two daughters married. What a foolish girl you are, Lizzy! Husbands do not grow on trees, you know! You must snatch them up when they become available – who knows when another may come round?

I shall need you and Jane to return to Hertfordshire a week before the wedding. There is so much to do! And you will have to have a new dress. I have sent word to your Aunt Gardiner, and she is expecting you. I am sure Charlotte won't mind – a sister's wedding is far more important than a visit to a friend! Mrs. Gardiner will take you shopping and remember what I told you Lizzy - you must give the men just a little something to tempt them, or they will not wish to see more! Mr. Bingley may have rich friends and cousins at the wedding and you want to make a good impression.

Your Mother

Elizabeth folded the letter with a shake of her head and tucked it in the drawer. Her mother would never change. At least there was some constancy in that, she thought with a small laugh.

After speaking to Charlotte about the necessary change in plans, she sat down at the little desk in the back parlor to pen her reply.

Dear Jane,

I am so pleased for you, dearest! You deserve every happiness in the world! I am only too happy to accommodate you, as I would be quite vexed if my favorite sister did all her wedding preparation without me. I have spoken with Charlotte, and I shall leave for London on the 7 of April. That will give us three weeks to shop and return to Longbourn in plenty of time for the wedding. I hope this plan is agreeable to you. I will write more soon.

Your sister,
Elizabeth Bennet

~

That night at Rosings, things were considerably less awkward. Darcy felt all the release of confession and was determined to enjoy this time with Elizabeth. He thought she had at some point felt something for him – he hoped he could revive it and make it grow. He set about his plan with precision and patience. He dressed carefully, purposefully wearing colors he knew Elizabeth favored. Colonel Fitzwilliam knew what he was about and was prepared to run interference with their aunt on his behalf.

If she could be won, he would win her.

When she arrived at Rosings, Elizabeth went straight to Georgiana's side. She wore the yellow dress from her first dinner in London, which did not escape Darcy's notice. She had a pearl pendant around her neck and her hair was twisted up in a style simple enough to do herself.

They sat in the parlor for half an hour before dinner, speaking comfortably, with Lady Catherine dominating the conversation. At dinner, Darcy sat on Lady Catherine's right, with a clear view of his cousin Anne directly in front of him. Colonel Fitzwilliam was next to Anne and Charlotte next to him. Georgiana was between Darcy and Elizabeth, with Mr. Collins on Elizabeth's right, across from Maria Lucas.

Poor Maria, she was so terrified of her surroundings and the threats from Mr. Collins that should she not behave properly, she would be sent home immediately, that she hardly said two sentences together, and those were to Charlotte. Mr. Collins took every opportunity to compliment Lady Catherine, Mr. Darcy, and Colonel Fitzwilliam, in that order, even though he was at the farthest end of the table.

Thankfully, Georgiana kept Elizabeth engaged in conversation most of the time, as Darcy was trapped speaking to his aunt, so she was able, for the most part, to avoid conversation with Mr. Collins. She took the opportunity to tell her friend of her change in plans.

"How long were you intending to stay at Rosings?" she asked quietly.

"I believe we are set to depart the first week of April, but I do not know the date exactly. Perhaps you could travel with us?"

"Perhaps. I will have to see if there is a post chaise available and if our dates align. We will speak more about it later."

After dinner, they retired to the drawing room where Lady Catherine insisted Elizabeth play for them. Glad to get away from the dominated conversation, she moved to the instrument with alacrity. Georgiana quickly stood and followed her, offering to turn the pages. A few minutes later, Colonel Fitzwilliam joined them.

She played for them the remainder of the evening, conversing with Colonel Fitzwilliam when possible, occasionally laughing at his jokes, while Lady Catherine was content to be worshiped by Mr. Collins and listened to by her favorite nephew. She criticized Elizabeth's playing multiple times, stating loudly that she would never be truly proficient if she did not practice more, and that she knew Mrs. Collins had no instrument, but she was welcome to play in the housekeeper's room. She declared she would be in nobody's way in that part of the house.

Elizabeth merely smiled and thanked her for her concern, and continued to play as Colonel Fitzwilliam made jokes about and did rough imitations of his aunt behind the cover of the pianoforte, much to the amusement of Elizabeth and Georgiana. She played until it was time to leave, said goodbye to her friends, and boarded the carriage to the parsonage.

~

Friday and Saturday passed by uneventfully, except for the call paid each morning on the ladies of the parsonage by the guests of Rosings Park. Not being formed for ill humor, Elizabeth quickly regained most of her natural ease with Darcy, except for the occasional flash of resentment when she thought too much about what he did and said about her family, but she could usually talk herself down fairly quickly.

Sometimes, she caught him giving her dark looks. They were reminiscent of the way he had looked at her in Hertfordshire, when she had thought he was searching for fault in her. Now, she thought he might be looking for something else entirely.

After church on Sunday, Lady Catherine invited the Collinses and their guests to dine at Rosings. This time, Elizabeth was seated next to Charlotte, on the opposite side of the table from Darcy and Georgiana and as far from Lady Catherine as possible. The message was clear: she had been demoted. Relieved the great lady didn't seem to be interested in quizzing her any longer, Elizabeth happily ate her dinner in quiet conversation with Charlotte.

After dinner, they sat down to play cards. They made up two tables, Mr. Collins, Lady Catherine, Mr. Darcy, and Anne de Bourgh at one table, Colonel Fitzwilliam, Charlotte, Elizabeth and Georgiana at the other. Maria Lucas was sitting out. The gentlemen were about to sit down, when Colonel Fitzwilliam asked Darcy to switch places with him, as he had something he wished to discuss with Lady Catherine. Darcy gladly obliged him and the games began.

"Fitzwilliam! What is it you need to speak to me of?" Lady Catherine demanded in a loud voice.

Maintaining both his volume and his humor, the Colonel asked her, "I wanted to know if you and Anne were planning a holiday to Bath this spring."

"A holiday? To Bath?"

"Yes."

"That is all? That is your important discussion?"

"Are you? Planning a holiday that is?" Colonel Fitzwilliam looked at her sincerely, awaiting an answer to his question.

Lady Catherine was not pleased. "No, we are certainly not planning a holiday to Bath. Whatever could make you ask such an insipid question?"

"I hear Bath is very nice this time of year. I was simply inquiring, that is all. Mother spoke of taking a short trip there later in the season."

"Humph! Of course she would! She always had more time than sense," she said derisively.

The Colonel merely smiled, knowing full well the extent of the feud between Lady Matlock and Lady Catherine. He was never one to brag, but he did believe his mother was winning.

"Oh, dear!" Elizabeth said quietly. She screwed her mouth up in concentration as she looked at her cards.

"Is everything alright, Miss Bennet?"

"Yes, quite, thank you, Mr. Darcy." She looked down, embarrassed she had spoken aloud.

"I do not know why everyone plays this game! I do not see what is so intriguing about it." Georgiana sighed as she made her play.

"I believe many look forward to what they may win," Charlotte answered her with a smile as she made a winning play.

"Perhaps you do not have a very competitive nature, Georgiana," offered Elizabeth.

"You may be right. I confess I have never cared for games where points are counted and the whole object is to win. If the game is not enjoyable in and of itself, why bother? There is more than the score to consider."

"Very wise words for one so young," said Charlotte.

"Very wise, indeed! What have you been reading, Georgiana?" asked Darcy in a teasing voice.

Elizabeth and Charlotte laughed, and Georgiana flushed and kept her eyes on her cards.

"Leave her alone, Mr. Darcy! She is quite right, after all!" Elizabeth smiled at Darcy, a familiar twinkle in her eye. He understood her perfectly. *That is the first time she has teased me since the ball,* he thought.

Darcy's mood only elevated from there, in direct correlation to his aunt's declining one. She did not like Darcy sitting away from her and Anne, especially when he appeared to be having a good time, much too good a time, and in the company of Elizabeth Bennet! She did not like how he smiled at her. And she did not like Fitzwilliam's ridiculous questions. This was what happened when you put men in the army; they became absolute imbeciles!

As the game wore on, Georgiana became more comfortable with Charlotte and began to speak more, to the delight of her brother. Elizabeth teased Darcy a few more times, always smiling at him as she did so, and he felt he had made definite progress.

~

25 March, 1812
Matlock House
London

Dear Miss Bennet,

I hope you will not mind, but Georgiana has informed me that you will be returning to London earlier than expected to shop for your sister's wedding clothes. I wish to issue an invitation for you to stay at Matlock House. It will be an excellent opportunity for us to get to know one another better, and if you are set on spending this time with your sister, please consider her included in the invitation. I would be happy to assist in the shopping, with your aunt of course. I found both your sister and aunt quite pleasant when I met them at Darcy House. As you know, I have no daughters, so preparing for a wedding would be very entertaining for me. I hope to receive your acceptance letter soon. I shall send my carriage to Kent for you if it is required, you need only let me know.

Sincerely,
Lady Matlock

Elizabeth smiled and shook her head as she refolded the letter. Lady Matlock really wasn't so different from her mother. Wealthier and better mannered, and definitely less shrill, but still just as determined to marry her off. At least Lady Matlock cared whether she liked the man she married.

The last few days had been very pleasant. She had visited each morning with Georgiana and the gentlemen, and often Georgiana would stay with Elizabeth while the men toured their aunt's estate. They had even all taken an open carriage ride around the neighboring countryside.

Colonel Fitzwilliam and Mr. Darcy had delighted in showing her and Georgiana all the sights and describing where they had been thrown by horses or played as children. Fitzwilliam was an excellent storyteller, as Darcy had promised, though she wondered if his stories were entirely factual. On more than one occasion, she had seen Darcy shaking his head or covering his eyes with his hand.

The parsonage had not been invited back to Rosings, but were expecting an invitation Sunday, as was the usual custom. Elizabeth and Darcy were nearly back to their previous level of comfort, even though there was the occasional moment of awkwardness.

It had been arranged that Elizabeth would ride back to London with Georgiana, Darcy, and Fitzwilliam on the seventh of April. She had joked that she had been offered so many carriages she was tempted to ride alone for greater comfort.

Only the Colonel had laughed.

~

Easter Sunday quickly approached and Mr. Collins was all aflutter as he ran through the house, ordering the ladies to dress faster and pin their hair quicker. Lady Catherine would not appreciate them being late, especially on 'such a sacred holiday'.

They were in fact quite early, and Elizabeth found herself wishing she had something to do as she waited inside the cold church. The sermon was dull and predictable, but blessedly short. Afterward, Mr. Collins rushed to the door to greet the parishioners as they left. When Lady Catherine walked past, he groveled obsequiously and wished her a happy Easter, to which she replied with a slight nod and an invitation to dinner. Mr. Collins was effusive in his thanks, and would have continued some time longer had Lady Catherine not walked away towards her carriage.

When they arrived back at the parsonage, an express rider was just coming into the lane.

"Express for Miss Bennet."

"I am Miss Bennet." Elizabeth took the letter as Charlotte gave the rider a few coins. She rolled her eyes in disgust when she saw the hopeful, wide-eyed expression on Mr. Collins's face. Elizabeth said a silent prayer that her father was well and broke the seal. Seeing three pairs of eyes on her, she excused herself to her bedroom.

28 March, 1812
Longbourn
Hertfordshire

Oh Lizzy! Why did you not tell me Lady Matlock had taken a liking to you? She has just sent a letter informing me of her invitation for you to stay at her townhouse! Think of all the men you will meet! Her eldest son is still single! And he has a title! Oh my Lizzy! Think how grand you will be!

Remember not to talk too much and try not to be impertinent. Men do not like wild women who roam the countryside alone and disagree with everything they say. Your father has consented to buy you two new gowns - your Aunt Gardiner will take care of it. Do not be a burden and make yourself agreeable. Oh Lizzy, how clever you are! Lady Matlock is a powerful friend indeed! Mind your manners and remember to give the gentlemen something to wonder about, but maintain your mystery. You must write soon and tell us of all the people you meet! Especially the gentlemen! Do try to find a handsome one, dear – they are so much more pleasant to look at.

Your Mother,
Frances Bennet

Elizabeth leaned back against the pillows. Only her mother would consider courting advice worthy of an express. She rang for a cup of tea and decided to take a much needed nap before going to Rosings. She asked the maid to inform Charlotte and Mr. Collins that all was well; her mother had just had something important to tell her, and not to worry. *Or rejoice*, she thought uncharitably. She lay down on the bed and relaxed, letting the sound of the newly falling rain lull her to sleep.

At Rosings, Darcy was preparing for an enjoyable evening. He had seen Elizabeth every day for well over a week. She seemed to have fully forgiven him and even looked happy to see him. However, she also looked happy to see Georgiana and Colonel Fitzwilliam. He had been maintaining a respectful distance while at Rosings or on the grounds to avoid angering his aunt, but when he was out he tried to pay more attention to her, and was livelier than usual, due largely to the fact that he was already comfortable with his cousin and sister.

After spending an inordinate amount of time preparing, he headed downstairs to meet their guests. Because of the rain, Lady Catherine had sent her carriage. He met them in the parlor, and quickly noticed Elizabeth was missing. His brow furrowing worriedly, he quietly asked Charlotte if Miss Bennet was ill.

"Not at all, Mr. Darcy. She will be along shortly."

Darcy was clearly confused as he looked out the window at the falling rain and wondered how she was going to arrive without a carriage. She couldn't possibly be expected to walk in this weather!

Darcy stepped toward the door quietly and snuck out before his aunt noticed. He quickly ran down the stairs to the entry, intending to seek out a footman to see if the carriage was being sent back for Elizabeth, when he was arrested mid-stride by a figure in the cloak room on his right.

Elizabeth had been sleeping deeply, thanks in large part to the steady beating of the rain, and had woken moments before they were to leave for Rosings. Mr. Collins pounded on her door, demanding she "be downstairs in three minutes", for the carriage would not wait.

Elizabeth leapt out of bed and looked around her darkened room, barely able to see the clock. Holding up a candle, she realized it was late in the afternoon, and she had slept nearly three hours. She quickly changed her dress and called for Maria to button her up the back.

There were still two buttons to go when Mr. Collins ran down the hall, grabbed Maria by the elbow and propelled her toward the stairs, yelling at Elizabeth over his shoulder, "We must not keep Lady Catherine waiting. Come now, Cousin, make haste!"

Swallowing the retort begging to leap out of her mouth, she grabbed a brush and stuffed a handful of pins into her reticule, and rushed down the stairs and into the waiting carriage. Luckily, she had put her shoes on already, or she would not have made it. The carriage lurched into motion before she was seated. *I wonder if he realizes Lady Catherine is not actually in the carriage, and probably would not notice the difference of a few minutes.*

Once at Rosings, an embarrassed Elizabeth stepped into the cloak room to fix her hair while the rest of the party headed upstairs to the drawing room. There, Darcy found her. He stood to the side where he was not easily visible and watched her brushing her long tresses in front of the mirror, her head tilted to one side.

Her hair was thick and full, with large waves that curled up at the ends. It reached almost to her waist and the deep brown color was rich and warm in the candlelight. Piece by piece, she brushed, twirled, and pinned, until all of it was piled atop her head.

Darcy stood mesmerized, watching her. He found it incredibly intimate and completely intoxicating. Realizing he was overstepping all bounds of propriety and invading her privacy, he stepped back and turned around, acting as if he had just arrived.

"Miss Bennet," he called as she came out of the cloak room, "I was just looking for you."

"Then you seem to have found what you were searching for," she replied with a smile. *I daresay I have*, he thought.

"May I escort you to the parlor?" He held out his arm.

She took it and asked, "You do not wish to know what I am doing down here all by myself?" She gave him a teasing smile.

Darcy blushed, wondering if she knew he'd been watching her. "Only if you wish to tell me, Miss Bennet."

She looked at him as if she were trying to make up her mind about something. "Very well. Mr. Collins cannot bear to keep Lady Catherine waiting, so I was forced to rush out before I was completely ready. I am afraid I took a nap this afternoon and slept longer than I planned. I woke up less than five minutes before we left." She smiled guiltily, which Darcy found more than usually endearing.

He smiled teasingly. "Mr. Collins would not wait for you?"

"I'm afraid not, and as I did not wish to miss an evening with friends, I came half-prepared. Are you very shocked, Mr. Darcy?" She raised one brow mischievously.

"Not at all, Miss Bennet. You would have been greatly missed, so I can only be happy you chose to come, regardless of your level of preparation. And I must say you look rather impressive."

"For dressing in five minutes you mean?" She laughed.

Darcy chuckled and turned his head sideways to look at her. He stopped walking half way up the stairs. "Uh, Miss Bennet, pardon me, but I believe you are missing a few buttons."

She looked at him quizzically as he gestured toward her back. She reached her free arm up and behind and felt the top of her dress. She blushed scarlet as she realized her top two buttons were unfastened. Elizabeth looked down and refused to meet Mr. Darcy's eye, silently cursing Maria and Mr. Collins and wondering how she was going to fix this before anyone else saw. Was coming without her hair done not bad enough?

"Please, allow me." Mr. Darcy released her arm and reached behind her, fastening one, and then the other button. If Elizabeth hadn't already been the color of a tomato, she would have quickly resembled one. The skin at the base of her neck tingled as chills flared up the length of her spine. Darcy's hands seemed to linger slightly longer than necessary, and when he was finished, their eyes met. They stared at each other for a long moment, barely breathing, neither saying a word.

A door closed loudly somewhere above them and they started, quickly remembering where they were. He offered his arm again, and they climbed the remainder of the stairs silently.

Darcy led Elizabeth to a seat in the parlor next to Georgiana and moved to the other side of the room. His aunt was speaking loudly to him, saying something about how he should come sit next to Anne, but her words barely registered. He stood looking out the window, his back to the room, his hands clasped behind him.

The way she looked at me, he thought, *she must feel something, she must!* Darcy relived every moment of their brief encounter. The way the light had played in her hair as she brushed it, the flush on her face when she realized her buttons were undone, the way her skin had reacted when he touched her, and the minutes they spent staring at each other on the stairs. He did not know how long it was, only that it was not long enough. She had seemed so open to him, as if she was his for the taking.

He'd nearly declared himself on the spot.

He had kept a respectful distance throughout the visit, not wanting to rush her and desiring to be sure of her complete forgiveness. He wanted nothing between them, and was willing to be patient and wait for her to regain trust in him.

They were called to dinner, and once again, Elizabeth sat at the far end of the table next to Charlotte, completely ignored by Lady Catherine. The meal was not overlong and they retired to the drawing room.

Lady Catherine sat on her throne in the center, Mr. Collins humbly worshiping at her feet. Usually, Darcy would sit near his aunt and away from Miss Bennet, partially to give Elizabeth space, but also because it was proper to give his aunt her due attention – he was her guest after all. But tonight, he quickly sat next to Elizabeth, causing Colonel Fitzwilliam to spring into action. Fitzwilliam sat near Lady Catherine and began to speak to her of music in an attempt to distract her from Darcy's nearness to Elizabeth.

Darcy and Elizabeth spoke of nothing in particular, but he sat a little closer to her than was usual, and did not often include Georgiana or Charlotte in the conversation, though they were near enough to be involved.

Charlotte was a shrewd woman, and she saw what was happening in front of her. She decided to give them as much privacy as possible by trying to facilitate conversation between Georgiana and Maria, which was stilted but progressing.

"Miss Bennet, tomorrow I have some estate matters to see to for my aunt, but Tuesday I shall be free all day. There is a ruin nearby that I believe you would enjoy seeing. Would you allow me to show it to you?"

"Of course, Mr. Darcy, I should like that very much."

They talked about their plans for the week, and eventually Elizabeth was asked to play. Darcy rose with her and escorted her to the pianoforte, and then sat down beside her, ready to turn the pages. Elizabeth's expression showed her surprise at his uncommon actions, but she maintained her ease and looked at him with a smile.

"What shall I play, sir?"

Darcy looked through the music, and choosing one he had always thought she played particularly well, he placed the music on the stand and resumed his seat. Usually, Darcy was a meticulous man, known for paying attention to details and maintaining his focus. He followed the music, intending to turn the pages at the correct moment, but he found being next to Elizabeth too distracting, and soon the time came to turn the page, and Darcy merely sat watching her, without the slightest idea of where she was in the song.

Finally, Elizabeth looked over at him and gestured with her head to the music stand. He quickly jumped up and turned the page, his arm and entire left side brushing against her as he did so. Elizabeth hoped no one noticed that she played the same chord progression three times through while waiting on him, or that she made a rather obvious mistake when he brushed against her.

He sat back down, ready to pay attention, but a few bars in, he was lost again. Elizabeth leaned toward him. "Shall I signal you when it's time to turn the page?" she whispered, intending to help. She wondered if he couldn't read music, but then why would he offer to turn the pages?

Slightly embarrassed, he answered her quietly, "Thank you, Miss Bennet. That would be helpful."

She nodded and continued to play, tilting her head to him when it was time to turn the page. Darcy quickly got over his embarrassment when he realized this method would allow him to watch her face without restraint or fear of discovery. At the end of the song, she turned to him with a smile.

"My fingers await your orders, sir."

"I've always liked this one, Miss Bennet."

Elizabeth looked at the song, noticing it was the same one she had performed at Lucas Lodged all those months ago. He had asked her to play it more than once in London, but she had thought nothing of it before. Now her mind was alight with suspicion.

She continued to play for another half hour, Darcy never relinquishing his position.

When the evening was over, Darcy walked them to the carriage and handed Elizabeth in, giving her hand a small squeeze before he released it. She smiled sweetly at him, and then she was gone.

CHAPTER 23

"Charlotte, whatever is the matter?"

It was Monday morning, and Elizabeth was in the back parlor writing to Jane when Charlotte entered, looking flustered and wringing her hands in front of her.

"Lizzy, I fear I have bad news."

"What is it?"

"Mr. Collins has just returned from Rosings, where he was meeting with Lady Catherine." Charlotte paused and took a deep breath. "It would seem that her ladyship is unhappy with you, Lizzy."

"With me? Whatever for?"

"She believes you are distracting Mr. Darcy's attention away from Miss de Bourgh."

"What? Is that what she said?"

"Not in exactly those words."

Elizabeth squinted and looked closely at Charlotte. "Charlotte, we are friends, you and I. Come, tell me what was said. I assure you I can handle it."

"Oh Lizzy, I am so sorry! Lady Catherine believes you are purposely trying to entrap Mr. Darcy into a compromising situation so that he will be forced to marry you. She called you a," Charlotte lowered her voice and leaned forward, "a common trollop. I am so sorry, Lizzy!"

Elizabeth released a short laugh and looked at her friend with relief. "Oh, Charlotte! I've never been called that before, but I shall not let Lady Catherine upset me! If that is all, I am not worried. Charlotte? Is that all?" Elizabeth's voice began to sound worried as Charlotte's face paled.

"Lizzy," she was so quiet Elizabeth had to move closer to hear her, "she demands that you leave immediately. She says she will not allow her family to be near such a one as you. I am so sorry, but Mr. Collins will not disagree with her. I'm afraid you must go." She hung her head as she said the last line, clearly mortified of her friend's treatment. "Immediately."

Elizabeth stood still and looked at Charlotte for a moment, not sure what to say. She had never been asked to leave anywhere in her life before, and wasn't exactly sure what the protocol for behavior was. She decided you can never go wrong with a dignified exit, so she held her head up and took Charlotte by the hand.

"It's alright, Charlotte. This is not your fault. Do not worry, I won't hold this against you." She squeezed her friend's hands. "Now, would you like to help me pack?"

Charlotte gave her a weak smile and they headed upstairs to Elizabeth's room, requesting her trunk on the way. Within two hours, Elizabeth's trunk was fully packed, a basket of food prepared for her journey by cook, and Mr. Collins had returned with passage for the post chaise.

The trunk was being loaded onto Mr. Collins's wagon to be taken to the village when a large carriage pulled up. Mr. Darcy quickly leapt out and directed the footman to load Miss Bennet's trunk onto his carriage.

Darcy greeted Mr. and Mrs. Collins and asked to speak privately with Miss Bennet for a moment. Mr. Collins was about to object when Charlotte stepped in and pulled him toward the house.

"Miss Bennet, I'm beginning to think you dislike my carriage. Please, if it is in some way deficient, I beg you to tell me so I may correct the issue." He smiled good-humoredly.

Elizabeth couldn't stop herself from smiling slightly. "I assure you it is nothing of the kind, Mr. Darcy. I seem to have found myself in need of a quick departure, that is all."

He looked uncomfortably toward Rosings. "Yes, I heard about my aunt's interview with Mr. Collins. How can I ever make amends for such behavior?"

"It was not you who did it, Mr. Darcy."

"Yes, but I am partially to blame." He looked at her quickly and back to the parsonage. "I understand you were to stay with my aunt, Lady Matlock, when you returned to town next week?"

"Yes, that was the plan, but now that I am arriving early, I will go first to my Aunt and Uncle Gardiner's. I do not wish to inconvenience Lady Matlock."

"I hope you do not mind, Miss Bennet, but I have taken the liberty of sending an express to my aunt in London. She will be ready for you when you arrive. Hannah is waiting in the carriage and will accompany you. I cannot allow you to ride post, Miss Bennet."

Elizabeth was too tired to argue, the rush of the last few hours having more effect on her than she would like to admit.

"Very well, Mr. Darcy."

"I am sorry we cannot leave with you today, but there is still some work to be done on the estate and we would not be ready in time, anyway. We may be able to leave at the end of week if the weather holds, and Colonel Fitzwilliam and I are efficient in our duties. Otherwise, we won't return until the seventh, as planned."

"I see. Then I will hope for clear skies for you." She smiled and stepped toward the house to say goodbye to Charlotte.

She hugged Maria and told her she would see her soon in Hertfordshire, curtseyed to Mr. Collins while avoiding eye contact, lest she say something regrettable, and finally came to Charlotte. The two friends embraced and promised to write, and when they released each other, Elizabeth saw tears glistening in Charlotte's eyes. *You may be secure, dear Charlotte, but you are not happy.* Elizabeth tried not to think about her dear friend's ridiculous husband and overbearing neighbor, and said a silent prayer that a true friend for Charlotte would emerge in Kent.

Elizabeth walked to the carriage, stopping just outside the door to curtsey to Mr. Darcy. He bowed over her hand and kissed it lightly. Though she couldn't feel much through her gloves, a heat moved through her hand up her arm.

"Safe journey, Miss Elizabeth." He smiled into her eyes and handed her into the carriage, squeezing her hand gently before he let go.

"Goodbye, Mr. Darcy," she said softly.

~

"How did Miss Bennet handle being sent off?" Colonel Fitzwilliam asked Darcy as they rode over the fields of Rosings, checking the drainage systems.

"She seemed to be fine. Mrs. Collins was not happy about it – she looked quite mortified, as she should be. What kind of person demands that a guest of another house be sent away?"

"Lady Catherine, that's who. I had a feeling this would happen. It's why I packed so lightly." Darcy gave him a look. "Well, she was bound to notice eventually, Darcy," he said with a shrug.

Darcy nodded. "The worst of it was that insipid parson. How anyone can stand to be around him is beyond me."

"What did he do now?"

"He had the nerve to tell me that I should have let Miss Bennet ride post, that Lady Catherine would be 'displeased' with my interference in an affair that was none of my concern." Darcy's face was twisted in disdain.

"Good God! He actually told you it was none of your concern?"

"Not so succinctly, but he eventually came out with something to that effect. He had the gall to tell me I should remove myself as quickly as possible so as not to encourage his cousin in her scheming! Can you believe it? Intolerable man!"

Colonel Fitzwilliam laughed loudly. "That is rich! To think that she would be trapping you! If they only knew you'd be too happy to be found in a compromising position and be forced to marry her. Oh, you'd love that!" The colonel guffawed loudly, slapping his knee.

Darcy glared at him. "Thank you, Richard. I'm glad to know you think so highly of me," Darcy said sarcastically as he looked away from his cousin and across the fields.

"Oh lighten up, old man! From the looks of it, it won't be long before we're hearing an announcement. Am I right?"

"We shall see, Fitzwilliam, we shall see."

~

They weren't the only ones thinking of Mr. Collins. As Elizabeth rode in the carriage, she thought over what he had said. The nerve of that man! What made him think he had the right to accuse her of such behavior?

He had suggested that she would never be invited to Rosings again, which he was sure she must feel deeply, but perhaps Lady Catherine would forgive her if she apologized and was properly humble. He spoke of Lady Catherine's condescension and rank, and how someone of her standing need not even acknowledge Elizabeth, and that she should feel honored by even the slightest of attentions.

Elizabeth fumed as she remembered Mr. Collins's words. "Cousin Elizabeth, it would be reaching incomprehensibly beyond you to attempt an alliance with a man such as Mr. Darcy. Of course, having refused the most generous offer you are ever likely to receive, and now having angered the house of de Bourgh, you cannot expect to marry at all."

Her only response had been a fiery stare.

Mr. Collins had gone on to say it was brazen of her to presume to importune Mr. Darcy so, and while he was in the company of Miss de Bourgh, and that surely, if he had encouraged her, which Mr. Collins was sure he had not, as Mr. Darcy, the nephew of his esteemed patroness, Lady Catherine de Bourgh, was an honorable gentleman and would never encourage one such as she beyond her station, he only did so out of politeness and a desire not to hurt her feminine sensibilities by pointing out her insolence in attempting to seduce him.

If Charlotte had not quickly ushered her husband out of the room, Elizabeth was not sure what she would have done. Insufferable, ridiculous, pompous man!

Charlotte had told her she would try to curb his tongue and keep him from spreading word of her dismissal. She felt it was the least she could do. Elizabeth was not worried overmuch. The only acquaintance they had in common was her father, and she knew he would only find amusement in the occurrence and wouldn't believe anything he said about her. Besides, Lady Catherine was certain to tell him not to mention it to anyone. She would not want the names of Darcy or de Bourgh sullied by unsavory gossip.

CHAPTER 24

Darcy stormed silently into his aunt's private sitting room.

"I would like a word with you, Lady Catherine."

She sipped her tea delicately, taking a full two minutes to reply. She sighed in an annoyed fashion. "Very well. I shall meet you in the study in twenty minutes."

Darcy strode out of the room silently without another glance in her direction.

Colonel Fitzwilliam saw his cousin walking past and quietly followed him down the stairs. Seeing Darcy disappear into Sir Lewis's study, he quickly returned upstairs.

"Come in," Georgiana called in response to the knock on her door.

"Come, poppet, you don't want to miss the show!"

"Richard, what are you talking about?" she asked in bewilderment.

"Your brother and our aunt are about to have a conversation in the study and I, for one, do not intend to miss it. Now come on!"

Georgiana leapt up from her seat and hurried to join Richard, who was already walking down the hall. They made their way down the stairs without making a sound and stopped just outside the study door. Fitzwilliam dismissed the footmen nearby and then sat on the floor, his long legs stretched out in front of him.

"What are you doing?" Georgiana whispered.

"I'm sitting. I suspect this will be interesting and long, and I am tired." He reached a hand up to her. "Come, poppet, sit down. No one will see you sitting on the floor. And if they do, I shall tell them you fainted."

Georgiana made a face and sat heavily by her cousin. "Thank you, Richard." She crossed her arms over her ribs. "And I do not faint!"

The colonel chuckled and signaled her to be quiet when he heard his aunt entering from the door in the next corridor.

"What is this about, Darcy?" Lady Catherine asked imperiously.

"The way you behaved toward Miss Bennet today was unacceptable," he said coldly, standing behind the desk with his hands clasped firmly behind his back.

She sniffed and looked away.

"She is a close friend of Georgiana's, as well as a friend of mine and Fitzwilliam's. In addition, she is Mrs. Collins's particular friend and guest, and Mr. Collins's cousin. Even one of these connections would make your behavior today completely objectionable, but Miss Bennet's relationship to so many in your immediate vicinity makes it unthinkable."

"Really, Darcy, when did you become so dramatic? Miss Bennet is no one, a poor relation, and a *distraction*." She spoke with her head held high, her back ramrod straight in the seat in front of the desk.

Darcy clenched his jaw and breathed in deeply through his nose. He could feel the muscles around his lips twitching and his eyes widening in anger, and he schooled himself to remain calm. A gentleman did not lose his temper with an aunt thirty years his senior.

"She was not your guest to dismiss, and you know it."

"Collins is my parson and required to do as I bid."

"He is a parson, not a servant!"

She flicked her wrist as if the difference was unimportant to her and kept her eyes on the carpet, giving her a false look of modesty.

"You cannot have everyone in the country sent away who does not bow to your every whim. You are too old to be acting like a spoiled child," Darcy spat quietly.

Lady Catherine's eyes shot up to meet his, her lips pursed in dissatisfaction. "I should have known you were no better than the rest of them. You are only a man, you do not have the ability to control yourself, but she," Lady Catherine nodded sagely, "she knew exactly what she was doing. Fluffing her feathers and shaking her tail for you! It was disgraceful!"

"Miss Bennet did no such thing," he replied quietly, his voice deceptively calm, but strong.

"That she had the audacity to flaunt herself in front of Anne, knowing the two of you are engaged – it was shameful. If you would hurry up and do your duty to Anne, I wouldn't have had to send her away."

Darcy ran a hand over his face and let out a stifled groan. "Lady Catherine, when have I ever given you the impression that I wish to marry Anne? For that matter, when has Anne ever said she wishes to marry me?"

"Anne knows her duty," Lady Catherine snapped. "And you know it was the desire of your mother for you to marry Anne. We spoke of it when you were children, barely out of your cradles."

"I told you years ago, I will not marry Anne."

Again, Lady Catherine flicked her wrist and looked towards the dark window.

"Lady Catherine, I tell you now, I will not marry Anne. Not now, not ever," Darcy said clearly.

Her eyes flashed and she glared at her nephew. "How dare you! You would deny the wishes of all your family, of your departed mother, and for what? For some bit of muslin from Hertfordshire?"

"Miss Bennet is a lady, a gentleman's daughter. And my mother never said any such thing! It is your wish, and your wish alone! It's time to quit pretending."

By now, both voices were raised and Georgiana and Colonel Fitzwilliam looked at each other with raised brows from their place in the hall.

"This is nonsense! You were formed for each other! Anne is perfect for you in every way!"

"Really? And what ways are those?" he asked with sarcasm.

"She is of noble lineage. She is the heiress of Rosings! She is more accomplished than a dozen Miss Bennets!"

"Really? And just what is Anne accomplished at? Is she a good dancer? Does she have a lovely singing voice? Can she play well?" Lady Catherine began to shake with rage as Darcy's voice became louder and more derisive. "She has no talent, no conversation, and barely an education."

Lady Catherine did not respond, but only stared coldly at him as her face went pale with anger.

"And whose fault is that, Lady Catherine? You have completely isolated her, filled her head with nonsense about moving to Pemberley to be my wife. She is completely unsuitable for the job and more importantly, she is not strong enough to be a proper mistress OR a proper wife! She would never be able to bear a child, as you well know. Marrying her to anyone would be giving her a death sentence, and yet to get what you want, you will stop at nothing. How can you be so callous to your own child?"

"You insolent boy! There is nothing wrong with Anne! She would make a perfect mistress and wife. It is clear that you will say anything to shirk your duty. You are without honor, without loyalty, and have no respect for your familial responsibilities! I am ashamed of you!" She was standing, leaning over the desk as she berated her nephew.

"*You* are ashamed of *me*?" Darcy let out a barking laugh that left his aunt speechless and wide eyed. "You, ashamed of me!" He smiled and shook his head, wondering if it was Elizabeth's influence that allowed him to see the absurdity in his aunt's words. "No Aunt, today, it is I who am ashamed of you," he said seriously.

Her face flushed red and she sank down to her chair.

Darcy continued, "Not only have you behaved appallingly to Miss Bennet and the Collinses, but you have used your own daughter for selfish gain, without thought to her happiness or even her health. What did you think would happen? Did you think you would eventually wear me down? That I would marry Anne and take her off to Pemberley, only to have her die after the first harsh winter, or worse, in childbirth?"

Lady Catherine looked away in an attempt to hide her guilty expression.

"Yes, that is what I thought. I know the will. Sir Lewis left the estate to Anne to pass on to her child. But if Anne never has a child? Well, if she dies without an heir, the estate reverts to the DeBourghs. And what if Anne passed before you? With the state of her health, it would not be surprising. You would be cast out, sent to the dowager's house and replaced by a new mistress of Rosings." He walked slowly to her side of the desk, his voice soft but with a dangerous edge.

"You just couldn't stand the loss of control, could you? You knew I would want to stay at Pemberley. Were we to marry, Anne would naturally move there. And you would remain here, queen of the castle. With any luck, Anne would give you a grandchild and your future as Mistress of Rosings would be secure."

Lady Catherine did not move. She looked straight ahead of her, her gaze never wavering from the landscape behind the desk. Her hands were folded neatly in her lap, one ankle tucked behind the other underneath her chair.

"Or did you think you would eventually gain control of Pemberley as well? How far did your little plan extend?" Her lips pursed almost unnoticed. "Ah, but I know more than you think I do, dear Aunt."

Her eyes snapped to him, then squinted in question.

"Yes, I know your little secret."

"What are you talking about?" she asked in a haughty tone.

In the hall, Georgiana looked to Fitzwilliam with wide eyes. He merely shook his head and gestured for them to continue listening.

Darcy sat down and leaned back in the desk chair. "When you were younger, you had your heart set on marrying George Darcy, heir to Pemberley. But he was never interested. So you married Sir Lewis instead, and then George married your little sister. You hated my mother. Everything you've said about knowing her wishes is a lie."

"How dare you! I was the better choice! ME! He should have chosen me! Anne was a weakling! How many stillbirths were there? How many miscarriages? She only gave him two children in fourteen years, and then she died and left him alone." Her voice was venomous and her expression was twisted like a knot in a rope.

Darcy went pale, then flushed a bright red. "Tomorrow, I will speak to your steward. A secretary will be hired and all important questions and information will be forwarded to Lord Matlock. I will finish what I started here, out of respect for the family, and then I and Georgiana will go back to London and not return. You shall not see either of us until you apologize for what you said about my mother and your ridiculous behavior towards Miss Bennet." He rose and stretched to his full height. "We're finished here. Good night, Lady Catherine."

His aunt spluttered and turned to watch him go, her protests falling on deaf ears. Before they could get away, Darcy opened the side door and nearly tripped over Colonel Fitzwilliam. He stopped for a moment to look at his sister and cousin, then stalked upstairs.

CHAPTER 25

Elizabeth's first few days at Matlock House were pleasantly spent. Lady Matlock was correct in assuming the sisters would want to be together, and Jane was quickly moved into the room next to Elizabeth's. Each morning, they would have breakfast with Lord and Lady Matlock, occasionally joined by Cyril, who was hardly ever there, and then the ladies would go shopping with Mrs. Gardiner.

Mrs. Gardiner and Lady Matlock were friendly to each other, and the four of them spent many happy hours looking at lace and fabric and choosing dresses that flattered Jane's coloring and figure.

Jane wanted to wear green for the wedding, but was convinced by the others that blue was more appealing on her and brought out her eyes. They settled on a decadent pattern to be done in blue with green trim and embellishments. Lady Matlock had gotten them in to see her rather exclusive modiste, who was to make the wedding gown. Mrs. Gardiner had been on a waiting list for an appointment for several months, so she took the opportunity to purchase a new gown for the occasion as well as a ball gown.

Mr. Bennet had provided enough money for Jane's wedding clothes and trousseau, as well as two new gowns for Elizabeth and a new dress for the wedding, as she was to stand up with Jane. Mrs. Gardiner was buying Jane two new nightgowns with robes as a wedding gift, and offered to purchase another gown for Elizabeth as well.

Unfortunately, Elizabeth was not having much success. Most of her attention was rightly focused on Jane, but she still needed to choose her own purchases. She simply could not find a fabric that she liked from the modiste's selection. It was their third day of shopping; Jane had chosen three dresses for her trousseau as well as the colors and pattern for her wedding dress, but she had yet to find the accompanying fabric for it and was feeling the same level of frustration as Elizabeth.

"I do not know why I simply cannot find the right thing!" Jane said exasperatedly. She was quite uncharacteristically irritated.

"Perhaps I could help you better if I knew what you were looking for exactly?" Elizabeth asked delicately.

"Oh, Lizzy! I know I am being difficult. I cannot describe it properly, I simply know that I shall know it when I see it." The older ladies smiled at her, remembering the stress of their own weddings and how finding the perfect dress suddenly seemed to be the most important thing in the world.

"Would you like to visit the drapers? They are likely to have a greater selection and we can have the fabric sent over," Lady Matlock suggested helpfully.

Jane lit up at the hope of finally finding what she was looking for when her aunt interjected.

"I have an idea." She leaned forward secretively, motioning for the ladies to come closer. "I should not be telling you this, and in such a place, but I have it on the best authority that a shipment of silk from the Orient, as well as a large consignment of muslin, has recently come into London – as recently as Monday. It is sitting in Mr. Gardiner's warehouse as we speak, awaiting delivery to the drapers," she whispered and looked at them conspiratorially, a sly grin on her face.

"Oh, Aunt! Could we?" Jane was trying to control her excitement, but after three days of searching through hundreds of bolts of fabric, this was very welcome news.

"I believe we can. What do you think, Lady Matlock?"

"I think I should call for the carriage." She rose with alacrity and instructed the assistant to inform the modiste that they would go to the drapers and that anything they found would either be sent over or brought back by themselves.

An hour later, the grand Matlock carriage was pulling up in front of a warehouse near Cheapside. The building was nondescript and had no storefront or shop, but had a well-kept exterior with a red door and a sign that read, *Gardiner Imports*, in neat gold letters. Lady Matlock had the appearance of a child sneaking cookies from the larder.

They were shown in by one of Mr. Gardiner's assistants, a young man of about twenty-two, tall and broad, and with quite a lot of brawn. He obviously spent a great deal of time working in the loading dock. Lady Matlock smiled and raised her eyebrows at Mrs. Gardiner, and Elizabeth wondered if she was seeing the beginning of a friendship.

Mr. Gardiner was out, but John, the young assistant with the tan skin and friendly smile, showed them to a room in the back where there were several crates standing on end so they were almost the same height as the ladies, their tops off for inspection, long, cylindrical bolts of fabric barely visible inside them.

"This just passed inspection this morning. Mr. Gardiner plans to check it later this afternoon and tomorrow it'll be off to the shops." He looked at the four women, all wearing expressions resembling children at candy shops. "Here are some step ladders so you can see inside. I'll be just outside if you need me." He smiled broadly and left, shaking his head. "All the pretty birds, lookin' for feathers!" he mumbled as he walked out, though he didn't seem to mind the intrusion of four pretty women *too* much.

"Well ladies, shall we begin?" Mrs. Gardiner asked.

"Yes!" the other three echoed in unison, each quickly grabbing a stool and heading for a box.

There were about twenty crates in the room, each filled to the brim with roughly a dozen bolts of fabric. They were all on the lookout for green and blue silk for Jane's wedding dress, as well as something that would complement it and suit Elizabeth. And of course, each woman was careful to watch for fabrics for herself as well.

Lady Matlock let out an unladylike squeal more than once as she ran to the door and called John back, requesting that he pull out three different bolts for her. Poor John was called in so frequently, he decided it might be wiser to just stay in the room, offering assistance where needed.

Elizabeth was leaning over her second crate, still not having found anything, when she came across a beautiful red silk. She had always loved red, but she was too young to wear it, so she usually passed it by. But this one was so lovely, she couldn't stop running the smooth fabric through her fingers. Lady Matlock was walking by and Elizabeth stopped her to show her what she'd found.

"Oh, Miss Elizabeth! You are quite right. This is lovely. I believe I would like some of this. John!"

The bolt was removed and set aside with Lady Matlock's others – a stack that was quickly growing.

"You would look wonderful in red, Miss Elizabeth."

"Do you think? I must confess that I have always wanted a red dress, but it is not the fashion for ladies my age to wear such a dark color." She sighed and looked down, obviously disappointed.

"Oh, tosh! It would make a lovely morning dress, or a dressing gown. A nightgown would be superb." She smiled at Elizabeth, who blushed slightly at the thought of wearing a red nightgown, and who she might wear such a thing for. "All in good time, my dear! Soon we shall be shopping for your trousseau, and we shall order you a red nightgown. Your husband will love it, I am certain!" Elizabeth's eyes widened as Lady Matlock patted her hand and returned to her search, mentally filing away her newly acquired information.

They continued the hunt for several more hours until the sun was low in the sky and the pile of chosen materials was high. The draper next door kindly came over and cut the lengths they needed, and Mr. Gardiner's secretary recorded everything and promised to have the bill delivered within a week. The fabrics were bundled and piled into the carriage, and Jane's wedding choices were sent straight to the dressmaker.

Since they were already in Cheapside, they dropped off Mrs. Gardiner and three very tired women returned to Mayfair. At dinner, they barely said a word, such was their exhaustion, leaving Lord Matlock to wonder if anything was amiss. When he finally asked how their shopping went, he was met by a barrage of information, from the variety of fabrics to the style of dresses to the sheer quantity of color choices, making him wish he had simply eaten his meal in silence.

~

Caroline Bingley had decided to host a dinner, and she included Elizabeth and Sir Malcolm on the guest list. The party was set for Saturday evening, and both Bennet sisters had replied in the affirmative.

Caroline dressed in one of her nicer gowns, though not the best, as she saw no reason to waste it if Mr. Darcy was not to be there. It was a small party, only fourteen people total, and she had secured the seat next to her for Sir Malcolm, and had placed Elizabeth next to him. She practiced a kind smile in the mirror for over an hour, while saying nice things about Elizabeth Bennet and trying to look sincere.

She thought she appeared believable.

Elizabeth and Jane arrived in the Matlock carriage, Lord Matlock absolutely insisting they take it. Elizabeth smiled at his solicitude and wondered if all the Fitzwilliam men were so inclined. Caroline Bingley saw the crest through the window and had to swallow the bile in her throat at the Fitzwilliam family's blatant preference for Elizabeth Bennet. She swallowed her anger and focused on her mission: attach Sir Malcolm to

Elizabeth. This was the perfect opportunity, with Darcy away and no one to interfere.

The guests all gathered in the living room and Caroline made the introductions. The only person Elizabeth knew besides the Bingleys and Hursts was Sir Malcolm, and he quickly made his way to her side while Bingley monopolized Jane.

"Miss Elizabeth, did you enjoy your holiday in Kent?"

"Yes, Sir Malcolm, it is a lovely county."

"And dare I hope that you are to stay in London more than a day or two?" he asked with a smile.

"Yes, I am to be here another three weeks, planning for my sister's wedding."

She wondered why he was still interested in her. Surely by now he'd realized that Jane was the woman Bingley had fallen in love with last autumn; the same woman who had such a terrible family that Darcy had felt obliged to separate Bingley from them. What could he possibly want with a woman of such bad connections and no fortune?

"Then I hope to see more of you." He smiled again, and Elizabeth politely smiled back.

Searching for something to say and not knowing anyone else to speak with, Elizabeth asked him about his estate in Staffordshire.

"Ah, Haverdene. What would you like to know, Miss Elizabeth?"

"Where is it located?"

"It is near the eastern border of Staffordshire, not far from Derbyshire. The nearest village is called Carlton, about three miles from the estate entrance. The estate itself is rather large, about seven miles around, and has a lovely river running through it, and a small forest filled with game."

"It sounds lovely. Do you ever walk through the forest?"

He laughed lightly. "I prefer to ride, but yes, I often go through the forest. I ride every morning as a rule."

"And what is your horse's name?"

Malcolm started. No one had ever asked him that before, at least not outside of a stable – and especially not a woman. "He is called Validus."

Elizabeth tilted her head to the side. "Latin for…strong?"

"Close – mighty." He smiled down at her approvingly. "Impressive, Miss Elizabeth."

"It would have been more impressive if I had gotten it right!" She smiled. "And what do you do when you are in town - unless you brought Validus with you?"

"No, he is safe at home. I often walk through Hyde Park. It is one of my favorite places in London. Do you ever walk there?"

"Upon occasion."

"Miss Elizabeth, I hope I am not being too forward, but it seems that every time I meet you, you are headed off to someplace else entirely, and I would very much like to see you again. May I call on you at Matlock House?"

Elizabeth flushed slightly from the earnestness in his voice and the expression in his light eyes. "You may call, Sir Malcolm."

As they walked into the dining room, Elizabeth on Malcolm's arm, she couldn't help but wonder what she had just agreed to. She had long ago acknowledged that she had feelings for Darcy, but she wasn't entirely sure if she trusted him. She had forgiven him and even understood his reasons, or at least understood how they made sense to him, but she wasn't sure if she would be able to get past his prideful nature. Yes, he had made great strides and had befriended her aunt and uncle, but was that enough?

She did not wish to be in a relationship where she was made to feel ashamed of her family; where they were not welcome in her husband's home, her home. She did not wish to be chosen in spite of her connections and expected to forget them except for the occasional visit and odd letter.

She wondered if Mr. Darcy would be rude to her mother and sisters and treat them as lesser than he. Beyond that, she wasn't sure he would ever even ask her. They were friends, surely, and he had shown that he liked her, but was there more?

She knew that Lady Catherine would not approve, and while she was currently a favorite of Lady Matlock's, that might change if Elizabeth went after her own nephew. It hadn't slipped her notice that Lady Matlock had conveniently left all her own family members off the list of eligible suitors.

Would Darcy be willing to stand against them? For her? She had nothing to offer, which had never bothered her before, but did it matter to him? Would he make such a sacrifice? She wasn't sure.

He had had several opportunities to declare himself and had not done so. The morning she left Hunsford, he had said that her leaving was partially his fault, but had not gone into any further detail. He neither affirmed nor denied his aunt's suspicions. She briefly wondered if he thought she might consent to be his mistress, for it was clear that he enjoyed her company, but she dismissed the thought almost as quickly as it came.

She made her decision: She would allow Sir Malcolm to call. It was not an official courtship, he had not made any declarations, and she did not believe she was toying with him. But he had made himself clear. He wanted to see her; he wished to know her better. She appreciated his candor and felt she knew where she stood with him.

Besides, she did like him and enjoyed his company. Sir Malcolm was the kind of man you could easily fall in love with if you allowed yourself, and Elizabeth imagined she wasn't the first to be on the receiving end of his smiles.

Sir Malcolm sat next to Caroline, and Elizabeth next to him. The man on her other side was Mr. Hurst, whom she knew from experience was not a good dinner conversationalist, so she anticipated talking to Sir Malcolm all evening, when he wasn't being monopolized by Caroline Bingley.

Caroline was in rare form. She was charming and almost sweet as she exchanged pleasantries and accepted compliments for the food. She turned her attention to Sir Malcolm and with a bright smile, asked, "Have you told Miss Elizabeth about Haverdene, Sir Malcolm?"

"A little, Miss Bingley."

"I'm sure we would love to hear more about it." She smiled convincingly.

He proceeded to describe his family's estate, answering Caroline's questions as he went. She made sure Elizabeth was listening and made efforts to include her in the conversation. She asked about the size of the house and the general appearance of it. She inquired after the stables and the horses, to which he answered that he thought he had one that would suit Miss Elizabeth well, causing the latter to study her plate.

Miss Bingley asked him about the neighborhood and the local wildlife, attempting to find topics that would make it sound appealing to Elizabeth. She wanted to know about the type and number of walking trails and asked after the gardens. He answered all her questions in detail and with enthusiasm, clearly proud of his home and heritage. He told the story of how his family became established at Haverdene and of his favorite views and trails to ride.

Malcolm was not interested in Caroline Bingley in the slightest, but he had been around her long enough to know that this was not her usual mode of behavior. He assumed she asked these questions for Elizabeth's benefit, hence his level of enthusiasm in answering them. He wondered why she was doing it, and the answer wasn't long in coming.

Caroline Bingley had only one motivation: to claw her way to the top of the ton by any means necessary. Her current plan to ascension was to become Mrs. Darcy, Mistress of Pemberley. If she was trying to match him with Elizabeth, it was not out of friendship. Caroline Bingley didn't have friends.

He had wondered if Darcy had taken a liking to Miss Bennet, but Caroline's current actions confirmed it. He smiled inwardly and thought of his old friend and him liking the same woman. He knew Darcy well enough to know that to him, family was everything. He would likely never go against them and take a dowerless bride, even if he loved her.

Stupid man, thought Malcolm. *Stupid, stupid man.*

Malcolm had liked many women through the years, but he was not constantly fancying himself in love, like Bingley, or separating himself from the fray like Darcy. He liked women; he was not ashamed to admit it. He enjoyed their company and liked to look at them, and dance with them, and hear them sing to him. Hence at balls, he generally danced every dance and was often sought after by matchmaking parents and eager debutantes.

He knew he was wealthy and single, young and good-looking, all of which made him a desirable match. However, he had never singled a lady out. Until he met a young woman in a book store. That occurrence was singular enough, but to find someone of the opposite sex who shared his interests, who could match him in intelligence, and who stirred his soul with her vivaciousness, was truly a wonder.

He was not naïve enough to imagine himself in love with Elizabeth Bennet after only a few meetings, but he knew he liked her and that he wanted to know her better – something he had not felt about a woman in many years. Only time would tell if more was to come of it.

CHAPTER 26

Late Monday morning, Elizabeth sat in the drawing room next to Jane, across from Sir Malcolm. He was genial and kind and perfectly mannered. At first they talked of the weather and eventually she asked him to tell her about growing up in Staffordshire. He described the county in detail, and Elizabeth listened interestedly. Eventually, they moved on to books and had a lively discussion about poetry. The half hour passed quickly, and Sir Malcolm was on his way.

Elizabeth retired to her room, needing to sort through her thoughts. She did not wish to lead Sir Malcolm on, but she also did not want to be silly and push away a perfectly good suitor whom she actually liked and who was in a position to marry her.

She found herself wishing the Darcys were already returned from Rosings so she might better decide on a course of action. Tomorrow was the seventh, and she eagerly anticipated their return. Oddly, she wished she could discuss her thoughts with Mr. Darcy. It was not the sort of thing one talked about with one's friends of the male persuasion, so she quickly ceased wondering about it as she pondered over what to do about Sir Malcolm.

~

Colonel Fitzwilliam, Darcy, and Georgiana returned on the seventh as planned, and Georgiana called on Elizabeth at Matlock House the next day.

"So how was the ball last night? You must tell me everything!" Georgiana gushed.

Elizabeth sipped her tea and replied, "It was as I expected. Your aunt introduced me to nearly every person in the room, half of whom I am sure I will never see again, and I danced nearly every dance. Mostly with nephews or younger sons of Lady Matlock's friends."

"Was Sir Malcolm there?"

"Yes, he was."

"Did you dance with him?"

"Yes, the fourth set and the last."

"Ohhhh. What about the others? Were any of them handsome?"

Elizabeth was extremely tired and had only had a few hours of sleep, and Georgiana was entirely too excited about last night's ball. However, she put her cynicism aside and humored her young friend. *I am becoming entirely too grumpy*. "Well, there were a few handsome ones. Mr. Hargrove was there again."

"The parson from Nottinghamshire?"

"I believe it's Northamptonshire, or is it Buckinghamshire? Anyhow, he will be at the concert tonight and has asked to sit next to me."

Georgiana giggled. "Oh! He must like you very much. What did you tell him?"

"I told him yes, of course. I didn't want to be rude. Apparently his family is old friends with your aunt's family."

"Lady Matlock is a Capshaw. Her father was the Earl of Rockingham. Her brother holds the title now, of course. Apparently they are a large family, but I rarely see them. Colonel Fitzwilliam could tell you more if you are curious."

"Is the colonel staying here or at the barracks?"

"He usually stays at the barracks, but when he has leave he stays here or with us."

"If I see him, I shall have to ask him about Mr. Hargrove, although I can't really see it going anywhere."

"Why ever not? Is it Sir Malcolm?" She tilted her head and leaned forward in anticipation of her friend's answer.

"No, it is not Sir Malcolm. I simply am not interested, that's all. And I don't really know that I would make a good parson's wife."

"What's wrong with being a parson's wife?"

"Nothing at all, I simply don't know if it's right for me. Somehow, I do not think I am virtuous enough for the job," she said with a smile.

Georgiana laughed. "What kind of wife would you like to be?"

"Hopefully a good one, and a happy one!"

"You must tell me everything that happens at the concert."

"I will try to remember each detail and relay it faithfully."

They talked of everything under the sun, spending nearly an hour on Lady Catherine's behavior at Rosings. The most informative part was when Georgiana told her how she had overheard an argument between Lady Catherine and her brother.

It was late one evening and she was about to retire for the night. However, that evening Darcy requested a meeting with Lady Catherine, and Colonel Fitzwilliam ensured they heard all of it.

Georgiana sat forward and told Elizabeth, "Prepare yourself for something very dreadful."

Elizabeth tried not to smile at her seriousness and nodded for Georgiana to continue. She began in a low voice, as if she were afraid of being overheard.

"Brother informed Lady Catherine that her behavior towards you was unacceptable. He said you were not her guest to send away, and that you were a close friend of mine, as well as his and Colonel Fitzwilliam's, and as such deserved respect. Lady Catherine said that she could behave how ever she wanted and that as her parson, Mr. Collins was bound to do as she bid."

Georgiana continued to tell her friend about the argument.

"Brother said he knew her little secret," Georgiana added, nodding with a serious expression.

"What happened next?" Elizabeth asked, knowing she shouldn't be gossiping but too curious to care.

"She said that if George Darcy had known what was good for him, he would have married her instead of her weak little sister, who had the audacity to die after producing only two children in fourteen years of marriage," Georgiana replied, clearly appalled at her aunt's speech.

Elizabeth put her hand over her mouth, her eyes wide at such unfeeling words, and from a sister, no less. After expressing how sorry she was that Georgiana had to hear such things about her own mother, her friend continued to tell her about the argument between her brother and aunt.

"I have never heard him speak so! His voice was so still – it was so unlike him. I've only ever heard him like that one other time – when he spoke of Mr. Wickham at Ramsgate," she added softly, tucking her head down.

Elizabeth squeezed her hand in support. "You do not have to tell me more if you don't want to."

"No, I'm alright."

Georgiana went on to tell her how Lady Catherine had stomped through the house, screaming at servants and shouting that Darcy would rue the day he crossed Lady Catherine de Bourgh.

Elizabeth listened enraptured, not sure if she should believe what she was hearing.

Georgiana went on to tell her that the next day, Lady Catherine had dressed Anne up in a frock with an incredibly low neckline, and had forced her to speak at breakfast, desperately trying to show Darcy what he was missing and equally hoping he would change his mind.

"It was all very awkward for everyone but Lady Catherine. Poor Anne was shivering and every time she pulled a shawl around her shoulders, Lady Catherine ripped it back, saying she would never get well if she continued to coddle herself." Georgiana shuddered at the memory.

Elizabeth shook her head and wondered at Lady Catherine's bizarre behavior. Georgiana continued telling her friend of her last days at Rosings.

Darcy and Fitzwilliam spent most of their time with the steward while Georgiana overcame her shyness and visited with Charlotte and Maria – anything to get away from Lady Catherine. When they rode out to look at the estate, Georgiana accompanied them.

A secretary was hired and the steward was given instructions to pass on all pertinent information and any questions he had to Lord Matlock.

It was with a joyful heart that the three left Rosings on Tuesday morning. Darcy looked back at the house, wondering if he would ever return. Surprisingly, he didn't mind the idea of not coming back.

Georgiana told her story with flair, and Elizabeth wondered if this was something she was picking up from Colonel Fitzwilliam. Georgiana apologized for her aunt's horrid behavior and said she knew Elizabeth would never do the things Lady Catherine had accused her of. Elizabeth thanked her and they embraced, glad to have the awkwardness out of the way.

Elizabeth couldn't wait to see Darcy. She wasn't sure if his fight with his aunt was because of her personally or simply the overt rudeness of the whole affair, which had then spiraled out of control. She began to wonder about his motives, which led to curiosity about his feelings, which led to difficult questions she did not want to think about. She wasn't ready to admit it, but a tiny bud of hope had begun to grow in her heart.

She called on Georgiana Thursday morning, only to find Darcy not at home. Lady Matlock was hosting a dinner the next night, so she would have to wait until then to see him. She desperately wanted to know what this all meant, and the waiting was torture. In the meantime, she took tea with Georgiana and told her about the concert the previous evening.

"Did Mr. Hargrove sit next to you?" she asked eagerly.

"Yes, just as he promised. He was very kind and solicitous. He spoke of music and told me of his favorite pieces and asked intelligent questions."

"Are you changing your mind about him?"

"Hmm, I think not."

"Elizabeth! You just said you had a pleasant evening with him!"

"I did not say pleasant! It was not unpleasant, but during the intermission, he asked me many questions that seemed strange to me."

"Like what?"

"Well, he frequently quoted Fordyce, which I must admit concerns me greatly, but he also asked me about living in a village, and how I felt about the duties of a parson's wife and whether I thought I could live on limited means. It was all so formal, like I was being interviewed."

"That does seem strange. Does he not care whether or not you love him?"

"I think he cares more whether I respect him and his position than for love. I suppose I should keep looking!" she said gaily.

"Do not worry. There is still Sir Malcolm."

"Yes, Sir Malcolm," she said thoughtfully.

~

Friday evening came round and Elizabeth dressed carefully in one of the new dresses that had been delivered that morning. Her hair was carefully pinned up by a maid, and Lady Matlock loaned her a pretty jade necklace with matching earrings to compliment her pale green dress. She wore a similar green ribbon round her waist and long white satin gloves, a band of matching green ribbon around her head, and rosette tipped pins in her coiffure. Her cheeks were flushed with excitement and her eyes sparkled in anticipation.

Bingley was the first guest to arrive. Of course, he immediately sat next to Jane and the two were nearly inseparable the rest of the night. Next was Sir Malcolm, who sat near Elizabeth, followed by a few others Elizabeth did not know, or had met and already forgotten.

Darcy arrived alone and walked directly to Elizabeth where she was speaking with Sir Malcolm. The gentlemen exchanged greetings and he bowed to Elizabeth before taking a chair nearby. Colonel Fitzwilliam came in and sat next to Malcolm, drawing him into conversation. Eventually the colonel said he wished to show him something in the library, and led Sir Malcolm out of the room.

As soon as they were gone, Darcy scooted his chair closer and looked into Elizabeth's eyes. "Miss Elizabeth." He drank her in, desperately wishing to tell her how he had needed her presence near him over the past week.

"Mr. Darcy."

They looked at each other silently for several moments, his eyes glowing with love, hers sparkling in anticipation and hope. Finally, he broke the silence.

"Have you enjoyed your time with my aunt?"

"Yes, she is very kind."

"She is. She was a close friend of my mother's."

"Yes, she told me."

"Has she?"

"Mr. Darcy, I hope I have not caused any trouble with your family. Please accept my apologies for upsetting your aunt," she said quietly.

Darcy stared at her incredulously for a moment, not believing she could really think herself to blame for anything that had happened. Then he realized what she was referring to.

"Ah, I see. You've spoken to Georgiana."

Elizabeth looked down. "She told me you've had a falling out."

"Miss Elizabeth, it was bound to happen at some time. Lady Catherine wishes everyone to do her bidding and obey her every command. I am not one to be told how to make decisions that are solely mine. We would have clashed at some point, you were merely the catalyst."

She didn't like the sound of that until she saw the smile lurking at the corners of his mouth.

"I believe you are teasing me, Mr. Darcy!"

"How can I resist when you make it so easy?" He smiled kindly. "Now, no more talk of my aunt. How have you been spending your time in town?"

"I have spent an inordinate amount of time shopping. I never thought I could shop so much in so few days!"

"I thought most ladies enjoyed a day of shopping."

"A day, yes, but every day but Sunday? I may never go again!"

He laughed lightly. "Miss Elizabeth, would you like to spend the afternoon with Georgiana and me tomorrow? I haven't had a proper cup of tea since you left."

It was her turn to laugh. "I would like to Mr. Darcy, but I am engaged to spend the day with my aunt and uncle tomorrow. But I am free Sunday afternoon."

"Sunday it is. Shall I pick you up at two o'clock?"

"I shall look forward to it."

Dinner was announced and he offered her his arm, which she took readily. They walked into the dining room and he settled her into her chair, which was conveniently located next to his. She looked at him quizzically as he sat, and he returned her look with a smile.

She did not catch Colonel Fitzwilliam watching them from the other side of the table, grinning slyly at Darcy, or see Mr. Darcy's small nod in response. She looked to her right to see Sir Malcolm sitting in the chair on her other side. He smiled brightly and apologized for not returning to the drawing room before dinner - Colonel Fitzwilliam had been showing him a saber in the library.

She looked toward the Colonel and he winked at her. She smiled and shook her head, glad to once again be in the company of friends.

Sir Malcolm asked her a question and they spoke for a few minutes, Elizabeth acutely aware of Darcy's presence on her other side.

After the first course was served, Darcy took the opportunity to capture Elizabeth's attention and began asking her about her sister's wedding, how the plans were going, and when she intended to return to Hertfordshire.

At a break in the conversation, Sir Malcolm interrupted, telling her all about a mare he had that he thought would be perfect for her to learn to ride with.

The first course was removed and Darcy took the chance to engage Elizabeth.

"Miss Elizabeth, I know this isn't the best place for such a discussion, but I wanted to suggest something."

"Yes, Mr. Darcy?"

"We were intending to return to Pemberley in June, as you know, but Bingley has just asked if he can change the arrangements. He and your sister will be in Scarborough in June and would like to come directly to

Pemberley from there instead of waiting till the end of July. It is not a long distance and makes more sense than returning to Netherfield for two weeks time, only to spend three days in a carriage back north. And I had wanted to be home a few weeks before visitors arrived."

"So what are your plans now?" she asked.

"I had thought to go on to Pemberley shortly after the wedding. I have spring planting to oversee and Georgiana is anxious to return. Then I may complete my business and have some time to relax before Bingley arrives in mid-June."

"I am sure I can travel north with my aunt and uncle. They will be leaving at the end of June, so I would likely arrive shortly after Jane and Mr. Bingley. Would that be better?"

This was not what he was hoping for. He had hoped to prolong his time with her, not shorten it.

"Actually, Miss Elizabeth, I was hoping you would consent to leave with us after the wedding." Her eyes widened. "I know it is a month sooner than planned, but would that suit you?"

He looked earnestly into her face and she quietly replied, "I must write to my father."

"Of course. I hope it can be arranged, Miss Elizabeth. Pemberley is particularly beautiful in late spring."

"I will do my best, Mr. Darcy." Elizabeth couldn't explain it, but she was beginning to feel breathless. The way he had looked into her eyes and the easy way he was speaking to her, as if she were a member of his family, was making her feel warm and a little nervous. In combination with the wine, she was feeling quite heady.

In an attempt to regain her equilibrium, she gave her attention to Sir Malcolm, occasionally answering a question from Darcy until dessert was served.

"Have you ever tried this, Miss Elizabeth?"

"I do not believe I have, Mr. Darcy." She looked at the torte on her plate, drizzled in a red fruit sauce.

"It is a mixture of raspberries and liqueur. My aunt refuses to let anyone see the recipe. Supposedly it was a secret of her mother's cook's, and she only serves it to very important guests."

"Then I am flattered," she teased.

"As you should be, Miss Elizabeth."

Elizabeth looked at the torte in front of her, enjoying the pungent aroma of the raspberries and the delicacy of the cream dolloped on top of them. She took a small bite and an almost inaudible sigh escaped her. Darcy watched her, enchanted, fighting the overpowering urge to feed her himself.

"What do you think?" he asked in a low voice.

"It is incredible. I see why she keeps it secret."

Darcy watched her eat in small bites, knowing he should look away, but not able to make his eyes obey his head. He had an overwhelming desire to touch her. Without considering her reaction, he reached his leg out under the table and touched her foot with his.

Elizabeth was about to swallow a bite of torte when she felt Darcy's foot press deliberately against hers. She startled and shifted reflexively in the other direction, her foot reaching out in front of her. Sir Malcolm's legs were long, and as she soon realized, he liked to sit stretched out. When her right leg jolted out and slightly to the side, she accidentally bumped into Sir Malcolm's foot with hers.

She couldn't speak with a mouthful of food and she could feel the blush spreading up her neck as she drew her foot back slowly. She demurely wiped her mouth with her napkin, took a sip of wine to restore her composure, and looked to her right to ascertain Sir Malcolm's reaction.

Malcolm, of course, thought she had touched his foot on purpose and took it as a sign that she liked him; it wasn't the first time a woman had flirted with him in such a way. He smiled slightly at her and returned to the conversation on his other side, moving his leg closer to hers so that their feet were touching under the table without her having to stretch out. *At least he is considerate,* Elizabeth thought dryly.

Meanwhile, Darcy knew he had startled her, but he also knew it would not do to not follow through, and he enjoyed the blush his action had created. He extended his leg once again and touched her left foot gently with his. This time Elizabeth didn't jump, but her face quickly flamed bright pink and he smirked in satisfaction.

Elizabeth did not know what to do. How had this happened? She'd been sitting calmly, trying to eat her dessert in peace, and now she was suddenly playing footsie under the table with two different men!

Oh, no! Sir Malcolm adjusted his position so that his entire lower leg, from knee to ankle, was pressed against hers. To make matters worse, Darcy had started rubbing her foot with his under the table. She remained completely still, trying not to move an inch – she did not want to encourage them.

She was shocked at their boldness, but then she remembered that she had made the first move with Sir Malcolm, or at least he thought she had. She briefly wondered if it would be considered rude to pull her leg away. Realizing it was an absurd question and that she would not find the answer to this dilemma in a book of manners, she looked helplessly down the table.

Jane was in conversation with Mr. Bingley, of course, and no matter how much Elizabeth willed her to, she would not look her way. Colonel Fitzwilliam caught her eye, and seeing her distress and embarrassment, he looked at her quizzically. She did not want to alarm him, so she smiled at him lightly and prayed for the meal to be over soon, before she died of mortification.

Elizabeth knew she should look at Darcy, but she could not bring herself to face him. She could feel his eyes boring into her, practically demanding she look at him, but she would not remove her eyes from her plate.

Finally, Lady Matlock stood and asked the ladies to join her in the drawing room. Elizabeth nearly leapt out of her chair in relief. The men stood as well and she was released from her awkward position.

As she turned to go, Sir Malcolm gave her a meaningful look and told her he would see her soon. She turned to Darcy, her eyes planted firmly on his cravat. She finally looked up when he said her name. She looked at him briefly, nodded at his promise to return to her shortly, and quickly made her way out of the dining room.

The gentlemen did not tarry long and soon joined the ladies in the drawing room. Elizabeth desperately wished to escape upstairs to her chambers, but she knew it was the coward's way out, and she resolved to find a solution to her predicament. She secured a chair near Jane, hoping that none would be available for the gentlemen and they would be forced to sit on the other side of the room.

She was not that lucky. Mrs. Humphreys had been on her right, but just before the gentlemen returned, she moved next to Mrs. Larkton and began chatting about their daughters.

Upon entering, Darcy quickly made his way to Elizabeth's side, taking the now empty seat at her right. Elizabeth cringed internally, but smiled politely. Sir Malcolm was not far behind, and when she saw him enter, Lady

Matlock called to Jane to come and sit near her, saying she had a question about her upcoming wedding. Now the chair on her left was free and Sir Malcolm sat down comfortably.

Elizabeth took a deep breath to steady herself and gathered her courage.

"Miss Elizabeth," Darcy and Malcolm both spoke at once, and Elizabeth looked from one to the other.

"Go ahead, Sir Malcolm," Darcy said. He turned his chair slightly so he was visible to both Elizabeth and his friend.

"Do you plan to play for us tonight, Miss Elizabeth?"

"I think not, Sir Malcolm. I'm afraid I am rather tired."

"I hope you are not unwell."

"No, not at all, Sir. I am merely tired. It has been an exhausting week."

"Do you still believe you will never shop again, Miss Elizabeth?" Darcy asked.

"I cannot say for certain, Mr. Darcy. But I can tell you I do not look forward to doing it again come Monday."

"When is your sister's wedding?" asked Malcolm.

"The fourth of May. I cannot believe it is so soon!"

"It is a big change, Miss Bennet. I know I felt it keenly when my sister married."

"Thank you, Sir Malcolm. I am really very happy for Jane and I have never seen her more content, but I will miss her terribly."

"At least you will see her over the summer, so you will not be too long parted," Darcy added.

"Yes. How long are they planning to stay at Pemberley?" she asked.

"I am not sure. Bingley usually stays six weeks or more, but I do not know about this particular trip. With you there, Miss Bennet may wish to stay longer."

"But I will not be there overlong, Mr. Darcy! I shall be back at Longbourn in August."

Darcy looked down and Sir Malcolm interjected. "Where does Bingley live? He told me he had leased an estate. Is it near your home, Miss Elizabeth?"

"Yes, Sir, it is in Hertfordshire. It is a lovely place, but I am not sure if he will buy it. He is only leasing it for the moment."

"Surely, with her family so nearby, Miss Bennet may wish him to buy it."

Elizabeth pursed her lips slightly. "Perhaps. I believe Jane's disposition would allow her to be happy in many places, though."

"Hertfordshire cannot have such a hold on you, Miss Elizabeth. I can't imagine you wishing to be settled as close as Netherfield is to Longbourn," Mr. Darcy said seriously.

"I will admit that it is possible to be settled too near one's family. I believe there are a great many places I could be happy." She looked from one to the other, wondering what they were thinking, and what they thought of her, and what they made of each other. What a fine situation this was!

They continued to question her back and forth, occasionally speaking over one another, each man wondering what the other was doing there.

Sir Malcolm felt Elizabeth had made her preference perfectly clear, and thought Darcy was being dense or stubborn in not removing himself.

Darcy knew only that Elizabeth had not moved away when he had touched her under the table and took that as an acceptance of his attentions, and wished Sir Malcolm would take the hint and leave off.

Later that night, after all the guests had gone and each of her attendants - as she'd come to think of them - had kissed her hand, smiled privately, and left, Elizabeth ordered a bath and gratefully sunk into the steaming water.

What a mess! She was going to have to talk to her Aunt Gardiner about this tomorrow. She had to undo this somehow.

But on the bright side, at least she knew how Darcy felt about her now. She went to sleep with a tiny smile on her lips.

CHAPTER 27

"Oh, Aunt! It was awful!" Elizabeth was sitting in Mrs. Gardiner's private sitting room Saturday morning, giving her a detailed description of the events of the previous evening.

Mrs. Gardiner stifled a small laugh and looked at her niece squarely. "I know these things are not considered proper, Elizabeth, but they are sometimes done, as you witnessed last night. I'm sure neither meant any harm. You said yourself Sir Malcolm thought you instigated it. He probably would not have continued if he did not think you approved."

"Yes, you are right." Elizabeth made a face and looked down.

"And what of Mr. Darcy?"

Elizabeth flushed slightly. "What of him?"

"He did initiate it himself. He is obviously interested in you, Lizzy. How do you feel about him?"

"Do you really think he is interested in me?"

"My dear niece! Do you not have eyes? He watches you constantly, has followed you all over the country, and makes every excuse to see you. He has invited you to spend the summer at his home. Are these not signs enough – even without his behavior last night?"

"What made him do such a thing?" Elizabeth wailed. She stood and began pacing in the small sitting room. "If he is interested, why did he not just say something?"

"Men often speak in other ways, dear. You will learn this in time. But I fear now you have a decision before you." Elizabeth sat and dropped her head into her hands. "You cannot court two men at once."

"Neither has asked for a courtship."

"I'm sure one of them will soon. And you will need to know what to answer beforehand. And remember dear, not everyone has a formal courtship. Mr. Bingley and Jane only courted for a few weeks before he proposed. They were in love before a formal courtship was even considered."

"Do you think one of them may just propose out of the blue?" she asked, slightly frantic.

"It is possible, I do not know either of them well enough to say. I do know, however, that men do not like to share their fiancés. I fear that if you do not single one out soon, you will lose them both."

"Oh! This is all so frustrating!"

"Elizabeth," her aunt said slowly, "you know which you prefer, do you not?"

"Oh, Aunt! They are both kind and generous and intelligent and interesting, and both are undeniably handsome and would be excellent matches, but..." she trailed off.

"But what, dear?"

"As yet, I am not in love with either, but I do believe I could love them, one more than the other. Though more is not the right word. Deeper, perhaps?"

Her aunt watched her as she paced back and forth to the window trying to sort out her feelings.

"I know you are not comfortable sharing your deepest feelings, Lizzy, but I do believe it would help you to talk this through."

Elizabeth took a deep breath. "Some time ago, I began to have a certain… regard… for Mr. Darcy. But then something happened and we did not speak for some time, and I was not sure that I could trust him, that I could be happy in life with him. I told myself that those things probably didn't matter anyway because he likely looked upon me as a sister or a dear friend. I recently began to suspect he felt something more for me, but I wasn't sure if he would act on it. Then last night happened – and now I don't know what to think! I feel that I could love him. That in fact, the only thing stopping me from being deeply and ridiculously in love with him is my own trepidation. I have not let myself love him! I think that if I were to let go, I could easily give him my whole heart." She looked out the window and her shoulders slumped as she toyed with her necklace.

"Sir Malcolm has been nothing but honest with me from the very beginning. He has never lied to me, nor offended me or hurt me. He has said he wishes to know me better. He is intelligent and has many interesting things to say. I enjoy his company and like him, but I do not feel anything deeper for him. Sometimes, I think that if I had never met Mr. Darcy, I could have been quite happy with Sir Malcolm. And I may still be. Neither has proposed or made me an offer of courtship. Sir Malcolm has yet to meet my family – he may change his mind. I do not believe he loves me, not yet. But from the way he looks at me, I think he would like to."

"And when Mr. Darcy looks at you?"

"When Mr. Darcy looks at me, it's as if we are the only two people in the world." She sat down in front of her aunt and clasped her hands.

"Aunt! What am I to do? After last night, Sir Malcolm believes I have singled him out and wish for his attentions. Mr. Darcy believes I willingly accept his. I have made an unbelievable mess!"

Mrs. Gardiner patted her niece's hand and gave her a warm smile. "There, there. Do not fret. We will work this out. The next time Sir Malcolm comes to call, you simply tell him that you were startled and kicked him by mistake, and that you did not want to be rude and that is why you did not pull your foot away. That is, if you have decided against Sir Malcolm." Elizabeth looked down. "You are seeing Mr. Darcy again tomorrow, are you not?"

"Yes, I am spending the afternoon with him and Georgiana."

"Perhaps he will take the opportunity to speak to you about his intentions. If he does not, you can always help him along." Elizabeth looked at her quizzically. "Simply drop Sir Malcolm into the conversation. Mention that he called on you last week and that you expect him to call again soon. Perhaps he will take the hint and tell you how he feels so that you may make a decision and move on."

"That is good advice, Aunt, but I hate to manipulate him into a confession. If he does love me, or holds a regard for me, I want him to confess it on his own. I would not wish to force such a declaration."

"I understand dear, and I know you will do what is best when the time comes."

~

That afternoon, when Elizabeth returned to Matlock House, she immediately retreated to the library. She chose a book that she was sure would distract her from her present troubles and started up the steps to her room. Jane was still visiting some garden or other with Bingley and the Hursts and would not return until after dinner, so Elizabeth would be spending a quiet evening with the earl and countess.

It was funny, but she was beginning to feel almost like a daughter of the house. She knew Lady Matlock had no daughters, but had always wanted one. She had confided in Elizabeth one day that she had had a baby girl, a short time after her son Richard was born, but her pains had begun early and the poor dear had not lasted above a day. She was buried at Matlock, and every year at the anniversary of her birth and death, her mother placed flowers on her grave.

As if that weren't enough, her next confinement was breech, and after two days of hard labor, and no movement felt from the babe, they had begun to lose hope. She had delivered a stillborn infant, another daughter, and had been unable to conceive again. The doctor had speculated that she was too damaged from the birth, but in her secret heart, Helen Fitzwilliam believed she simply could not take another heartache, so her body had mercifully spared her.

Any momentary annoyance Elizabeth had felt with the countess's machinations was quickly allayed, and she hoped that her willingness to share this season of her life, and even Jane's willingness to let her share in the wedding preparations, had gone some way to heal the ache in her heart.

"Miss Elizabeth!"

"Lord Matlock!" Elizabeth stopped on the stairs and curtseyed to her host.

"Are you off to read?"

"Yes, I thought I might relax for a little while before time to change for dinner."

"Would you like company? I was about to sit in the blue sitting room with a book as well."

"Thank you, milord. I would like that."

She turned and led the way to the back of the house where there was a small but comfortable sitting room, decorated in smoky blues and filled with light from the north facing windows. Lord and Lady Matlock rarely received guests there, but used it as a private retreat for the family and close friends.

The two sat, Lord Matlock in a large wingback chair, where his dog, Rex, quickly curled at his feet. Elizabeth sat comfortably in the corner of the settee and opened her book.

Lord Matlock looked out of the corner of his eye at the young lady residing in his home. Her presence in their lives had come quite unexpectedly, but he did not regret it. He knew that Helen had felt the loss of daughters acutely. Her sister and brother each had two sons, so she was not even granted the relief of nieces to spoil.

Because of Lady Catherine, a close relationship with Anne was out of the question, so that left Georgiana as her only outlet for maternal affection. It had been wonderful for Georgiana to have someone fill the place of mother in her life, especially someone who had been so devoted to her own mother.

However, Georgiana's remarkable resemblance to her departed friend often pained his wife, and though she would never be so indelicate as to say so, as her husband, he knew. He had, on occasion, heard her call his niece by his sister's name, only to quickly correct herself. He understood her pain, as he missed his younger sister as well.

Thus, he was grateful for the presence of Elizabeth in their lives. She reminded him of Anne in some ways. They both had a joy for simply living that he had always admired, and a well-developed sense of humor. Elizabeth could not look more different, though, and he noted it with relief.

If she had a fortune, or if he had a small estate to bequeath his younger son, he thought she might do for Richard. It would be lovely to have her for a daughter. But alas, he thought the two had a more sibling-like relationship, and he would be content to have her as a close friend of the family.

Henry ceased his daydreaming and went back to his book, only to be interrupted by his wife a few minutes later. She was followed shortly by the butler, who announced they had a visitor. Removing to the front parlor, they were all equally surprised when the butler announced Sir Malcolm.

"Good day, Sir Malcolm. How nice to see you again." Lady Matlock graciously directed him to a chair between herself and Elizabeth.

"The pleasure is mine, milady. I must admit to this not being a typical parlor call."

"Oh? And to what do we owe the honor of your visit?" Lady Matlock asked, clearly intrigued but also amused.

"I have come to ask Miss Elizabeth to join me for a walk in the park. It is a lovely day and I thought she would enjoy the sunshine."

"I'm sure she will be very happy to accompany you. Elizabeth, why do you not fetch your things while I keep Sir Malcolm company?"

Elizabeth nodded, knowing resistance was futile and realizing this would give her a perfect chance to speak to Sir Malcolm about the events of the dinner party.

Five minutes later, a maid was set to chaperone, and she was stepping out the front door on his arm. Lady Matlock smiled broadly as she sent them on their way, her husband chuckling silently and shaking his head behind her.

"And just what is so funny, Henry?" Lady Matlock asked with her hands on her hips.

"He gave her a quick peck on the cheek and smiled. "Nothing, my dear, nothing at all. Though it is a shame women are not allowed in the military. Your gift for strategy could be quite useful there, I think."

Lady Matlock huffed until he turned away, then smiled to herself as she followed him back to the sitting room.

~

Sir Malcolm Rutherford was a mysterious man. Accounts of him ranged from rake to philanthropist, from loving brother to disobedient son. He was a friend to many and a stranger to no one. He was on every guest list and sought after at every dinner party. He was always impeccably dressed, but never a dandy; lean, but not overly thin; strong, but not overly broad. He sat his horse well and filled out his dinner coat nicely. His jet black hair fell in silky waves across his worry-free brow and his ice-blue eyes could pierce without damaging.

Such a man inspired camaraderie in his fellow gentlemen and admiration in women both young and old. After the passing of his father, he began to spend less time in town and more time at his estate with his mother and younger sister, both of whom doted on him excessively. He was still seen in town occasionally, but he was subdued, restrained, less wild in his pursuit of pleasure.

After his mother passed a few years later, he disappeared altogether, only to resurface in a year with his sister, now a woman in search of a husband, on his arm. Within a year she was married to an Earl, and he was free to return to his former ways.

But he did not.

Thus began the mystery of Sir Malcolm. Even though he was in full possession of his fortune and was known to be free of encumbering debts, he did not continue his previous ways of staying out all night and sleeping all day. No, he went to his club and played chess with his father's contemporaries. He attended hunting parties in the country. He was present at select balls and dinner parties and was polite to all in attendance and flirtatious with the young maidens and a few lucky widows, but he remained closed – hidden – unavailable.

What made Sir Malcolm even more vexing was that he could be startlingly direct at times, which never failed to catch one off-guard, as most had gotten used to his more circumspect behavior of the last few years. He was always charming, and yet always at arm's length.

Then, when one least expected it, he would come closer, eliminating the distance between the parties, and shocking the recipient with his sudden candor. Thus was the case for Elizabeth, who at times did not understand him at all, and at others found him refreshingly honest. However, even she did not expect his honesty to go quite this far.

"May I ask you a question, Miss Bennet?"

"Of course, Sir."

"I'd like to know if your heart is engaged?"

"That is a highly inappropriate question, Sir!"

"I know." He looked at her steadily and they kept walking along.

"Most men would ask if I was being courted or if I was seriously considering a suitor. Your question is unexpected."

"I realize that. But I think it best to get to the heart of the matter whenever possible."

"And may I ask to what these questions tend?"

"Certainly. If I am to win your heart, I first need to know if it is available for the winning."

She looked at him, a light blush on her cheeks. "You are bold, Sir."

"Fortune favors the brave, Miss Bennet."

"And what if my answer is no and my heart is available. What will you do then?"

"Actively pursue your heart, naturally." His voice was smooth, light, natural, and completely unnerving.

"Pardon me, Sir, but there is nothing natural about it. Most men seek only a fortunate alliance with an amiable woman; the heart rarely comes into play," she replied as she attempted to keep her flustered feelings from showing on her face.

"But that is not what you want," he replied steadily.

"No, it is not. I had always hoped to marry for love. Mutual respect and esteem in a relationship are essential for lasting happiness." She spoke quietly, focusing on the path ahead of her.

"A wise philosophy I think."

"And what if my heart is engaged? What will you do then?" She looked up, her chin slightly raised.

"If he is worthy of you and returns your regard, I will bow out gracefully and hope to remain friends. If he is not or does not, I will wait patiently for you to recover from your wound and try again."

"You seem to have given this a great deal of thought."

"And you seem to be avoiding the question."

"You are astute, Sir Malcolm. The truth is, I do not know. Sometimes, I think I am as free as a bird, and others I feel my heart is not mine to command."

"That must be confusing."

"You have no idea."

"Fear not, Miss Bennet. I will not disappear at the first sign of indecision. I am a patient man. I can wait."

She smiled brilliantly at him. "You cannot know how nice that is to hear, Sir Malcolm."

~

"Tell me everything you know about Sir Malcolm," Elizabeth said abruptly as she walked into the sitting room.

"Well you certainly don't waste time, Miss Elizabeth!" answered Lady Matlock. "Sit down and let's have some tea, then we can discuss the baronet. I assume you enjoyed your walk?"

Lady Matlock poured while Elizabeth sat working her skirt in her fingers, her only answer a lift of one arched brow.

"Has he declared himself then?" Lady Matlock asked.

Lord Matlock lowered his book slightly and peered over the top.

"He may as well have. He asked if my heart was engaged and if he might begin the pursuit of it."

"Oh my! That is good news indeed! And what was your reply?"

"I asked him to be patient."

"Really? Whatever for? I thought you liked Sir Malcolm?"

"I do like him. I am just not sure if I wish to marry him. If I consent to a courtship, it is likely he will propose, and I do not wish to have a scandal come down round my head if I publicly court and then refuse him."

"Why on Earth would you refuse him?" asked the countess in astonishment.

"I do not know!" Elizabeth responded, her voice bordering on hysteria. "That is why I wish to know more about him and why I asked him to be patient. I cannot honorably consent to a courtship if I do not think there is even a possibility of accepting a proposal, and I cannot know that until I know more about him."

"Alright dear, I understand you, now calm down." She handed Elizabeth a plate of biscuits which she began nibbling on nervously while Lady Matlock gathered her thoughts.

"Let me see, where to begin... I first met his mother, Lavinia Granger, shortly after I married Lord Matlock. She was a few years older than me and a very nice woman. We were not of the same circle, but she had recently become engaged to Sir Robert Rutherford and was in town for the season. She was not well received at first, her family had fallen on hard times, but everyone eventually gave in, as they always do. They just have to throw back their heads and howl for a little while, but then they come round.

"She was a very bright woman. She used to hold salons in their townhouse during the season. We would discuss art, literature; it was a very small group, but I was fond of her and the discussions were stimulating. Sir Malcolm is the same age as Richard, their fathers were at Cambridge together and friends for years. He was always a sweet boy, though a bit mischievous. He and Richard would get into some interesting scrapes together. Malcolm and Darcy became friends when they were all at school together as boys. I believe they are still close."

"Yes, I believe you are right." *Oh Lord, this is not going to be easy.*

"Anyway, he was a bit wild in his younger days, but what young men aren't? He seemed to level out considerably when his father died. He was always close to his mother, and he stayed by her side while she was grieving – it was quite endearing to watch. After she passed on as well, no one saw him for well-nigh a year, until Arabella came out. Their aunt handled everything, and I believe she still advises him. But don't worry, dear, she is a friend of mine," she said with a wink and a pat on Elizabeth's knee.

Oh, dear.

"He is known as a good man, fair and honest, he's never been caught in any underhanded dealings. Lord Matlock informs me he is not one for gaming or drunkenness, which is important in a husband." She raised her eyebrows meaningfully. Lord Matlock hid behind his book, not wishing to be drawn into the conversation and hoping his wife had forgotten his presence.

"I quite agree." Elizabeth took a deep breath. "So everyone agrees he is a nice man without any skeletons in his closet?"

"I believe so, dear. I'll certainly keep my ears open and let you know if I find out anything else."

"Thank you, Lady Matlock. I think I'll have a short rest now. I'm rather tired from my walk in the park."

"Of course dear. And don't worry over much. When the right man is before you, you'll know. You'll see it in his eyes."

Elizabeth nodded and went upstairs, feeling a headache creep up her neck. It wasn't until she was lying down that she realized the incident at the dinner party had never come up. *Oh, well. It is likely immaterial after that conversation.*

Lady Matlock turned to her husband. "You can come out now, Henry."

Lord Matlock dropped his book and looked at his wife. "Whatever do you mean, my dear? I have been right here all along."

"And conveniently hiding behind your book." She smiled wryly at her husband as she rose and took his hand. "Come my love, I believe it is time to dress for dinner."

Lord Matlock looked at the clock and saw dinner was more than two hours away. He smiled when he saw the gleam in his wife's eye. "Yes, I believe I will be quite hungry this evening." And he dutifully followed her upstairs.

~

Elizabeth looked at her closet, trying to choose what to wear. Lady Matlock was out, and Jane was spending the afternoon with Miss Bingley, poor thing, so there was no one to ask. She eventually settled on a lavender gown. She knew Darcy had seen it before, but it was flattering to her coloring and the neckline was just right; not so high it was prudish, but not low enough to be garish. One of the housemaids helped her dress and fixed her hair in a simple but elegant style. She put her pendant around her neck, grabbed her bonnet and gloves, and headed downstairs.

Darcy had said he'd pick her up at two, which she thought meant he would send the carriage for her, even though it would take longer to hitch up the horses than to actually drive the short distance. She looked at the clock in the drawing room; it was ten minutes till two. Darcy was generally early and never late, so she decided to go ahead and put on her things. As she was tying her bonnet ribbons, the butler stepped in to announce Mr. Darcy.

She looked up in time to see him striding into the room.

"Mr. Darcy!"

"Miss Bennet, you look surprised. Were you not expecting me? You haven't forgotten our appointment, have you?"

"No sir, of course not. I am merely surprised to see you here yourself. I assumed you would send the carriage."

"I said I would pick you up, did I not?"

"Yes, you did."

"Shall we then?" He held out his arm and she walked toward him, quickly slipping on her gloves.

As they stepped outside, she did not see the carriage. "I thought we could walk today. Do you mind?"

"I believe you already know the answer to that, Mr. Darcy." She smiled at him.

When they arrived at Darcy House, he ushered her into the library. Before they could sit down, tea was brought in with a plate of lemon biscuits. She smiled happily and began to serve the tea. As she handed him his cup, she asked if Georgiana would be joining them soon.

"She is out with Richard. She'll be joining us later."

Elizabeth looked up in surprise, her eyes wide. They were alone – in his house with no one but servants about. Suddenly her mouth went dry and her throat constricted. She knew she should say something, but she couldn't form words. *Was he going to declare himself? Was that why he had orchestrated this meeting? But I haven't decided! I am not sure yet!*

Elizabeth had mostly decided in favor of Mr. Darcy over Sir Malcolm for a courtship, but she was not yet ready to commit to a marriage with anyone, and she experienced the occasional moment of doubt over her decision. She still had some lingering questions about what life would be like with him, and her feelings had yet to outweigh her concerns.

"Miss Bennet, are you unwell?"

"I am quite well, Mr. Darcy. Thank you."

"Miss Bennet, I hope you are not overly distressed by Georgiana's absence. She intended to be here, but Richard stopped by unexpectedly and whisked her away."

So he did not orchestrate this. Elizabeth began to relax, chiding herself for overreacting.

"It is quite alright, Mr. Darcy. I'm sure you and I can find a way to keep ourselves occupied until her return. We are good friends, are we not?"

He looked at her intently, wondering if she had any idea of the effect her words had on him. "Yes, Miss Bennet, we are good friends."

She smiled and took a bite of her biscuit, slightly discomfited by his scrutiny.

"Actually, that is something I wanted to speak to you about," he said lightly, looking around the room and ending on her face.

"What is, Mr. Darcy?"

"Our friendship, Miss Bennet."

"Oh."

"I was wondering if, hoping really… that you might... that you would want to perhaps become even better friends." He leaned forward as he sat on the edge of the chair, his legs wide and his elbows propped on his knees.

"Better friends?" she echoed, a nervous feeling taking hold in her stomach.

"Yes. I know I have hurt and offended you in the past, and I know that you have graciously forgiven me. I understand that trust must be rebuilt, and I would like for us to have an opportunity to get to know one another better, for you to get to know *me* better, in the hope that you can fully trust me one day." Elizabeth looked at him wide-eyed, at a complete loss for words. "Because I fervently hope that one day, hopefully some day soon, we will be much more than friends." He looked deeply into her eyes and Elizabeth forced herself to speak.

"More than friends?" she squeaked.

"Yes. Much, much more. What say you, Miss Bennet?"

Elizabeth stared at him, searching his eyes for she knew not what, but finding sincerity and affection there.

"I think I would like to know you better, Mr. Darcy."

CHAPTER 28

The following Friday, Mr. Bingley organized a picnic near the pond at the park. Jane and Elizabeth, Georgiana and Mr. Darcy, Caroline and Mr. Bingley, and at the last minute, Colonel Fitzwilliam, were in attendance. Rugs were spread under a large tree near the water and servants laid out a large selection of cakes, breads, and cold meats. Wine flowed freely and the group of friends laughed and talked. Even Miss Bingley was somewhat pleasant, likely due to her proximity to Mr. Darcy, who only tolerated her presence because he knew she would be leaving early to attend a prior engagement with her sister.

After nearly two hours had passed, Caroline Bingley was collected by Mrs. Hurst, and Mr. Bingley spirited Jane away for a walk around the pond. Georgiana went to feed the ducks with her cousin, and Mr. Darcy quickly sat next to Elizabeth, who put down her book at his approach.

"May I assist you in some way, Mr. Darcy?" she asked him sweetly.

He scooted nearer and answered, "Perhaps, Miss Elizabeth. Tell me, if a lady is being courted by a gentleman, does she like to hear compliments?"

"I suppose she would."

"Then may I say how enchanting your hair looks in the sunlight?"

"You may," she answered softly, as her cheeks turned a soft shade of pink. Darcy smiled at her reaction.

"I'm going to enjoy courting you."

"Is that what you're doing?"

"Of course. Hadn't you noticed?"

She looked at him wide eyed, then at her lap.

"Well, I am. Quite seriously."

"I had noticed, Mr. Darcy," she said quietly.

"Good. Do you still plan to leave for Hertfordshire in a week?"

"Jane and I will leave Saturday next. Then it will be little more than a week until the wedding."

"I imagine things will be very different after your sister is wed."

"Yes, they will be. I will miss her terribly, but I am very happy for her," she said lightly, but with a hint of melancholy. "At least I know that she is marrying someone she loves and who loves her in return. I believe she will be very happy with Mr. Bingley."

"I agree. They are well suited to each other and should make one another happy."

"I'm glad you think so, Mr. Darcy."

Darcy did not like the slightly serious turn the conversation had taken and attempted to return to lighter territory.

"Come now, I think that is enough of this 'Mr. Darcy' business. I am beginning to feel like a school master. Will you not call me by my name?"

She smiled archly. "Do you prefer Fitzwilliam or William?"

"I answer to either, though Fitzwilliam can be a mouthful. Only my closest family calls me William."

"Oh." She took a deep breath and added, "I think it could be confusing having you and the Colonel around and both being called Fitzwilliam. May I call you William?"

"Please do. May I call you Elizabeth?"

She felt warm under his steady gaze. "Please do."

He reached his hand forward to where her hand rested on the ground. He gently traced a line down her fingers and across her knuckles, and finally began drawing shapes on the back of her hand. Her cheeks were a soft pink and her neck felt hot. The nerves on the back of her hand were at full attention and soon, her entire right arm was tingling.

"Elizabeth."

She tore her eyes away from his tantalizing movement and looked across the pond, at a squirrel running up a tree, at a child running down a hill in the distance. She looked everywhere but at him.

"Elizabeth. Will you not look at me?"

She shook her head vigorously.

"No?" He sounded amused. "Why ever not?"

She pursed her lips and looked to her left, doing her best to ignore the man who was slowly driving her mad with his incessant drawing on the back of her hand.

"Are you angry with me?"

She shook her head.

He continued his movements, using his entire hand to stretch out over hers as each of his fingers raked slowly from the tip of her nails to her wrist.

"Are you unwell?"

There was definitely amusement in his voice now.

She squared her shoulders and shook her head.

"Are you angry with Fitzwilliam? He has been a bother today."

She tried to hide her smile and again shook her head.

His hand now sat warmly atop hers, his thumb wrapping around her wrist and stroking the delicate skin he found there.

"Did you know your skin is incredibly soft?"

This time her mouth quirked a tiny bit, but she was able to control her smile.

Again, she shook her head.

"It is. I must confess to you that I often wished to touch you last autumn when we were in Hertfordshire together."

She stiffened in surprise and barely stopped her mouth from gaping open.

"What would you have done, had I simply reached out and touched your hand?" he asked softly.

She remained silent, her eyes fixed on the water.

"Would you have slapped me for my impertinence?"

She pursed her lips and tilted her head to the side, as if in thought, but still would not look at him.

"Never mind, do not answer that," he said with a grin.

"Elizabeth?" He leaned forward and whispered in her ear, suddenly serious and very close. "Do you have any idea how lovely you are?"

One last time she shook her head, her movement small and slow.

"Well, you are," he whispered hotly. "So, so lovely."

He traced his fingers up her forearm and down again. His touch was light, like a feather, and she began to wonder if she had imagined it. Slowly, she turned her head toward him and met his gaze.

And then she saw it, and suddenly, she knew. It was in his eyes.

~

Elizabeth was still unsettled about Sir Malcolm. A week had come and gone since their last conversation, and she had yet to have an opportunity to speak with him alone, and she was beginning to fret about it.

He had called twice at Matlock House; once when the drawing room was full of other callers, and the second time Elizabeth herself had been out, so there had yet to be a chance for private conversation. She had seen him at a concert, where he sat across the room with his aunt, at two dinners, where he sat at the other end of the table, and finally at the theatre, where they spoke pleasantries amongst their parties during intermission.

Elizabeth waited eagerly for a chance to speak with him privately, but it seemed as if fate were conspiring against her. Before, when she did not care two figs whether she saw Sir Malcolm, he had been everywhere; sitting beside her, turning pages for her, and always finding his way to her in a crowd. Now, when she wanted to speak to him, he was nigh on impossible to reach! She lamented the fact that a woman could not make a simple call on a man, and felt all the perverseness of his never being where she wanted him to be, when she wanted him to be there.

The next day, Elizabeth was walking in the park with Jane when she saw Sir Malcolm striding towards them. They greeted each other politely, and Jane graciously fell back to walk with the maid who was accompanying them while Elizabeth stepped up to walk with Sir Malcolm.

After a fortifying breath, she began.

"Sir, you have always been honest with me, a trait I appreciate more than you can know, and now I feel I must be honest with you."

"This sounds serious, Miss Elizabeth," he responded.

"A week ago, you asked me a question about my heart."

"Yes?"

"At the time I was unsure of my own feelings, but I feel I must tell you now that my heart is engaged. I'm sorry, Sir, but I thought it was best to tell you the truth."

"I guess it is not engaged in favor of me then?" he asked with a wry smile.

Elizabeth looked down. "No, Sir. I am sorry," she said quietly.

He tipped her chin up with a finger and smiled softly. "Do not worry, Miss Elizabeth. We shall always be good friends, shall we not?"

She smiled with relief and nodded. "Yes, I would like that very much."

"And with any luck, you'll change your mind and I'll be first in line."

Elizabeth gasped slightly in surprise until she saw his mischievous grin. She glared playfully and then said, "As your friend, I will forgive your impertinence."

Sir Malcolm laughed and took her hand in his. "You will be missed in London, Miss Elizabeth." He placed a soft kiss on the back of her hand.

"I shall miss you as well, Sir Malcolm," she said softly, giving him a gentle smile.

CHAPTER 29

"Lizzy, you have been gone too long. I haven't heard two sensible words together since you left," Mr. Bennet grumbled as he made his play on the chess board in his library.

"Papa, you know Mary can be sensible some of the time." She made her move and looked innocently at her father.

"Ha! That is the funniest thing you've said all day, my dear! I grant you she isn't as silly as the other two, but she is far from sensible."

A few minutes elapsed in silence as they played, Mr. Bennet gaining a clear lead over his distracted daughter.

"Papa, there is something I have been meaning to talk to you about."

"What is that, my girl?" he moved his rook and looked up from the board.

"You know I have been invited to spend the summer at Pemberley."

"Yes, you wrote me of it, as did your uncle. Though you may not enjoy yourself with such an unpleasant man about. Are you sure you want to go?"

"He's not so unpleasant really, not once you get to know him. He is perfectly amiable." She moved a pawn as her father scrutinized her.

"Have you actually come to like the man, Lizzy? After what he said about you?"

"He did not mean it, not really, and he has apologized for it. We have become quite friendly."

"I see. Has his behavior toward you changed so much?"

"Not so much. I have simply come to know and understand him better. I fear my earlier judgment of him was not sound."

"I gather you are referring to the story told you by the nefarious Mr. Wickham. I've had a visit from your Uncle Phillips. He informs me that the man is a blackguard and a gambler. You seem to have had a lucky escape, my dear."

"Yes, Father."

They played silently for a while longer and Elizabeth decided to again broach the subject of Pemberley.

"Papa?"

"Yes, Lizzy?"

"About going to Pemberley this summer," he looked at her shrewdly, "the Darcys' plans have changed."

"Have they?" he said with mock surprise.

"Instead of leaving in June, they will go to Derbyshire shortly after Jane's wedding. Mr. Bingley's cousin is getting married in Scarborough and wishes him and Jane to be there, so they want to go to Pemberley earlier than planned. Obviously the Darcys need to be there to greet them."

"I see. And what does this have to do with me?" he asked plainly, focusing his attention on the game. "Check."

Elizabeth looked at the board ruefully and back to her father. "They wish for me to travel with them – in May. It would be more convenient and comfortable, and much less expensive." She watched the board carefully, not meeting his gaze.

"Do you wish to go with them?"

"Yes, I do."

"Why should I allow my daughter to travel over a hundred miles with a man I hardly know and his sister whom I have never met? That does not sound quite right, now does it?"

"You will meet Miss Darcy when they arrive for the wedding. And her companion Mrs. Annesley will be with us. And there will be a driver and a footman. I will be quite safe. I daresay safer than when I have taken the post."

He looked at her from under his bushy gray brows. "You will let me know if Mr. Darcy does anything improper, Lizzy?"

"Mr. Darcy will not do anything improper." She repressed an eye roll.

"Just because you like him now does not mean he is not a man."

"Very well, Papa. I will let you know if anything untoward occurs, though I am sure it will not. Mr. Darcy is a gentleman."

Mr. Bennet sniffed and moved his piece.

"There will be no sense at all in this house, with Jane married and gone and you spending the summer in Derbyshire."

"I may go?" she asked hopefully.

He released a long sigh. "Yes, you may go."

She smiled brilliantly. "Thank you Papa!"

~

27 April, 1812
Darcy House
London
Dear Elizabeth,

I am so pleased that you will be accompanying us to Pemberley! The trip will be so much more exciting with you there! I have much to tell you, but Brother suggests I save some conversation for the journey since we will have endless amounts of time and no real diversions, so I will refrain for the moment.

As for the particulars of our journey, we wish to leave the day after the wedding, as early as possible if that is amenable to you. Fitzwilliam has included an itinerary of all the places we will stop so your family will know where you are. Please let me know your favorite foods and I will ask Cook to include them in the basket for the carriage. Remember to bring a cloak. Even though it is summer, it can be chilly in the carriage if there is a strong wind or much rain, and we occasionally travel into the night. I will bring a few extra books from the library so there will be plenty to go around. There are always blankets and a pillow or two if you wish to sleep.

The journey is long, but Pemberley is worth the trouble. I cannot wait for you to see it! We shall arrive in Hertfordshire on the 1 of May and will call the following afternoon. Until then, I remain,

Your friend,
Georgiana Darcy

Elizabeth refolded the letter and turned her attention to the missive that had been tucked inside it.

Miss Bennet,

Please find enclosed the names and locations of the various inns we will be stopping at during our journey north. My sister and I could not be more pleased at your joining us. I am greatly looking forward to your visit to Pemberley and furthering our friendship.

F.D.

She tucked the missive into the drawer of her small desk, but not before noticing the strong, neat handwriting and the evenness of his lines. Hers always tilted up slightly. *Ever the fastidious master,* she thought with a grin. She grabbed the list of inns and went downstairs to give it to her father.

The next few days passed swiftly and soon the Gardiners arrived. Three days later, Mr. Bingley, his sisters and Mr. Hurst descended on Netherfield. The women of the party kept their distance, attending only those functions which they were bound to out of obligation to their brother.

Bingley hosted a family dinner four days before the wedding. Caroline refused to acknowledge the Gardiners with anything but a small nod, but was otherwise polite, though clearly not enjoying herself. Oddly, she placed Elizabeth next to her at dinner.

"Miss Elizabeth, did you enjoy the season in town?"

"Yes, Miss Bingley, I did."

"I believe Lady Matlock took you to several functions. Did you enjoy the society?" she tried to hide it, but the disdain in her voice was thinly veiled.

"Yes, she did. I met a great many people."

"Was Sir Malcolm a frequent guest at Matlock House?"

"He called and attended dinners, yes."

Caroline faltered slightly, knowing she had never been invited to any of Lady Matlock's functions, but pressed on. "Lady Matlock is an incomparable hostess." Elizabeth smiled slightly. "Does she encourage Sir Malcolm's attentions towards you?"

"That is a private matter, Miss Bingley," Elizabeth said in a firm voice.

"Pardon me, Miss Elizabeth. I meant no offense." Caroline finished her dinner without speaking again to Elizabeth, a small smirk on her face, believing she had her answer from the blush on the lady's cheeks.

~

Two days later, Elizabeth snuck out of the house early in an attempt to escape her mother and her mad wedding preparations. If she was forced to tie one more bow, she would not be responsible for her actions.

A mile and a half later, Elizabeth stopped under her favorite tree. She spread her cloak on the ground to protect her from the dew and sat down, her legs stretched out in front of her, reclining on her elbows. She reached into the small bag she had brought with her and grabbed an apple, taking a large bite as she enjoyed the early morning sun. When she finished it, she threw the core into the brush and laid back, closing her eyes as she rested her hands on her stomach. She drifted to sleep listening to the scurry and rustle of the creatures in the surrounding fields.

Darcy had escaped the house early, or rather escaped Caroline early. Since he'd arrived the night before, he had heard nothing but complaints about the Bennets, and what a trial it would be to be connected to such a family. He had heard enough and retired early, along with Georgiana and Bingley.

He secretly hoped he would see Elizabeth out walking. He hadn't seen her in a week and was desperate for a glimpse of her. As he rode in the fields bordering Longbourn, he slowed his pace, looking for a bonnet moving through the landscape. He saw nothing but a bright yellow patch under a tree in the distance. He scanned again, and when he came across the yellow patch of what he thought were daffodils, he saw something move. He rode closer and realized it was a young woman, lying under the tree. Smiling to himself, he dismounted and tied the horse to the post, quickly climbing over the dividing fence.

He approached quietly, not wanting to startle her. When he was only a few feet away, he stopped and looked at her sleeping form. Her bonnet was on the ground next to her, its ribbons flapping in the breeze. Her hair was up, but a few strands had escaped their pins and a dark curl lay across her cheek. Her yellow dress glowed in the sunshine, the skirts billowing up slightly when the wind blew. He saw a narrow ankle where her skirt had come up a few inches and couldn't keep from staring, though he knew he should look away.

He stood watching her for some time, reveling in the peace that filled him at the sight of her and the sense of intimacy watching her sleep gave him. Finally, he advanced toward her, not knowing the best way to wake her. He could not leave without speaking to her. And what if someone else was to happen by? She was not safe there alone. At least that was how he justified his presence to himself.

He knelt near her head and gently whispered her name, "Elizabeth."

She made a small sound and shifted, but did not wake. He slowly reached his hand out and removed the stray curl from her face. Then, ever so gently, he stroked her cheek with his hand.

"Elizabeth," he said a little louder. She released a contented sigh and smiled lazily, turning her head so her nose nuzzled gently into his palm.

Darcy watched her, mesmerized, until quite unexpectedly, she kissed his palm and mumbled, "Stay." She smiled and settled back into sleep.

Darcy lost all ability to think properly and could focus on nothing but the way her lips had felt on his skin. He briefly wondered if she knew it was him who had touched her and called her name, then decided he did not care – he had been the recipient of her affection and he would enjoy it, whether it had been deliberate or not.

Realizing she was not going to wake, he put his riding coat on the ground next to the tree trunk and sat down, his legs stretched out in front of him, his back against the tree, and reached into his pocket for the small book of sonnets Georgiana had given him for his birthday. He sat next to her, silently keeping watch, for another half hour before Elizabeth began to stir.

She opened her eyes slowly and blinked into the bright sun. She propped herself on her elbows and looked around, wondering what time it was and how long she had slept. When she looked over to her right, she jumped when she saw a pair of black riding boots. Alarmed, she followed the boots up until she met the smiling face of Mr. Darcy.

"Good Morning, Elizabeth. I trust you slept well?"

"Mr. Darcy! What are you doing here?" she asked, sitting up and straightening her dress.

"I was out for a ride and I saw you lying here. I could hardly allow you to sleep unprotected, so I waited for you to awaken," he said simply.

Elizabeth automatically reached to her hair and sighed inwardly when she realized several pins had come undone. She quickly began re-pinning her hair and asked Mr. Darcy, "Why did you not awaken me, sir?"

"You seemed too peaceful to upset. I have not waited overlong. And I must confess I was hoping to run into you when I rode out this morning."

"Were you?" she asked with a bright smile.

He looked into her beaming face, relishing that her smile was finally for him, and answered, "Yes, I did not want to wait until this afternoon to call with Georgiana. Then I would have to share you with a room full of people." He set his book down and rested his hands on his lap, unabashedly watching her fix her hair.

"You may have a point there, Mr. Darcy. I'm afraid nothing is being discussed at Longbourn but the upcoming wedding. I must confess it is why I escaped out here this morning. I cannot talk any more about lace!"

He laughed with her. “Do you nap as a rule on your morning walks, Elizabeth?” he asked with a raised brow.

“No sir, this is something I do rarely. I did not even intend to fall asleep today, but I am afraid I was up rather late talking with Jane last night, and I did not get much rest.”

“You must be trying to squeeze in as much time as possible together before she leaves with Bingley.”

He looked so kind and understanding, as if he really cared about her feelings for her sister. “Yes, we are spending as much time together as we can. I will miss her terribly when she is married and gone.” She thought for a moment and said, “I am glad you found me this morning, Mr. Darcy.”

“You are?”

“Yes.” She looked at her hands where she was twirling a piece of grass. “May I make a confession?” she asked softly.

“Please do.” He resettled his seat and straightened his shoulders, eager to hear what she had to say.

“I was hoping I would run into you today. I knew you had arrived yesterday, and I also did not wish to wait until this afternoon to see you.” Her cheeks flamed red as she told him, and Darcy’s face lit up, thrilled at her desire to see him and endeared by her innocence.

“Then I am glad we found each other. Elizabeth,” he hesitated, “I fear I must make a confession of my own.”

“Oh?” she raised her eyes to look at him.

“When I came upon you earlier, I did try to wake you. I called your name. You did not stir and that is when I decided to wait.” She flushed slightly, but did not appear upset as she looked at him.

“That is not much of a confession, William.”

“No, it is not. My confession is that when I saw you lying here, I wanted to waken you – with a kiss.”

“Oh.” She looked into his eyes timidly, then grew bold from what she saw there. “Why didn't you?”

“I did not wish to frighten you when you woke to such a strange sensation.”

“I am awake now.”

“So you are.” He moved toward her slowly, his eyes fixed on her mouth, his steady approach making her alive with anticipation.

He raised one hand and touched her cheek softly, then brought his lips toward hers until they were only a breath apart. He looked into her eyes and watched them close slowly, preparing to savor her first kiss. He gently pressed his lips to hers, taking his time and drawing out each sensation as it coursed through him.

Elizabeth felt heat. Hot and tingling in her lips, a burning feeling that only seemed to get hotter just as she thought it had reached its peak. She felt a hand on her cheek, holding her to him, and slowly his other hand slipped round her waist to press her closer. Tentatively, she moved her lips against his, attempting to mimic the motion he was using. She felt a sort of grumbling sound in his chest where her torso touched his and she instinctively pressed against him, wanting to be close but not able to get close enough.

She felt something warm and wet pushing against her lips and opened them in response. She felt his tongue trace her upper lip and then her lower, feeling the tickling sensation it produced but not wanting to laugh. His hand on her back was moving up and down, daring a little lower with each stroke.

She had risen to her knees and before she knew what she was about, she had pressed herself completely to him and wrapped her arms around his back. Her left went up into his hair to grasp the soft waves there while her right clutched desperately to his jacket.

Darcy broke from her lips and kissed her jaw lightly, moving down her neck where he planted soft, lingering kisses.

"Elizabeth. My own Elizabeth." She smiled at the love-drunk sound of his voice and the heat of his breath on her neck. "Be mine. Be mine, Elizabeth, no one else's. I cannot live without you."

She froze at his question and stiffened slightly as she ran his words through her mind. Was this a proposal? Or was he requesting further liberties? Before she could decide or reply, he was speaking again.

"My darling, marry me. Marry me and be my wife and my lover and the mother of my children. Be the mistress of Pemberley, as you are already the mistress of me. Be mine, Elizabeth. Say yes."

He resumed kissing her neck as a thousand images whirled in her mind at once. She, Elizabeth Bennet, wife of the most powerful man in Derbyshire. Intimate confidant and (gulp) lover to the heavenly, handsome, maddening man humbling himself before her. In an instant she saw long trips in summer to the seaside and breakfast under a mountain of feathers and white linen sheets. She saw them surrounded by dark haired children, a son with her eyes and his strong jaw, a daughter with her smile and his blue gaze. She felt a warm sense of contentment come over her, an unquestionable feeling of right-ness, and knew this was where she belonged.

"Yes, Fitzwilliam. I will be yours."

Instantly she felt his mouth crashing against hers with none of the gentleness of before, but with a hunger, a fierceness she had not known existed. She opened her lips to him and let him delve deep inside her, returning his fervor as best she could. She felt a stirring in her bosom where he was pressed hard against her and a warm, sinking sensation in her lower belly. His arms were around her back, crushing her to him so tightly she could hardly breathe, but she did not want him to let go. She wrapped her arms tightly around his waist and held him as close to her as she could, feeling the hardness of his chest and the firmness of his hips against her softer body.

They remained locked together longer than either was aware of, but eventually released each other and began a slow walk back to Longbourn.

"I should speak to your father," he said as they moved along the path.

"Must you? I do not want to take away from Jane's day at all. She has waited so long for this."

He smiled down at her. "I see no harm in waiting until after the wedding."

"William, will you think me terribly indecent if I asked you not to mention anything just yet?" His brows rose. "It's just that if my family knows we are engaged," she couldn't help smiling at him as she said it, "I'm afraid Mama will not allow me to accompany you to Pemberley, for she will need me here. We would be forced apart, possibly until the wedding, and my mother will be relentless."

He thought silently for a moment. "I see your point. I do not wish to leave you in your mother's clutches without my protection. Ow!" He rubbed where she had pinched his arm and smiled at her mischievously. "But mostly, I would miss you terribly. We have only just been reunited. I do not know if I could leave you again." He stopped on the path and turned toward her, caressing her cheek softly and leaning down to give her a light kiss.

She sighed as he pulled away. "I would miss you, too. Would it be so terrible to send my father a letter once we are at Pemberley? You could tell him you proposed there."

"I do not like lying, Elizabeth, especially to your father," he said seriously.

"Very well. I shall simply have to retract my acceptance. I have decided that I will need some time to think over your proposal, Mr. Darcy, before I can give you an answer. A fortnight should be enough time," she said with her chin in the air as she marched away from him.

"You teasing little minx." He quickly caught up and pulled her off the path behind a tree, kissing her determinedly while he pinned her against the trunk. "Do you still need to think about my proposal?" he asked as she clung to his shoulders breathlessly.

"Hmm, maybe just a little." She giggled as he growled and kissed her again, this time running his tongue in circles around her own and suckling her bottom lip.

"And now?"

"Maybe a week's time will suffice."

He kissed her again, firmly, and clutched her so close to him she could hardly breathe.

"And now?"

"Not fair, Mr. Darcy. You must remember that if you speak to my father immediately, it will be weeks, perhaps months before we can do this again."

Boldly, she ran her hand lightly up the front of his waistcoat, then skimmed her fingers across the skin at his neck where his cravat ended. She traced the lines of his face with her fingers, all the while looking into his blue eyes with her brown. She saw the desire, the inner conflict, and the surprise he was feeling at her actions. Slowly, tenderness and awe blossomed in his eyes and he grabbed her hand with his own, placing a kiss in her palm.

"Alright my love, if that is what you want. But I must speak with him at least regarding the possibility of a proposal. My honor demands it."

She smiled and stretched to kiss him delicately on his chin. "Alright, Fitzwilliam. I accept your compromise."

CHAPTER 30

The next twenty-four hours flew by, and before they knew it, Jane and Elizabeth were preparing for bed on the last night Jane would be a Bennet. Elizabeth was brushing her sister's hair, the two of them giggling over a childhood memory, when Mrs. Bennet burst into the room, Mrs. Gardiner close on her heels.

Fanny was obviously frazzled, and Mrs. Gardiner led her to a chair before taking a seat herself. Jane and Elizabeth looked at them wonderingly, curious to know what was going on.

"Jane, I must speak to you. Lizzy, you may as well stay, too and spare me the trouble of having to repeat this before your wedding, if you can ever find a man to take you," she said exasperatedly.

They looked at each other in alarm, Jane's eyes wide as she realized what her mother was about to tell her.

"Now girls, it's time you learned about the duties of being a wife." They sat down next to each other on the bed, Jane clutching Elizabeth's hand tightly. Mrs. Bennet began without preamble. "On your wedding night, you should take a bath; it will help you to relax. Put on a new nightgown - something alluring." Mrs. Bennet motioned with her hands while Jane closed her eyes in embarrassment.

"Drink a glass of wine beforehand, it will help with the pain. Now, your husband will come to your chambers and you must lie down on the bed - it's best to blow the candles out; the less you see, the better," she said with such a look of wisdom and surety in her own words, "and he will remove his trousers, and possibly his shirt. Mr. Bingley likes you very much and you are very attractive, Jane, so he may wish to touch and kiss you before he begins."

Jane stared at her mother with wide eyes, desperately praying for this conversation to be over as she clutched Elizabeth's hand even tighter. Elizabeth bit her lip to keep her composure.

"Now, you have never seen a man disrobed before, and if you do not want to, you should keep your eyes closed. He will become inspired," her hand moved upward, "and will enter your womanhood and spill his seed. He may act as if he is in pain, but I assure you he is not." She rolled her eyes at her sister in law.

"Now, the first time you will feel some pain and there will be blood, but not too much. Keep a towel by the bed to cleanse yourself. Simply lie still and let him do as he wishes, and it will be over soon. Afterward, he will thank you and return to his chambers to retire for the night. He may wish to sleep with you, especially in the beginning of your marriage as it will be more convenient if he wishes to have you more than once in a night."

Jane's chin dropped as her eyes met her sister's, both open wide in surprise. *More than once in a night? How…?* Elizabeth mentally shook herself at the idea, and then at the disturbing realization that she had just learned something about men from her mother.

"It is your wifely duty to bear your husband an heir. The more he lies with you, the sooner you will become with child. Your husband will avoid your bed on Sundays and during your courses, and of course when you are with child or ill. Once you have given him an heir, it is alright to cut back on the amount of time you spend together. A headache is a believable way to avoid relations." She nodded at them knowingly.

"Now, do you have any questions?" She looked from one to the other, like a rabbit popping up from a hole in the ground.

Jane and Elizabeth stared at their mother with mouths open and eyes unable to blink. Realizing Jane could not speak, Elizabeth said, "Thank you Mama, that was most instructive."

"Only a mother's duty, child. Now get to bed. Mr. Bingley will not want a red-eyed bride, now will he?" She kissed Jane on the head and left the room, happy to have that done with.

Mrs. Gardiner quietly stood and closed the door behind her sister-in-law, then came to sit across from Jane. "How are you, dear?"

Jane's eyes shifted to look at her aunt, but she could not speak.

"It is not all exactly as your mother says. That is some women's experience, yes, but the act of love can be quite pleasant, especially when you love your husband, as you do, dear." She gave Jane a small smile and continued, "There will be some pain the first time, yes, but if you are relaxed it will not be so bad, and it does not last long. Mr. Bingley loves you very much and will be very gentle with you. Let him guide you, trust him, and don't be afraid to follow your own instincts. He will not hurt you. Love is a gift, and the act of love is very special. Do not let it be ruined by ill-founded fears." Jane nodded, tears of anxiety in her eyes as Elizabeth rubbed her back to comfort her.

"Do you want to ask me any questions? I promise to be honest with you."

Jane was silent for a moment and finally said, "Just one. What did Mama mean when she said 'become inspired'?" She looked at her aunt with a quizzical expression and Mrs. Gardiner's eyes opened wider. Elizabeth giggled and whispered in Jane's ear. Jane's eyes snapped wide open and her mouth dropped.

"No! It cannot be! Whatever am I going to do with it?" Elizabeth couldn't help but laugh, and Mrs. Gardiner was equally unsuccessful in restraining herself. Eventually Jane joined them and said through her giggles, "To think it is like the animals in the barn! Who would have thought?" They laughed until their sides hurt, and finally went to sleep.

~

Jane's wedding day dawned brilliant and glorious. Jane was fretted over by her mother, who was constantly running through the house, waving her handkerchief and calling for her smelling salts. Finally, Jane found a minute alone with Elizabeth.

"Lizzy, I need your help with something."

"What is it, Jane?"

"I want you to keep Mr. Darcy and his sister away from Netherfield tonight." Elizabeth gave her an odd look. "Not for the whole night, but at least until after supper, or perhaps late enough that I will be asleep."

"Jane, what's going on?"

"Oh, Lizzy, I shall die of shame! Everyone will know what we are doing! I cannot have guests in the house when I am… becoming a wife! Caroline and the Hursts are already going back to town after the wedding breakfast, so it will only be Mr. and Miss Darcy. I cannot be the hostess on my wedding night!"

Taking Jane's hands in her own, Elizabeth said calmly, "Do not worry Jane. I will invite the Darcys to stay here for the afternoon. Better yet, I will ask them to walk with me to Oakham Mount. Then we will come back here for supper and I won't let them return until it is late."

Jane's expression relaxed. "Thank you, Lizzy!"

"Do not worry, Jane. I'm sure Charles will ask Mr. Darcy to stay away. You said yourself that he is a very thoughtful man. And Mr. Darcy is quite conscientious as well. I'm sure they have considered it." Elizabeth stroked her arm gently.

"Oh dear! I feel as if my entire life is changing in an instant! I'm so glad you will be beside me, Lizzy. I don't know what I should do without you!"

Elizabeth gave her a wobbly smile and they walked down the stairs together.

~

At Netherfield, Darcy briskly walked into Bingley's dressing room. "You needed me, Bingley?"

"Ah, Darcy! I wondered if I might ask you a favor?" Darcy nodded. "After the wedding breakfast, would you mind staying away for a bit? With my sisters gone back to town, I don't want Jane to feel as if she needs to play the hostess on our wedding day."

"Of course, Bingley, we wouldn't wish to intrude. I've already thought of an alternative. Might I borrow your gig this afternoon? I thought I might take Georgiana for a drive."

"Of course, of course."

"I'm sure the Bennets will invite us for supper, so we won't be back until late. And our rooms are in the opposite wing – too far from the master's suite to hear anything -" Bingley's face began to grow red - "so tell your bride not to worry. We'll go straight to our rooms – you won't even know we're here. And we'll leave first thing in the morning, so you should breakfast in bed." He winked at Bingley.

"Oh, not you, too! Just wait – one day it will be your turn and we'll see who's laughing then!"

Darcy laughed as he ducked out the door before the cuff link Bingley threw at his head could hit him.

~

The wedding was perfect; the sun shone softly through the stain glass windows, leaving the chapel in a haze of warm light. Jane was beautiful, her blue eyes shining as she swept down the aisle on her father's arm. Bingley wore an enormous smile, balanced by the scowl on his sisters' faces.

Darcy stood beside him, tall and officious, disliking being in front of a crowd. He occasionally stole a glance at Elizabeth where she stood next to Jane, careful not to stare and draw attention to himself. Elizabeth flatly refused to look at him. She knew if their eyes met, all would be obvious to anyone who was watching, and since they were standing at the front of a rather full church, the chances of being observed were high.

Afterward, they walked the short distance to Longbourn for the wedding breakfast. Mrs. Bennet had truly outdone herself. There were trays upon trays of elegantly presented food, endless bottles of wine, and a table filled with prettily iced cakes and fancy pies. Jane and Bingley stood near the entrance greeting guests as they arrived. Speeches were made, toasts were drunk, and after a few hours, the bride and groom left for Netherfield.

After most of the guests had gone, Darcy invited Elizabeth to drive out with him and Georgiana. Grateful he and Mr. Bingley were giving Jane the privacy she so desperately needed, Elizabeth happily spent the next few hours showing them the countryside surrounding Meryton. The Darcys had supper at Longbourn, where, thankfully, her sisters were too tired to be much bother.

Mrs. Bennet, however, seemed to have boundless stores of energy. After more than a month of planning, weeks of hectic fittings and consultations, and the completion of the event itself, she still had the energy to discuss loudly how grand her daughter would be, how Netherfield was the finest house in the county, and how she hoped Mr. Bingley would buy it for her dear Jane. Jane had always been so beautiful, of course she was destined to marry a rich man. Had she not said so since she was an infant? And Mr. Bingley was so agreeable! How fortunate that her Jane was married to such a handsome, wealthy gentleman.

Elizabeth tried to ignore her, attending to Georgiana, who looked quite shocked but was holding up well, at the opposite end of the table. She stole a few glances at Darcy, who had turned his head away from Mrs. Bennet and was deep in conversation with Mr. Gardiner across the table from her. Elizabeth was thankful she had some relatives of whom she could be proud and silently thanked her mother for not arranging the seating, allowing them to choose their dinner partners.

After the meal, the ladies sat down in the drawing room while the men went to Mr. Bennet's library. Mr. Gardiner, having an uncanny knack for knowing when he was and was not required, busied himself at the far end of the room, while Mr. Bennet and Darcy sat near the low burning fire.

"Mr. Bennet, I wonder if I might speak to you about something of import."

"What could that possibly be, Mr. Darcy?"

"I wish to court your daughter, Miss Elizabeth," Mr. Bennet stared at him, "and then I wish to marry her."

Mr. Bennet's eyebrows shot up. "You want my Lizzy?"

Darcy answered steadily, "Yes, sir, I do."

"And may I ask why you have taken so sudden an interest in my daughter? I was led to believe you did not find her tempting in the least." Bennet steepled his hands and sat back.

Was he never to live that comment down? "I have favored your daughter for some time, Mr. Bennet, since last autumn when I stayed at Netherfield. It is not sudden at all, I assure you."

Mr. Bennet looked at him amusedly. "And does she return your regard?"

"I doubt she feels as strongly as I do, but I do not believe she is indifferent to me, either."

"I see. Have you asked her for her hand?"

Darcy cringed slightly at the slight falsehood. "I had hoped to secure her hand this summer, which is why I wished to ask for your consent before I traveled to Pemberley."

"Hmmm. You've thought of everything, haven't you, Mr. Darcy? I suppose I ought to ask you all the usual questions. I'm sure you know what they are, so why don't you just tell me and if any information is lacking, I shall ask." He waved his hand dismissively.

Mr. Bennet was enjoying toying with him, much like a barn cat with a mouse caught by the tail. Darcy was not used to being treated in such a fashion, but he put his indignation aside for the sake of Elizabeth.

"Well sir, I have an estate in Derbyshire, as you know. It brings in 10,000 pounds a year. I have a house in town, which your eldest daughters have visited, that I inherited with the estate. I am the eldest son and have no brothers; my sister Georgiana is my only living immediate family member. Everything is owned free and clear by me. There are no mortgages on any of my properties, and I am not fond of excessive gaming or drinking, so there is not likely to ever be. I also have various other investments in shipping, textiles, etc, and a few smaller estates in Wales and Scotland, which earn another 4,000 pounds on average."

He leaned forward, elbows on knees, his voice earnest. "I will provide generously for your daughter. She will want for nothing and will have unlimited access to whatever she needs. I plan to settle 20,000 pounds on her when we wed, and her allowance will be as high as she desires."

Mr. Bennet's eyes widened slightly, but he was determined not to be impressed. Darcy continued, "I assure you, sir that I love you daughter very much and will do all that is in my power to ensure her happiness."

He looked squarely into Mr. Bennet's eyes until the older gentleman spoke. "And what of later? What if there is no heir? Is your property entailed upon a cousin?"

Ignoring his snide tone, Darcy answered him civilly. "The property of Pemberley is entailed to the extent that it cannot be separated, but it is not entailed away from the female line. If I were to die without an heir, Pemberley would immediately fall to my sister Georgiana, and on to her eldest son. If we have daughters and no sons, our eldest daughter would inherit. Elizabeth would be well provided for in the event of my death. She may live at Pemberley as long as she chooses, and if she so wished, the dower house is large and comfortable, and she would have rights to it until her death. Any children we have will be well provided for as well."

"Again, Mr. Darcy, I must say you seem to have thought of everything. I will not dally with you." *Any longer*, thought Darcy. "Lizzy has always been a favorite of mine, and she will not be easy to part with. But she will not accept just any man, even one as well-qualified as you, so I advise you to make sure you know what you are about before you ask her." He gave Darcy a meaningful look.

Darcy tried not to show a smirk of satisfaction. "So I have your blessing, sir?"

"You have my consent – IF Lizzy agrees to it. I will withhold my blessing until I speak to my daughter. Does she know about this conversation?"

"I will discuss it with her as soon as I have the chance."

"If I know my Lizzy, she will want to keep this quiet as long as possible, so I shall refrain from sharing this with Mrs. Bennet until I hear from her." Mr. Bennet rose. "Shall we join the ladies?"

CHAPTER 31

Elizabeth wandered through the garden at Pemberley, marveling that within a few months, this would be her home and her responsibility. She ran her hand over the blooms on the hydrangea bushes and cut a few blossoms to place in her room.

She let her mind wander over the last several days.

She would never forget the first time she saw Pemberley. Georgiana had fallen asleep and Darcy had enticed her over to his side of the carriage. She had soon followed Georgiana into the land of nod, Darcy's arms wrapped tightly about her. She awakened to his voice in her ear.

"Elizabeth. Dearest, wake up. We are nearly there. Wake up, Elizabeth."

Elizabeth slowly opened her eyes and looked around. Georgiana was asleep across from her and Darcy was next to her, his arms wrapped around her, his solid chest beneath her head and shoulder. She felt his breath on her temple as he spoke to her.

"I am awake. Where are we?"

"We are in Pemberley Woods. We'll be home in a quarter hour."

Elizabeth smiled at his choice of words and looked out the window at the passing trees. The land was much harsher than Hertfordshire, that she could tell right away. The contrast of gray stones and dark fir trees was striking. They were on a hill and she could see into the distance one hill after another, all covered with dark trees, the space between them broken up with fields and pastures dotted with sheep.

Soon they stopped and he led her down a short footpath, taking her hand as soon as they were out of sight of the carriage. They quickly came to a clearing and Elizabeth was met with a breathtaking view of the great house, backed by a ridge covered in dense trees, the massive park surrounded by lush woods.

"Oh, William! It's breathtaking!"

"Do you like it, Elizabeth?"

"Like it? I can hardly find the words to describe it."

The house itself was large and made of a light colored stone, sitting peacefully at the far end of the valley before them. There was a stream running in front of it which swelled into a small lake, reflecting the house in its waters.

"This is Pemberley," he stated simply, gazing out across the land of his fathers. Elizabeth turned to watch him, noticing how stately his profile looked and how all his features seemed to relax here. There was a peace about him that was not usually present. Finally he turned to her. "Does it please you, Elizabeth?"

"I am delighted. I have never seen its equal." She looked at his eager face and felt, not for the first time, that she had some bit of power over him, and she was overcome with the desire to make him happy and bring a smile to his face. "It is truly beautiful, William. I will be very happy to call it home."

He smiled and stroked her cheek softly before leading her back to the carriage.

She clipped a few more flowers for her basket and smiled, thinking how fortunate she was to marry a man that she loved and who loved her in return, and one who had such pleasant relations – well, excluding Lady Catherine of course. Mr. Bingley was a very nice man and Elizabeth did sincerely like him, but every time she thought of Miss Bingley and Mrs. Hurst, she gave thanks again for Georgiana.

After being at Pemberley for a few days, Georgiana had begun to suspect something was going on between Elizabeth and Darcy, but said nothing. When they told her of their engagement, she had jumped up and down crying, "I knew it! I knew it!"

After several minutes of sloppy kisses on cheeks and tight hugs, Georgiana had run from the room to tell Mrs. Reynolds, the housekeeper, who had been speculating along with Miss Darcy on the nature of the relationship between the master and Miss Bennet.

Elizabeth laughed slightly at the memory. She had never seen Georgiana more animated. Fitzwilliam had promptly written to her father to inform him of their formal engagement, and Elizabeth had written as well, telling Mr. Bennet how happy she was and how much she was looking forward to becoming Mrs. Darcy.

Mr. Bennet had replied with his usual sardonic wit, and Darcy did not think he sounded overly happy to be parting with his favorite, but Elizabeth read between the lines and ensured him that her father was happy for her, but sad to see her go. Mr. Bennet also promised to let Elizabeth inform her mother of the engagement herself, something she was not sure was a blessing.

She sighed again as she wandered into the house with her basket of flowers. Funny, Pemberley already felt like home. Darcy had sent off letters of announcement to Colonel Fitzwilliam and Sir Malcolm, and Elizabeth had written to Jane and the Gardiners, all of whom sent their warmest congratulations and hopes for the couple's happiness. The announcement would not be in the paper for a few weeks yet, and Elizabeth was putting off telling her mother for as long as possible. Preferably not until Jane arrives.

But now, it was time to go inside and meet Mrs. Reynolds for a tour of the mistress's chambers.

~

"Has this tub always been here?" Elizabeth asked as she looked at a large, gleaming copper tub.

"No, Miss Bennet. Mr. Darcy ordered it in London last winter and requested it be installed here. The ottoman was moved here from another sitting room."

"Last winter? Which month?"

"February, Miss. I received a letter from him informing me of its arrival around the seventh, I believe."

"Thank you, Mrs. Reynolds. Is there anything else I should see of the mistress's chambers?"

"Yes, Miss Bennet. Follow me."

Elizabeth and Georgiana followed her through Ann Darcy's old chambers, looking under dust cloths and exclaiming about furniture pieces. Mrs. Reynolds was very knowledgeable about the history of Pemberley and told them which pieces came from where and which had been Mrs. Darcy's favorites.

"She loved this dressing table. It had been a gift from her mother when she came out, and she had it brought over from Matlock." Mrs. Reynolds looked wistful as she gingerly touched the gleaming wood.

Georgiana approached the piece slowly and reached out to touch the warm red wood. Elizabeth watched her friend carefully and came to a decision.

"Mrs. Reynolds, I believe the dressing table in the room I am in now is more suited to my height. I would like that one moved in here, and if Miss Darcy does not object, we can place Lady Ann's in her room. It is only fitting that a daughter have her mother's favorite piece, just as she is preparing to come out herself."

Georgiana looked at Elizabeth with shining eyes and the two quickly clasped hands.

"Thank you, Elizabeth," Georgiana whispered.

Elizabeth gave her hand a squeeze and Mrs. Reynolds led the way into the sitting room with eyes cast down.

~

"Enter!"

Elizabeth stepped into Darcy's study and immediately slipped behind his desk to plant a kiss on his cheek.

"What was that for?" he asked as she settled into the seat across from him.

"No reason. Can I not wish to show affection to my betrothed without having a particular motive?"

"Of course you may – your displays of affection are always welcome. Have you completed the tour of your new chambers?"

"Yes, I have. I think I will like them very much. I'm considering papering it in yellow. It would be so bright and sunny in the morning. What do you think?"

"Sounds very cheerful – like you. But you know you may decorate however you wish – it is your room to do as you will."

"Yes, but I believe you will often be there, too, and I do not wish you to be uncomfortable." She spoke evenly, but her blush told of her embarrassment on this particular topic.

He looked at her steadily for a moment, then responded, "That is considerate of you. I am fond of yellow, especially on you, so go ahead with your plans."

"I did not know I was gaining such an agreeable husband," she teased to lighten the suddenly heavy mood. "Perhaps you could tell me what you do not like so I will know what to avoid in my redecorating."

He steepled his fingers in front of his face and places his elbows on the desk. "Hmmm. I do not like peach. Lady Catherine had an entire drawing room done in it and I found it quite nauseating."

"I can imagine. Any others?"

"I am not particularly fond of gold and overdone or ornate furnishings. I have been wanting to change the green and gold drawing room in London for some time now, but did not have the slightest idea what I would change it to."

"I will remember that for the next time we are there. Any favorites I should know about?"

"I have always liked red. Actually, I think it would be very becoming on you."

"You do?" she wondered if she should tell him she had always wanted to wear red, but her mother would never allow it. Perhaps she would order a red dress as a surprise.

"Yes, it suits you. Are you going to redo your study as well?"

"Yes, I believe so. I haven't decided on anything yet, though. I will have to give it some thought. Fitzwilliam?"

"Yes?"

"May I ask you an odd question?" she asked looking at her hands.

"You may ask me anything. What do you wish to know?"

"I just wondered why you ordered a new bathing tub for the mistress's chambers last winter. Mrs. Reynolds said you ordered it in February."

He let out a ragged breath and leaned back in his chair. "I knew how much you liked baths and thought you would enjoy it."

She looked at him askance. "How did you know I liked baths so much?" she asked with a mixture of indignation and curiosity.

"I have very loyal servants, my dear, and when I asked if you were comfortable and enjoying your stay, they happened to mention you seemed particularly appreciative of the large bathing tub. That's when I ordered the new one for Pemberley."

"I do not know what to say. I will be certain to guard my tongue around the servants in future. Did you know you wanted to marry me in February then?"

"I believe I have always wanted to marry you, since the day you wandered into Netherfield with your petticoats six inches deep in mud. But yes, that was about the time I realized I could marry no other and decided to propose to you," he told her with a small grin.

"Oh. Why did you wait so long?" she asked, slightly disbelieving.

"Well, it is hard to propose to someone who is not there." She looked down at her hands. "I had planned to ask you the night of the ball at Matlock House, but as you know, events led to a different outcome, and I waited to ask until I was sure of your affection."

"You were going to ask me the night of the ball? When we returned home or at the ball itself?"

He smiled that she now referred to his houses as home and answered her question. "I had planned on asking you to join me in the library before we retired, and I was to going to ask you in front of the fire. I had always thought of it as our room – it seemed a fitting place."

"I, too, have thought of it as our room. I am sorry your original plan did not work out. How disappointed you must have been!"

"Yes, I was. And angry and confused and a host of other emotions I do not wish to recall. But it is behind us now. Now you are mine and there can be no running away," he said with a sly smile.

"You need have no fear on that count. I find I have no desire to run away from you."

"Elizabeth?"

"Yes, dear?"

"What would you have said? If I had asked you the night of the ball, what would your response have been?" he asked softly.

She took a deep breath. "I cannot say for certain, of course, but I imagine I would have asked for some time to think it over. I did not realize I had come to care for you in that regard until I was leaving London. I realized I would not have felt so betrayed if I didn't care for you." Darcy winced at the mention of his poor behavior. "But I probably would have accepted you... eventually."

She smiled and walked round to his side of the desk, putting her hand on his arm. She kissed his cheek and walked out of the room, saying goodbye over her shoulder as Darcy stared after her, his head tilted slightly to one side in contemplation.

~

Finally, after a week of procrastination, Elizabeth decided she could put off writing to her mother no longer. With a deep breath, she sat at the writing desk in her sitting room and began a letter to her mother, followed by another for Charlotte.

Longbourn, 4 days later

"Hill! Hill! My salts! Kitty, Lydia, Mary! Where are those girls?" Mrs. Bennet ran through the house, waving a letter frantically above her head.

"Mr. Bennet, Mr. Bennet!" She burst into the bookroom. "Can you believe it? Our Lizzy? Engaged to Mr. Darcy! Ten thousand a year!"

"Yes, dear. I am aware," he answered drolly.

"Oh, how you delight in vexing me! How could you not tell me sooner? Oh, you teasing man!" she called over her shoulder as she left a grinning Mr. Bennet alone with his books.

"Mary! Where are your sisters? Lydia cannot go to Brighton now. We must prepare for the wedding!"

"They have gone to visit Maria Lucas, mama," Mary answered plainly.

"Come Mary, put on a better dress. We must call on my sister Phillips and Lady Lucas." She began up the stairs, an unsmiling Mary in her wake. "This will show those upstart Lucases. What is Longbourn to half of Derbyshire and ten thousand a year!?"

Hunsford Parsonage, the same day

Charlotte sat in her parlor re-reading a letter from Elizabeth, a particular passage receiving more attention than the rest.

...while I am sure this is no surprise to you, my friend, I am sure it will be to your husband and his noble patroness. I shall not presume to tell you what actions to take, but may I suggest a trip to Lucas Lodge in the very near future? You may find the air there more agreeable than that of Kent...

"The trunks are all packed, madam."

"Thank you, Daisy. Make sure James knows to be ready in the morning. I will depart at first light."

"Yes, madam."

Charlotte looked at the letter she had penned to her husband. It was unfortunate that a parishioner was on his deathbed and that Lady Catherine had seen fit to send Mr. Collins to comfort the family in this time of need. He would likely not return before she left. Mr. Collins would have to take comfort in the fact that his wife was needed by her family due to a "most urgent matter". She trusted he would not ask too many questions.

He rarely did.

~

Blackburn, Matlock, Derbyshire, 2 days later

Lady Matlock sat at her writing desk and eagerly opened her latest letter from Elizabeth. She hadn't heard from her in nearly a fortnight and was becoming concerned. Halfway through, she caught her breath and dropped the letter.

After taking a moment to compose herself, she picked up the letter and re-read the section that had so shocked her.

…I cannot tell you how happy I am! Fitzwilliam is everything I could ever want in a husband, and I have every confidence that we will be deliriously happy together. We plan to wed in August, in Hertfordshire, and would be so happy if you could attend. Your friendship and guidance has meant so much to me, and I truly appreciate everything you have done on my behalf. Your kindness will always be remembered…

Lady Matlock first felt indignation and a little anger. She had introduced Elizabeth to countless suitable men and she had turned them all away. What made her think she had the right to poach amongst her own family?

But after several minutes' deliberation and another perusal of the letter, she was softened by Elizabeth's words of love for Fitzwilliam, joy at their engagement, and gratefulness for all her assistance. She had hoped to see Darcy make a splendid match, both of affection and fortune, but she grudgingly admitted (to herself only) that she was being a bit of a hypocrite and decided to put on a brave face and seek out her husband in his study. Perhaps he had a letter from Darcy.

"Helen! Can you believe this?" Lord Matlock waved a letter in front of her. "Darcy is engaged to Miss Bennet!"

"I know. I've just had a letter from Elizabeth." She sighed and sat down in front of his desk. "What do you think?"

"I was about to ask you the same thing," answered Lord Matlock. "You know her better than I. Will they do well together?"

"I believe so. Now that it is before me, I wonder that I never thought of it before."

Lord Matlock nodded. "I would wish she was better connected and had a substantial dowry, but at least she is a good sort of girl, and Darcy certainly seems wild about her." He gestured to the letter again. "Well, as wild as he ever seems about anything. So I do not need to talk Darcy out of it?"

She raised an eyebrow. "When has Fitzwilliam ever been talked out of anything?"

Matlock smiled fleetingly. "Good point. Well my dear, when shall we leave for Pemberley?" he asked, knowing his wife would want to see them for herself.

"Tomorrow I think. Nothing like a little surprise visit to celebrate an engagement." She smiled mischievously.

Matlock laughed. "You are positively devious, wife!"

"Yes, and you love that about me." She smirked as she left the room to pack for their trip.

Getting Darcy and Elizabeth together may not have been her idea, but it would not stop her from taking credit for the match, or from assisting with all the wedding preparations. After all, she was the closest thing Darcy had to a mother now and Elizabeth was her protégé. Who better to handle all of the details?

~

The Hurst Townhouse, one week later

"Anything of interest today, Caroline?" Louisa asked her sister as she entered the breakfast parlor.

"Nothing of note as yet. Lady Clayton has thrown another scandalous dinner party, but that is nothing new," she huffed, bored, and continued reading the society pages, a dainty floral tea cup in one hand.

Several minutes passed in silence until the sound of breaking glass broke into the stillness.

"NO!"

"Caroline, whatever is the matter?" asked Louisa in a worried tone.

"It can't be. It simply cannot BE!" shouted Caroline.

"What cannot be?" asked her sister.

"That conniving, two-faced, stupid little HOYDEN! How DARE she?"

"Who?"

"He's mine! MINE!" Caroline stomped her foot and clinched her fists by her side, her face a bright magenta.

"Caroline, what on earth are you speaking of? Who is a hoyden? Who is yours?"

Taking a shuddering breath, her temples throbbing, Caroline said through clenched teeth, "That country chit and Mr. Darcy." Her nostrils were flared and her teeth almost chattered from her restrained rage.

"Eliza Bennet?" Louisa asked in surprise. "And Mr. Darcy? Really?"

Even the sight of her sister in an apoplectic fit could not restrain Louisa's delight in fresh gossip. Her eyes lit up at the thought of the ruckus this would create in society, until she remembered that she herself was now connected to the Bennets through her brother's marriage.

"Louisa, tell Mr. Hurst it is time to visit his brother in the country. I'm suddenly feeling a need for fresh air. I shall be ready to leave after breakfast tomorrow."

Caroline marched out of the room with her head held high, so high in fact that Louisa wondered how she could see where she was going.

~

Rosings, Kent, later that day

"How long has the mistress been going at it?"

"Over an hour now." A loud crash shook the wall behind the footman. He smiled at the young maid. "Don't worry, she'll calm down eventually and then hopefully she'll be off to London and we'll all have a bit of a holiday.

Crash!

"What got her so upset?" asked the maid.

"You didn't hear?" She shook her head. "Looks like Mr. Darcy's gone and got himself engaged – and not to the young mistress."

The maid's eyes widened. "How long do you think she'll be going on?" Her words were punctuated by the sound of heavy glass being thrown into a fireplace and shattering into tiny pieces.

"Awhile, I guess. Care for a walk, Mina?"

She smiled. "Thank you, Thomas. I'd like a walk."

She took his arm and followed him into the back garden, only starting slightly when another boom shook the wall beside her.

CHAPTER 32

August 5, 1812
Wedding Day of Fitzwilliam Darcy and Elizabeth Bennet
9 pm

Elizabeth sat in front of the mirror, brushing her hair slowly. She had long ago dismissed the maid, wishing for a few minutes of solitude before her groom would join her. She looked at herself in the mirror and wondered that she didn't look any different. She felt like a new person. She had a new title, a new name, a new position in society, a new home, a new family. It seemed only fitting that her reflection would be different as well, but her same brown eyes and chestnut curls looked back at her.

"Mrs. Darcy," she said quietly. She smiled slightly and took a deep breath as she thought about the events that had led to her new title.

Lady Matlock had proved herself to be efficient and decisive – not that anyone had ever doubted she would be. She wasn't at Pemberley a full day before she took over the wedding plans, and before they knew what had happened, Darcy and Elizabeth had a wedding date in early August, and instead of Hertfordshire, the wedding would take place at the Pemberley church. Darcy's family had been notified and nearly all planned to be in attendance – minus Lady Catherine, of course. But then, she had not been invited.

Jane and Bingley arrived a fortnight later and the Bennet family came in mid-July. It had been a hectic time, filled with social engagements and wedding preparations, with barely a moment to herself.

Looking at the silver brush with her new initials engraved on the back of it, Elizabeth forcefully pushed back the unpleasant memories of her mother embarrassing her in front of Mr. Darcy's family, and of Lady Matlock winking at her as she gifted her a blood-red silk nightgown the night before. She would think of nothing humiliating or disconcerting. She would focus on the fact that she was now a married woman, and that she had a loving husband who would be by her side all her days.

She smiled softly as she thought of Fitzwilliam. He would be here soon. She stood up from the dressing table and blew out the candle. She went around the room, snuffing candles and turning down lamps until there were only lowly lit lamps on either side of the bed. There was no fire due to the August heat, and her windows and balcony door stood open to allow a breeze to sweep through.

She loosened the belt on her white silk robe and went to stand on the dark balcony, letting the cool night breeze refresh her heated skin. This particular night gown had been chosen by her aunt and she felt that it flattered her and was appropriate for their first night together as man and wife. She did not yet feel bold enough to wear the red one, but she suspected she would soon enough.

After several minutes spent staring at the moon's reflection in the stream, she heard a light tapping and then the gentle sliding sound of the door to her room opening. Soon, a pair of warm arms enveloped her from behind and she leaned back onto a firm chest.

"How are you, my love?" he asked quietly.

"I am well. How are you, my darling?"

"I've never been better."

"Really? And why do you suppose that is?" she asked, unable to suppress her urge to tease, even on this night.

"Today, I attained my heart's desire." He leaned his head forward and kissed her neck softly.

She inhaled sharply at the sensation.

"William?"

"Yes, my love?"

"Nothing," she said quietly as she shook her head.

"What is it, Lizzy?"

She turned in his arms and buried her face in his chest.

"I suppose I am a little nervous," she said in a muffled voice.

"Lizzy." He grasped her shoulders and held her away from him, stroking her arms gently. "Do you have any idea how lovely you are? My sweetest Elizabeth, will you not look at me?"

She raised her head and looked at him shyly.

"My love, look at you! You are so beautiful! All the times I imagined this night, but this..." His eyes raked down her figure. He reached her feet and swept his gaze back up, his color rising as he stopped at her breasts.

At first she felt self-conscious from his perusal, but as he continued she began to feel bold, and when he flushed she realized he was just as overcome as she was. Slowly, she stepped back into his arms and reached around his waist. She tilted her head up for a kiss and he stroked her cheek, then the hair at her temple.

"Elizabeth, my own Elizabeth."

"Yes, Fitzwilliam, I am yours."

"As I am yours. I promise you now, Elizabeth, there will never be another. It will always be you."

She understood his meaning as she glanced at the bed to her right. "And I will always be yours. I promise."

He led her to the edge of the bed. "Come, my dearest, loveliest Elizabeth. Let me show how much I love you, how much I need you."

As he reached to pull her to sit by him on the bed, she stayed his arm. "Wait," she said firmly.

His brow furrowed in concern and disappointment. "What is it?"

"I want to tell you something. I… I just want you to know…"

He tilted his head and she ran her fingers along the side of his face. He grabbed her hand and kissed her palm softly. "What is it, my love?"

"I must tell you that I – that you are so… that you are dearer to me than anyone else. You have my whole heart, William. And I know that you feel passionately for me, but know that I also… I feel… you are so wonderful! And I am so happy!" She smiled radiantly through her nervous speech. "I want you to know that I love you dearly, beyond anything I ever imagined I could feel for anyone. I want you to know that I give myself freely – tonight. Not because it is my wifely duty or your marital right, but because I want to belong to you, in every way. I am not frightened. A little nervous, I do so want to please you, but I am not afraid. I trust you. Completely. You are everything I could ever wish for and I… I just want you to know how much I love you!" She grabbed at the silk of her robe in frustration. "Oh, there don't seem to be the right words!"

He grabbed her fidgeting hands in one of his own and cupped her cheek with the other. "I understand you perfectly, Elizabeth. That is why there is an act of love. So that we might show each other everything we cannot find words for."

She looked at him with questioning eyes. "You will show me what to do?"

"Of course, my love. But I do not think you will need much instruction; your instincts are perfect so far. I love that you told me what is in your heart. I will treasure your words always."

She smiled and he saw pure love and adoration in her eyes. "Make me yours, Fitzwilliam."

EPILOGUE

Darcy took Elizabeth to the Lakes for a wedding trip, and he soon saw the advantages of pleasing one's wife. He set out to indulge her daily, and she reciprocated in the most delightful ways. He now understood the sometimes bemused expression he saw on some of his recently married acquaintance and why Bingley was so jovial during their last visit, even beyond his usual cheerfulness.

Elizabeth was a delight. A charming, lovely, sweet, enchanting temptress. He found himself smiling at the oddest times, and while never one to become giddy or foolishly grin at nothing, he did catch himself, on more than one occasion, on the cusp of releasing a very un-manly laugh. He would not call it a giggle exactly, but its very presence did unnerve him somewhat.

Elizabeth was no less pleased with her husband. He was her rock, her protector, her provider, and her dearest friend. She feared nothing and counted on him for everything. The material advantages of her marriage were not important to her beyond her daily comforts, but he provided something infinitely more valuable to her. He knew her, understood her tastes and preferences, and went out of his way to show her a view he thought she would appreciate or purchase a book he thought she would like.

She was doted on, cared for, and thoroughly loved. Her independence did not balk at his solicitude as she thought it might, for he was neither high-handed nor officious with her, but careful to ask her opinion on matters that concerned her. He trusted her completely and it showed in every touch, every show of confidence, and every word said in her praise. She found that her love for him grew daily, and that just when she thought she could not care for him more, he did something unexpected and her heart grew in affection for him. She was always quick to show her regard and her husband was exceedingly happy with this aspect of his wife's disposition.

A few months after their wedding, a joyful Elizabeth told her husband that she expected she was with child. Early the following September, shortly after their first wedding anniversary, Elizabeth gave birth to a rosy baby boy, whom they called Bennet. He was followed in quick succession by his brother Richard, a decidedly large baby – which Elizabeth wasted no time in blaming on her taller-than-average husband. Next came Madeline, Henry, Helen, and Jonathon in two year increments.

Jane and Charles Bingley were just as happy as everyone predicted they would be. Within a year of their wedding, they were blessed with a daughter, christened Elizabeth. They then bought an estate in Yorkshire and moved only thirty miles away from Pemberley. After getting settled, Jane increased again, resulting in their second daughter, Margaret. She was followed twenty months later by a son and heir, a fiery-haired boy called Charles.

The Bingleys were happier than even they thought they could be, and Jane and Elizabeth delighted in the knowledge that their children would grow up together. It was because of their closeness that Elizabeth noticed and then became worried when Jane began increasing rapidly when young Charles was two years old. Jane became so uncomfortable and short of breath that she was forced to lie down for the last six weeks of her confinement. Finally, she delivered two healthy girls, Jane and Marianne.

Mrs. Bingley (in a very un-Jane-like display) swore she would never be the same again and vowed to not have another baby. Poor Charles felt so badly after his wife's ordeal that he promised to stay away from her, even going so far as to move into another room in a separate wing to keep temptation at bay.

He kept his word for nearly five months before succumbing, once again, to his angel. Jane was fortunate, however, and it wasn't until the twins were celebrating their fourth birthday that she delivered a healthy, bawling boy, christened William after his uncle. The delivery was blessedly easy and afterward, Charles was allowed to remain with his wife in *their* rooms.

Two years after they wed, the Darcys hosted a house party. Among the guests were Elizabeth's sister Mary, the Bingleys, and a Mr. Hargrove from Buckinghamshire. Or was it Northamptonshire? Elizabeth wasted no time in introducing the parson to her very single sister. His position, morals, and upright standards attracted Mary, and her piety, seriousness, and perky bosom (not unlike her sister's) attracted him. Eight months later, a very pleased Elizabeth attended their wedding.

When she was seventeen, Lydia Bennet was caught kissing a militia officer behind the stable and was promptly sent to stay with Mr. Bennet's sister, Sarah Gordon. Horrid Thomas Gordon had inherited his father's estate and Michael had joined the Royal Navy. Thomas's wife and Lydia tolerated each other to a degree, and when Michael returned home with three of his fellow officers for a long visit, the young Mrs. Gordon wasted no time pushing Lydia toward the eligible sailors.

Four months later, a rather robust and glowing Lydia wed Commander Henry Jackson. Commander Jackson found much happiness in being aboard a vessel for long months at a time, then returning home to his young and vibrant wife, only to leave her again in a month's time. They lived in Essex and had three daughters, which Mrs. Bennet blamed on the water. If it weren't for all the sea air, and all the unhealthy, salty water, she knew that her darling girl would have done her duty and provided a whole flock of sons, she was sure of it.

Catherine Bennet wed a vicar she met in Yorkshire while visiting her sister Jane, whom she had grown considerably closer to since the latter's marriage and defection from Hertfordshire. They courted simply and wed quickly, then proceeded to have three sons in four years. Mrs. Bennet was exceedingly proud, and for the first time, Kitty had her mother's favor over her younger sister.

Charlotte and Mr. Collins were blessed with only two daughters in seven years of marriage. Mr. Collins was not pleased, especially after seeing how prolific his cousins were, and with so many boys among them! Even the plain and dour Mary had had two sons after only four years of marriage. He could not comprehend how they were so much more successful at begetting heirs than he. Perhaps it was Charlotte? She was seven and twenty when they married. Could she be too old to bear sons? Of course, it never occurred to him that he might want to visit his wife's chambers more than once a week if he wished for more offspring.

Charlotte was happy with her two daughters, Catherine Ann, who unfortunately had the look of her father about her, and Rose Charlotte, who was a more delicate version of Charlotte herself. Sadly, she never did become Mistress of Longbourn. When their youngest was but three years old, poor Mr. Collins became ill with pneumonia after a severe cold he contracted while trying to deliver spiritual edification to Lady Catherine during a heavy rain. After three weeks in his bed, he succumbed to the illness, and Charlotte became a widow at six and thirty. She and her daughters moved to a cottage on the Bennet estate so that she might be closer to her family and her daughters could be raised near the home of her childhood.

Mrs. Bennet was so thrilled to see her daughters well married that she was constantly in some sort of over-excited fit. Five daughters married! And to such wealthy, agreeable gentlemen! Even Mary had found a husband, and was now on her fourth confinement. When she thought of Lydia's young commander, such a handsome sailor, oh my!

She was so proud, nary a conversation went by that she did not exclaim to her neighbors of the good fortune of her daughters and the great beauty and accomplishments (and inheritances) of her grandchildren. One day, while expostulating to Lady Lucas, she became so excited that she fainted clean away. She was removed to her chambers and three days later, Mrs. Bennet was no more.

Mr. Bennet remained a widower for the rest of his considerable time on earth. Mr. Collins had been the last generation of a three-generation entail, and with his death, and his lack of heirs, Mr. Bennet had a change of heart. Where he previously was resigned to losing his estate, he now felt inclined to fight for it, and with the assistance of his sons-in-law – and Mr. Darcy and Mr. Hargrove's combined political influence due to their families – the entail was broken and Mr. Bennet was then free to leave his property to whomever he chose.

He thought it fair that since he had no sons, his home should go to his eldest grandson. Bennet Darcy was already in line to inherit Pemberley, so the next eldest grandson, Richard Darcy, became the heir to his grandfather's estate. He felt it only right that his favorite child's son, the one who had most enjoyed Longbourn and knew every tree and stream, should inherit the family home. The fact that Richard had both his mother's expressive eyes and lively disposition only endeared him more and was further evidence that Mr. Bennet had made the right decision.

Mr. Bennet found that without a wife to hide from, his bookroom was no longer as appealing as it had once been. He took great pleasure in having his three eldest grandsons, Bennet, Richard, and Charles, visit him each summer, and showing them the land of his fathers and the home that, though often neglected, he loved. With a Darcy set to inherit the Longbourn Estate, Mr. Darcy chose to invest in new equipment and farming techniques, considerably raising the earnings of the property. And of course, without Mrs. Bennet's constant entertaining and bills from the dressmaker's, much of the income was now able to be saved, creating a profitable estate with full coffers for the young Darcy to inherit.

Colonel Richard Fitzwilliam blushed prettily when told his cousin's child would be christened after him – which Darcy only teased him minimally about – and he accepted the role of godfather with honor. He stood up with his brother Cyril at his wedding to the wealthy daughter of an earl, and watched silently as his brother continued his loose ways, despite the presence of a pretty wife at home. He congratulated Cyril when his first daughter was born, and condoled with him when his wife died shortly after the birth of their second daughter.

Richard seemed content to remain on the outside, near his cousins' or his brother's families, and his mother feared that he would remain so forever. She introduced him to every heiress she had an even passing acquaintance with. When that failed, she broadened her search to ladies who were well connected, but not well dowered. Eventually, she cast her net to include those even remotely suitable, some with small dowries, others with less than stellar pedigrees. She conferred with her husband and they were able to use a portion of her own dowry, which was for the dowries of daughters they never had, to purchase a house in town. They let it out for the time being, but Lady Matlock vowed that as soon as she saw Richard showing interest in someone, anyone, she would tell him about the home they had purchased for him and the subsequent freedom that would allow him.

Her wish was to come true in an unexpected way. Richard had become friends with the Gardiners through Elizabeth and Darcy, and he was frequently invited to dine. Being a soldier, he was not nearly as proud as his brother the viscount, or even as his noble, though kind, parents. He had no problem rubbing elbows with those who worked for a living, for he knew that although he had a generous allowance from his father, he too earned his own bread.

It was at one such dinner party that he was introduced to a Mr. Duncan, a middle-aged man who was known for his considerable success in industry. More interesting to Richard was Mr. Duncan's daughter, a Miss Amelia with auburn hair and porcelain skin. He thought her eyes were the greenest he had ever seen and her voice was like a soothing rain to parched land.

He made quick work of calling on her, and soon he was asking her father for a formal courtship. After witnessing his cousin's happy marriage to a poor woman, and his brother's miserable existence with an heiress, he knew which he preferred. Permission was granted and Richard was faced with telling his mother of his intentions toward the daughter of a man actively involved in trade. His parents were not happy at first, but upon the realization that Richard would not change his mind – and upon learning of her dowry of forty thousand pounds – compounded with the fear of losing him forever, they agreed to meet her and try their best to like her.

It was difficult at first, but they grew to respect Amelia and she them, and soon an engagement was announced, followed three months later by a wedding. Richard resigned his commission, and he and Amelia moved into the house his parents had purchased and quickly filled it with four children, two boys and two girls, who were doted on by their grandparents.

Oddly, Cyril never did remarry. His estate had the benefit of his late wife's dowry and did not need another, and he was not overly fond of the married state. So it was that upon his brother's early death, Richard Fitzwilliam became the eighth earl of Matlock, a position he had never wanted nor aspired to. Amelia Fitzwilliam, a woman born of trade, became a countess and successor to a long line of highly influential women in the ton. It was no surprise that she found an ally and friend in her new cousin Elizabeth, and between the two of them, they navigated the murky waters of London society with their dignity intact.

Caroline Bingley was so enraged after hearing about Elizabeth's engagement and Darcy's betrayal that she stayed in her room for a month. Once the news of the wedding was released, she threw herself heartily into the little season. She laughed and flirted with every eligible man over twenty-two and under fifty. By the end of the year, she had secured two offers of courtship and one proposal. She accepted the latter and moved to his estate in Warwickshire, a pretty property smaller than Netherfield but larger than Longbourn.

There, much to her chagrin, she proceeded to have five daughters in nine years. Her marriage suffered only slightly less than her figure after so many confinements. Finally, in her twelfth year of marital cohabitation, she produced the much longed for son, named John for his father. Her husband was so pleased, and her illness during her pregnancy had been such that both her marriage and figure improved, and Caroline Hutton, nee Bingley, found a measure of contentment, spotted with the occasional dash of joy.

Louisa Hurst finally did her duty and fell with child, but before her son was born, Mr. Hurst choked on a chicken bone and despite heroic efforts on the part of a footman, it could not be dislodged. Louisa gave birth as a widow and remained on her husband's estate until her son came of age. The heroic footman loyally followed her thither and, according to her brother, Louisa was said to be content and even happy. Sometimes, she would not be seen by anyone for months at a time, but she did not seem to mind and society did not seem to truly care. Her son grew up well with the other children on the estate, three of which looked remarkably similar to him and had rooms in the same hall as he, but being a happy child, he never questioned it.

Lady Catherine refused to acknowledge Elizabeth until she produced an heir, and her desire to see the boy could not be quenched. They established a tentative peace which was once again shattered when Ann deBourgh died of consumption in 1816. Lady Catherine blamed Elizabeth, stating that if Ann had married Darcy, she would have lived. This made no sense, of course, and Darcy was beside himself with anger at Lady Catherine and her ridiculous need to place blame on everyone but herself. However, Elizabeth could only feel pity for a grieving mother and refused to take offense at anything the older woman said.

Lady Catherine would occasionally visit the Darcys in London, though neither ever traveled to the other's estate again. Sometimes she would speak to Elizabeth, other times not, depending on how angry she was feeling that day. Mrs. Darcy chose to see it for the ridiculous spectacle it was, and they continued on in this manner until Lady Catherine's death. Even on her deathbed, she protested her illness, saying she likely would have lived longer than everyone present had her maid not come into contact with a rather sick groom carrying typhoid fever.

Georgiana was beyond pleased to have a sister she adored and a brother who was so happy he was actually caught smiling on more than one occasion. The winter before she came out, which was postponed a year due to Georgiana's desire to be with Elizabeth during her confinement, the Darcys hosted a Christmas ball at Pemberley. Georgiana was allowed to attend and dance with the family as she was already seventeen and would be presented in the spring. To her surprise, young Miss Darcy found herself drawn to a tall, thin man with ice blue eyes and jet black hair. Being such a close friend of the family, he was allowed to dance with Georgiana, and by the end of their set, neither she nor Sir Malcolm was unaffected.

Elizabeth saw it all and was not surprised when, the day after her coming out ball in April, Sir Malcolm was at the door, requesting a courtship with the (now eighteen) Georgiana. After a year of courting and engagement, they were wed at Pemberley. Darcy was pleased to have his sister settled so close to him and with such a trusted friend, and Elizabeth was glad to know that both her friend and sister had found happiness.

Sir Malcolm and Lady Georgiana Rutherford had three sons and two daughters; the girls were the image of their mother, with honeyed curls and large blue eyes. The second and third sons were almost copies of their father, but by some strange stroke of fate, their first, Robert, had the look of his Uncle Darcy about him.

Elizabeth found this all very funny when young Robert, who looked more like her husband every day, began to show signs of affection for Jane's daughter Marianne, whom everyone said was spectacularly similar to Elizabeth in appearance, though not as much in temperament. As the three families grew up near each other, and Robert and Marianne seemed to grow closer and closer, she could not help but cast her memory to the past and remember her own courtship to her beloved husband.

Even after twenty-five years of marriage, she was still blissfully happy and completely devoted to her now gray, but still handsome, husband. She had always thought him to be of an even temperament, one not prone to change or whims of the moment. But he had surpassed even her expectations as a husband. He had proven himself to be a steadfast and loyal companion, a tender and passionate lover, and wholly devoted to her happiness and their success as a couple.

The wife of Mr. Darcy had such extraordinary sources of happiness necessarily attached to her situation that she had, upon the whole, no cause to repine.

THE END

ABOUT THE AUTHOR

Elizabeth Adams loves sunshine and a good book, dreams of living in a villa on the Mediterranean one day, and is a horrible gardener, though in her mind, she has a green thumb. This is her first book.

For more information, outtakes, and a peek at what's coming next, go to ElizabethAdamsWrites.wordpress.com.